The

ANTIQUE DEALER'S DAUGHTER

LORNA GRAY

A division of HarperCollins*Publishers*
www.harpercollins.co.uk

Harper*Impulse* an imprint of
HarperCollins*Publishers*
The News Building
1 London Bridge Street
London SE1 9GF

www.harpercollins.co.uk

This paperback edition 2018

First published in Great Britain in ebook format by
HarperCollins*Publishers* 2018

A catalogue record for this book
is available from the British Library

ISBN: 9780008279592

Set in Birka by Palimpsest Book Production Limited,
Falkirk, Stirlingshire

Printed and bound in the UK by CPI Group (UK) Ltd,
Croydon, CRO4YY

For my family

Chapter 1

I have been taught that I must appreciate the origin of a thing before I can truly understand its meaning. This is because my father has a passion for antiques and he is a man obsessed by the written record, the provenance that proves where an item began its life and charts its path through time. For him, provenance does more than add value to a precious object by declaring it to be a genuine relic from some notable moment in history. It ties him to long-gone human lives. It gives him a chance to touch what they have touched and take their stories as his own.

Very well – put in those terms, the provenance of my story is this: I grew up in London and my teenage years were an unspeakable mess of war. I belong to that unheroic generation of girls who were too old to be evacuated with the smaller children but too young to lend my weight to the war effort. While older women were called up to save the nation by building aeroplanes or tilling the land or were generally being terribly useful in the WAAF or as a WREN, I did nothing very useful at all. If anyone has ever wondered who did the mundane work behind shop counters after those brave women

1

went off to be busy elsewhere, the answer is that the ordinary, everyday work was fulfilled by girls like me.

At the age of fourteen I left a life of disrupted lessons in a dingy air-raid shelter for a daily journey to work in Knightsbridge. I watched through dirty bus windows as, day by day, the bold London landmarks that had charted my youth fell prey to the destructive power of the Blitz. And I did nothing.

Now, though, the war is over. The recent past has grown a little brighter; a little clearer. The whine that was once the sirens and dogfights of yesteryear has become, these days, really nothing more sinister than the shriek of black swifts that tumble playfully in summer skies. Although, even their cries have been silenced of late. This is because the little birds left about a week ago to pass onwards on their migration and their departure has been a fitting companion for the decision I made last Saturday. The one where I gave notice to my employer and decided that after two years of peace it was time to stop worrying that childhood had made me a passive witness to conflict. It was time I took my life off its war footing and found what hope this adult life could bring.

Unfortunately, before announcing this grand scheme to my parents, I really ought to have remembered that I am abysmally poor at speaking what I feel under pressure.

I know now what my father suspected. After all, I've already mentioned that my father believes that the key to everything lies in understanding the past. So if I'd hoped to get my parents to listen to what I really wanted to do with my future, I should have chosen an easier excuse than my determination to stop living each day like London in peacetime was just the same as war and always stifling.

It probably wouldn't have made any difference anyway. My parents found it far more digestible to deduce that their young daughter had been made restless by the after-effects of an unfortunate romance. And since I couldn't entirely refute it, the only compromise we could agree on was the exchange of this urban post-war stagnation for an altogether different kind of peace in the form of a long overdue visit to a spinster cousin in the timeless Cotswolds. My parents saw her as a usefully dithering older relation who would act out the time-worn part of a cautionary tale and save me from tripping into bitter independence. I thought my parents were mistaking me for someone else. My life so far had not exactly been renowned for its brave choices. The fact I'd let them argue me into coming here was proof enough of that, I should have thought.

Anyway, irrespective of all that, I'd have stood a rather greater chance of receiving this cautionary experience had my cousin actually been at home when I arrived.

In fact, by her absence, my cousin is responsible for many things. Had she met me at the bus stop as she had promised, I wouldn't have been forced to walk the two miles alone with my case to her tiny cottage at the bottom of this dusty valley. If she'd been at home when I finally arrived here, I would have had her company instead of nothing but the mile upon mile of blue sky – a novelty in itself after the smogs of London – and my only neighbour wouldn't have been the deserted single-storey building that stood just beyond the turn of the track about a hundred yards upstream, firmly dispelling the fantasy of a simple life passed in a rustic hovel. My cousin's company might also have eased the disorientating sense of loneliness after the important bustle of leaving London, which was only broken by the distant telephone that proceeded to ring on and off for the next three hours.

She certainly might have known who the owners were and decided to do something about it before the sun dipped below the ridgetop behind me. And if she had, when I finally gave in and took it upon myself to labour my way back up that trackway with the view of at least seeing if I could be of any use, I could have either escaped or averted this fresh proof that conflict stalked everywhere, even in peacetime. I certainly wouldn't have found an old man lying flat out on his garden path beneath peas and feathery carrot-tops, with a wound to his head.

Chapter 2

He wasn't alone. I arrived at the moment that the fellow who had been trying to help him had to rapidly set him down on the crude stone slabs of the path because the old man's weight had grown too much.

I was beside them before the old man had even stopped falling. Despite my first impression, this was not an act of war. There were no armies here, no great propaganda campaigns to tell us which nations were on the side of right. I had to make up my own mind and all I saw was a poor old man who had lately bashed his head and made it nearly to his own front step before abruptly succumbing to the shock. I remember his face vividly. There was a greyness to it. His skin was creased by age, with fine woolly hair over the top. He was wearing the coarse shirt and heavy brown trousers of the ordinary countryman. His garden path was a narrow line between overcrowded beds and he stirred a little as I reached his side. One side of his face was gritty from his fall. There was a smear of blood on his right hand that spread to my arm as he watched with that blank instinct that comes from partial consciousness while I dropped into a crouch and examined him.

5

I don't remember the second man. He remains an infuriatingly formless shape in my memory of that day. The image has been subsequently enhanced by the memory of other encounters in other places at different times, but that day I only saw the way he was tugging ineffectually at the fallen man's gardening coat in an attempt to make the old man rise and that he surrendered the invalid's care to me just as soon as I reached his side. He did it with relief, it seemed to me. I remember the hasty instruction he gave to stay and do what I could, and the way his dirtied hand briefly patted my shoulder as he slipped out past me towards the gate. I heard the breathless urgency in his voice as he said that he would fetch better help. I barely looked at him. My eyes were all for that semi-conscious old man and the awful graze on his temple, and the flies that clustered everywhere.

It was about three minutes later when I caught again the renewed ringing of that solitary mark of human companionableness – the still distant telephone – that it dawned on me how strangely the man had made his exit. I also realised just how brutally silent everything else was. The telephone wasn't close by; there were no telegraph wires reaching across this disordered triangle of five or so dwellings, but that persistent drone was near enough to prove the point. Clearly, wherever the other man had gone, he certainly hadn't gone to call the doctor.

Suddenly it felt utterly exposed to be crouching over the old man like this. We were enclosed in a cocoon of greenery where anyone might be watching us and yet we might not see them. It was a very raw means of lurching into the sudden twist of considering what had really happened here. My search of those blazing shadows was stilled between telephone rings when the rattle of a car engine rose like a skylark on the air.

The busy traffic of London was unknown here. This single car claimed the entire valley as its audience. I'd thought at first it was departing; that it showed that the man was making his departure even more final. But the thread of sound became more defined, pausing only for the brief mumble as it met a gate across the lane, before continuing its ascent once more from the valley bottom. Now it was running along the ridgetop just above the village. I had the awfulness of waiting here with the sudden sense of my uselessness if it should turn out that this car was carrying the man back to us. I didn't know what it would mean for me if he should return in an entirely different spirit to the sort that brought assistance. Because I had no doubt at all that if no one had been near enough to answer that telephone, certainly no one would hear any shout of mine.

The car didn't veer harmlessly away to leave me with nothing but a sense of my stupidity for cringing here while better help passed us by. I waited, braced amongst the bees to do Lord knows what, while the whining engine turned off the lane at the plain stone barn and dropped into the village triangle.

It stopped. A voice spoke to another inside the neat little burgundy runabout and then a man and his small white dog got out.

He wasn't the man who had left me here on this path. This man was tanned and fair-haired, or at least had ordinary hair made fair by the sun, and he was of that age, about thirty, where these days you could be reasonably certain he'd encountered harder scenes than this during his war service. He certainly reacted quickly now. Quicker than I did. I shot to my feet and he'd passed me with a hand to my arm to set me to one side before I'd even spoken. Somehow I'd anticipated more discussion first. So I staggered there and dithered while he dropped to one knee by the old man's side, and felt I ought to be barring his path or helping or something; and discovered instead that he was harmless and I wasn't needed, and found time to notice the ugly streak down my wrist and to reel from it and feel a little sick.

A voice demanded my attention. It was the driver of the car. He'd climbed out and now he was standing in the gateway and saying, 'You must be Miss Sutton, I presume? What's happened to Mr Winstone here, do you know?'

It was a relief to be recalled to the gate by the car driver's questions. It was like stepping out into a summer's day. Behind me, the invalid was still befuddled and his crooked old hand was bloodier than ever where it had touched his head. The small cottage that loomed over him was made of crumbling stone, and so were its neighbours on this narrow terrace. I was rubbing heat back into my skin, a gesture of general uncertainty about my role here and whether it really was right that I was surrendering responsibility for Mr Winstone's welfare to the kneeling man like this, and I had to shudder as I discovered what lay under my grip for a second time.

The man I met at the gate prompted me into speech. He ducked his head to meet my eye – his eyes were brown and alert and he was very tall. This was a deliberate attempt to establish control. He wouldn't have known it but the technique was familiar. It was amiable enough but it wasn't far removed from the methods the air-raid wardens had used to instil calm in panicked slum dwellers after they had abruptly discovered a void where the house next door had been.

I imagine the technique had been well used in the London Blitz, but it certainly didn't work on me now. This man woke me to the disquiet that lurked within and I forgot the stain on my arm and said with a voice made sharp by suspicion, 'What do you mean *'presume'*? How do you know who I am? And who is he?'

Along the path, I saw that Mr Winstone had managed to sit up and was feeling his head and talking, or possibly cursing, to the younger man, who was resting on one knee beside him amongst the spilling geraniums. Old Mr Winstone spoke in the elongated vowels of the West Country. The younger man had a tanned hand lying easily across the point of his other knee with a finger hooked into the collar of his enthusiastic dog. His manner was intense and restrained to gentleness all at the same time. His accent was softer than the old man's. He looked and sounded like a working man; rough clothes over strong limbs.

In quite a different tone, the taller man by my side told me calmly, 'He's Danny Hannis. Bertie Winstone's son.'

Briefly, very briefly, my gaze flickered from its watch on the path to this man's face. His mouth formed a benign acknowledgement of the difference in names. He amended, 'Stepson. Danny was in town to pick up a part for the tractor, so it made sense to come home with me. He knows I take my car on a Wednesday. I know who *you* are because we don't get many visitors to these parts and, besides, I'm a friend of your cousin. She didn't tell me directly that you were coming, but word gets about. I'm Matthew Croft, by the way. How did you find him like this?'

There, amongst the patient answers to my questions, was the real question of his own.

I stopped trying to goad myself into a distress of helplessness and looked straight at him for the first time. He was older than his friend by a few years in a way that made him too old for me but probably very suitable for my cousin. Since my mind was still clearly struggling to let down its guard and determined to record every detail it could now, I also happened to notice that his hair was fair, his eyes were very dark in this violet sunset, and his clothes and general demeanour made it seem more likely that he was on his way home from a day in the office rather than a day in the fields.

When my mind finally decided after all this that it was time to answer his question before he had to repeat it a third time, I found myself saying on a note of disbelief, 'There was a man. He went that way.' I pointed my hand towards the corner of the lane, with a vague bias for the direction it took along the ridgetop past that barn towards the gated section and downhill, perhaps, to the valley bottom. 'He had a pale jacket ...'

I caught Matthew Croft's expression. It broke through my seriousness and left a rueful smile in its place. I was not, it seemed, destined to be a very valuable witness.

Danny Hannis must have lately arrived at pretty much the same conclusion about his stepfather. Mr Winstone didn't seem to know who had left him on the floor either. Danny's swift glance along the path towards his friend was like a brief release of concealed impatience. It came in a blast and then his gaze moved on to me. At this range his eyes looked blue or perhaps green and very clear indeed. And rather too sharp. He saw the blood on me. His look began as a question but it was a shock to see my own suspicion reflected there upon his face.

I heard myself saying quite automatically, 'You know, since that fellow is presumably not coming back again to pick up Mr Winstone after all, shall we have a go at patching him up ourselves?'

It was for once the right thing to say. Suspicion evaporated for all of us. I saw Matthew Croft's nod. He beckoned and I heard the creak behind as a youth scrambled out of the car and we all bustled Mr Winstone into the house. Inside, this place was no bigger than the average worker's terrace in a London slum and if Danny Hannis lived here with his step-father, it amazed me that there should have been enough space for him. The old man himself was settled into the dipped seat of an armchair and the younger men propped him there while I scurried into the equally diminutive kitchen to scour my skin free of that revolting stain. There was no tap, only a stone sink and a jug of water drawn from the village pump, but there was soap and a good cloth and at last my skin was pink and clean and I could stop acting like a shocked bystander and think of going back and offering help in the other room.

I didn't stay there for long. I found myself being sent back into the kitchen very smartly on an order from Matthew Croft to do something useful like preparing warm water using the kettle on the stove.

The ancient cooking range was the sort that had to be lit in the morning and kept lit all day if any cooking was to be done, even in summer. It was sweltering in that tiny space and it took about ten minutes to heat the water. I reappeared in the doorway with a basin and a clean cloth in time to make Danny Hannis abandon the question he had been about to ask and rise instead from his crouch before the old man. 'Come along, Pop,' he said with that slight slant to the voice that men use to imply considerable care. 'Bear up. What's all this you're saying about water? You didn't get a good look, I suppose?' This last was meant as a question for me without so much as turning his head.

I couldn't tell him anything about any water beyond the basin in my hands. There was no need to say anything about burglary either. I'd overheard them eliminating that much and, besides, both the kitchen and this equally tiny living room were perfectly clear of signs of invasion. I might have still held out some hope that the departed male had merely been an awkward neighbour helping the old man home after a fall. Except that I could see now that my usefulness in the kitchen had the air of being inspired by that all too familiar division based on gender – and therefore presumed fitness to bear the hard truth.

I also believed Matthew Croft had only encouraged Danny to ask me his question in order to pave the way for giving me firm thanks and sending me on my way. I could tell they'd discussed this from the way Danny reacted when I repeated the all too brief description of a male with dark hair and a pale jacket. He hadn't expected me to have anything to add. I was, in fact, forgotten at the instant I began speaking and Danny Hannis returned to his crouched position before the armchair. His hand went out to Mr Winstone's where it rested upon the arm of his chair, and he fixed the old man with the most compelling concern I have ever seen and it shook me.

I heard him repeat for what had to be the hundredth time, 'What happened to you, Pop? What could possibly motivate someone to bash you over the head?'

And if I had ever really felt I might need to stay to defend Mr Winstone from this man, the feeling was dispelled here. There was, beneath the search for information, genuine bewilderment in his voice.

It was at that moment that fresh voices came from the path and the owners of them entered through the front door. And when I say these newcomers brought a sharp return of tension, this feeling was based on Danny's reaction rather than mine.

Chapter 3

The first to come in was a woman in her mid-thirties, who matched Matthew Croft in being rather taller than the norm for her sex. She stopped on the threshold, took in the oddity of a scene where the old man was sitting in his armchair surrounded by his stepson, a friend and a stranger. Then she stepped in and moved Danny aside from his place before his stepfather's chair with a murmur and a familiar touch to his wrist.

She was the sort of woman who might have posed for any of the propaganda photographs that had proliferated during the war; the sort where capable women in crisply tailored uniforms were caught in the last dramatic moment before setting off on a mad uncharted flight across England in order to deliver a new aircraft to its crew. Now she was asking Danny Hannis to explain how the old man could pass from being well and unharmed at her house a few hours ago, to this. I gathered she was a Mrs Abbey, who lived a short distance away. She was not only an older and decidedly more self-assured woman than I; she was also braver. Her hands went straight to the wound on Mr Winstone's head.

The other woman had a less practical reaction. She was a motherly sort of person of about fifty. She wasn't overweight, but comfortable with very fair hair of that sort that barely shows grey set in tight curls around her head, and she was clearly Danny's mother and Mr Winstone's wife. It was the combination of Mrs Winstone's concern and Mrs Abbey's uninterrupted bossiness that led me to realise that Matthew Croft hadn't actually been practising that time-worn method of instilling calm by organising any stray womenfolk into running errands in another room. Just me.

It must be said that I didn't really mind. This part of my discovery wasn't what mattered here. Because I must admit that, to an extent, I'd understood why he should have thought that Mr Winstone's distress hadn't wanted a stranger's invasive fussing. It hadn't slipped my notice that there was something intensely personal about the old man's confusion and the care that had been given here. And I would have gone easily when I'd realised what he wanted. He needn't have thought I would have stayed to argue the point like some fearsome busybody or, worse, some frightened young thing needing to be shielded from the dread of walking home.

What did matter, though, was that when I saw his easy acceptance of Mrs Winstone's right to ask any questions she chose, it served to make me very aware of the difference in his friend's behaviour to Mrs Abbey.

I'd thought Danny Hannis had been preoccupied but reasonably pleasant before. I didn't believe he had cared about me, beyond that effort of establishing my value as a witness to a distressing scene. Now I was unobtrusively watching him from my place in the kitchen doorway. Mrs Abbey had placed him against the wall beside his mother and I became acutely aware that while he was answering some of his mother's agitated questions, the ones that weren't answered by his friend at least, his attention was all for the other woman. Perhaps it was the unforgiving light – there was no electricity in this village to beat back the coming dusk – but I thought he was watching her and wearing that shuttered expression a man gets when he is uncomfortable but constrained enough by convention to keep from expressing the feeling out loud.

I wouldn't say that his expression conveyed dislike. His mouth seemed able to form a smile readily enough when Mrs Abbey directed some comment at him. I might have worried that his unease lay in a wish to keep her from hearing the details of what had befallen Mr Winstone, except that he seemed to be making no effort to prevent his mother from thoroughly dissecting the lot.

Mrs Abbey was teasing some of the crusted hair aside to permit a clearer view. She was the sort who demonstrated the unbending practicality of one who was very much in the habit of getting on with things because no one else would be doing them for her. I thought she bore the shadow of what might have been wartime widowhood in the lines about her mouth and the neat order of her clothes. Presently, though, Danny Hannis and I both could see that the woman's decisiveness meant she was probing vigorously at Mr Winstone's head when she might just as well have left it alone.

Revulsion, both from her actions and the man's strange powerlessness, made me lurch into saying to Matthew Croft,

'Did you want me to clean up Mr Winstone? That is why you asked me to fetch hot water, isn't it?'

Matthew Croft was standing very near me in the gloomy space between Mr Winstone's shoulder and the sideboard that was set against the kitchen wall. He turned his head as I added haplessly, 'I worked behind a chemist's counter for six years; that must be a training of sorts for this kind of thing, mustn't it?'

Heaven knows what I was thinking, saying that. It was purely a product of unease. Or an impulse to interfere since this other man had sent me scurrying for the hot water in the first place, or be helpful, or something. I regretted my offer just as soon as my gaze returned to the mess Mrs Abbey was uncovering on Mr Winstone's head because it was, in fact, my idea of a nightmare to begin dabbing that crusted hair.

Luckily, Matthew Croft was seemingly oblivious to the way Danny might have thanked him for seizing this chance to diminish Mrs Abbey's control of this room. He was also consistent in his effort to manage the stresses that had been working on me, as I now understood he had been doing all along.

I found myself being relieved of the steaming basin and then returning to the kitchen on a fruitless hunt for antiseptic. It was a charade, for him and for me, because he had no real idea of there being any antiseptic and I went straight to the sink in this rustic back room and used the curiosity of peering through the window above it as an opportunity to undertake an equally fruitless search for the house that sheltered the distant telephone.

I perceived a high garden wall, the stunted church tower and perhaps the roof of a distant barn and that was all. I pretended that I was looking out as a means of soothing away the intense strangeness that was coming in waves from those people behind me. It was also a way of escaping the vision of untrained hands running over a head stained with all that drying blood. In truth, I believe I was really bracing myself, all the while, for the news that Mrs Abbey had been sent in after me.

I'd thought she would be. If Danny had really wanted to exclude her, he might have taken this chance to ask her to help the stranger find whatever it was that Matthew Croft wanted. I found my hands were gripping the smooth stone rim of the sink in readiness for the turn to meet her. But I didn't need to. Because in that room behind me, I knew that she had taken the basin straight out of Matthew Croft's hands and now she was dabbing at a clot on Mr Winstone's head with that neglected cloth.

In this room, the homeliness of a ringing telephone made me think of doing what I ought to have done in the first place. I reset the kettle on the hot plate and boiled it to make Mr Winstone a strong cup of sugary tea.

I had barely made it when I was called back into that cramped room again by the clear mention of, 'Miss Sutton.'

It was Danny giving my name to his mother. Mrs Winstone had finished bewailing the time she had wasted languishing in the clutches of the girl who set her hair and instead was wondering who had found her husband. And Danny was now requiring me to repeat my pathetically unsatisfying description of male with dark hair and a pale jacket and it made this crowded house suffocating because the description didn't inspire recognition in anyone and I didn't know why Danny should suddenly have thought to include me. It wasn't enough to imagine that he had simply wanted the witness to speak for herself.

Danny took the teacup from me and left me stranded while Mrs Winstone beamed at me. She did it in that shattering way people have of being utterly admiring of acts of kindness that are only ever foisted upon a person by circumstance. Somehow that sort of appreciation always jars for me. I didn't want gratitude for an act that any civilised person would have done. And I didn't want to have my own small intervention swelled into the status of a noble deed when I thought there were already quite enough tensions in this room without pretending that the incident hadn't simply been a normal every-day blunder. Particularly when the utterly dismayed perpetrator of it had quite clearly cared enough afterwards to bring Mr Winstone home.

I must have spoken at least part of that thought out loud. Presumably the less defensive part. Mrs Winstone turned to her son. 'This didn't happen here? Mrs Abbey, did this happen at your house? Did this happen at Eddington?'

All eyes turned to Mrs Abbey. It happened with a suddenness that would have made my face burn crimson. I thought the lady displayed creditable poise when she only paused in her ministrations to say with sympathetic understanding, 'Bertie visited us today, but I'm afraid I can safely promise that he wasn't in my little yard when I stepped out to run my errand to the shop about twenty minutes after he left. I wish he had been. I can only say, Mrs Winstone, just how relieved I am that I encountered you and extracted you from your hairdresser's house – otherwise it might have been another hour yet before you'd come home to find the old man like this.'

Mrs Abbey wasn't congratulating herself on her timely intervention. She really did care, I think, about the delay. But as she finished I saw her gaze flick curiously over Mr Winstone's head because Matthew Croft spoke almost immediately with a clearer question of his own for the old man. 'Were you at Eddington to repair the pump?'

The question was so abrupt that it came out like undisguised suspicion, though I didn't think he meant it like that. It was simply that he wasn't bound as Danny was to this woman and he wanted to know if this explained the reference Mr Winstone had made to fiddling about with something to do with water.

'*Of course* I wasn't working on the pump.' At last Mr Winstone spoke and his voice was as battered as his head. Five people were suddenly united in thought as we watched a veined and arthritic hand lift to sweep a shocked teardrop from the corner of his eye. A faint rattle of grit scattered to the floor. 'That's the boy's job. Why aren't you listening? Mrs Abbey only needed me to take a look at something in the house as I was passing by.' He rounded on his stepson. 'And I was only asked to help because you weren't there. I told you this earlier. You know she always has something that needs doing. It was afterwards that I stopped at the turbine house.

Now I've got to get on. Mrs Abbey here is adamant that she's going to take me to the doctors and I've got plenty to do first. It's bad enough that you ...'

The old man's voice tailed off into a jumbled agitation about his wife's supper. He gave the impression she was very particular about meal times. I saw the blankness ripple across Danny's face as he realised that his stepfather had at last recalled the site of his incident. I also saw the bemusement that followed as his mother slipped into real shock and began engaging everyone in a needlessly circular discussion of alternative meal choices if they were going to be late back from the doctors. And it was then that I realised that Danny did mean to use me to manage Mrs Abbey after all.

Mrs Abbey had suggested that the old man should see the doctor. Now Danny was intending to use my presence to save himself from having to tell this woman that he and his friend had already planned to use the car for precisely this purpose, and she wouldn't be coming along.

I could tell he was about to suggest that she should walk me home. It made me wonder what kind of hold this woman had over such a man that he was contorting himself into peculiar strategies just so that he could avoid offending her. Because clearly he had no concern whatsoever about what should happen if he irritated me. It made me wonder if this uneasy tiptoeing was someone's unhappy idea of love. And whose.

And still Mrs Abbey's long fingers were lingering over that crust of blood in Mr Winstone's hair.

She really was making the wound bleed again. Just a little,

but all the same this was ridiculous. I was standing by the immaculate little sideboard and it struck me that the gloriously open front door was just there. It was barely three yards or more away if I slid along the mantelpiece behind Mr Winstone's chair. I didn't care what use Danny Hannis thought I might be. I didn't know any of these people and I wasn't obliged to bolster the numbers of bystanders so that Mrs Abbey could be grouped with me and with all due politeness barred from trespassing upon their visit to the doctor. And it certainly wasn't for me to stage-manage this scene so that the particular bystander in question wouldn't know it was Danny's choice to cut her out of their plans.

I turned my head and abruptly discovered that Matthew Croft's eyes had followed me as I passed him. I was beyond the barrier of the armchair now and it was hard to make out his features in this dark and busy room. I was near the small window that looked out over the garden and I didn't think he was having the same difficulty reading mine. I didn't like to think what he might be seeing there. He was trying to ease his way around the chair after me. He was moving quite swiftly. He meant to speak to me. I thought he meant to stop me from going. He was probably intending to assume responsibility for directing my movements again, as though someone needed to manage my shock for me after this distress. He was going to insist that I had some company, and for the sake of his friend he would probably decree that it should be Mrs Abbey. Only that woman was scolding her patient loudly. Her voice swamped all else; deliberately, I think.

She'd just been promising again that soon she would finish

22

dabbing at his head when she told Mr Winstone clearly, 'Don't dramatise, Bertie. I know what you're hinting at and I really don't think this could possibly mean we're set for a return to all that awfulness we had at the beginning of the year.'

She made Matthew Croft freeze in his pursuit of me. His head turned. She had the attention of the whole room when she added, 'It's such nonsense when we know full well this fellow today was one of those squatters from the camp. Who else could it have been? Dirty people. I always thought it was only a matter of time before something like this happened. Unless you're going to tell us he had a limp?'

I thought she meant that last part as a joke. I saw a corner of her mouth twitch as she dropped that bloody rag back into its bowl with a soggy slap. I saw her hold up her dirtied hands, looking for somewhere to wipe them. She swiftly stepped through to the tiny kitchen to claim a towel while nobody moved. Then she stepped back into the room again and gave a shake of her head at the foolishness of it.

'No,' she said firmly. 'The only connection this has to that sorry business is the charge that might be laid at the squire's door because he went away and allowed those rough vagrants to settle here unchecked. If only the old fool would come home where he belonged, he'd do something about that dirty camp and we wouldn't need to be haunted by anyone, dead or living. Although, of course ...' There was a furtive pause while she scrubbed her hands a little more before she added on a secretive whisper, as if none of us were listening, 'between you and me I can't imagine how he can come back when certain neighbours *will* persist in reminding him of his loss.'

It was an exceedingly odd statement. But my surprise was nothing to everyone else's reaction. They weren't surprised; they were dumbstruck. It left Matthew Croft stranded in the middle of the room and she had even silenced Mrs Winstone. But it was Danny's reaction now that shocked. The gloom in this house was consuming everyone, but I could still see Danny. I could identify him from the intensity of concentration that passed from him to that woman.

Danny's stillness now had an entirely different quality from the awkwardness that had prevented him from halting her dominion over his father's treatment. His expression also swept away the fantasy I had been harbouring that there was a secret between them and it was love. The expression on his face was blank like that of a person facing a sudden resurgence of defensiveness that ran deep; deeper even than Mr Winstone's wound.

This was because Danny could tell as well as I that the odd turn of Mrs Abbey's speech had the taste of revenge on someone, but it wasn't meant to rebuke Danny for his manoeuvrings over taking Mr Winstone to the doctor. I thought this was directed at Matthew Croft for his rudeness in dissecting Mr Winstone's visit to her house, although, to do Mrs Abbey credit, I didn't think she had meant her remarks to have this impact. This wasn't within her control. Something very nasty began to build in the damp corner beyond the fireplace and it grew bolder when Mrs Abbey straightened.

She was flushing and trying to act as if she hadn't said a thing. She knew she'd made a mistake. She attempted to make amends by urging Mr Winstone onto his feet and then there was a sudden rush of life back into this room as stronger hands than hers lunged to keep the old man from falling. There was a scuff as the armchair was moved aside and then a decisive lurch of men across the room towards me and the door.

I was outside before I knew it. They were driving me along from behind. After all that anticipation, the fresher air of a dusky August sky was no relief at all. The shadows chased me out. These people were disturbing me far more than any brief distress of finding an old man on his path and I thought I had remembered now what old business Mrs Abbey had stumbled into talking about. My cousin had mentioned something like this in her letters.

The squire was an old army man and my cousin called him Colonel, presumably because my cousin didn't owe him the same deference he got from those who deemed him lord and master. Her letter had mentioned the tragedy of a son's death in some sort of incident in the winter. She'd implied that the loss had shattered the entire community, and I'd witnessed proof myself now of its wounds. But having said so much, my cousin's letter had declined to convey the rest, in part due to her preoccupation at that time with her own mother's death and also to supposedly preserve tact and to save misunderstandings later. And also, I'd thought, to irritate my curiosity in that infuriating way people have when they have something they wish they could talk about but don't want to be the gossip who tells you.

As it was, I wasn't quite sure I wanted to find out the rest quite like this. There was an additional hint within my cousin's letters that a local man had been caught up in the mess and I thought I had some idea now of who that local man might be.

Mrs Abbey began to rapidly retract her judgement of the old squire's neglect of his estate. It was too late though. It was horrible but it was as if Mrs Abbey had accidentally summoned the dead son, poor man, and it was his shade, or at least the shadow of his end, that crept after us from the house.

Now she was bustling ahead and chattering about her wretched squatters instead. And all the while I thought the strangest thing of all was that no one simply swept it all away with the obvious retort that Mr Winstone hadn't been hinting anything at all. The poor man could barely recall meeting me on his path; he certainly wasn't giving graphic accounts of the terrors that had walked him home and connecting them to any old business that could affect people like this.

Mr Winstone was scuttling along behind her, between his helpers. He wasn't terribly steady on his feet. It was only after they had made it through the gate and past me to move on towards the car that Danny said something rather dry that made the ugliness that had been working its tentacles after them along the path sharply turn on its heel and climb out over the garden wall. He said that he was glad that someone was on hand to give such a well-founded explanation of how his stepfather's injury today had stemmed from that scene in March, because this was the first mention he'd heard of that tragedy for almost six months. His dry humour was for his friend's sake. I knew it was because it drew that man's attention from the immediate task of preventing the invalid from pitching headfirst into the side of the car. I saw Matthew Croft right the old man and then turn his head to give a surprisingly warm grin. And then I was only left with the puzzling realisation that while I had been watching and worrying over the reasons why a man like Danny Hannis might find himself unable to risk offending Mrs Abbey, I really should have been noticing that she didn't like his friend at all.

She was, however, perfectly, convincingly repentant. She knew she'd made a crass mistake and if she didn't, she certainly found out when it cost her the right to accompany Mr Winstone on his trip to consult the doctor. I felt almost sorry for her when she joined me just as the men were depositing their charge in the passenger seat. She had been roundly excluded from the crush as Mrs Winstone organised herself into the back seat. Danny was folding himself in beside his mother without so much as a glance for the neglected neighbour. It became all the more humbling when the small dog clambered in after them. The only person who didn't go was the wavy-haired youth Freddy, who was hovering by the bumper in that helpful way people have when they desperately want to be useful but have no idea what to do. I thought he was waiting for orders and it belatedly occurred to me that Matthew Croft had been intending to offer the boy as my companion when he'd been trying to organise my walk home.

I didn't mean to give Matthew Croft time to remember. I was a few yards away, at the limit of the pockmarked garden wall, and I would have left there and then except that Mrs Abbey had her hand on my arm as she told me earnestly,

'You've been badly shaken by your brush with this fellow, haven't you?'

She was speaking as though nothing else mattered beyond Mr Winstone's injury. Perhaps nothing else did. They all knew each other, these people, and the slip about a man's death must have been made by others before. I played for the same indifference while carefully dodging away from that clutching hand of hers. After all, it had last been seen grasping a bloody rag.

I remarked lightly, 'Shaken by that man? No.'

She looked disbelieving. 'You kept dithering in and out of the room all the time that we were talking.'

I conceded the point with a faintly worn smile. Rightly or wrongly, I soon took advantage of a disturbance within the car to make my getaway from all of them. That telephone was ringing again – that blessed reminder of noisy things that belonged in the companionable bustle of my familiar city life – and I went to it like it was a lifeline.

Chapter 4

Suddenly it wasn't as late as I'd thought. I supposed escape might feel like that. The large house that stood on the opposite side of the triangle was still touched to warmth by the last of the day's colour. It wasn't the one that was ringing. That was coming from the other side of the village; in the space after the church but before the turn where the lane coursed away downhill. This grand house was the steward's house and it was where my cousin had lived and grown until her father had died and her mother had retired to the cottage. I'd only visited these parts once as a child and that had been when I was eight. I barely remembered it but I did remember the village boys who had waged cheerful war with my cousin's older brothers while my cousin scolded and I trailed about behind the lot of them like a pathetic undersized shadow. It was possible that Danny Hannis had been one of them.

The house seemed to be a boarding house for farm workers now. There was a steady stream of them passing between the steward's house and what I'd taken earlier to be a derelict farmyard, only now it was flooded with light and crowded with men and tired carthorses. This, suddenly, was the bustle

I was used to. Here the crowds took the form of dusty males ranging along the lines of various low stone walls, smoking and drinking weak beer. The farmhands were all, to a man, tanned and wiry. None of them wore a pale summer jacket. I suspected that most weren't wealthy enough to own one.

Freddy didn't own one either. He caught up with me before I'd even reached the point where the track veered to the right, downhill to my cousin's cottage, or left around the lower limit of the churchyard and towards that telephone. He grinned at me as he fell into step beside me. He was all limbs and amiableness. 'I don't mind walking with you, Miss.'

The boy matched my sense of escape. He was on that cusp between childhood and manhood. He was aged perhaps fifteen and his face had the unsymmetrical structure of a teenage boy whose features were just beginning to settle into the mould of the man he would become. He wasn't tall. He was perhaps my height and no more, but he had an endearing air of doubtful friendliness; warm and cheerful because it was in his nature to be so, but doubtful because perhaps other people didn't always welcome it.

A certain sense of this boy's niceness after that room full of adult complications made me protective but perhaps less tactful than I ought to have been. I remarked, 'I'm going to answer that telephone. But I'll be very glad of your company if you can explain to me precisely how it happens that there is so much danger tonight that I must let you escort me about the place, and yet somehow once I'm home I'm supposed to be perfectly happy to send you merrily onwards to your own home alone.'

He wasn't offended. He told me simply, 'My home isn't just downstream from the turbine house Mr Winstone mentioned.'

Ah.

I confessed sheepishly, 'That's my cousin's nearest neighbour. I thought that little brick hovel was somebody's cottage.'

I made Freddy laugh. 'Absolutely it is. And did you notice that it comes complete with running water laid on beneath the floorboards? You should be careful who you say that to. The turbine house is a matter for local pride. It gives light to the farmyard and the Manor. And it would give power to the steward's house too if we had a man in there at the moment. We're as modern as you like here.'

But not so modern, I thought, that anyone thought to mind the traditional distinction between the luxuries experienced by the land-owner compared to those of his tenants.

Then Freddy added doubtfully, 'Did you say you were going to answer that? It's in the Manor. Someone should be there.'

That told me what dwelling had the boldness to possess a telephone in this humble place. Its busy farmyard yawned in the gloom beneath us, where life hummed from every ancient stone and sagging roof, and stables for carthorses nestled against the rear wall of a massive stone barn. Below, the trackway descended into stillness. So did the cobbled surface that curved along the front of the enormous barn and veered left at the corner of another. There was no farmhouse attached to this enclosed run of buildings. There was no reassuring glow from watchful windows to oversee either route. Moths and shadows were the only traffic on this trackway. And the memory of Mrs Abbey's summoning of ghosts and odd strangers, which to these people was also the correct description for me.

I dithered and spoke before I'd thought. 'You'd think that Mr Winstone would be able to name this man if he'd ever met him before, wouldn't you?'

Freddy only said politely, 'Miss?'

The real worry burst out and it matched the blazing colour that still just touched the sky behind the darkened curve of the opposing valley hillside. I said bitterly, 'I can't believe I didn't hear anything. I must have been at home when it happened. I was outside, sitting on my cousin's front step. The turbine house would have been just out of sight around the bend of the track and I heard nothing. I must have followed them almost step for step up the hill and yet I saw nothing. There was nothing at all except the endless murmur of that telephone.'

I turned suddenly and chose the lane above the barn. I could hear my old friend that telephone still, but rather less insistently against the muffle of that great stone barn. Now it was a forlorn note of neglect. The farmhands were all going home for the night and not one of them thought he should answer it. I knew why. It was someone else's job and, besides, after the tension I'd encountered in that room after the mention of the Colonel's son, I could guess that none of them would dare.

I wondered if Danny might. Only he wasn't likely to be released from his care of his stepfather for a while yet.

The Manor stood a little aloof from the village. We scurried along the frontage of that vast stone threshing barn and passed its gaping void of a vacant doorway. The cobbled drive rose past the stone barn to nose onto a narrow yard that was lined to our left by another older, rougher barn and on our right by the beginnings of parched garden terraces. No beans or cabbages were tended here. Above all this towered the Manor, a building that thrust up old weathered Cotswold gables all along its western face. Mullioned windows studded three floors and hundreds of tiny diamond panes of glass were each turned crimson by the last glimmer of daylight. It was all at once bleak and the most beautiful house I had ever seen.

A sudden doubt made me ask, 'Freddy? Where is the doctor's house?'

Freddy didn't know I was thinking about that man again. The one who had been supposed to be going to fetch help. The boy told me innocently, 'They've gone to the next village along. A place called Winstone.' He caught my look. He grinned. 'Mr Winstone's kin took the name when they travelled into Somerset sometime around the dawn of the universe and in the time since, nature and work have conspired to carry him back again. Him and Mrs Winstone have been married for nearly twenty years, I think.'

Freddy was also unaware that part of this determination to answer the telephone was the tantalising idea that the Manor might be about to gift me the opportunity to speak to my cousin. I might be able to ask her advice before consigning myself to the silence of a solitary night in her cottage. The invitation was certainly lingering there in the air.

The kitchen door was unlocked in a manner that implied someone ought to be at home. I hallooed as one was meant to upon trespassing into a private house, but then I stepped in and found the light switch. Its garish yellow glare revealed a cavernous void that showed very little sign of regular use. The whole place confirmed Mrs Abbey's statement that the Colonel was spending his bereavement elsewhere.

It made me say to the boy, 'Didn't you say someone still lived here?'

He was looking pale in the harsh electric light. I made him come inside so that I could shut the door before all the summer insects could swarm in after us. This little piece of practicality made him muster the words to reply, 'The house-keeper.'

His voice was very small. His wide eyes were taking in the clean surfaces and empty stores. The farmyard might not have been as derelict as I had supposed, but here the abandonment was real. It was not, however, so old that dust was yet filming the bare surfaces and still that wonderful beacon of life was justifying our intrusion by persisting shrilly.

I followed its call through to where the high beams of the kitchen dropped into the cooler air of a narrow dining room. The light from the kitchen was strong, but this place was made oppressive by walls of panelled oak. Almost the entire space was occupied by an enormously long and very old banqueting table. I didn't need my father's training in the trade to recognise its value. Nor did it require his skill to identify the ancient mechanism for a spit-roast within the equally massive but decrepit fireplace. It too was gloomy in that way that spoke of a livelier past long neglected.

By the time I had proceeded through the turns of an impossibly dispiriting passage, the caller had given up and so had I, nearly. I couldn't find a light switch and the array of paintings that belonged to the era when young gentlemen took grand tours had swiftly given way to the cold metal of old muskets and gin traps. Then I emerged into the loftier space of a broad Georgian stairwell and here was salvation in the form of an elegant table lamp. The moment it was lit, it felt as if I had stepped out of a museum and into a home. I had been beginning to feel thoroughly unwelcome in a place that preferred to be left alone to sleep and dream of the lingering weight of the son's death. There was also, predictably enough, a growing sense of unease brought on by the memory of that unlocked door and the realisation that the man who had dropped Mr Winstone almost by my feet might have taken flight this way. The feeling was made worse when I checked the shadows in the passage behind me and realised that Freddy had not followed me here.

That wonderful table lamp saved my ebbing confidence; saved everything. A small stack of letters had been collecting by its side for a matter of a fortnight at most. Here I was in a space where a white plasterwork ceiling hung high above at the level of the attic floor. Glass consumed the entire end wall of the house except for the black rectangle that was reserved for a wide front door. Dusky blues shot across the sky outside and the lamp sent rainbow hues racing after them across the chequerboard marble floor. This place was no monument to mortal decay or the lair of a dangerous man; more the tidy corner where the family ought to have been, only they had lately but temporarily stepped out for a while.

The caller obliged me by trying again and drew me at last to trace the sound through the doorway that stood opposite in the narrow portion of wall at the foot of the stairs. If the entrance hall was welcoming, this room was glorious. A vast and elegant bay window faced full west over gardens and the lip of a drop that plunged away so suddenly into the valley below that it was almost powerful enough for vertigo. This view was at last the peace and glory of the countryside.

I lifted the receiver from the thoroughly modern Bakelite telephone, which stood on the expansive desk. I said, 'Hello, um—' I scanned about me frantically for something that would help me recall the family name, if I had ever been told it. The oval portrait of an attractive woman in dated clothing on the nearest bookcase was no help at all. With an effort I dredged up an image of the platter of post. '— Langton residence?'

'At last.' This was the operator. She sounded beyond exasperated as she hastily retreated from the conversation to allow the caller, male, to say tersely, 'Hello? *Hello?*'

'Good evening,' I replied politely, repeating after a moment, 'The Langton residence. May I help you?'

'Where the devil have you been? I've been trying for days.' My politeness was wasted. The man on the other end of the line was clearly intending to make absolutely no concessions for basic civility. He was also, as it turned out, unwilling to leave me room to actually answer him.

I began, 'Well actually I—'

'Where's Mrs Cooke? Why isn't she there?'

'I'm afraid I don't know Mrs—'

'What on earth do we pay you for if you don't know where she is?'

'You aren't actually my employ—'

'Hang on.' The voice became muffled as a hand was placed over the mouthpiece. 'I don't know, sir. I'm trying to find out, only there's some dim-witted—'

'*Sorry?*'

The voice came back into clarity. 'Pardon?'

'Ah,' I said sweetly, 'I'm sorry, I thought you were speaking to me there.' There was a momentary silence. Now that I had his attention, I resumed my idea of crisp orderliness. 'This is the Langton residence, only I'm afraid no one is here who can take your call. I'm a neighbour, you see, or rather the guest of a neighbour and I only stepped in because the telephone was ringing again. It's been going all afternoon and I'd have answered it sooner only then there was a bit of a crisis in the village and I've only just heard it again now. I thought I'd better come in to answer it anyway. Just in case it was urgent, you understand.'

There was a pause when it dawned on me that I was explaining all this without having the faintest idea who this man was. Then it was proved that I hadn't really been explaining anything as far as he was concerned. Just as I was about to ask this distant male his name, I heard him say on a faintly wearied note, 'I'm not entirely sure I do understand, actually, no. Who did you say you were again?'

In the background at his end I heard an older man's voice adding something pettishly. I ignored it and said, 'Emily

37

Sutton. I'm staying with my cousin, Miss Jones. At least I'm staying at her house while she's in h—'

'Well, Emily, I'm not sure what you—'

This time I interrupted him. Perhaps it was being sworn at, ridiculed and then called 'Emily' like some half-trained parlour maid that made me brave. I mean, anyone who was local knew my cousin as the daughter of the old steward, even if they had no reason to know me. And, besides, even at this time when war had done away with all sorts of obsolete social conventions, strangers could still expect to rank enough for a 'Miss'.

I said, 'I'm sorry, but I didn't quite catch who *you* are.'

I was perhaps a shade hostile. It was slowly dawning on me that this man would want something from me. So when he told me he was Colonel Langton's son I'm afraid I simply said impatiently, 'You can't be. He died.'

I think I was imagining this might be some extension of the scene I'd just left by Mr Winstone's house, or perhaps I was comparing this caller with the sort of chancer who occasionally tried to convince my father that the rare and valuable antique he'd just listed for sale was in fact their long-lost family heirloom and theirs by right. Any moment now, this man would lead me into making a fresh statement about the family just so that he could parrot it back to me later under the guise of genuine knowledge before he set about coercing me into popping some supposedly meaningless family trinket into the post for him.

Only this man did none of it. After the smallest of hesitations, the caller replied calmly, 'That was my younger brother. The Colonel's other son.'

And my cousin had feared that a lack of tact would cause misunderstandings.

Through a stomach-gnawing fog of embarrassment, I heard him add, 'This is Captain Richard Langton.'

'That's nice,' I remarked faintly, while frantically trying to calculate how one addressed a captain. I finally tacked on as an afterthought a vaguely military, 'Sir.'

'Thank you. And now that we've cleared that up, perhaps we can return to the original question?'

'Which was?'

'Where is Mrs Cooke?'

I was coiling and uncoiling the telephone wire about my fingers. I had to stop it before I twisted it into a permanent state of tangle. I told him, 'I'm afraid I don't actually know who Mrs Cooke is. The house looks shut up to me; there is no one about and the kitchen doesn't look particularly well stocked, although admittedly I can only relate the impression I got on my dash through from the garden. As I've already said, I only answered the telephone because it's been ringing all day—'

'Yes, yes; and you only heard it ringing because you're visiting your aunt Mrs Jane or something like that. Please don't let's go over all that again.'

'My cousin. Miss Jones of Washbrook.'

'All right; Miss Jones. But that still doesn't solve my problem.'

'Which is?' I'd been right about one thing at least. He was going to ask something of me.

'Perhaps you could deliver a message to our driver?'

'Is it an emergency?' I don't quite know what made me ask that. I suppose it was a legacy of the shock of finding Mr Winstone at the end of what had already been a very long day of travelling. I was wary of what fresh demands this place would make of me.

The question certainly puzzled Captain Langton. He said on an odd note, 'No. It is quite important though, Emily.'

Again the address of the parlour maid or the charwoman. Though probably I deserved it this time. I was after all only here because I hoped to make free with his telephone in order to call my cousin just as soon as he gave me room to do so. Biting my lip, I agreed.

'Good,' he said briskly. 'Could you tell him that he's to collect my father from the solicitor's office in Cirencester at eleven o'clock on Thursday? Heavens, that's tomorrow now. That shows that I've spent all week trying to set this up. My father intends to go home for a while to ...' He checked himself. 'No, those details don't matter here. What does matter is that he's met by the car tomorrow. Do you know our driver, Bertie Winstone?'

Oh Lord.

'I'm sorry,' I said inadequately. I really hadn't handled this conversation very well. 'Mr Winstone has had a bit of an accident. I'm afraid I've just left him as he was being whisked off to be patched up by the doctor. I have to tell you that I really don't think it likely that he'll be fit to drive your car tomorrow. Or any car, for that matter. I really am very sorry.'

'You'll have to speak up. There's an almighty racket going on here. Did you say Bertie has had an accident?' The man was hard for me to hear too. A persistent drone in the background was blurring his voice.

I told him what had met me during the course of climbing the hill to answer his call; that is to say, I gave him the bare facts about the whole neighbourhood being deserted all day, about finding Mr Winstone, the lucky timing of Danny Hannis coming home, the likelihood that the attack had taken place at the turbine house and, finally, I don't know why, that I had met several of my cousin's friends, including Mrs Abbey. I believe I might even have mentioned something about the loneliness that had inspired my walk up the hill in the first place. Apart from that, it was, I realised, the first time I had willingly given Mr Winstone's injuries the title they deserved and called this thing an attack and not an accident. It was a peculiar kind of shock and yet somehow it lessened it to be telling this man and the Captain certainly took the information very matter-of-factly. I suppose as a military man such things might seem more commonplace and as a son he was certainly inclined to be more concerned with the news that his father was going to be beset by yet more inconvenience.

He was asking me, 'Is it still working, though? The turbine, I mean. The house still has electricity?'

'I'll have to check.' I presumed he was wondering if the house was even fit for his father to inhabit. He was very practical, this Captain. Whereas I think his orderly mind flustered mine, or perhaps he just made me conscious of the way the evening's shocks had shaken me. I finally realised what I'd said and corrected myself in a rush. 'No, I won't need to check, sorry. I switched on the light in the kitchen when I came in. So, yes, the house still has electricity. But won't that be from the batteries anyway?'

I was gabbling, confusing myself, but it didn't matter anyway because he was saying something else and then I was distracted by the sight of Danny's dog dashing by on his own business, past the window. He had obviously been left behind after that last ruckus in the car. I saw now that another small village clustered on the opposing hillside. The cottages were distinguishable by the yellow smear of oil light in their windows. To their right, another single streak of colour was shining lonely above the straggling woodland that trailed upstream from the unseen hollow where my cousin's cottage stood. Apart from these few specks of life, the valley was solemnly left to the trees. Proving the point, an owl hooted from one near by. It made me realise that the Captain was still waiting for me to answer his last question.

'Yes, sorry,' I added hastily, then I realised I didn't actually know what I was supposed to be answering. 'Pardon?'

'I was just saying that Bertie was lucky that you happened by. I should have guessed myself that no one would be on hand to answer my call if the housekeeper wasn't home. The few village men will have been up in the fields, and the women and children too for that matter. They're starting to gather the barley, I believe, and you should know I say that with all the confidence of one who hasn't the faintest idea about the timing of these things. It was all still laid to sheep pasture when I last lived at home. Did you say Mrs Abbey was there too?'

My hand was fiddling with a pencil now since I wouldn't let it toy with the telephone wire. I had to bend beneath the desk to retrieve it when the pencil rattled to the floor. I asked, 'You know her?'

'I should do. I've written her enough letters over the past few months. She's one of our many tenants, or at least she is when she pays. We allow her a little grace because of her husband. It must have been a shock, discovering Bertie like that.'

I was busily thinking that Mrs Abbey hadn't spoken terribly nicely of his father for one who owed him a debt of gratitude. I said, 'I expect it was, but it hasn't really sunk in yet. It didn't really happen to her anyway, if you know what I mean. She only arrived later as a spare part to Mrs Winstone's return.'

'Actually,' remarked the Captain mildly, 'I believe I was meaning you there.'

It was then that the caller proved that he hadn't been as insensitive as I'd thought to the strain of my evening. He'd simply been calming about it for my sake, and perhaps because he was practical and limited by being on the other end of a telephone.

'But anyway,' the Captain added, then his attention strayed as the noise increased on his end of the line, like when a door is opened and the bustle from outside briefly rushes in. With equal suddenness, his attention returned to me. 'Look, I've got to go. My father's train is about to be called.'

'Is that Paddington?' Abruptly the sounds clarified to be those of a busy station. I ought to have recognised them, having departed from the same London terminus myself that morning.

The Captain was saying rapidly, 'My father is staying in a hotel tonight and he'll get a car from there in the morning. He can do anything that needs doing for Bertie tomorrow. Lord knows what my father will do for his lunch, but I suppose that's minor in the general scheme of things and will simply have to be added to the list of things he'll address when he gets there.'

'And what about Mrs Cooke?'

He understood in an instant. 'If you're feeling brave, feel free to have a quick look about and raise a hue and cry if you find anything awry. I'll give you the name of my father's hotel, just in case.' He gave it to me and I had to jot it down on the corner of the desk's large sheet of blotting paper. 'But,' the voice in my ear continued, 'I shouldn't worry. You said it yourself, the kitchen is bare. She's probably just gone off to visit friends and hoped we wouldn't notice. And if she hasn't, well, my father will be back tomorrow. Either way, try not to worry. I hardly think this is anything *you* need to worry about.'

'Nothing to worry about at all,' I remarked more dryly than I intended. 'Except what your father would say if someone wasn't going to the shop to get his lunch.'

He laughed. It came as something of a surprise after an evening of serious tones. Then he thanked me and said, 'I suppose you could consider it a temporary employment? Will you do that? We can put your fee on account.'

In the background I could hear the noise of that train station again. In a very odd way, I didn't want him to go. I suppose it was because this man was like a little touch of the familiar and the end of this conversation would leave me alone with my thoughts and the task of summoning them all in an effort to explain all this to my cousin. Embarrassingly, I thought he sensed it because he said rather distractedly as the sound behind him intensified, 'Listen, if it will make you feel more easy, we'll speak further about all this tomorrow, if I can manage to find the time. And by the way,' his attention briefly fixed on me again before he went to help his father find his train. 'I'm sorry I was rude to you. You can put that on account too.'

Then, having stunned me with his sudden apology, which left no room for reply as he moved to end the call and I prepared to rest my own receiver on the cradle, I heard his distant voice add an urgent, *'Hello?* Emily, are you still there?'

'Yes?'

'I should have asked. Did you get Bertie to a doctor?'

'Yes,' I said. 'I mentioned it just now. As I left he was being parcelled off there by his son and—' I was interrupted by the surprise of Freddy appearing in the doorway and switching on the light. After the easy gloom of nightfall, it was blinding.

Oblivious to the way my eyes were stinging, the voice by my ear prompted impatiently, 'And who? Quickly please.'

'Mr Croft.' I said it thoughtlessly. Then I remembered Mrs Abbey's barbs and realised what I might have done. Impulsively I added, 'I'm sorry, Captain.'

But the apology wasn't really for the sake of the sharp exclamation that was transmitted down the telephone wire only to be followed curtly by something like: 'Why on earth ...?

Oh hell, I really have to go. I wish ... Thank you for this, I think ... but really, of all the people ... Why on earth did you have to involve *him?*'

As I say, it wasn't the strength of the Captain's oath that shook all thought of disappearing housekeepers and injured old men and even my plan of telephoning my cousin from my head. It was the way the garish light had revealed that all the Captain's sentiments had appeared first on Freddy's face; and had intensified there just as soon as the boy guessed who was on the other end of the line.

Chapter 5

Freddy's face regained colour almost the moment we stepped back outside into the warm evening and I was relieved to see it. There was no question now of dithering to telephone my cousin in the hope that she'd suggest I gave up the cottage and instead take a room in a hotel near her in Gloucester, nor did I spare much thought for worrying about strangers or the whereabouts of Mrs Cooke. This was more vital; this was my responsibility because I had brought him here.

The sense of it lurked in knowing that the time I had spent seeking that telephone was the time that had preyed on Freddy's nerves until he had finally grown desperate enough to come inside to find me. His decision must have been prompted by a premonition of something very terrible indeed. I knew it had because the release as we left by that kitchen door shone in the flush that burned the boy's cheeks. This was a kind of bravery that hurt. It was all wrong that such a kind, harmless youth like this boy should have ever known fear enough to think it necessary to overcome the memory of it in this moment for the sake of me.

I could see now that my cousin's description of a wintery incident with the Colonel's younger son had misled me. Her letter had led me to imagine something along the lines of an over-bred buffoon caught up in a tragic accident involving the March bad weather. The winter had been a chaos of deep snows and extreme freezes but, all that aside, several things were now very clear to me. The first was that the fracas in March was no more an accident than Mr Winstone's collapse on his path. The second was that while my cousin had at least hinted that the chill of last winter had left its mark on the whole community, it had taken their reaction to Mrs Abbey's mistake to make me realise the shadow of what had befallen still lived in this place. For Freddy, it dwelt in that house if not in that beautiful room with the bay window. And now there was a chance that the family was set to be brought back into his sphere again and a trace of the dread that haunted Freddy was even detectable in a grown man like the Captain. In the man it took a different form, but all the same, even in the Captain's voice I thought there had been a glimpse of something that came strangely close to fear.

I could hear it in the boy's voice now when he asked above the creak of the valley gate as it was opened and pressed shut, 'They're coming back then?'

'They are,' I confirmed gently. 'Or rather, the Colonel is.'

I took Freddy swiftly onwards down the hill because I didn't know what else to do. True twilight had descended in the time that we had been indoors and the hillside was a picture of warm summer tranquillity. I eyed my companion carefully as we neared the valley bottom. His face was angular in this

48

light; sharp beneath unruly hair. He didn't seem so much afraid now as resolutely expressionless as we passed beneath the scented dark of the small plantation of pines.

'Did he say *why* the Colonel was coming back?'

I noted that Freddy didn't consider himself one of the Colonel's subjects. It was left to men like Danny Hannis to pay the squire his due deference. 'No,' I said carefully, 'Captain Langton didn't say why. He didn't have much time because the train was being called. I imagine his father wants to come back and check that the harvest is progressing as it should. I do remember that he said something about the barley.'

'Oh, is that all?' He said it in that flat way youths have of dismissing something desperately worrying quite as if it didn't matter at all. Then he said briskly, 'They're taking in a late cut of hay at the moment. The corn's behind because of the late summer.' It was said in a rush of an apology because he didn't like to contradict. Then he asked in an altogether brighter way, 'Do you think we should go and have a look at it?'

This last question was because we had reached the last turn of the track above the turbine house. The brickwork was rendered in crumbling plaster and it shone white before us against the curling black line of the stream. Now that I knew, this tiny hut really was quite unlike a dwelling. It was also unlike any electricity station that I had ever known. The power stations of London were great smoking beasts with towering black pillars for chimneys. This small brick house straddled a neat platform and water made a faint shushing sound some-where beneath, where it was released following its racing fall through a pipe from a pond high up by the village. Further downstream I could just make out the broader area of the ford and, a short way beyond that, the end wall of my cousin's cottage shone grubby silver where the trackway rounded the base of the hillside.

'We can take a little detour to the turbine house to have a look, if you like.' My agreement was given doubtfully. Then I perceived the fierce concentration in Freddy's face and wondered if people persisted in asking him questions, probing what he knew, and it was this little inquisition he was presently bracing himself for rather than any particular concern about our recent trespass in that house. Immediately, I found I would like to examine the turbine house very much. 'I know it would make me sleep more easily if I knew we'd done our bit to check that poor Mr Winstone has really left no sign behind.'

The change in Freddy's demeanour was instant. It was, I thought, a reassuring sign that the boy's life did not appear in general to give him much sense of fear but all the same I expended significantly less effort on looking the part of a valiant sleuth as I followed him over the last of the roughened hillside and worked rather harder at staying alert to signs of life.

There was no one here. The hut's rotten door was locked. The single metal-framed window with its flaking white paint was securely fastened and nothing could be made out through the filthy glass. Concealed within would, I knew, be the neat little turbine and an array of vast batteries that stored the generated power for future use. It was all wonderfully clean and efficient, and also decidedly exclusive.

My voice sounded loud in the hush of a sleeping valley. 'Don't the villagers mind that their houses stay dark while all this awaits someone's return to the Manor?'

'Not really. It's very old. It's always been like this.' Freddy seemed surprised by my question, which in turn surprised me. It seemed an odd mixture that he should dislike the Colonel and his family and yet apparently easily accept this. Freddy wasn't set to be a revolutionary. He was just a boy who was very afraid that the Colonel's return brought the threat of fresh harm to his tall and caring Matthew Croft.

We were peering for footprints in the baked mud of the bank above the stream. There was nothing there but the neat little hoof prints of thirsty sheep, at least nothing that we could see by starlight. There was nothing here to shake the overriding sense of my own care for this boy. I found that I was saying clumsily, 'Mr Croft didn't kill him, did he? Didn't cause the son's death, I mean?'

I shouldn't have said it. I had only meant to establish the limit of the bad feeling between the Langton family and the other man before adding something reassuring, but the boy beside me, naturally enough, completely misunderstood my intentions. He was suddenly very ready to be angry.

'No! Of course not.' He stood there glowering at me in the night, hands balled into fists by his sides and hair all dishevelled again. This really was something that he was asked all too often. It also, I think, cut far too close to a memory of a near loss of his own.

'Well then,' I persevered gently. 'I really think you needn't worry any more. From the way Captain Langton reacted when

51

I mentioned Mr Croft by name, it seems to me that the family is just as desperately keen to avoid an encounter with that past as you are. You mustn't think the Colonel means to create a fuss by coming back, or that his return is designed to bring fresh upset for Mr Croft. Captain Langton was …' I searched for a sensible way to put it. 'Well, to be brutally honest, he sounded like a normal human being who'd had a bit of a shock when I mentioned that Mr Croft was helping Mr Winstone. You *can* believe me, Freddy. Really you can. So don't be afraid for Mr Croft any more, Freddy, please.'

The boy blinked. I'd surprised him. He hadn't expected my only objective to be plain reassurance. But he did, I saw with relief, understand it. For a moment, his fierceness had made him seem suddenly very young indeed. Then he abruptly relaxed.

Shyly, like a guilty child after a fit of the rages, he gulped and said quietly, 'You're very nice, Miss.'

'Not really. It's just the truth.'

'You hope,' he retorted, but he was only contradicting me for the sake of form. Then he abruptly abandoned the search of the riverbed and led the way across rough ground towards my cottage.

A drowsy bird twittered in one of the taller trees. It set off a cock pheasant, who set off another, and so on until the warning cry barrelled up and down the valley in a relay from one tree to the next. There were an awful lot of pheasants up there. Their voices mapped the twists and turns of the valley far beyond the point where it curved away into the smothering oblivion of darkness.

It made me think again that I really ought to walk Freddy home. I said as much and he sniggered with that boyish confidence that never fails to charm. 'It would pose a bit of a problem though, wouldn't it, Miss? We'd be up all night walking each other back and forth.'

We were at my garden gate. I set a hand on the weathered wood and tipped my head thoughtfully at him. 'You don't seem very nervous.'

I saw him shrug with hands in pockets. His attention was on a pebble he was turning underfoot. Tangled hair was falling over his brow as he said, 'You said yourself that the fellow brought Mr Winstone home before he met you and bolted. There's not much point in being afraid of a man like that. He probably didn't mean to hurt Mr Winstone anyway. He's probably just a vagrant who came back from the war a bit strange and Mr Winstone caught him unawares.'

'You think it was one of Mrs Abbey's squatters?'

The boy's gaze lifted. 'Well,' he said simply. 'No one who knows Mr Winstone would do it, so it must have been. Goodnight, Miss.'

And on that practical piece of reasoning, he left me and loped complacently off into the gloom. I walked rather less energetically into my cousin's house and bolted the door. It was, I thought, one thing to be giving reassurance to a frightened youth about the way Captain Langton had spoken of Matthew Croft, but it didn't do much for my own worries about letting the boy go. Responsibility always did take the form in me of a vivid awareness of the present set against all the things I should have done before but hadn't. It was complicated marriage between duty and an enduring feeling of guilt that stemmed from all those childhood moments that had long passed and the knowledge that there would never again be a chance to repay what I owed to those people, so I'd better act well now.

But committed as I was to the idea of playing a fuller part these days, it must be said that helplessness was sometimes still preferable to the occasional experience I have had of the other end of the spectrum; the sheer chill of sometimes acting calmly where care and duty had united to override every other serious principle. Those were the moments that brought me into an acquaintance with the dark things in this world that I would otherwise have quite cheerfully ignored, and I hated them.

They made me wish I could run away. They saddened me. The idea that this life was placing me in the company of conflict filled me with a sense of hopelessness for the future and an urge to seek peace elsewhere. It was the principal motive for this visit to my cousin's house, after all. Only now I had the memory of the other responsibility that had met me today; the one that had led me to pick up an old man from his path and brought me into an encounter with the long list of other worries that went with this place. So at this moment I was contemplating leaving this place again tomorrow and walking the two miles to the bus stop with a view to riding into Gloucester and joining my cousin, as if peace might be found there instead.

The single thing that checked me was my other fear; the one where I am afraid I will discover a few years from now that instead of finding the tranquillity I crave, I've actually developed a terrible habit of dramatising the more ordinary parts of life and fleeing from them for absolutely no good reason at all. So really I had no intention of going anywhere.

Except, of course, to bed and the hope that tomorrow would be an easier day.

Unfortunately, as it turned out, I also have a habit of falling into naïve optimism, and in this instance the lesson came in the form of a light knock upon the front door at about eleven o'clock as I prepared to go upstairs at last.

My visitor was Mrs Abbey and I'm afraid to say that for a brief childish moment I was tempted to feign deafness and leave her out there. But then maturity or responsibility or pure idle curiosity or whatever it was dictated that I opened the door and let her in.

As first entrances went, hers wasn't favourable. The first thing she did as she stepped in a slinking manner out of the dark and along the cramped hallway was to eye the proliferation of oriental vases on the narrow shelf that snaked away at head height into the kitchen and remark, 'I see Miss Jones hasn't yet brought herself to clear away the old lady's ugly knickknacks.'

They were very ugly and it was, I realised then, absolutely no wonder that I'd been running a long argument with the past and loneliness tonight. These feelings dwelt here in this house. Each of the rooms in this cottage was consumed by the fuss and clutter of a dead person's tastes. In the hallway, my aunt's commemorative plates joined a flight of ducks to soar away up the stairs. In the tiny sitting room, fading cross-stitch samplers competed for space with Victorian day beds and fragments of broderie anglaise. Upstairs, in the room designated to be my bedroom, there was just enough space between the display of thimbles and the miniature hazel hurdles for my suitcase and the bed. I've never met anyone before or since who could compete with the scale of Aunt Edna's commitment to traditional crafts. All the time that I'd been working myself up towards going to bed, I'd struggled to convince myself that her shade wasn't watching from the collection of shadows on the coat rack. She'd died six months ago and in hospital rather than here, but I wasn't entirely sure she wasn't the sort to indulge in a spot of haunting all the same.

Suddenly, in an unexpected way, Mrs Abbey's bluntness made me like her. It made me lead the way down the short step into the kitchen and I should probably explain why my cousin Phyllis wasn't presently in it herself. The explanation for her sudden trip to the city of Gloucester had been left for me on the front step in the form of a note dated yesterday with instructions on where to find the key. Cousin Phyllis was trapped in hospital by the inconvenience – her words not mine – of a broken wrist. A friend of hers had scrawled a postscript upon the envelope with the information that the doctor was intending to keep Phyllis for a day or two yet and that this friend would drop by at some point to see that I was managing.

I thought for a moment that Mrs Abbey was the author of this postscript and that was why she was here. I even had the horrible suspicion that this woman was actually here now to break the news that my cousin's bicycle accident hadn't been an accident at all, and I had to add another act of violence to the day's tally.

But she didn't. She had nothing to say on the subject at all. She was far too busy proving that she was at least a little bit of a genuine gossip because she was enjoying the horror of the attack on Mr Winstone and the inconvenience of Eddington being half a mile on from here and the irritation that certain self-important gentlemen didn't consider it necessary to drop a woman home.

'Did you help them ferry Mr Winstone to the doctor after all?' My bewilderment wasn't easy to hide.

Eyebrows lifted. In the greasy light of the oil lamp on my cousin's kitchen table, her hair looked more frayed about the edges than it had been before. The yellow glow was casting her cheekbones into strong relief and it made the shadows under her eyes stronger. She looked tired. But no weariness could affect her presence. She was, as I have said, rather tall and immaculately clad in a navy skirt and jacket, and she had a jaw that implied considerable strength of will and carried its own kind of beauty. There was, I'd noticed, something about the confidence of women of that age – all over thirty – who knew these days exactly what they were capable of and wore it as easily as a dash of lipstick.

Mrs Abbey's mouth only formed a little smirk as she conceded, 'If I'd gone with them on their little jolly to see the doctor, they'd have insisted on driving me straight home and I'd have been safely tucked up under the sheets by now instead of bothering you on your doorstep. No, the truth is I'm here because it's getting horribly late and it's still a long way home and I've done something rather foolish.'

The smirk eased to show a brief gleam of teeth.

I repeated blankly, 'Foolish?'

She leaned in to confide dramatically, 'I went to where *it* had happened and to see if this vagrant had left any signs behind.'

Ah. She wanted to discuss her squatters again. I disarmed her as best I could. 'It's not foolish at all. Freddy and I did exactly the same thing. Would you like a cup of tea?'

It was only after I made the offer that I remembered that my cousin's kitchen was like Mrs Winstone's house. Here too we were dependent on an ancient cast-iron range for any cooking. My parents' home in Putney had running water, gas and electricity laid on. This kitchen had a big stone sink without taps, a tiny window that looked out onto the privy and the single luxury of a full jug of water on the sideboard waiting to be used. Unfortunately, I hadn't lit the beast of a range yet and it was going to require a minor war to get it going. Then Mrs Abbey chose that moment to break the latest shocking news of the evening. She actually laughed at my offer and said, 'No tea for me, thank you. I know where you get your water.' Then, seeing my face, added, 'You did know it came from the stream, didn't you?'

I'd been drinking from that jug all afternoon. While I was hastily resolving to boil the water very thoroughly from now on, Mrs Abbey drew out a seat at my cousin's tiny table.

The kitchen was whitewashed on both walls and ceiling

and the clean austerity of the room was a direct contradiction of the clutter that swamped the rest of the house. I moved to the sideboard and propped myself there. Now that I'd let this woman into my home and gone through the brief flutter of companionship I had time to wonder why she was here at all. I prepared to let the silence stretch. I was beaten by Mrs Abbey's sly sideways look and murmur of, 'How did you get along with Freddy?'

Her manner puzzled me. It was the sort of tone a woman might use while probing an illicit liaison, only this boy was barely fifteen. I said helplessly, 'He seems very nice.'

'Didn't you find him a little simple, poor boy?'

This was what she was probing. 'No.'

'I suppose you didn't know him before, did you? That's one thing that can be said for Matthew Croft, he's certainly improved the boy.'

'Mr Croft isn't his father, is he? I mean, he's not Freddy *Croft?*'

This question amused her. She laughed. 'He certainly isn't. Matthew married Mrs Croft in the spring. Or Eleanor Phillips, as was, I should say. And she isn't his mother either.'

I conveyed my enquiry with a look. The name was not one that had made its way into my cousin's letters. Which, to be frank, meant my cousin liked her.

Mrs Abbey added cheerfully, 'Her farm is the one just up the lane from the village. You'll see her out and about exercising her horses. Or, at least, usually you do but I haven't seen her ride for a while. Freddy's helped her with them since he was evacuated here. He's from London, like you. Although perhaps not quite like you. His former home is presently a flat piece of ground in one of those cleared spots around the East End.'

'And is yours?'

'Pardon?'

'You, me and Freddy; we're all from London. It's starting to feel more like home by the minute.'

Mrs Abbey looked askance at my comment. It made me realise what it was about this visit that felt slightly out of kilter with my expectations. She wasn't here for tea. She wasn't really here as my cousin's friend and she certainly wasn't quite succeeding at becoming mine. That was the point, I realised. The problem here wasn't so much that I didn't think that I would like her but that I felt she wasn't quite letting me know her. I might have decided that I thought she was wrong for sifting through so many subjects just as soon as she entered the house but they were all shifting so rapidly from genuine humour into sharp edges that I still couldn't say that even these rather harder gossipy kind of comments were truly giving me a clear measure of who she was.

Actually, there were two things I could tell. The first was that she didn't have a very nice way of repaying the way everyone tended to be kind to her. And they did it without seeming to like her very much either.

I also could tell that she was only prepared to allow a discussion on her old life amongst the barrow boys of the London East End in that it gave her a chance to return to a discussion of those squatters.

'Sweet of you, Emily, dear,' she remarked with the crisp elocution that comes from superior schooling at an early age, 'to imply that I rank amongst the Freddys of this world as an evacuee but actually my old home was levelled years ago for a new gas works. But if it's Londoners you want, you'll find this place feels even more like home soon. There's a whole bunch of émigrés in a camp a mile or two away at the old air-raid look-out station on the Gloucester road.'

Her little conversational turn was so neatly done it made me smile. I understood at last why she'd been so keen to talk about Freddy. His origin would have brought us to this point if my comment about hers hadn't.

I was standing with my back to the cast-iron stove leaning against the rail that dried the dishcloth. Mrs Abbey's attention didn't enjoy the subject of the squatters for long. Her mouth was already running on to fresh sympathies for the old Colonel and his prolonged absence which had allowed the squatters to arrive unchecked. At least, I thought she meant to seem sympathetic. What she actually said was, 'Silly old coward. The whole family knows how to make a mess of things, so I suppose we shouldn't expect them to step into the breach about this. I suppose your cousin told you about young Master John Langton's antics and passed them off as if they were just a little misstep?'

I stilled against my prop of old metal while she added a shade sourly, 'Everyone does it. It's a great conspiracy of silence out of respect for the old man, but I can tell you that nothing the son did should ever be classed as forgettable. They have no right to do it to him. Master John was unreasonable, beautiful, vibrant and terrible and he gambled everything, including his life here, as if they were just counters to be won and lost. At the end, those fearsomely blue eyes—'

'Mrs Abbey, don't.' The plea was sudden but forceful. The way that her voice dwelt on the man's nature was almost like a caress.

My urgent interjection came as she drew breath to start telling me about how John Langton had died. Only I already knew how he'd died. He died like anyone does losing a game they had intended to win. Unwillingly.

She persisted, 'Didn't *you* say tonight that the man you saw was tall and dark?'

Now Freddy's white face was in my mind, and the way the Captain had sounded when I had unwittingly dredged up the memory for him. When I didn't manage to formulate a reply, she added it for me. Musingly, seriously, she added, 'Yes. Yes, you did. When you were telling Mrs Winstone that you'd seen him on the path you said that he was wearing summer clothes that were too good to belong to a farmhand, that he had black hair and was tall. Lean, was it?' This was as I corrected her. 'Well that's just another way of saying tall, isn't it? And if he should have happened to have a limp ...?'

'I—'

She was sitting there with her hands spread on the table. It was the sort of manner a person contrives when they think they're being very daring and I didn't like it. I suppose I was easily spooked tonight. Her mistake in Mr Winstone's house had sent all sorts of shadows racing about the room and Aunt Edna's slightly mad collection had accompanied me all evening. I certainly didn't need Mrs Abbey to begin conjuring the dead man's shade from the corners again now.

I told her more clearly, 'I don't want to know about it. Don't you think it might be time for bed?'

She didn't take the hint. She told me with relish, 'Master John had a physical weakness in one leg. He took a riding accident in his youth and his body never quite allowed him to forget it. Its waxing and waning was a barometer of his darkest moods.'

I think she could tell I was about to protest rather more precisely. She turned her eyes to an ugly vase on the high shelf before she said with a different kind of eagerness, 'Of course, if you're about to tell me that the man on Mr Winstone's path today *didn't* have a limp and piercing blue eyes—'

'You think I remember the colour of his *eyes?*'

'— There is someone else who matches that description, who didn't die last March. Someone who is also tall and capable and to whom, for all they say he was innocent, everyone was happy to attribute all manner of violent tendencies until young Master John's death put it clear out of their minds ...'

Her gaze returned to me. It actually made me laugh. 'Mrs Abbey, if you mean to hint at Matthew Croft, I have to tell you I think you'd do better to stick to the version that blames the squatters. There must be someone amongst them who matches your description of tall and dark with blue eyes.'

For a moment I thought my tone had shocked her. Then I realised that she was just amused by my tart adoption of her idea of Mr Winstone's attacker. It didn't really matter what

I said I thought he looked like. She knew what I'd told them at the village.

With rather more frankness and rather less play at scandal, she asked me with a coolness that was the most authentic curiosity I'd had from her, 'When you were with Freddy just now, did you see anything? Find anything he'll feel obliged to tell the others?'

Oddly enough I appreciated the honesty of this open question. She wanted to know what we had found because if Freddy lived with Matthew Croft and Freddy told him that we'd searched the spot, she knew perfectly well that the information would not be returned to her. The exclusion almost explained her visit here, except that this might have just as easily waited until the morning.

I told her the truth. 'We tried to look about but it was dark and more than a little unnerving. We didn't find any great clues, if that's what you're asking.'

Mrs Abbey wasn't smiling in the lamplight. This was the real woman and she was deeply alert for something. I could feel its energy emanating from her; building in hard waves ready to break. The thought came unbidden – ready to break like anger.

'Mrs Abbey,' I began tentatively, 'Why don't you like Mr Croft?'

Her gaze flickered and cooled to a wry smile. 'I wasn't very tactful earlier, was I? That man ... well, that man is everything John Langton can't be. He's alive and he's frustratingly reserved. He won't talk about what happened, regardless of how I ask – and don't look like you think I'm only probing for the sake of gossip because, believe me, I knew young Master John and of all the ways we could manage what went wrong, this conspiracy of silence so that we never dare to even *speak* his name is the worst kind of healing. There isn't even a grave where we can lay his ghost to rest—' Something passed across her face like a settling of control. Afterwards, her words were steadier and less inclined towards revelation. I still wasn't allowed to know her. 'And to crown it all, that man refuses to buy my old car that's mouldering in my barn.'

Her mouth plucked into amusement. I mustered a vague smile in return as I was meant to. Then she asked in her own version of my earlier hesitancy, 'Emily, dear, tell me the truth. Did you really see as little as you declared earlier? Or are you just displaying the practical city-dweller's approach to a drama and walking swiftly by on the other side of the street?'

'Do you mean to ask if I'm minding my business in case someone minds it for me? What do you think?'

Mrs Abbey hadn't meant to offend. At least, I presumed not. She said benignly, 'I think it's very unfortunate that poor Mr Winstone can't remember the man's face ...'

'... Since that just leaves my description and I barely saw him at all.' I finished the point for her. Foolish honesty made me add, 'Although, I should say that I think I'd recognise him if I saw him again.'

I didn't expect Mrs Abbey's demeanour to transform to decisiveness quite so abruptly, but it did, all the same. The change might almost have been with relief. This feeling was certainly running high. She was suddenly dragging out a wristwatch on a broken strap from a pocket. I suppose it mattered to know that I knew enough that this man might be identified and caught; in a strange way I suppose it promised safety even if this night had to be got through first. And that in itself was a clue to her real purpose here, because then she was telling me about the footpath to her little farmhouse and doing one of those funny twists people do when they mean to point out its location only to find themselves waving a hand at the impenetrable screen of a wall. This was the reason why she was here. At last I understood that she wanted to feel in control and at last I was allowed to know the reason for all this odd circular conversation that she patently didn't really enjoy. She'd given herself a fright at the turbine house and couldn't quite bring herself to face the long walk up a darkened path to her farmhouse alone.

'You could stay,' I offered doubtfully. 'Unless your hus— someone will be out looking for you?' I'd almost said husband then and saw from the way she jumped that I'd cut rather too close to that deeply private pain. For a moment she stared at me with that vacancy of expression that a person gets when they've been tested unexpectedly on an unhealed wound.

Then the moment passed and she was saying with elegant amusement that was also very genuine, 'What, will you make room for me amongst all the Welsh love-spoons? No, I've got to get back. It's practically neglect as it is and if I hadn't been foolish enough to meet with Mrs Winstone by the shop I'd have been home hours ago. The path from the ford is very overgrown—'

'Let me just fetch a jacket,' I interrupted, 'and a torch.'

I stood up from my lean against the stove. Mrs Abbey's eyes followed the movement. In the lamplight, her face was wan. 'As easy as that? You're coming with me?' Her voice was odd. Shaken would be the best term I had for it, as though guilt strode in on the heels of getting what she wanted.

I pressed my lips into a hapless line. After all those musings on responsibility, this particular question didn't even require debate. There were some things that you would agree to do without forcing a person to ask first.

I moved past her into the hallway. She rose to follow me and seeing her afresh in a different light I was startled to perceive the faint sheen of moisture on her skin. There was an energy to her movement that had nothing to do with her endlessly shifting humour. She had that look of exhaustion where she was growing so tired of her lot that she was coming out the other side. She was very glad I'd offered to come with her. It hadn't been temper before. I'd mistaken it. This energy came from the unpleasantness of being horribly spooked by her night-time prowling and the release of finally admitting it.

I found the torch as I struggled into my shoes. It was jammed inside a large and genuine Grecian urn that stood beside the elephant's foot umbrella stand in the hall. The umbrella stand was inevitably a mark of the old lady's taste, but the urn might just have been my cousin's. Phyllis's war had been a rather different experience from mine.

Having lingered silently beside me for the past five minutes while I searched, Mrs Abbey abruptly spied a different object of interest. My suitcase was standing at the foot of the stairs where I had left it many hours before. She asked in a curiously strong voice, 'Have we driven you away?'

I didn't quite trust myself to reply. It was too complicated. So instead I blew out the last of the lamps and stepped out into the surprisingly well-defined landscape beneath a starlit night in August. My companion took the torch from my hand and waited while I fumbled with the key. It was an enormous thing and I had a vague suspicion my aunt had taken it, lock and door and all, from a church somewhere. I only hoped the church had been a more willing participant in the transaction than the elephant who had supplied the umbrella stand.

The night air seemed to revive Mrs Abbey. I heard the increase in the rate of her breathing while I struggled to turn the key. With the sort of embarrassed haste that, in my experience, is commonly used when one has just found a lost object in one's own pocket after initiating an extensive communal search, I heard Mrs Abbey say, 'You know, I don't really need you to come with me at all. I'm bothering you unnecessarily. I'll just borrow the torch, if I may, and return it tomorrow if I catch you before you go. Otherwise, I'll leave it for Miss Jones. Goodnight. I'll be quite safe, and thank you for the company tonight.'

She left me standing there so swiftly that I didn't even have time to formulate a protest. Or perhaps I was relieved to believe her and let her go. The garden gate clanged shut and then I briefly saw her shadow as a darker shape against the white streak of the stone track. There was a brief flash from the torch as she found the path beside the ford and then the light was extinguished long before her shape was swallowed by the scrubby woodland at the base of the hill. Wood smoke that wasn't from my stove hung in a silver mist on the silent valley air. The idea of darkness in this desolate place really took on a very different quality compared to the sooty gloom I had known in Putney.

Closer by, something rustled in the dry stalks of the bean plant behind me. It made me shiver and step back in through that heavy door very rapidly indeed. What, I wondered, had she been so afraid was waiting for her out there that she'd come to find me, only to abruptly change her mind? Because she had been afraid for a while there, I knew she had. It had been the only feeling she had shared, but it had been genuine. And then the feeling had passed for her with a suddenness that had carried its own kind of violence.

I bolted the door and checked all the windows. This house was wonderfully secure. No intruders would be working their way in here except in the same manner as the one who had lately stepped in after knocking on the front door. I shut out her visit like I shut out the night. It was, however, impossible to shut out the overwhelming sense that I had just escaped something, only I didn't know whether the relief had really been hers.

Chapter 6

This new morning began with company and friendliness, where yesterday had ended with loneliness and worries. The nearby shop – and by nearby I mean at the end of a heating two-mile walk to the bus stop and beyond – stood a few doors down from Mrs Winstone's hairdresser in a sunken lane with sheep pasture beyond. The most sinister thing I encountered in that busy place while I made the sacrifice of funds and rations for the sake of the Colonel's lunch was the welcome offered by the shopkeeper and her mildly mildewed husband and the collection of respectable mature ladies who used the shop as a waiting room for the doctor's house next door. They seemed to take their slice of gossip as a kind of tithe on users of the public telephone.

Which meant in a way that it was perhaps fortunate that I failed to reach my cousin on the ward telephone at the hospital. If I had, I'd have unwittingly filled the assembled ears with enough gossip to keep their mouths working for the next few days at least. Instead, I only got to speak to a nurse, who wouldn't even confirm that there was a Miss P Jones on the women's ward at present. The most she would say was that the telephone trolley would be on the ward for the patients' use at six o'clock this evening and I could try again then, which wasn't terribly useful since sometime in the course of last night I had discovered the idea of achieving a different and more enjoyable kind of flight in the form of going down to join Phyllis today. It would be typical if it turned out that as I travelled down on the bus to Gloucester, she should be travelling up towards her home.

I'd left my suitcase at the Manor. It would save at least part of this long walk if I decided to make the trip anyway. It was a good job too because I knew I'd never have found the courage to climb back up out of the valley otherwise. The walk back to the village on its own seemed designed for exhaustion. It was hot already and a heat haze was casting mirages amongst the tall masts of the wireless station by that bus stop. Only one car passed me on the long lane and it was fortunate that I had about a mile's warning before it came into view because, unbelievably, it nearly ran me over. It barrelled down into a dip between farm buildings like a rude black beast of a bull and sent a chip of stone flying up onto my ankle while I politely waited on the verge. Then it vanished around a bend and took the roar of its motor with it.

I thought I'd found it parked in the massive stone barn that flanked the Manor farmyard. No one was in the village again and the farmyard had renewed its camouflage of dereliction. I'd walked that way round to the Colonel's kitchen door after doing my duty by knocking on Mr Winstone's door first. He wasn't there. No one spent their days at home here.

The long black nose of the enormous car was occupying

the cusp between light and shade beneath the great gaping threshing doors of the barn. A touch to its bonnet proved that the engine was warm. Movement emerged from the depths within and it was Danny Hannis's dog. He sauntered out from the left-hand wing of the barn. It was now that I saw that this great building was no longer dedicated to grain processing. Half of the space within was consumed by the unmistakeable profile of a shrouded steam engine. The other bay housed rusting hay rakes and implements and a very expensive modern grey tractor which looked similarly like it had already worked very hard for its keep.

There was no sign of the man but the dog was a curious soul. He supervised me as I abandoned this dark cathedral for farming technology. He was with me when I caught the distant murmur of a voice beyond the turn of the other barn; the older one that sagged beneath the weight of its years and ranged further up the hill to meet the Manor kitchen.

It wasn't a happy voice. It was a low stutter of 'm's, like a moan. My first thought naturally enough was of Mr Winstone. My second was for that missing housekeeper.

There it was again, to my left behind a low door into this second barn. It was a low mumble like an injured soul might make, or a hostage, bound and gagged. It made me grasp another concept of horror. The one where a forgotten woman lay unheeded for days on end.

The cobbled space between house and barn was empty. So were the long terraces of the garden. There was no other sound of life here. Other than the dog, I mean. He was at my heels and the only sound he made was the faint click-click of claws on the cobbled ground.

It was the stuff nightmares are built on. I had to ease open the door into an ancient space. I had to wake to the guilt of knowing I'd meant to look last night for conclusive signs that the housekeeper really had left, only I'd been distracted by the way Freddy had appeared. The door was set on surprisingly well-oiled hinges between ancient walls several feet thick. Within was a long narrow stone-flagged passage that ran like a cave along the painted face of wood-panelled stalls and loose-boxes and pillars that supported a low hayloft. This barn had been a tithe barn in its former life – a vast storeroom for a medieval wealth of grain – but its recent job had been to house the Manor stables and, like the rest of this place, its grandeur stood as a monument to neglect after the loss of the son. A set of heavily bolted carriage doors stood at the far end as a bar to freedom and daylight. All the Manor buildings seemed to have issues with good light. The only light here came from about five unglazed slits spread along the barn's length and the small open door by my side. Dust hung in the narrow beams of sun-shot air, waiting for a breeze.

Mrs Cooke the housekeeper wasn't here. No one was, at least no person. The murmur came from a lonely goat living in quiet luxury in the stable that was tucked at the end of the row beneath the steps to the hayloft. I'd never met a goat before. This one had his own lancet window and he was a friendly beast, albeit slightly alarming when his head suddenly appeared at eye height, with his front feet hooked over the stable door. He was also rather too interested in the forgotten parcel of groceries in my hands. I left him with a promise to return later with the scraps.

The dog left me at the kitchen door. Alone again in the dry stillness inside I laid out my collection of salad stuff and wondered just how exactly I expected this meagre fare to do for the squire's lunch. Then I remembered that the note my cousin's friends had added to her letter had included the name of the woman who would sell me eggs. It seemed that someone lived by day in this place after all. She was tiny and crabbed and the luxurious cluster of eggs she unearthed in a vacant cowshed behind the steward's house was a far cry from the paltry one egg allowance Putney residents had enjoyed each week provided that they were in stock. Our transaction was also mildly illegal but I was hardly going to complain, particularly when she was kind enough to give me butter and half a loaf of bread for the Colonel's lunch too.

Phyllis's letters were always a source of information. Apart from the recent missive that was presently lodged in my suitcase and bore the crucial invitation to visit and directions to her door, I also had the memory of a hundred or so more that spanned the years and had come from various corners of the world. She was, as implied by my father's use of the unattractive term *spinster*, an unmarried woman of independent habits. But I didn't think she entirely warranted the term when she was in fact only thirty-one and, besides, I thought it a terrible way to summarise the contribution made by a woman who belonged to that generation of intellectuals who were recruited immediately in 1939 to lend their expertise to the various specialist branches of the War Office. Phyllis had been called up to do something very interesting with maps; her background was in geography.

My letters to her were the childish musings of a girl penned during the quiet times at the chemists. Phyllis's bold and witty replies were invariably written from obscure locations made even more obscure by the heavy hand of the censors, until they said only that she was well and that the weather was fair – meaning Scotland, I thought – or bracing – perhaps Shetland – or enjoyably temperate, which I took to mean somewhere hot and therefore foreign. The impressive Grecian vases nestling amongst her mother's clutter in the hall told their own story about where that might have been.

Unfortunately, I had neither my cousin nor one of her letters to guide me now. I was setting the hardboiled eggs to cool in a fresh pan of cold water – indoor taps in this kitchen, of course, presumably drawing spring water from a delightfully hygienic cistern – when I heard a clunk from the depths of the house. It manifested itself into a clatter from the floor above, followed by the bang of a door slamming at the front of the house. It reverberated along the passage and into the dining room and from there to me in the kitchen. It even made me cast an anxious glance out through the window in case a sudden squall had blown in, which it hadn't, and then it made me recollect my suitcase left any old how by the kitchen table, as if I were expecting the Colonel to invite me to stay.

I moved to retrieve it and found it wasn't there. But someone was indeed at the front of the house. Scurrying through the gloom of the dining room and then the passage, I learned that the bang had been a door being flung open. I'd assumed it had been the sound of it blowing shut. The distinction mattered because now I found the weighty front door thrown wide, letting in sunlight and flies, and a man heading up the stairs.

He was a short man in a dark suit and he had a suitcase in his hand. My suitcase.

He was oblivious to me. He seemed intent on marching upwards two steps at a time. There was a car outside, black and ordinary, like a cab the Colonel might have taken from his solicitor's office. I reached the curving scroll at the foot of the banister as the driver's foot disappeared out of sight.

I called some form of surprise up at him and set foot upon the stairs, I believe because I thought he was a respectable cab driver taking the passenger's bags to his room and he had somehow managed to confuse my bags for the Colonel's and it was my duty to correct the mistake. Only then the nature of the man's gait changed. Before it had been confident, decisive. Now, at the sound of my voice, he snapped round and charged with a clatter of footfalls back into view again. I heard his breathing. Rapid and light and not very friendly at all. There was a rush and a thump and a lasting impression of the beautiful plasterwork on the ceiling as I reeled for the banister. I thought for a moment he must have launched off the top step and landed on me. Then I thought he must have bolted blind straight past and caught me with the case. Finally I realised he hadn't done either and had the sudden cringing discovery that the man was beside me.

This space was light. White walls, white plasterwork and blinding sunlit glass. The tan case swung above me at about the height that might batter my head. There was a moment when a hand caught in my hair. Then it let me go with a suddenness that shocked almost as much as the impact had, leaving me to discover pain beneath my arm that would later reveal itself as a vivid bruise and also to taste the unpleasantness of a cut lip where I had bitten it while clutching painfully at the solid support of the wooden rail.

There was a crash below as he charged out through the door and missed his step, to turn an ankle where the stone flags met gravel. Then there was a roar as an engine kicked into life. I twisted there, hanging from my wooden anchor, catching my breath, and watched as a battered black Ford veered unevenly away up the curve of the drive towards the lane. I thought he turned right at the end, downhill.

I did nothing. The only thing I could state and did state later with any confidence was that this imposter's bald head was most definitely a long way removed from Mr Winstone's lean attacker.

Chapter 7

It was easy to trace where he had been. He'd allowed himself some time, I think, to search the house before our encounter in the stairwell. The evidence implied he must have been on the point of leaving until some sudden recollection drew him to race back inside with the bang that had brought me scurrying. It occurred to me that perhaps he had left some telltale mark behind, made some error that would allow us to identify him, and that was why he had dashed back in – in a determined effort to retrieve it.

If so, it wasn't in any of the downstairs rooms. He'd left doors swinging into the little room that opened from the wall beside the little table with the lamp on it – a library – and also the study where the telephone stood. At the swift glance I cast in through the door of each, the shelves of the library were untouched, but perhaps the bottles on the drinks trolley in the study were fewer than they had been. He had, of course, also made a thorough tour of the kitchen and helped himself to my suitcase.

The door of the kitchen was probably how he had got in. I'd bolted the front door firmly as I'd left with Freddy last night and it showed no signs of a forced entry now. I bolted it firmly once more and crept upstairs. I know why I went stealthily, as if I were myself a burglar. It was because the house suddenly felt cold and alien again and I wished I wasn't here.

Upstairs I found a series of three or more closed doors and a long passage that served as a gallery with a further collection of doors just distinguishable at the far end. It was darker again up here and the whole place smelled of mildew and old polish.

I was being watched. Not by the balding man or any possession of his. There was nothing to indicate he'd even been up here before the moment I caught him on the stairs. Instead, my audience was the row upon row of photographs on the wood-panelled walls. Hard Victorian gazes judged me severely as I passed. The women had sharp noses and the menfolk wore unattractive beards that sat beneath the jaw. Then I was greeted by the woman from the photograph in the study downstairs, this time glamorous in her Great War wedding suit. In the next she was smiling tiredly with black hair and extraordinary deep-set eyes and a very young boy in her lap and a badly concealed bulge around her middle. The same eyes were met in the portrait that followed this tranquil family scene, but this time in a young man. Even in hand-tinted colours in this gloom, the intelligent blue gaze of her teenage son shone out of the shifting features of one who might have been designed for the life of a musician or perhaps an orator. I knew which son this was. The clue was in those eyes and the height which matched Mrs Abbey's idea of a ghost. He was older in the next and this portrait gave an even stronger sense of the handsome face with a flair for drama, yet here I thought I could perceive a tinge of something colder, sadder. Harder. Perhaps it had been taken after the accident that had lamed him. Even so, even with the slightly defiant challenge of the supple lines of that mouth it would, I thought, have been easy to have liked him.

By contrast, the next photograph showed a different kind of man. He was young, perhaps nineteen or twenty. It came with a peculiar twist of pity that I observed how unexciting this person seemed compared to the brother who had looked so much like their mother. It proved how misleading an impression could be when it was formed purely by hearing a voice on a telephone. The present man must be older. His voice had led me to imagine a man with easy confidence and my mind had countered it by presuming he would turn out to be the sort of officer whose chin retreated into his neck just as his forehead advanced on his hairline. This young man in the photograph was neither. His brother burned; this man was subdued, a level gaze in a blandly unemotional face. He was followed by a sequence that captured the career of his father – a senior military man distinguished by an ever-increasing collection of medals – and I thought I could perceive something of a similarity between the Colonel and his older son, particularly in the set about their mouths. Neither looked like they smiled easily. Above it all I was remembering my complaint about Mrs Abbey and how hard I found it to be certain I knew who and what she really was. I suspected the same rule would apply to this man.

The floorboards at the end of the row creaked. I had drifted down the length of the gallery, to be standing just shy of the black corner where a second, narrower flight of stairs turned out of sight up to the attic floor. That sense of trespass returned violently. It carried the message that at any rate I ought to know precisely who and what the younger brother was. He was dead and the sort that left a terrible memory for his neighbours.

The thought dawned that it was not my job to find the traces left by that imposter. The air up here was not still and settled after his invasion. He was here, brooding and silent, and waiting for me to climb onwards from this unexpected encounter with the images of masters past and present. I whirled and raced for the lifeline of the telephone downstairs and the police station that could be reached through it.

I was woefully unprepared for the sudden tilt of my heart as I reached the stairs and a man emerged from the blaze beaming in through the freshly unbarred front door. His figure took form below, ascending as I prepared to race downwards.

I snatched at the banister rail. Only he wasn't charging into the attack like a burglar. He was running his hand along the rail himself as if he had every right to be there as he climbed steadily towards me. There was a stick in his other hand. The sight forced my mind to swing violently away from the dread of a renewed confrontation with a returning imposter to a jolt that was altogether less tangible; less easily digested in the light of day. At the heart of his silhouette, I could feel he was watching me. For a second my legs actually carried me down a few more steps, as if I might attempt my own version

81

of the wild leap down the stairs and bolt past him for the door.

Then in the next second my mind sharply observed that my appearance had surprised him just as much as he had surprised me. More than that, I saw that he had noticed my impulse to escape and was instinctively bracing himself to put out that arm to intercept it. It made him real. It made his shape become more solid. My hand tightened on the banister, snatching me to a halt where my feet weren't quite yet ready to do the job themselves. He stopped too; or rather the instinct that threatened immediate action passed into something less intimidating as he read the manner of my appearance more clearly. And then my eyes adjusted to take in his features.

'Emily, I presume,' Captain Richard Langton said from his position about seven or so steps beneath me, and placed himself firmly in the land of the living. 'Why are you up here?'

Like his portrait on the wall, the Colonel's older son was unsmiling. Below I heard a mutter from a more aged person who was passing from the stairwell into the passage and onwards towards the kitchen. Outside, beyond the newly opened front door, a man was dragging cases out of the back of a shabby cab and stacking them on the drive.

The Captain's steady climb reached me and I stepped aside to allow him to retain his grip on the banister. I remembered the sense of pity that had met my examination of his portrait and was disorientated by it. It stole my capacity to speak sensibly. I said in a shaken rush, 'You're limping. For a moment I thought—'

Later I would be forever grateful that intelligence briefly

put in an appearance and checked the end of that sentence. I had been about to say that for a moment I'd thought he was his brother.

Instead, I found that he was surveying me with the sort of calm scrutiny that scorched. I imagine he saw a silly young woman in a summer frock with a pale face and standing on the stairs in a house where she had no right to be. I saw that he was a good few years older than the young man in his photograph. He didn't tower over a person as his brother must have done, but was tall enough to have seemed nicely built had it not been for the debilitating distraction of the cane, and I had the slightly embarrassing thought that the voice on the telephone had been an indication of the presence of the real man after all. He wasn't wearing a uniform. His ordinary single-breasted suit over shirt and tie would have done for any reasonably wealthy man of the day.

So much I grasped as he turned his attention to my question. I heard him say with creditable mildness, 'I sprained something tangling with an idiot who was running for the same train. It'll ease off soon enough. What *are* you doing up here?'

Then, sharper, 'There's blood on your ear.'

I put a hand up. My fingertips came away stained with a thin film, like grease. I had been bashed about the head by my case after all. The memory went through me like a bolt. Followed by the memory that I had been on my way to telephone for the police. I found that my eyes must have drifted past him onwards down the stairs at the thought because his head half turned to follow my gaze as if unsure that I wasn't acknowledging a presence beyond him. There wasn't anyone there, of course. His gaze slowly returned to me, watching me more closely. I imagine he was wondering if my sudden desire to move onwards was driven by the shame of snooping. I had an overwhelming urge to show him my empty hands, palms uppermost.

Instead I scrubbed away the blood on my fingers and gabbled anxiously, 'There was a man. In this house. I was preparing your father's lunch and he was in here. He stole my case. I'd only left it here while I went to the shop. I came through into the stairwell and he ran past me into a car – he'd been looking about the house, I think. He'd been into your library and the study. I came up to see what he'd been doing upstairs. I don't know who he was. After what happened to Mr Winstone last night I thought, well … I don't know. He bashed me as he took off and, as I said, he took my case.' A hesitation before I added nonsensically, 'It had all my clothes in.'

I had to suddenly reach past him for the banister. Not because I was in any way unequal to the distress but because my words were coming out so quickly that I ran out of breath. I found that his hand had flashed to my elbow to steady me. It was done with the same instinctive reflex that would have formerly intercepted my flight. It meant to save me from tipping head first down the stairs but it hurt too because his walking stick was trapped beneath his hand and my flesh.

Now I really was breathless. He steadied me for a moment and then said, 'All right now?'

'Yes. Yes, fine now, thank you.'

He let me go. I stayed propped against that vital solidity of the banister. Then he said in a tone of some doubt, 'Did you say someone came in here to steal your *bag?*'

'My suitcase, actually. It was only left in the kitchen while I went to the shop.'

'Very well, your case,' he amended calmly. 'But *why?*'

I was calm again myself now. I turned my back against the banister and said plainly, 'I haven't the faintest idea. He'd been in the library. And that office to the right.' A waft of my hand. 'I was about to go in there myself to telephone the police when you arrived.'

I saw something snap in his expression. An indefinable shift in his attention. 'Show me,' he said. And suddenly, uniform or no, I really was face to face with a career soldier.

The cane was dropped against the banister and the long coat that had been draped over his arm was hung there above it. There was no sign of the limp now as he went with me down to the white and black chequerboard tiles on the ground floor.

He hesitated when he reached the threshold into the room that housed the telephone. For a moment I thought he was anticipating something that waited for him in the room beyond.

I was seeing the room for the first time as he must; as a person familiar with it must, I mean. There was the same warm sunlit glow and today it cast into relief the pretty feminine décor of a woman's drawing room that was only superficially supplanted by its later incarnation as a man's study. This had been his mother's room and her personal choice of paintings still hung on the wall; two landscapes in unattractive brown. My father would have loved them both. I was more conscious of the masculine touches that overlaid the woman's tastes. They belonged to the young Master John as Mrs Abbey had called him, and they also belonged to the dread that had flooded Freddy's face as he had approached this very same threshold last night.

It was the same memory that this was the brother's domain that checked the man beside me now. But the Captain had better mastery of his feelings than the boy had, where calmness might manage the job better. He only asked me unnecessarily, 'In here, you say?'

And stepped into the room.

I watched him as he surveyed the untouched surfaces and shelves of this space. I found myself recalling the photographs on the gallery wall and realising that I'd misread him there too. The idea I'd had that he was a cold, bland man beside the insatiable, charming energy of his brother was a lie. I'd read that grey portrait as calm but it was only calm if the manner of the control itself served to prove the energy of the thoughts beneath. I don't mean to say that he displayed an unhealthy tendency for concealment. In fact, I believe it was the opposite. This was a man who had the intelligence to feel but also to take responsibility for his manners and to govern them, particularly at times like the present when a young woman had surprised him in his house.

Of course the contrast to this was the intimidating idea that instinct might be the force that unchained responsibility for him. It made me wonder if the physical part of his life in soldiering was the moment that measured reason twisted into the freedom of pure reflex. In short, I found myself wondering if he enjoyed the liberation of violence.

It was a bad moment for the Captain to turn and spy me waiting awkwardly on the threshold, fingers toying blindly with the grooved wood that framed the doorway. My mouth began to frame the tentative suggestion that perhaps he should undertake the act that had motivated my flight from the gallery upstairs and it was time to call the police. It would have marked a conclusion to my part here for both of us. Then he caught as I did the crescendo of speech in the passage behind me and beyond the stairwell. The sharp rattle of raised voices in there was accompanied by the unexpected yip as a dog barked.

In a moment he was past me, a hand lightly brushing my sleeve in encouragement to follow, and perhaps reassurance. He met the commotion in the claustrophobic gloom of the passage. I was behind him. We weren't witnesses to another assault though. At least not one by a human. Danny Hannis was there with a captive white blur wriggling away under his arm. He must have just snatched his dog up after it had been discovered attempting to worry the old man's ankles. The Colonel was there now beyond him, a bullish head on a short neck, who must have once stood taller than his son. He was the sort of man who in his youth must have strutted about grim-jawed with all the might of his military training, but now he was reduced to being all torso and frail limbs. He seemed to develop a list as he marched along the passage towards us to the point that his shoulder veered helplessly into a line of gin traps. He was brandishing a fist like a prize fighter. I wasn't quite sure who he was preparing to beat: the dog or the farmhand.

The Captain curbed it all by saying quite cheerfully, 'Hello, Hannis,' before adding, 'Father, do you have to announce your return by battering an estate worker?'

'Particularly when the estate worker in question only came in to see what Miss Sutton was up to.' Danny was not, it must be said, particularly cowed by the Colonel's anger. Perhaps it was a common enough mood that no one here thought to take it seriously.

'What was she up to?' I felt the Captain's gaze switch curiously to my face.

Danny abandoned retreat to tell him quite coolly in a tone that was rather unpleasantly man-to-man, 'I saw her go nosing into the tithe barn and then here, and then that car dashed off.'

There was something there that uncomfortably gave the suggestion of suspicion. I tried to hide my irritation. The Captain, on the other hand, really did conceal nothing. I felt the readjustment quite plainly as he reconsidered my flight from the gallery upstairs. It made my cheeks flush quickly and hotly since, on the subject of behaving oddly, Danny was rather more guilty than I, given the fact he must have been hiding in the machine barn while his dog had escorted me on my way.

I told Danny, 'In which case you'll be interested to know I thought I was looking for Mrs Cooke. Only I found a goat instead. And since we're talking cars, did you have to nearly run me down in the lane with that beast of a machine?'

I felt my mouth work into silence in a peculiar way as it dawned on me just as soon as I spoke that of course it hadn't been Danny who had roared along the lane at me. It had almost certainly been the bald-headed imposter arriving to begin his search. I risked a glance at the Captain. He'd guessed it from the change in my expression. That control was in evidence again on his face. This time from the cool turn of his gaze towards me his manner appeared to wish to project itself onto me. Well, as it was, I could appreciate the impulse that might drive a son to shield his ageing father from the shock of learning that his home had been invaded, particularly coming as it did in the wake of a belated return to the site of recent bereavement and the added distress of Mr Winstone's attack.

I did my best to help. I stood there mutely and let the Captain tell me briskly, 'Hannis isn't allowed to drive the car. Something about the nature of his cornering has put my father off. I can't imagine why.'

The remark made Danny's grin return briefly in the dark. There was concealment somewhere in there of a different sort that seemed like a conspiracy to avert a different stress for the old man. I thought Danny knew I'd noticed. He added with perfect blandness, as if pre-empting another accusation, 'And before you ask, it can't have been Pops behind the wheel just now because the doctor took one look last night and prescribed bed and quiet. So with that in mind, he's gone into town with Mum on the bus.'

There was no grin this time, but beneath the rough hair, his eyes gleamed. We attempted a general movement towards the light of the stairwell. Only unfortunately, for all the old man's air of increasing infirmity, the Colonel was still as sharp as a tack.

As he stepped out into the better light of the space beneath the stairs from the peculiar tomb of violent implements that seemed in some way a physical representation of his grief, I saw his face clearly for the first time. In other ranked soldiers I had met, even when dressed in ordinary clothes, their profession had always been distinguishable by the peculiar suppleness around their mouths when they spoke; something like an exaggeration of the movement of the jaw that belonged to men who spent a lot of time in the officer's mess and got a lot of practice at guffawing. I couldn't imagine this old soldier had ever guffawed in his life.

His son didn't look like he belonged to that class either. He certainly wasn't smiling when his father queried coldly, 'You saw this man?'

Because I was stupid, I asked blankly, 'Which man?'

'Father, this is the young woman who made me run for the train. Miss Sutton.' Just beyond my right shoulder the Captain's voice was low and mildly persuasive, as though his father was in danger of bullying me like he did Danny Hannis. For a moment I thought the son was saving me, but when I turned my head I found that although his eyes were a considerably less dramatic shade of hazel compared to his father's grey, at that moment they shared rather too much of the family intensity for my comfort. There was something odd there; a kind of dismissive impatience when he added, 'I think, Emily, you said you were about to prepare my father's lunch?'

Flushing, I said lamely, 'Why yes, I—'

'This man who nearly ran you down.' The Colonel's interruption was decisive. 'He was here? At this house? Was it the same fellow who ...?'

He meant to ask, of course, if this were the same fellow I had encountered on Mr Winstone's garden path. Standing by the table with the lamp on it, the old man's gaze was unwavering. I couldn't help answering now. I risked a glance at the Captain as I said awkwardly, 'He wasn't the same man.'

I caught the moment the son raised his eyes to heaven.

The Colonel was waiting. I could see that he was used to having his orders obeyed. I could also see that his hand was trembling a little where it hung by the polished lip of the table. I said unwillingly, 'He looked like a city man who had taken a wrong turn off the main road.' I couldn't help the stray of my eyes towards the Captain's own city attire. There was a twitch of enquiry in response to the unintended insult. I added hastily, 'I mean his suit was grey and he wasn't terribly tall and he was balding.'

'Age?' This was from Danny.

'About fifty, I think. He had a pappy complexion.'

'Pappy?' The Colonel frowned at the term.

'You know, fleshy but soft, like a shrivelled potato.'

'You have excellent powers of observation.' I believe the Captain was mocking me. Little did he know how much I had been privately congratulating myself for learning the lessons of yesterday and managing to commit this man's features to memory. The Captain asked, 'And what did he take, do you know?'

He'd asked me this once before. He knew what I would say. 'Nothing that I know of,' I said, 'except my case, of course. He took my suitcase.'

'Yes, yes,' the Captain agreed impatiently, 'and with it, all your clothes. So that when we next see you, I presume you'll be clad in your aged aunt's wardrobe, which last saw the light of day in the era of bustles or something like that. Have pity for me while you do it. I wasn't planning a trip to the country when I dropped Father at the station yesterday and my change of mind came up on me, shall we say, rather abruptly and without leaving time to pack.'

'You needn't have come at all,' remarked the old man tersely while revealing for the first time the first glimmer of the parent beneath. He was fond of his son. That weakness in his hand wasn't fading though. It suddenly struck me that it was perhaps deliberate that the Captain was keeping us loitering in the lee of the staircase. A few steps more would confront the old man with the open door into the younger son's study and I thought I knew by now what effect it had. To lay it before the old man like this just as soon as he'd arrived would be an awful welcome.

'Hold on a minute, Emily.' I must have moved impulsively to shut it because the Captain put his hand out. I think he thought I was running away. His gesture held me there while he said to his father, 'Do you want your cane? I've taken it upstairs already. Emily? Perhaps you might ...?'

Perhaps he'd understood me after all. And perhaps he knew his father well enough to know that it wouldn't help to let the old man know why we were, in effect, managing his entrance to his own home. I nodded my agreement and turned to slide through the gap between the Captain and the painted triangle that screened the space under the rising stairs. Then the Colonel's voice addressed me so that I turned again and found myself briefly faced with the panel of glass beneath the stairs that proved to be a historic gun cabinet. Sporting guns from the ages were locked inside, gleaming with oil, and an awful lot of rotten old shooting sticks with deer's feet for handles.

I was turning again to face the Colonel as he asked, 'Do I understand correctly that you saw both these men? This fellow today and the man who struck Bertie? Has your stepfather remembered anything useful, by the way?' This last question was barked at Danny.

Danny shifted the weight of the little dog in his arms – who was now hanging like a deadweight in protest – and said blandly, 'Not really. To be honest, now the excitement's worn off and people have stopped fussing over him, the only thing Pop can really remember with any clarity is the sight of Miss Sutton's face looming over him on the path.'

'Poor man,' I sympathised automatically, before I'd thought. But really I was wondering why Danny had said it like that. Why he'd felt compelled to add this little mention of my part in Mr Winstone's collapse in the manner of an amusing aside and yet I could tell in an instant that it meant something to the Captain. I couldn't read Danny's face because his eyes were downcast as he ran his free hand over the dog's head in an easy caress, but I could read the Captain's. He was staring at me as though he'd just discovered a lie while he said clearly, for his father's sake, 'Well, it doesn't seem anything important was taken today. Do you want to step outside with Hannis, Father, and give your orders about where to take your many bags?'

And then the impasse was broken by a flurry of movement which bore the old man to the door and outside and the Captain to the study door. He shut it decisively. A hand gripped the handle firmly while his eyes followed the departure of his father and then as soon as he was sure the Colonel was out of earshot, his attention rounded onto me. I was hoping for an easing of tension; a recognition at the very least of our mutual charade. I wasn't prepared to meet suspicion. And I wasn't remotely happy to perceive the tone in his voice when he said, 'What are you doing here, truly? I mean *who* are you? What is your profession?'

I gaped. The lie he thought he'd discovered was very specifically mine. It made me bluster, 'I beg your pardon? What have I been doing? I've been here talking to you on the telephone, I should think, and running errands, that's what.' His head tilted. He expected an answer to each of his questions. I added a shade tartly, 'I haven't got a profession. Formerly I was a chemist's assistant. In Knightsbridge.'

'And your father? What does he do?'

The rapidity of his hard questions was strangely shocking. It was the unfriendliness of them. I understood that he didn't know me and might wish to understand better who had been letting herself into his father's home, but I didn't know what this particular course of his suspicion meant. I told him, 'He's a supplier of antiques to the nobility. Or, at least, he was. He's trying to retire.'

'So he's also a person with a former profession. I see. And this cousin of yours?'

'Cartographer.' Surprisingly, this was given by Danny Hannis. We'd both thought – the Captain and I – that Danny was already outside, but there he was, bending on one knee before the front door, dragging a string from his pocket to act as an improvised lead for the dog. Without lifting his head he added, 'At least, that's what she is when she's not being a strange solitary soul living in the shadow of her dead mother.' Now the head lifted. 'You know her. She's the daughter of old Steward Jones. He clipped our ears for poaching fish from his pond and when he died old Mrs Jones retired to the cottage in the valley. That was about the time you last spent a long spell at home ... I mean, it was about ten years ago.'

I expected the Captain to soften a little at this laying out of my credentials. But he didn't. He listened impassively while Danny told me cheerfully, 'I meant to say. Your cousin's bicycle was left in my workshop after her accident and she asked me to give it to you. Said it might be useful. It's outside the kitchen door, leaning against the far wall. She's set to be let out tomorrow so you can tell her that you got my note and managed to get eggs and milk as directed.'

Then his mouth twitched in a manner that implied either sympathy, solidarity or ridicule before he swiftly escaped outside to receive his orders from the Colonel, leaving me to fight a battle with the Captain that I couldn't even imagine a need to begin.

I tried to establish a little more clarity as the Captain moved to ease the front door closed. I said reasonably, 'Don't you think it's time we called the police?' Then I added haplessly in the face of his stare, 'Isn't that what one normarily does at a time like this? When one isn't being whatever it is you suspect me of?'

I actually expected him to smile at that, particularly given the way my brows furrowed in the wake of spotting my own little peculiarity of speech. But it turned out the illusion I'd been suffering that I understood his idea of calm was made of very brittle stuff. I didn't know this man at all. And didn't want to. I thought I preferred the sort of soldier who smirked and guffawed.

This man manufactured a stare that made it seem he thought I had run mad. It was a very strange defence. I was helpless as he said, 'No police.'

I said quickly, 'I appreciate that you want to protect your father but why are you——?'

I meant to ask why he was systematically belittling the pretty fundamental loss of all my clothes, let alone the seriousness of my account of an invasion into his house, but he interrupted with a very bland question of, 'Do you understand?' Then I had to stand there feebly while he pursued his own course. 'I expect you think I'm overstepping my authority here but, really, you foisted that role upon me when you decided to embroil any passer-by who happened to be in the vicinity in the rescue of my father's driver.'

We were back to unhappy mentions of Matthew Croft again. I whispered his name.

The sunlight through the glass beside the doorframe touched one side of the Captain's face. It should have softened his features but it didn't. 'Spot on,' he said. 'Since you got there so swiftly, I imagine you must have already digested every sordid detail of my family's history with that man, so you cannot be at a loss now to understand why at this moment I'm here when I ought to be in London and why I couldn't possibly allow you to wreak further havoc in this house. Haven't you done enough?'

'I haven't actually.'

'*What?*'

'Heard the full sordid details.' That startled him. He'd thought I was finally admitting darker intentions. It seemed he was absolutely failing to understand me too. It was unexpected. This was not a common experience for me. I told him with a greater sense of sympathy for the feeling that was driving him here, 'Barely anyone has said a word. And besides, I haven't asked. I have no interest in knowing what happened in that room or what Mr Langton did. And I don't want to hear any unpleasant insinuations about Mr Croft either.' I lifted my chin rebelliously, just in case he meant to defy me there. 'Based solely on my own brief dealings with that man, I have to tell you that I actually quite like him.'

That, suddenly, made the Captain smile. In the midst of his worries about his father, I'd made him laugh. 'In that case,' he said, 'I suppose I'd better not ask what opinion you've been forming about the rest of us.'

It was a concession of sorts. Then he gave a little sigh and tension fled too. A hand lifted to run through dark hair. He said with considerably more gentleness, 'Look, please try to see what's happened here from my point of view. I don't really mean to accuse you of anything. I believe you really have acted in good faith. It's just that I've come here at great inconvenience because of something that was said by a young woman I've never met and now she's announced that we have to add an intruder to the list. If you knew how the past few months have been for my father you'd know just how horribly convenient that sounds.'

A strange chill went through me as his head lifted and he told me frankly, 'Now, I can't stop you from reporting the loss of your case to the police, and I certainly will be encouraging Mr Winstone to report his assault. In fact, he's probably already done it, so I hope you're ready to give a full and thorough witness statement when our local constable comes knocking. But,' he added, becoming severe again, 'be aware that you never had access to this house. Tell them you were robbed outside, tell them it took place anywhere – on the moon if you like. But *do not* mention this house.'

He continued by making a rough list. 'Don't mention your food in the kitchen, the telephone conversation with me in my brother's study or any of it. Please. I really cannot have the police calling on my father. It's bad enough that Bertie's attack loosely connects my father to Matthew Croft. I can't have it made worse by having this house in an official report. You have no idea of the distress it will cause when it gets out. Which it will inevitably do. Please?'

Now he'd surprised me. I'd expected him to claim my silence with threats. Instead he'd dared to trust that the high significance he placed upon his father's needs would rank as sufficient justification for overriding mine. In a last show of defiance, I muttered to my shoes, 'I'll send *you* the bill for replacement clothes, shall I? Since I won't be depending on the law to return them.'

I looked up in time to see a different kind of concentration flicker behind those eyes, followed by perhaps the first instinctive feeling I'd seen him reveal that day and it wasn't violent at all. There was the smallest glimmer of warmth. I'd obviously just revealed some part of me too. 'Do that. And Emily?'

'What?'

'Did you really say 'normarily'? You do know it isn't a word, don't you?'

'It's an accidental contraction of normally and ordinarily,' I said bravely. This was something that happened whenever I got myself into a position of trying to speak my mind and only ended in entangling myself instead. It irritated me that I'd slipped into doing it now. 'I can't help it. You've already scored your victory. Do you have to make me feel like a child too?'

I'd like to pretend I managed make a grand exit then and left him staring dumbfounded at my magnificent wake from his place in the stairwell. But instead I glanced back briefly as I reached the passage towards the dining room and, to be honest, there was something awfully humbling about seeing this man wreathed in all that sunshine while his father and a man and a dog bickered cheerfully about luggage behind the glass outside, turning alone to face whatever fresh battle awaited him within the bright, pretty setting of that study.

Chapter 8

I have often wondered if I am the sort of person who tends to make things unnecessarily dramatic with the force of my own emotions. But lately I have tended to believe it is more complicated than that. I think that sometimes it is my better feelings that keep me from making bigger mistakes. I didn't march back to the bus stop to idle away three hours until the second and final bus of the day came. I didn't feed the resentment from my ejection from the Manor or use it as an excuse to relieve all the other stresses of the morning either. I'm already a woman who is haunted by the grander wrongs I have encountered in life – there are plenty of real opportunities to feel wretchedly at fault if one only looks for them after all – and I certainly didn't need to add to the burden by participating in the more immediate idea of tit-for-tat that grows all too often from smaller trespasses upon basic civility.

I suppose the simple truth was that I was haunted enough by things that I couldn't control, so I certainly didn't wish to add to the list by including things I could. So instead I shed the lot by feeding a few scraps to the goat as I'd promised, then I wheeled the bicycle gingerly down the hill back to my cousin's cottage and took the water jug from the cool of the kitchen to find the spot in the stream above the ford where the sheep didn't spoil the banks.

The hour that followed began with an introduction to yet another man. This one wasn't balding and wasn't attacking anyone either. He was robust and friendly and he was interrupted in the act of propping his motorcycle against the verge outside my cousin's gate as I returned with a brimming jug.

Constable Rathbone accompanied me inside. He was flushed after his race down the track from the other direction – the route that rose from the cottage through dark green trees and a gate onto a lane – and his hair had been swept into chestnut curls around the base of his helmet by the wind. He was here, as the Captain had foreseen, because Mr Winstone had reported his assault early this morning and this proved that it was a good job I'd put off racing for that bus because it really would have been suspicious if the main witness had taken off before she'd even left a name and forwarding address.

The constable sipped my tea and took notes while I recounted a simple statement of what I had found on Mr Winstone's garden path. The kitchen was an inferno because I'd had to light the stove to boil the kettle and the room was only made bearable by the breeze that was wafting in through the open front door. Through the course of the policeman's questions I learned that he was a true upholder of the law and by that I mean he gave the impression he might be very efficient at setting-to with whistle and truncheon if he were called to suppress a civil disturbance. I had a suspicion, however – and it was borne out by the fact that he had not yet visited the supposed site of the attack – that when it came to the investigation of a crime, his training only went as far as recording the bare facts of the case ready to hand over the lot to a detective from the county force. I supposed PC Rathbone might prove to be capable of rising to the task of arresting his man if the brute were to be caught in the act of doing something irrefutably guilty. But quite honestly the good Constable Rathbone didn't give the impression that he had any idea of actually going in hunt of him.

In a way it was fortunate Constable Rathbone wasn't much of a detective. He had finished his tea and was folding away his notebook and reaching to collect his helmet from the kitchen table when we heard a car roll to a halt on the trackway outside. There was a creak as its springs met a hollow and silence as the engine died. Naturally, I went to look. I was half hopeful that this was a cab bearing my cousin home from the hospital. It wasn't. The chrome bumper of a black bonnet peeped at me from beyond the screen of the garden gate while I hovered near the mass of coats hanging in the hall. Aunt Edna didn't seem to be stalking me from amongst them today.

But a real living person was hunting me. The sound of a car door swinging on its hinges travelled through the open front door. It was followed naturally enough by the thump as the car door was shut again, only, instead of hearing next the crush of dry stone underfoot, there was a cough as the engine kicked urgently back into life. The driver had climbed back in again. He made his car perform a quite extraordinary turn in about thirty rapid shuffles back and forth before dashing away again around the bend towards the lane where the gate had been left swinging. It was the black Ford and the swift about-turn had occurred when its bald-headed driver had stepped around the front of his car and found himself being presented with a close view of a policeman's motorcycle.

I stood there too stunned to really register shock. Quite honestly, it had never occurred to me to think that I was the common theme in this run of oddness rather than the Manor. Only here I was gripping the coarse folds of one of many aged coats, merging with them, really. And thinking that I'd met bombs and war, and wasted years dreading that all the human nastiness that ran like a vein through the whole lot might persist into peacetime, and yet at the same time I'd still happily been convinced that none of it had ever been specifically directed at me. Now, though, this man had apparently taken to calling on my doorstep just as soon as I'd left myself with no real chance of catching any bus anywhere and I was feeling as though this one thing were about to prove that my attempt to find a little perspective here was set to be horribly skewed the wrong way. Where I had meant to assert once and for all that nastiness had no place in my daily life at all, these people appeared determined to prove that it very specifically did.

'Changed his mind, did he?' PC Rathbone joined me in the hall, small eyes in a sunburnt face wrinkling comfortably at the now vacant trackway. 'Oh, no, here he is back again.'

The policeman was oblivious to the fact that this was an entirely different car. I couldn't quite see its nose well enough to say what make of vehicle it was, but this time the gate was carefully pushed shut and the black bonnet that drew to a halt at the end of my garden contained the unmistakeable might of a very powerful engine. It seemed that I had been partially right to think the Manor owned its share of this strangeness because here was its representative arriving in person at my garden gate. It must be said that the news didn't exactly come as a relief.

Willpower made me shake off the clawing grasp of musty coats and the proximity of the amiable policeman and step out onto the path. My hands met and gripped the weathered wood of the gate and I waited there while the car creaked and Captain Langton climbed out. I saw him hesitate fractionally as he saw me there, but then he turned to press the car door shut. Unlike the other man, this man didn't even quiver when he stepped around the nose of his car and his eyes fell upon the policeman's motorcycle.

His eyebrows lifted a fraction though when I didn't open the gate for him. Instead I leaned across it with my weight on my hands to tell him in an unfriendly whisper, 'PC Rathbone is here asking about Mr Winstone's injury. And did you see the other car?' I could tell from the brief drift of his attention towards the empty lane that he hadn't. 'It was the man from the Manor but PC Rathbone thinks you're him. He didn't notice that the other car drove away and you've arrived in a different car. Are you sure you want to see him now?'

I stopped myself from turning this round into a plea to stay with a fierce jerk of determination. I was, I think, expecting the Captain to make his excuses to leave. I suppose I was encouraging it. I couldn't see a way for him to come in without having to either lie or make me explain that he was not the same man that the other driver had been. And despite his repeated requests for discretion, I didn't quite think lying was his usual habit. At the same time it was suddenly hitting me with the kind of tension that makes every part of the mind ache that I ought to really be wondering why that other man had called here, and how that man had known where to find me at all and what I would do if the burglar was only waiting for these people to go before coming back again.

To stop myself from seeing this second man as my salvation, I made myself wonder what he wanted from me now.

It was a fair question. The Captain was scrutinising my unsmiling face; trying to trace that hostility to its source. He hadn't come here expecting this. I suppose he'd presumed the manner of my exit from his house hadn't quite paved the way for plain unfriendliness.

I thought for a moment he might be imagining that I was trying to send him away without talking to the policeman because I was afraid of betraying that I was actually a party to the bald man's actions. The Captain's own features were carrying a question. But when his mouth finally moulded itself into speech, it wasn't to announce his departure or add fuel to my increasing sense of isolation. It merely asked, 'Are you going to let me in?'

I let him in. I stepped sideways with my hands still gripping that gate so that it swung on its hinges. Then, with one final guarded glance at my face, the Captain stepped past me onto the awkwardly narrow space of the path and on into the hallway of my cousin's house. With no steps to climb, there was no sign of the faint unevenness in his stride now. I eased the gate shut and followed. I was in time to hear his opening greeting to the policeman. It was astounding after all he had made me swear not to say.

The Captain said coolly, 'I don't believe we've met. Captain Richard Langton. Has Miss Sutton told you about her encounter with an unusual car today? No? You should know that there is a man in this neighbourhood who has taken to driving about at speed and indulging in near-misses with pedestrians.'

I thought his manner was designed to carry meaning for me, I don't know why. Well, actually, I did know why; I just didn't like it. It struck me that this steady release of information was the Captain's way of exerting control over me and this scene, and the idea was deeply, unreasonably offensive. I didn't want to be cast in a passive role here. Not even when the act itself might have been intended to assure me that he believed that my nervousness belonged to something more complicated than the guilt of being caught red-handed meeting his burglar. The Captain might have been exposing our secret to the policeman purely to reduce the threat I might pose if he should prove to have been wrong about me. But it was more likely that the Captain thought the threat to me was unmanageable enough that I needed to be sheltered by someone like him; someone like an experienced soldier who would choose for me which decisive action to take. Any minute now and he'd be telling me not to worry again.

I approached as the policeman asked him seriously, 'Really?'

PC Rathbone drew out his notebook again and licked the tip of his pencil. 'Can you describe the car?'

The Captain had heard my tread on the step and was gracious enough to step aside slightly to allow me to join them in the gloom of Aunt Edna's coat-rack. There seemed to be some expectation that I would answer. Both the men fixed their gazes upon me. But when I drew a hesitant breath, the Captain recounted crisply, 'Black paintwork. A Ford perhaps, but I shouldn't think it was locally owned since there aren't many cars of any sort round here and the driver is dressed like a neat little businessman. Aged about forty, sorry, fifty.' A nod to me. 'He called at the Manor earlier. Apparently he picked up one of Miss Sutton's bags and gave her a fright and now he's just turned up here.'

He was, I noticed, continuing the theme of making light of the loss of my things and I didn't like that either.

But I didn't do anything about it. I stood there, hugging myself and mute, in my cousin's hallway while PC Rathbone swelled complacently. 'Perhaps this little chap called here to make his apologies and saw my machine outside and took fright himself?'

The policeman's lower lip was puckering in an enquiring sort of way. I felt compelled to say in a voice made tight and rapid by something that came close to temper, 'Perhaps. But you should know that the man wasn't all that little and he really had no reason to take my case.'

It was then that I saw the expression behind the Captain's eyes quite suddenly. He'd been hiding it before behind his calm assertion of command over these proceedings. I knew now this had simply been his own natural urge to establish order here while he calculated how far my ongoing hostility implied my efforts towards secrecy were indicative of a separate, deeper complication. And his urge to take charge was contradicted by his appreciation for my protection of his father. I added nothing more and watched him read the faint slackening of my lips.

There was the barest flicker of recognition in that hazel gaze. Then the Captain waited as the policeman jotted down a few notes. As the last line was written and the notebook snapped shut, the man from the Manor added, 'You'll naturally be adding this house to your round later, won't you, Constable?'

The notebook was put away in a breast pocket. 'Naturally,' agreed the policeman. Then he dragged his helmet from under his arm and set it upon his curly crown. He stepped neatly past the Captain and then me and out onto the path. He turned back momentarily on the threshold. 'By the way,' he asked. 'Did this man take anything else from the Manor?'

I felt the Captain's hesitation behind me like a whisper in my mind. I felt compelled to say, 'I expect Captain Langton hasn't had time to look properly yet.'

And then PC Rathbone was passing through my gate and settling himself onto his motorcycle. He wasn't really interested in any of this anyway. The Captain didn't leave. And hostility didn't quite go either. Now that the tricky business of managing the rival impulses of protectiveness and truth to a policeman was over, this other part of my experience at the Manor still wanted something from me, even if it wasn't a guilty confession. I felt it with the same insistence that had made a strange bald man briefly linger with me on the staircase there. That time the man had abruptly changed his mind and left, clipping my ear with my own suitcase as he went. This man didn't move. I watched the policeman go and then I carefully avoided acknowledging that the Captain was in turn scrutinising me. Unexpectedly, there was doubt here still and a sense that he was finding the contrast between my withdrawal now and my almost naïve helpfulness on the telephone very hard to read.

It made me deliberately voice what needed to be said. With my eyes still on the now empty trackway, I observed, 'You told the policeman about our visitor.'

The Captain laughed. Contemplating the same view that captivated me, he said, 'I'm not a lunatic. I might well have begged you to help me keep my father away from official notice but I was hardly likely to disregard the news that this man has now taken to calling at your house.'

His friendliness was my cue to shut the door and put an end to all that tension and I moved to do it, only to realise it would leave us together in a very intimate setting. Too intimate. I'd expected my unease to go with the policeman only it hadn't, or at least distrust had changed into a very different kind of nervousness. It was because I suspected that, for him, friendliness was just another way to take charge. Which was a very unkind thing to think but still it most definitely felt too close to be shut up with him in here in this tiny house with its tiny rooms and even smaller kitchen, waiting for him to smoothly lead me towards hearing whatever he'd come here to say. So instead I stood there with my hand on the open door and I told him, 'No, perhaps you weren't. But you might have made more of the theft of my baggage.'

'I was thinking you might yourself.'

This was said more coolly. It drew my gaze at last. His expression was bold, clear. It wasn't an accusation but he meant me to answer the question that hung over my behaviour. He proved it when he remarked, 'You stepped in when the policeman asked that last awkward question.' A deeper intensity of interest that carried the faintest of concessions towards real gratitude. 'Why did you do that?'

I replied rather coldly, 'It strikes me that I ought to be asking you to explain what was taken, since I've obviously saved you from having to lie to a policeman. Only I don't want to know. I can state quite firmly that I really don't. If it is the sort of thing you couldn't tell the policeman I don't think I should know either.'

For a moment the Captain was actually disconcerted. It clearly grated to have his integrity questioned. 'Don't say it like that. Please. My idea of the seriousness of what I stepped into an hour ago escalated the moment that fellow turned up at your garden gate and I don't know why I didn't tell PC Rathbone. It's in part this damned sense this place gives that one careless word will cause my father a whole deal of fuss. But,' he added, 'at least this particular oversight is easily remedied. Thanks to you I will be able to tell the man later.'

I believed him, I didn't know why. The Captain had been urging concealment from the start but all the same I believed him when he said this place was the sort to fix shackles upon a person. Only in my mind the ties of his sense of duty and

110

the history of this place had more the appearance of a snare. There was still the impulse to shed the lot and be rude by ushering him away to his car.

I felt beneath my fingertips the rough pitting of a scrape in the old oak of the front door. In a voice that was certainly softer if not yet ready to move beyond that to true warmth, I asked, 'Why *did* you come to see me? You didn't know I was set for an interview with the police, did you, so it can't have been because you wanted to act as a censor upon what I said in my statement? And you can't have known the burglar was about to knock on my door.'

He told me plainly, 'It was the fact you took the trouble to make up a plate of bread and salad stuff for me on your way out. Is that a terrible thing to say?'

My expression made him laugh. 'Obviously it is,' he remarked, still smiling a little. 'Well, the long and the short of it is, I'd had a terrible night followed by an even stranger morning and in the midst of it all, the young woman who seemed to be the principal cause of my unplanned arrival here took the time to leave some lunch for me. It was,' he added more seriously, 'a reminder of a simple bit of humanity and, I might say, a sobering experience.'

As olive branches went, it was a good one. It was utterly disarming. It made me willing to smile at last myself. It shook away the expectation I'd had that he was only here to assure himself that I was keeping my promise of silence. It proved that he hadn't come to bully me a little more. Unfortunately, his apology also had the effect of removing my control over this scene once and for all.

It gave me room to fully experience that other, less willingly acknowledged fear that resided beside the one that belonged to the visitation of that other man in the black Ford.

That car had carried the usual dread that I was going to be made to confront some of the darker aspects of this world. This other fear belonged solely to this Captain. It began with the realisation that I'd bristled right up to the moment that I'd shown that I cared to help him manage the toll this burglary would take on his father, and at that moment I'd let him glimpse what nervousness really lay beneath. There was a very faint trace of that protectiveness in his manner still and this time it was directed at me rather than his father. It was disconcertingly unexpected. It was made all the more confusing because I thought it was an instinctive part of his nature rather than a conscious decision to be kind. It was like being wrapped in a tender touch. Except that this was again an encounter with the decisive habits of a soldier. He knew I had been frightened and now I had to deal with the familiar expectation that I was set to receive soothing platitudes and the supposedly reassuring news that he hadn't come here to force me to hear what he wanted me to do for him next. Because, to a man like this, I had never been judged capable of doing anything of any use at all.

Very deliberately I focused on the simple social nicety that was probably all he really wanted from me anyway. 'Tea?' I asked, and walked ahead of him into the kitchen.

We took our tea outside. I'd mistakenly directed him out there with the idea that there were some folding chairs beneath the window, but there weren't. Luckily he didn't seem to object to me sitting on the warm stone of the front step while he leaned against the doorframe and we both turned our faces to the sun and sipped our tea.

After a while, memory suddenly prodded me into asking, 'Wouldn't you prefer to find somewhere to sit inside? On account of your sprained ankle, I mean.'

I glanced up at him to catch the brief shake of his head. He told me, 'I'd rather stand, if you don't mind.'

I didn't mind. I was sitting with legs stretched out and idly crossed at the feet and revelling in the blazing scents of an English vegetable garden at the height of its summer glory. This was what the Manor lacked.

'I lied to you earlier.' He waited until I lifted my gaze to him again. 'When I said it was a sprain. The truth is, I was a little taken aback that you'd noticed. It's the usual sorry story of an old injury that flares up if it takes a sudden knock. Unfortunately, in my case, an old injury that won't quite resolve itself is the sort of thing that ends a career and I'm working very hard to keep mine. So please don't let on that you know.'

'Why are you telling me at all?'

'I'm trying to say I'm sorry. For being rude to you again.'

I returned my gaze to the gravel by my step. I had been rolling it and ordering each grain in that abstract way people have when they are really thinking deeply about something else. Such as how confidently he wore his citified clothes – not with the sort of confidence that makes a person swagger, but the sort where they firmly believe they are fit to meet anything, wherever they are. Whereas I was pretty sure I was looking very much out of my element, and wearing my only remaining frock in the whole wide world, and a tired one at that.

I deliberately made my hand mess up the little lines of stones and told him easily, 'You don't need to apologise to me. You weren't to know I wasn't ... well, whatever it is you suspect me of.'

'Suspected, Emily. I wondered if you were from a newspaper. Or at least tied to one – hence all the questions about your family.'

The insinuation was so unexpected that it made me laugh. I thought he was almost smiling himself as he added, 'The thought had crossed my mind that your sudden arrival and interest in prowling about the attics of my father's house might well have been because you were a woman with a nose for a good story. I've even wondered if you were the sort who would be prepared to create a bigger one if the connection forged by Bertie's assault between my father and Matthew Croft proved too tenuous.'

There was something mildly flattering about the idea he had been accusing me – idly at the very least – of actually orchestrating something on the grand scale of a scheme like that. My voice was suddenly itself again. Friendly and cheerful. 'Good heavens. Has that happened before?'

'Not directly like that, no. But if you discount the part of the unknown female, not dissimilar. And the consequences were, shall we say, dangerous for the health of all concerned.'

That shut off my mirth like a switch. I twisted so quickly to look at him that my tea slopped. He didn't, it must be said, look like a man who was confessing to the use of his hands

for the purpose of silencing a journalist. The injury was probably more personal than that. Presumably his father again.
'Heavens,' I said again, more sincerely. 'I'm so sorry.'

'Don't be.' A glimmer of a smile before I turned away once
more. 'Or at least if you must feel sympathy, keep it for people
like you who've had the misfortune of touching an old wound.
I think for once I have been worrying about this more than
my father does. The problem has its origins in the period
before my brother drew all eyes to him, so at least I can't
blame him for all this, and I am finally learning now to
understand our value to the newspapers and how to keep it
from preying on my sense of proportion. Or, at least, I thought
I had but, as you say, my behaviour today proves the contrary,
perhaps.'

A wry twist had entered his voice. He knew I hadn't said
that at all. His willingness to confide a small hint of the old
habits that had influenced his recent behaviour was like a
deliberate defiance of the distrust that had lurked between
us since his arrival here. A peculiar pause slipped in afterwards
like a shy beginning of better ease only, from the way he spoke
next, it seemed more probable that he was securing the careful
rebalancing of peace before the next distress worked its way
in. I had a sudden sharp suspicion that he was steering me
towards something. Then he only said gently, 'I didn't mean
to treat you like a child, you know. How old are you?'

With deliberate tartness I told him, 'Twenty-one. Just. How
old are you?'

He was unfazed. 'A considerably more experienced twenty-
nine.' He was teasing me. Beside me, I saw one trousered leg

move to cross over the other as he relaxed in his turn and leaned back more comfortably against the wall. I heard the clink as he reset his teacup upon its saucer and set the pair of them down somewhere to one side. Then he said, 'Were you serious when you said that you don't want to know what else the man took besides your case?'

It was done so smoothly that I might have believed he was only making idle conversation. Only that suspicion lurked there waiting to return me to tension. From the tone of his voice I could imagine that he had his head back against the warm brickwork and his eyes closed against the heat of the sun. I didn't turn to check. I said rather too firmly, 'I was. Not unless it explains why he should have come to find me now.' Clearly it didn't since the Captain remained silent. Now I turned my head. 'You know, I really don't know who he is. I don't know why he came to your house. I swear it isn't me who brought him to this place. I can't see how it has turned out to be anything to do with me at all.'

An eye opened against the glare and rolled down to me. He wasn't accusing me of anything at all. He asked, 'Did he follow you to this cottage, do you think?' He was being very matter-of-fact. I liked him for it. It made it easier to relax. Until it dawned upon me in almost the same moment precisely who he was.

I was sitting here on the front step to my cousin's modest little cottage while the squire's son drank tea and listened as I talked as though we were equals. It was a mistake born of that wonderful glimpse of the familiar that the ringing telephone had given me yesterday. The truth was that in town our paths would quite frankly have never even crossed. Here they had and purely because he was – to borrow a phrase from Mrs Abbey – the new young master of these parts. I realised belatedly that this must simply be the Manor's equivalent of a pastoral visit to a needy cottager – he didn't want anything from me at all – and I was making a terrible faux pas.

First I answered his question hastily, 'No, I'm absolutely certain he didn't follow me. It took too long for him to get here. I think he must have gone through my bag at last and found the letter from my cousin. I can't see how else he thought to come here.' I added by way of an explanation, 'She'd written the directions to her house in it.'

And having brushed off that concern just as quickly as I could, I added rather more formally, 'Are you sure you wouldn't prefer to sit somewhere more comfortable? I probably shouldn't be keeping you anyway, having already ruined your day by dragging you out of London in the first place.' I made to get up, but as I lifted my hand with its teacup – to keep it clear of my knees while I rose – I felt the tug on the delicate china as his hand moved to intercept.

He said, 'I've already said I'm sorry, so please don't do this. Don't run away.' And he took the teacup from me to set it down beside his own on the broad windowsill to his left. Across the faint rattle as china met brick, he told me with rather too much perception about the real cause of my discomfort, 'I'm not trying to frighten you about this man. And you don't have to talk about him if you don't want to, or justify yourself to me either. I'm not accusing you of anything any more, or trying to wade in where I'm not needed. This isn't my home, you know. I've no intention of stepping into my brother's shoes and acting the part of the new master about this place. And that means I can freely make a promise to leave off undermining the tranquillity of a certain young woman whose only mistake was to expend an absurd amount of energy sorting out a few homely comforts for my father.'

It was there again; the question that I thought we'd left behind. It was the urge to ask me why I'd done it at all. And the uncomfortably exacting suggestion that it wasn't enough to simply answer that he'd asked me to.

As it was, he didn't ask that. Instead, and a shade too promptly for it to escape feeling like a fresh accusation, he asked, 'Why are you here? And don't tell me it's to holiday with your cousin because Hannis has already told me that she's in hospital.'

He must have caught my raised eyebrows as I settled back into my place on the front step, for all that I thought I had turned my head away. I heard him assure me wryly, 'This isn't a test, you know. I really am only trying to make conversation.'

My attention snapped back round to him. 'Are you?' I asked. Then I relented. I didn't want to distrust him any more and this was the price. I told him, 'This *is* a holiday. I didn't even know Phyllis was in hospital until I arrived here yesterday and was met by Danny's note. And anyway, what else do you call a trip that was supposed to be a change of scene, a brief get-away from the old life in town?'

'You don't intend to go back, though, do you?' He was quick, this man.

'How can you tell?' I asked. I knew why.

'I remember your decisive remark earlier about having no occupation. You don't intend to go back to – what was it? – a chemist's shop in Knightsbridge?'

I was sitting with my weight propped upon my straightened arms now and my hands laid palm down on either side of me upon the stone front step. The stone, the sky, everything, was ablaze and tension eased with a simple exhale of breath. The Captain wasn't going to presume that I was taking a last solo holiday before preparing for a marriage because there was clearly no ring, so instead, since he had obviously committed to memory everything I'd said, he was going to ask the next inevitable question in the line for a single woman of my age, which was whether I was set to take over the reins of my father's business now that the old man was hoping to retire. And I'd give my reply as a parody of the Captain's own remark about being unwilling to step into his brother's shoes and tell him that I felt the same about antiques. Only that wasn't strictly true.

I'd ruled out that career for myself when I'd insisted on leaving school at fourteen. Even then, the routine of running my father's shop would have been the most respectable choice and back then I might have been meek enough to have accepted it, but my father had been slow to offer it. He'd thought a few years of hard work in the real world would do me some good, rather than rewarding the abandonment of my education by letting me laze within the cosseted life of the family business. He'd also been wary of introducing a young daughter into a shop front and restoration workshop fundamentally occupied by men. My father knew it was the sort of path that led to an unwise marriage at a painfully young age. Which, I thought, made it all the more ironic that my father was now in the position of being ready to give almost anything if I would only choose the nice safe route of staffing his shop and thereby put myself in the way of a nice tame future with his favourite apprentice.

Today, in this pleasant sunshine, the man beside me, with the very different kind of presence, followed the predictable path. He asked that expected question about my future in the antiques trade. Only then I surprised myself by answering completely differently. Perhaps it was his easy self-assurance that made me brave enough to tell him, 'I could go back, actually. I could manage the shop once I've finished indulging in improving stays with long-overlooked cousins. It's what I'm supposed to do. But Dad doesn't really need me there. He never did. One of the apprentices has survived his national service and has come back primed and ready to run the whole lot. I'd rather not get in his way.'

'This counts as an improving stay?'

He'd caught my slip about the truth behind this visit. I wasn't in the habit of lying, as such, but I will admit that I tended to find it hard to stay true to my purpose if there was a choice between saying what I thought and hurting someone I cared about, or saying what they wanted to hear and, through that, picking the route that was quietest. It was cowardice, I supposed. So it was perhaps lucky for me that this man wanted to hear what I thought I ought to say. And there wasn't really any danger that I would hurt him with this.

'Very well,' I conceded. 'The truth is, my parents are pursuing the much-exercised route of giving me the chance to experience a few hard knocks in the wider world before it's too late and I'm out in it with no chance of return.'

He was quick with his reply. 'I should have thought,' he remarked dryly, 'you'd experienced quite enough of the wider world as it was, growing up through the past few years in London. Haven't your parents left it a bit late to take fright and evacuate their daughter to the country?'

I grinned. 'You think I'm here like a forlorn child with my name on a tag about my neck, waiting for an aged relative to claim me? Not a bit of it. My father isn't really an overbearing sort of parent, you know. It's me that is torturing him. I gave him a fright by first telling him that I was going to leave school and aim for adulthood at the age of fourteen; and then again as soon as I reached sixteen and I took to filling the gaps left in the dance halls as well since the older women were stumbling into hasty marriages with their brave RAF men in between bombing runs. Now I'm a grown woman and confusing him all over again by giving up the job I had to argue my way into taking in the first place and, actually, this visit to see my cousin wasn't his idea. It was my mother's. And besides all that, it was my choice to come here too.'

If he noticed my defensiveness about the course of the decision-making, he didn't show it. I cast him a shy glance. 'Did your ...?' I began then flushed. 'No, sorry, never mind. Ignore that.'

My companion prompted calmly, 'Did my what?' When I only shook my head mutely, he added, 'Do you mean to ask if my father is similarly dictating my choice of career? No. The Langton name has been put to many different enterprises, good and bad, but when it came to joining the army I found – how shall I put it? – well, without going into the details, it was easy to find this was one aspect that was purely me. I had the expectation from an early age that I would follow in Father's footsteps and by the time I was about your age I was already there.'

I remarked carefully, 'When you were my age you must have been getting ready to fight.'

He confirmed, 'I was in my first command at the outbreak of conflict.'

I'd been right; he did find honesty easier than I did. There was not even sadness there, nor regret for the state of war. There was assurance and a sense that the military life was a vital part of this man's idea of self-worth.

I stirred restlessly. Suddenly a whisper of that old distress crept close again. I knew I'd asked but there had been a reference to his brother in there somewhere. And perhaps the shadow of something else that was too deep for the cautious gossip recounted by my cousin's letters. It seemed to me that even if he didn't find it sad, to me there was something awful about a man being brought up to believe that a hard, destructive career such as his was the counterbalance that restored his value. Unfortunately, I think the Captain noticed my flinch. I could feel his gaze on me as he observed, 'You do try very hard for peacefulness, don't you? You don't want to talk about our little balding friend any more than you have to. And you really didn't lie when you said you won't hear the gossip about my brother ...'

He had noticed that I'd shied from his reference to the weight that rested on the Langton family name. He must have noticed that I'd shied from his mention of war too. It struck me that he really did make a habit of considering all the subtleties of everything that was said. All along he'd been working to solve the puzzle of who I was and lead me into explaining the cause of my unwillingness to discuss the darker aspects of what had happened at the Manor. I suppose he was afraid it meant something more serious was afoot. So he'd given himself time to study me and this was the result. Well, he must know I was a harmless fool by now.

'I do try for peacefulness.' I mimicked his phrasing a shade bitterly. 'If you must know, my decision to pay this visit came just after I made the mistake of mentioning to my parents that, amongst other things, I think I'm a pacifist. Or a conscientious objector, or something like that. At least, I would be if I were a man and required to do something about it. It's not a particularly socially acceptable thing to confess at the moment, is it? So much so my father took it as a sign I was concealing something else. I'd abandoned the nice safe prospect of a future in his shop and left a perfectly respectable job at the chemists, and according to him, it's not like me to do that without having the nice logical prop of marriage or retirement to make the decision for me. He became convinced that a severe emotional loss must have slipped in somewhere along the way and he just hadn't noticed before now. And since I'd just been ranting about seeking peaceful solutions, I could hardly stand and argue the point, could I?'

I knew it sounded feeble. It made me finish on a lame note

of excuse, 'The truth is I can't even see my mother's cat with a mouse without wishing to intervene.'

I turned my head. He saw my defiance – I knew this would be seen as a challenge to a man who made war his business. He also saw that I was ready to be humbled. He didn't do it. Perhaps it was the mark of a soldier that he didn't make a stand on a point that was already won.

Instead he took that same note of practical calm as he remarked, 'Forgive me, but haven't you got something the wrong way round there? I had understood that the basic principle of avoiding conflict meant that you *didn't* intervene. Unless your philosophy is based solely on the premise that you possess sufficiently superior strength to render all opposition futile. What would you do if the cat were the size of a tiger and you couldn't just pick him up?'

It was a fair point. He would naturally think along the lines of irrepressible nature, both within the cat and its victim, and of solutions being dependent on superior force so that all sides might be cowed into perfect peace. And perhaps he was right and I wasn't a true pacifist. Something certainly cut too close to a nerve that had already been set on edge by the bizarre contradiction of wishing this man would go away, changing my mind and then reverting again just as soon as he began to talk about his career, only to find myself at the same time really, really treasuring the experience of talking seriously like this.

It made me say with a better attempt at honesty than before, 'Tell me that peace means days and nights spent hiding in holes while the danger that is raging outside switches between the fury of a foreign power trying to reduce an entire city to embers and our own people who are cheerfully picking through the smouldering rubble.'

'You mean looters?' My slur had startled him. His manner had suddenly grown harder to match. Perhaps he felt I'd meant the point as a personal barb. I supposed people like him tended to be kept safely anaesthetised from that particularly commendable of aspect of our resilience to the Blitz. It wouldn't do for a soldier to realise that the people for whom he was laying down his life were utterly, entirely, ordinary and flawed, and therefore potentially undeserving of the sacrifice.

It cooled my readiness to be defensive. It curbed whatever I had intended to say next. I wasn't trying to hurt him. I was simply trying to explain the rest. I added with a wry smile, 'It really is quite unfortunate, don't you think, that I've come here to establish a little calm, to shake the dust of a ruined city from my boots, so to speak, and within the first twenty-four hours I've received absolute proof that the war might end and the world might change, but absolutely nothing alters human nature.'

After a moment, the Captain observed mildly, 'Bertie's attack and the little invasion at the Manor really have frightened you, haven't they?'

The sudden steadiness in the Captain's voice after its momentary roughness made me jump. Now I realised with a peculiar little shock that his protectiveness was there again in a faint whisper, and sympathy without ridicule.

'Actually, no,' I told him with an odd little shiver. It had jolted my mind more than it ought to hear the attack on Mr

Winstone grouped with the loss of my bag. It's shameful to admit but I'd almost forgotten about yesterday in the effort of tiptoeing around talking about today. 'Or, at least, the truth is I'm not really upset about them. It isn't really about those people and what they've done. It's about me and the fact that I'm desperately hoping everything will be different now – now the war is over, I mean – only I'm afraid nothing is going to be very different at all. Days like yesterday prove it. At least, I think they do.' A hapless smile. 'I know this feeling begins with the knowledge that war made people like you give up something profoundly personal for the sake of a mass of people you'd never even met and—'

'And now you're afraid it's your turn? Because you know we fought for ourselves too.'

His interjection rather derailed what I had been meaning to say. Probably for the best. So instead I agreed and conceded an easier truth, 'Perhaps. But yesterday, Mr Winstone was a stranger to me. When I found him on his path and the fellow who'd dropped him there slid away, I don't know what I'd have done if that man had come back.'

'Screamed the place down, probably,' the Captain remarked in the same lighter tone, 'until someone came to help. Or else discovered just how much physical force you're truly capable of exerting under extreme pressure. And I should say that it fully explains why you should have been left feeling quite so unsettled, since neither of them are remotely appealing prospects. Not when the one implies unbeatable odds, and the other is an introduction to a part of oneself that doesn't bear contemplation on a quiet summer's day in the country.'

He'd surprised me. I'd expected him to either assure me that there had been no danger at all or to smile and contradict my attempt to measure the assistance I had given to an old man against his own experience as a soldier. I hadn't expected understanding like this.

'Quite,' I agreed. I found myself smiling suddenly. 'I know I have my limitations, but I honestly don't know how capable I am of rising to the defence of a stranger in the way that has been routinely demanded of people like you. I've never even had to learn how far I would go to save someone I truly cared about, and quite honestly, my hope for a different kind of life ahead really, really depends on never being required to find out. So there you have the truth of my pacifism. The cowardly confession of a woman who managed to get all the way through a war without being called on to do anything useful and who is desperate to keep it that way now that she's an adult and she's got no more excuses.'

An uncomfortable pause while my gaze returned to its steady examination of the contents of my cousin's garden and then, abruptly, I lurched into answering the question he'd really been asking all along. 'And that is in part why I didn't tell PC Rathbone everything about my lost suitcase just now – it wasn't purely because I can appreciate your wish to protect your father. At least not fully. It's because I can't bear to feel indebted for something I won't ever repay, not even when it's the person's job. If I'd told the policeman about all this, he'd have been obliged to take steps for my safety and fuss and worry and then I'd have to admit this was more serious than I want it to be. I'd never be able to get things onto a normal track.'

This time when he spoke, it was in a very odd voice. 'You really do mean that, don't you?'

'Probably,' I replied. I shook it all away with a decisive little squaring of my shoulders. I had my hands clasped about my knees now. I turned my head over my shoulder to look up at him. 'And,' I added with a wry grin and an easier slide into truthfulness, 'I've unexpectedly explained my motives far better to you than I ever managed for my parents, so if I still haven't managed to explain myself coherently I'm afraid you'll just have to make up the rest for yourself.'

'I understand you.' The confirmation was given in a manner that suited the sudden shift in mine, but there was something in his steadiness that told me I'd revealed more about myself in those last few lines than all our past words together. His expression wasn't really betraying any of the reactions I might have expected, but I thought I'd suddenly crossed over from the girl he couldn't comprehend into the woman he understood only too well.

Then he straightened from his lean against the wall. His manner was suddenly decisive. I saw his glance at his watch. He was about to go and suddenly I didn't like it at all. I didn't want to be left alone with the worry about deciding between keeping watch from behind a locked front door or making a dash through quiet lanes for the shop where I might telephone for a car to carry me down to Gloucester. And, of course, I knew I would never be able to escape the one real worry, which was that I was destined now to spend the rest of the day re-running what I'd just laid bare to this man, and finding far too many reasons to feel ashamed.

The Captain was asking me crisply, 'What do you plan to do now since you can't stay here? Will you catch a train home?'

'Go home? No.' My initial surprise and then the twist of amusement that formed my negative made my cheeks burn. I thought that had given away rather too much of my feelings too. I always had felt that I'd never been particularly hard to read. This was proof of it.

'Well then, Emily, this is going to sound more than a little ridiculous after all but turning you out of the house earlier, but actually I'd like your help. And don't look at me like that. It's true.' There was a brief hint of a reassuring smile. 'Have you eaten, by the way?'

My mood lifted to match his. 'I have. I took the remaining two eggs for my lunch.'

'Good. Well, my proposal is this: Tomorrow I have to go into Gloucester for a meeting and I thought you might like to come along and call in at the hospital to see your cousin. From what I know of hospital stays, I imagine she'd appreciate the sight of a friendly face. That's the bribe. The fee is that today, after all I've said about refusing to play my brother's part here, it just so happens that I've committed myself to acting out the role of the squire's son to the extent of running my father's errands. Today that involves making contact with various people who by virtue of being either staff or tenant or both are deemed the Manor's responsibility. I've spent an hour already speaking to all the people who could be reached by telephone. Now I've got to go and see the next person on the list and I'd be very glad if you would come with me. Don't ask me why because I think I'd better not say. Let's just allow that, amongst other reasons, I've been made aware through an intensive run of correspondence in recent months that some of our tenants possess a certain habit for tying people up with little chores and although I hope I'm not susceptible, I really haven't got the time to find out I'm wrong. Will you come? Please? We can add your fee to the account. Otherwise, you can cut your losses on your trip here and I'll drive you now to meet the next London train ...'

There was something bewildering about the frankness of his offer. It was like he really was hoping I would choose to go with him. It made it easier to do what I wanted, somehow.

And in making that choice, it was with a lighter feeling than I might have expected that I belatedly went to pay the visit to Eddington that Mrs Abbey had briefly been determined to get me to make late last night.

Chapter 9

'Were you Blitzed, Emily?'

The question came out of a companionable silence. I turned my head from the scene arcing away beyond the glass in the passenger window to the driver beside me. In the main, experience had taught me that when a person wondered if someone was 'Blitzed', they were meaning that this person had lately taken to acting irrationally, hysterically and excessively sensitively. The term was only ever applied to excitable females, usually out of their hearing and more often than not accompanied by a discussion of their emotional state that would end with a condescending variation of *'never mind her. She was Blitzed, poor dear'*. Meaning, I supposed, that the poor woman's weakness of mind was owing to the misfortune of having had a great bomb land above her head. This was not necessarily quite what this man was asking, but all the same ...

'No, I wasn't,' I said. 'But thank you for drawing attention to my unnecessarily complicated view of things. I think what you're actually meant to do here is reassure me by observing that everyone likes things to be safe and kind and nice, and

131

naturally finds it really challenging when they're not; and that I mustn't be ashamed of taking things excessively to heart. But never mind.'

He glanced sharply left, only to catch my grin and smile a little himself – why on earth I'd thought this man would be bland – before easing the car off the lane that ran high on the opposing ridgetop and into the darkness beneath a group of vast chestnuts. Sunlight flickered and then we were free again and rolling gently along a rough trackway between cattle fields. The Manor stood a few miles away on the opposing valley hillside, a yellow beacon and just slightly aloof from its neighbouring cluster of cottages and barns. The part of the valley bottom that was shelter to my cousin's cottage was a long way below and screened by trees.

I was nervous without knowing what I was nervous of and yet exhilarated, as though I had unexpectedly been gifted a pleasure trip. Even the rotten stone walls in this little slice of countryside were the stuff of picturesque postcards. I felt the Captain's glance graze my face again.

He remarked, 'You've found yourself to be utterly under-prepared for what's happened here, haven't you?' There was a pause as he negotiated a steep turn down into a walled farm-yard. Eddington had the same air of history and abandonment as the Manor farmyard. The Captain told me, 'That's good. Because you're meant to.'

Now it was my turn to smile, but incredulously. The car drew to a halt. He added, 'It's easy to get the impression that the recent conflict ought to have turned all of us into experts at handling any crisis and to feel belittled when you get caught on the hind foot. But it's right that the sort of unpleasantness you encountered yesterday and then again today as a person who is being drawn in from the periphery isn't the norm for you. It gives me hope because it means that such things remain so rare and so unpredictable that it's impossible to prepare for them. And with that in mind, speaking as one with a certain degree of experience, please, for the sake of your happiness, don't even try. It really can't be done and in this instance, when war is irrelevant and you're dealing with something plainly criminal, toughening up just means denying all proper feelings, which doesn't do any of us any good.'

Then he climbed out and came round to open my door. I noted that he called it 'unpleasantness' rather than anything more severe. And also that he dubbed my presence in these scenes peripheral. I thought his choice of words was deliberate. He meant me to understand that I really ought to rank all this small and unworrying, and it occurred to me to wonder if he meant that I was permitted to relax into the part of innocent bystander solely because his experience made him think he had to take responsibility for whatever this was. I also wondered what form his experience took if he could measure preparedness against happiness in those sorts of terms, but he didn't give me room to ask.

Mrs Abbey's house was the next surprise here. I had been expecting it to match her person – a strong personality and well presented. But instead it was the brittle energy that had run as an uncertain undertone through her gossiping last night that was nakedly displayed today. The lady who opened the battered front door was unkempt and tired and not remotely pleased to see us. She also had children. Three wild-looking boys aged roughly seven, five and three. No wonder she'd been determined to get back last night. And no wonder that the Colonel allowed her a little grace with her rent. This whole crumbling place reeked of the loss of her husband.

Mrs Abbey met us in her doorway with an impression of the shabby defensiveness I remembered from the depressed mothers in the slums. Her eldest boy too was standing glaring before she grew impatient and sent him dashing away through the grimy passage that ran between the house and the barn to the tall boundary wall. Then she turned her attention to me.

Specifically me. She had no particular reason to recognise the Captain if she'd only encountered him through his letters as the Colonel's current deputy since the other son's death, but even if she didn't know the Captain, she clearly knew this big black car and I thought it very peculiar that she should ignore him for the sake of making a show of pretending that all along I'd been in disguise and concealing a career as the old man's agent. She told me crossly, 'It's no use to me that you've come today to pry into the squire's business. Why didn't you tell me you were his vanguard last night instead of coming here in all this state now? I mean, you can say this for the young Master. He was the man in charge of collecting the squire's rents, but he was also practically a friend to me and if he'd been here, we'd have had plain dealing and someone with the clout to see to the repairs that need doing.'

I thought she was making the point that she was unused to visitors, she didn't know the Captain and she didn't feel like she needed to try to know me. And she certainly didn't want last night's drama calling personally at her door now that our nervous kinship had been burnt away by the normality of a morning's chores.

If I really had been the Colonel's agent, I might have observed that amongst all that it was clear she hadn't yet discovered gratitude for her landlord's patience with regards to her arrears. But I wasn't. I was just me and now we were meeting here and her present home consisted only of a square yard within a high boundary wall with a barn and the house set against it in a yellowish stone that was crumbling like dry cheese; and I was finding that, rather than blaming Mrs Abbey for her rudeness about the Colonel, I was suddenly wondering how she came to be paying rent to live here at all.

Presumably following a similar train of thought, the Captain asked her as we were led in through a narrow hallway, 'When did you move here?'

His manner of speaking showed curiosity rather than offence. He didn't seem to mind that she'd left her landlord's son no room to introduce himself before she invited us in. Inside, the Eddington farmhouse was dark but better furnished. The right-hand room was a living room and every one of the chairs and tables was an original from its era. I imagined they must be her own. The house was set with its rear against the easternmost wall of the yard and no windows pierced this rear face, just dampness from stonework that was spongy even at the height of this roaring summer.

Mrs Abbey's temper must have eased as she reached the better backdrop of her private possessions. She was ready to at least acknowledge the Captain now and by the time she answered his question she was confident enough to worry about the state of her hair. She was tidying it in the reflection of a weighty mirror set on the wall between tasteful but faded watercolour paintings as she told him, 'We moved here three years ago. My marital home was Gloucester. You can imagine the boys' delight when we exchanged urban conveniences for this scene of rural luxury where the nearest shop lies at the other end of a stiff two-mile walk.'

She patted one last section smooth and turned. Her attention to her looks ought to have seemed mannered and designed purely for the interest of the gentleman, but it wasn't. She wasn't courting him. This wasn't a saucy play for power. She was already sure of her control. She'd established her dominion here just as soon as she'd relegated him to the status of my driver on her front step. Instead, I felt again the faintly humbling authority of a woman whose capabilities must rival my cousin's, although admittedly I now knew this woman had no real connection to the formidable heroines of the propaganda photographs. Mrs Abbey must have been a young mother early in the war, so she wouldn't have actually been required to contribute any more than I had. I thought, in fact, that Mrs Abbey's air of competence came from that far harder school of education; the sheer hardship of bringing up three children in this rotten place on her own.

'Sit,' she told the Captain. 'I'll make tea. Miss Sutton? Will you help me in the kitchen?'

The Captain didn't sit. He moved to the mantelpiece to entertain himself with her display of family photographs while

I followed her curiously across the narrow passage past the cluttered base of the stairs. I wasn't expecting my arrival in the kitchen to be greeted by a Mrs Abbey who was clutching the kettle and buoyant and utterly my friend.

She leaned in to confide with a lively whisper, 'I know who he is. And I can guess that he's here to soothe the malcontents on his father's estate because the Colonel's come home. It wouldn't do, I know, for us to meet the old man without receiving a little bit of coaching about our due humility from the son first. So I thought it would do him some good to have a little set-down.'

I couldn't help casting a wide-eyed glance back across the gap of the stairwell, but the man she was speaking about was absorbed by his examination of an ornament on her mantelpiece.

Mrs Abbey was laughing at me. There was a clatter as she placed the kettle on the stove. Her cooking conditions were even worse than my cousin's. Her stove was set against the wall opposite the door and it was rusting, with a ridiculously small drop hole for the fuel. It had been designed for coal when Mrs Abbey only had wood. She turned there, tipped her head at the void of the hallway and told me, smirking, 'It's been a long time since that man in there abandoned the business of running this place to his brother, and I'd be willing to lay money on the fact he's only paying lip service to picking up this business now. But,' she added on a suddenly cool note, 'what I'd really like to know is why *you're* here. I thought you were catching a bus. Did something happen?'

Playfulness died like it was on a switch. Her manner meant

to imply concern, I believe, but it fell far short of it. I thought her sharply blazing impatience as she waited for my answer more interrogative. She looked worn in the diffused light of her kitchen. That strain was here still; the energy that had run like a nervous current through her departure from my cousin's cottage last night.

I found myself reaching a hand across the tabletop towards her to ask in a voice that found urgency and forgot to whisper, 'Mrs Abbey, did you get home without mishap last night?'

In my mind was that rustle of the undergrowth and the vivid sense of the mile or so of dense thorny woodland that I now knew straddled the hillside between her home and mine.

She didn't pale, though, and reveal her distress. Nor did she confess that all this jumping about from rudeness to friendship and back again was merely a result of the fact that the arrival of the Captain's car had presented her with guests that she did not want.

She shook off the demanding stare and crept closer. She treated my question as of all things a sly deflection from a truth that might have been betrayed if I had answered hers. She was very close. Her mouth dipped teasingly as she leaned to give a daring whisper into my ear. 'A word to the wise, Emily dear. They're all thieves one way or another and the whole estate is mortgaged to the hilt.'

I was utterly, completely, taken aback. So much so I collided clumsily with her kitchen table. It was large and cumbersome and the kitchen was tiny and there was a boy there too – the smallest child with angelic fair hair and blue eyes who was clattering about with a toy in the corner where the cooler end of the rusting cooking range met the heavy stone sink. I steadied myself and, in doing so, took a small step back and managed to say, 'I beg your pardon?'

She straightened. Then she confided in a rather more ordinary voice, 'Master John Langton was, I can tell you with some confidence, a thief of hearts as well as the illicitly acquired contents of other people's houses.'

I was supposed to be shocked, but at that moment, suddenly, I barely cared about her hint about the womanising. I was too busy discovering the awfulness of my reference to the looting I'd witnessed in London. No wonder the Captain had jumped as though I'd struck him. He must have thought for a moment that I'd been attributing personal blame. Now I was feeling like I was straying horribly close to the sort of prying I'd declared I wouldn't do when I couldn't help asking her, 'John Langton was a thief?'

'They say that when he died some paintings came to light that had been lost from a house during an air raid. Despicable if it's true, isn't it?'

My slur upon looters got worse.

And yet, the worst part was actually the way she added her next. She lowered her voice to a whisper again and added, 'The squire always seemed to hope that a respectable marriage would set poor young Master John on the straight and narrow, but although he was perpetually the toast of elegant young ladies, he could never quite get away from giddy dreamers. Now I'd be fascinated to know how that man *there* does these days, wouldn't you?'

There was a tilt of her head towards the open doorway. She confided darkly, 'I imagine our Captain Langton is pretty down on his luck since young Master John ensured the family name became synonymous with mud and everyone knows the country house belongs to the bank. Perhaps that's why he persists in acting the part of the determined soldier. Perhaps he hopes the part of the poor wounded war hero'll remedy the damage done to his reputation, if you know what I mean.'

The suddenness of the change in her from nervousness to this hard relish left me flabbergasted. It felt like I'd been walked into a trap. This had been the motive behind her sudden desire to form a womanly enclave in the kitchen. Her hands were moving, sweeping back the curls of hair from her face in a manner that seemed at last designed to emphasise her womanly beauty, like a star of the silver screen cast by age into playing out the final dramatic scenes of a brilliant but jilted villainess when she firmly believed that by rights she ought to have still ranked as the heroine. I had to wonder suddenly, with a sharp pang of doubt, if her turn of phrase had been deliberate when she had implied that she had reason to know John Langton's history.

Perhaps it had been designed to lend weight to her other insinuation. She meant to imply that the same Langton blood ran in the elder brother too, but since bankruptcy and dishonour had come into the frame, it was likely that he would have a considerably longer wait until a usefully affluent marriage came along. Frustration would be his main bedfellow now. And perhaps foolish young women who took to travelling about the countryside with him in his car.

Awfully, my revulsion must have been written plainly upon my face. It gave her the excuse to belatedly put out that hand across the table to press mine. 'Take care, Emily dear. You're probably just about pretty enough for the Langtons. Perhaps, after all, you should have taken that bus home?'

I was snatching my hand back. I was retreating towards the door. I didn't know where this commentary on the Captain's romantic ambitions had come from, and the compliments to my person were absurd. The assault on my sympathies was matched by the expression in her eyes, like the desperate triumph of a woman who wasn't actually in control of herself at all. This was the mania of a woman who was so busy thinking of something else entirely that anything might be said.

I was at the doorway. The middle child was there on the bottom step of the stairs, sullenly picking at some damp plaster with a pencil. I believe I was retreating towards the Captain, not because I in any way wanted him to hear this, but because I needed the reassurance of a comparison between rational conversation and the scene I'd just left to prove to myself that something really was awry here. There was, after all, every possibility that the woman was just an obnoxious gossip and I was merely a timid prude. Mrs Abbey was following me with a tray of tea things. I'd have said she was scuttling in pursuit of me except it was even more absurd than all the rest.

The Captain was still at the mantelpiece. He watched my hurried return and then Mrs Abbey as she set her tea tray down behind me on the sideboard with a suppressed clack.

His eyes, when they swept over my face and onwards to Mrs Abbey's, were utterly calm. So much so that I had the sudden horrible task of debating inwardly whether or not this carefully observed patience in a man who had a long list of things to do – but finding himself first being ignored then left waiting while Mrs Abbey proved her little bit of power by keeping me gossiping – was only being polite at all because he wished to hide the fact that he had heard. And yet, I was sure Mrs Abbey's insinuations could not have travelled the gap of the hallway. Her voice had been too deliberately staged as a private whisper and it had been done for my ears rather than his.

I dithered helplessly just inside the doorway at the back of a rather worn Queen Anne chair while he stood there at the mantelpiece looking, well, indecipherable and then he spoke across the room to Mrs Abbey. 'Has Miss Sutton told you that my father has called a meeting with his tenants tomorrow at midday? In the Manor farmyard, if you can manage to get there for that time?'

I wished he hadn't mentioned my name. Apart from the fact that I couldn't have possibly passed on the Colonel's message since this was the first I'd heard of it, I felt as if this sudden choice of addressing me formally actually emphasised the ease with which he usually dispensed with social distinctions to call me merely by my first name. Irrationally, since Mrs Abbey couldn't possibly know this, I was certain that she too must feel the change. I felt myself straighten beneath the touch of her glance before she turned to test the condition of the tea.

The Captain was cocking his head at the run of photographs on the shelf by his elbow. 'Is that man Mr Abbey?'

The question jerked Mrs Abbey's eyes to the only picture in the row that contained a youngish man as though the thought stung. The rest of the gilded frames contained either the children or older people who were, presumably, the grandparents. After that first jolt of surprise, I saw Mrs Abbey only gaze at the photograph in question for a moment before abruptly collecting herself. She gave the Captain a surprisingly brave smile. 'Taken on holiday at Weston-super-Mare.'

The man in the photograph was well groomed with smoothly creamed hair, which, judging by the shade of sepia, must have been a mid-brown. His eyes were set in comfortably fleshy cheeks that spoke of office work. Most significantly of all, he bore absolutely no resemblance to either the man I had seen on Bertie Winstone's garden path or the man who had made off with my luggage and, if the Captain had listened at all to anything I had said, he must have known this. I thought that this photograph was proof of the principle that like attracts like because there was something faintly effeminate in the curl about this man's mouth that was mirrored on our hostess's lips as she stepped around my chair with a teacup in her hand and added huskily, 'Happier times.'

And it seemed rudeness wasn't only limited to her because I was a little startled when the Captain merely gave a mild agreement and reached out a hand to accept his cup. I instantly found myself speaking what he hadn't; voicing my regrets for her loss only to fade to a mumble when it was clear that Mrs Abbey didn't want them. When I moved to take my own cup from the tray I discovered that the Captain was watching me. Brown eyes curious in a guarded face. He covered the moment by addressing the first of many questions to Mrs Abbey about Bertie Winstone; about his visit here yesterday and the work Mr Winstone had done for her.

It turned out that this, at last, was the Captain's real manorial duty. I wished very much that he'd told me before that he'd been coming here for the sake of asking this. His gaze raked mine once more, briefly, just before he asked Mrs Abbey why she'd chosen to go to the shop frequented by Mrs Winstone. He was observing that surely there was another, nearer shop in the village just a mile or two along the ridgeway. I could guess from that glance that he knew I must be made uncomfortable by this. And he was sorry, but he was going to pursue it anyway. Absurdly, I suspected that he even wanted me to feel the unbending nature of his resolve, just as Mrs Abbey did as he questioned her.

I looked away when Mrs Abbey remarked rather tartly and not without justification, 'To be honest, Captain Langton, if you can ask me why I would walk all that way to the shop at Winstone, you're obviously not a man who has often had to stand in a queue for your groceries. If you were, you'd appreciate the distinction between one shopkeeper's sweaty leaves and another's succulent greens. And we haven't, you'll have noticed, much soil in that yard for growing our own.'

For once, I was rather more on her side than his. I found my gaze drawn to the middle boy, who had crept from the bottom step into the doorway. I turned to him fully and he whispered something. My voice was gentler than my mood, purely because of the way the child shrank just as soon as he had my attention. I asked him mildly, 'I beg your pardon?'

The boy was lean and undersized and had a sulky air, like a boy who frequently did wrong when he meant to do right and was stubborn enough to stick to his purpose either way. But not enough to speak it out loud. The oldest child piped up enthusiastically from the front door, 'He fixed it yesterday. Do you want to see it?'

It transpired that Mr Winstone's visit here yesterday had been for the purpose of repairing a rope swing. It was a swing that was, in my opinion, slung very dangerously close to a derelict well.

We'd been bustled outside, or at least I had. The boys had led me at a gallop past a more useable well that lurked at the heart of the farmyard. This well had a heavy bucket on a long rope and mossy alpines growing from every crevice, and it must be said that it left me feeling not even the smallest speck of jealousy after seeing the source of Mrs Abbey's drinking water compared to mine.

The children raced past it, past the furthermost tip of the long barn and through a gap in the wall made when someone had carted away the stone to build anew elsewhere. We were in a second yard, even more derelict than the first. There was hardly any wall at all here, and nettles and trailing fronds of vicious brambles were growing from the cracks in the hard-standing. In the corner, where tumbled stone met the shade of the hilltop and a fringe of woodland, was another broken old well and a great ash tree with a rope dangling from its drooping bough.

The Captain wasn't with us. In the moment of following me he'd been barred at the threshold by fine fingers clutching at his sleeve. I'd heard a murmur of 'Just a moment, *Langton.*' It had carried a softness with it that was completely out of place. It made my skin crawl. I thought she'd uttered the name like that before, and not necessarily for this brother.

The boys wanted me to admire the rope. They wanted me to admit that it was a very fine rope and the log that Mr Winstone had secured to the end of it as a seat was a remarkable addition. They weren't impressed when I dared to observe that it wasn't terribly safe to swing so close to the unguarded well. Quite appropriately, my comment was met with an agreement from the children of the sort that was only ever given to very stupid adults who stated the obvious and implied yes, of course it wasn't safe. It was a swing.

'That's delightfully dangerous.' The Captain's voice was just behind. I tried not to jump guiltily as I turned to find him reaching past me for the rope. He must have followed me quite swiftly after all. There was no explanatory glance for me but his manner was brisk and inoffensive. The boys were delighted to show a man their toy. Sunlight dappled across the Captain's shoulders as he dutifully tested the strength of the rope with his weight and asserted that the knot securing the seat was firm. 'Just don't fall into the well. Put a board across it or something.'

Needless to say, the boys nodded their agreement very seriously.

Now the Captain did look at me. 'Ready to go?'

I followed. I hadn't quite decided what I would do now,

since I had no intention of trailing meekly along to his next interview, but I certainly wasn't going to stay here.

'Emily, dear.' Mrs Abbey's soft voice called me back as we passed the tip of the barn. After the dereliction of the second yard, this square with the serviceable well and the relatively robust boundary wall seemed positively grand. I turned a shade reluctantly. I'd had enough of her warnings against romantic entanglements. What I wasn't expecting to find was that the restless, unceasing energy that had first met us at her door was back and in full unadulterated earnest. This was raw. This was fear and it had been with us the entire time. I didn't know what the Captain had said to her after her unguarded use of his name, but it had certainly had its effect. I thought she was still mistress of the feeling, but only just.

Mrs Abbey drew near when I waited for her. She stood there in the lee of the high boundary wall where it cut into the hillside above us. Trees fanned their shade across her and towards the lip of the well.

She began by saying on an accusatory note, 'You didn't tell me about that man.'

'Which man?' I was losing track of who I ought to be gossiping about, whether Mr Winstone's attacker, the balding man, the Captain or his criminal, philandering brother. I was also distracted by the way her hands had grown incapable of remaining still. First they rested on her hips, in the next moment they were wrapped across her middle, then toying with the button on her left cuff, only to finally settle upon reaching out and scooping the youngest child – who had introduced himself over that business of the swing as Ben – into the curve of her arm against her side.

She said rapidly, 'The Captain told me that the man has taken the accounts ledgers from the squire's office. That's why the Captain's here now – he's got to go round all the tenants named in those books to warn them that this man may come a-knocking. He's called on you already?'

Desperate. That was the way to describe the pattern of her speech now. It burned against my own discomfort at suddenly learning the truth of what had passed between them just now. Not rebukes or signs of irritation, but a warning.

And through it all, Mrs Abbey found the time to be the first and only person to actually acknowledge the impact the loss of my entire wardrobe would have on me. She said quickly, 'If you're not catching that bus and you need a change of clothes while you're here, I expect we can find something that will fit. It'll cost you a fortune to replace them all, won't it; and even that expense only comes if you can get your clothing coupons to stretch beyond the usual two or three things, isn't it?'

She drew a quick breath and added, before I could interrupt her with thanks and commentary on my approaching patronage of second-hand shops, 'And yet, I suppose it will be helpful to the police that you got a good look at the man who bashed old Bertie Winstone over the head at long last?'

'It will?' I asked blankly. Her sudden eagerness had startled me. I was stupidly slow to comprehend. Then she gave one of those encouraging nods that hurry a person's thoughts along and I realised the mistake. I said hastily, 'Oh. No. They're not the same person.'

She didn't, however, respond in quite the usual way. She looked at me as though I'd lied. Her hand curved around the head of the little boy, smoothing his hair, nervous and protective. Then she said with stiff disbelief, 'You're sure? I thought they were, from what Captain Langton just said.'

I suppose no one liked to hear there were two criminals in the area: a brute and a thief. And I disliked finding myself suddenly exchanging information as if we were back in the kitchen and gossiping. I told her firmly, 'The man I saw stepping away from Mr Winstone was tall and lean, just as you said last night. This man today was the opposite. He was stocky and balding with a grey suit, like a travelling salesman.'

'And you're certain, I suppose? I thought you said the man last night wasn't tall. As you said before, the idea that he was tall was mine. Whereas *I* recall that you said he was quite short really?'

Her insistence made me smile, but not in an amused way. I conceded unhappily, 'Perhaps he wasn't all that tall, I think. But the man today was very different. And he had a distinctive taste in yellow alma mater schoolboy ties.'

That last was a sudden recollection. The image was suddenly vivid and brought with it a physical memory of that brief but intensely bitter anticipation I'd felt as he'd paused to grip me on the stairs. Or perhaps it was the way my nerves recoiled from the sting of Mrs Abbey's sudden grip upon my wrist now.

Her hand was locked over mine. Her voice was an urgent murmur. 'Emily ...'

We were disturbed by a more distant echo of my name as

the Captain called to me over the roof of his car. He used my first name too and rather less patiently. In a way it felt like a rescue. Or perhaps that was just wishful thinking to countermand the inconvenience of having that degree of intimacy implied here. I turned my head to acknowledge him.

When I turned back I saw the flicker. I saw the lift of her chin that was driven by a feeling more complicated than fear.

My silly bout of nerves evaporated again and reformed into something rather wiser, almost quickly enough for pain. I felt my eyes narrow as, instead of bridling at the implication she too had noticed the Captain's use of my name, I began seriously, trying to be bold, 'Mrs Abbey. Is something the matter?'

The change in her own demeanour was demonstrated by her grip. Instead of pinching the skin of my wrist any further beneath tightened fingers, she merely gave my hand a brisk pat. Like a bossy aunt does when the child has said something foolish. 'What? No. Of course not. Only, with this man around, if you happen to see my children out, will you keep a kindly eye on them?'

The cheery way she was speaking now implied she was asking for the sort of care that involved nothing more valuable than an occasional good morning or a share of my sweet ration if I should meet them at the shop. She was very good at shifting from one feeling to the next, so I answered the intent within her request rather than the manner of its delivery.

I said firmly, 'Without question.'

Relief didn't show on her face. I saw her cast a glance down at the boy beside her. Sandy-haired, bright-eyed and bored out of his mind, only wishing to be released so that he could join his brothers in a race through the dingy passage by the house. Mrs Abbey smoothed this last child's hair and then let him go after them. Her anxiety about imposters in the neighbourhood did not seem to extend to keeping her children close by. And probably they'd been alone here last night.

It was a very disconcerting note to leave on. Particularly when, as I dropped into the passenger seat beside the Captain, it dawned on me that in asking and failing to gain a fuller picture of her state of mind since her late-night walk home, I really ought to have been also asking the rather more mundane question of whether she might return my cousin's torch.

Chapter 10

After the strangeness of our visit and the endless waiting that must surely have irritated him no matter how well he hid the feeling, I had expected to find, somehow, that the Captain was angry with me. But there was no temper in the way he steered the car in an arc around the crumbling wall of the well and then up the short rise onto the trackway above the farmyard. The car went with a smooth acceleration that was admittedly quite fast, but really implied only readiness to get on with the next job in hand.

There wasn't even any temper in the way he spoke as we approached the heavy dark of the chestnuts that marked the turning onto the lane. He asked me as if it were only a matter for idle curiosity, 'What were you and Mrs Abbey talking about so intently just before we left?'

'Her children,' I replied promptly, biting my lip. 'I promised I would keep an eye on them.' And found suddenly that anger was lurking in me instead. I couldn't fully tell what he'd meant by the question. I didn't know if he now disliked the promise I'd given or he disbelieved me when I implied that this was all we'd said. I only knew that I had become so bewildered by all the contradictory questions that had crowded in through the course of my various exchanges in that rotten farmhouse that my mind was abandoning the lot and simply answering the injustice of having to feel like I'd done something wrong.

In an effort to disguise my rising frustration, I said shortly, 'Wherever did you get this monster of a car anyway?'

'It's a Lagonda and I didn't get it anywhere. My brother did.'

I saw his grimace. He knew that his answer had carried a sting. His foot eased its pressure upon the pedal and allowed the car to slow a little for the curve ahead. Over the deafening rattle of the rough trackway, he told me quite blandly, 'Technically, it's my father's car now. Luckily for us, Bertie's been religiously topping up the tank and a few spare cans with his petrol allowance over the past months, so I've got enough fuel to run about the countryside on Father's errands, and then that's it. It'll have to be sold. My father doesn't want it and I don't need a car in London. I couldn't run a thirsty beast like this anyway since I'm not yet in the habit of exploiting my position in the army to claim more than my basic petrol ration under the guise of having official duties.'

I was watching him, so I caught the swift sideways glance as the dark beneath the trees enfolded us in its shroud. And, in that last second before the brakes bit ready for the junction onto the lane, I saw the truth about his mood.

I saw that his restraint was as much about control as Mrs Abbey's drama had been. She wasn't unique in being disturbed by the private conversation they had shared and it wasn't for her alone to feel the shock of our visit. But while her distress was all put into nerves and slander, here was withdrawal and a hard control of a different kind that was presently focused very firmly on keeping his worry contained and well shielded from me.

He still didn't believe me or my part in this. But while I digested that unpleasant reality and all its implications in terms of what it said about how my general nature must be perceived, I saw something else. I saw his reserve and caught a brief, devastating glimpse of what true loneliness was. I saw the deep, dark isolation of a mind used to facing battle alone.

Concern welled so fiercely that I forgot myself. For him there was something here more grave than even I knew. A hand reached for his sleeve. *'Richard!'*

I surprised myself. I certainly surprised him. A quick drift of his eyes ran left to the touch I had laid upon his arm, and then on towards me. Then again and a curse as they widened and made my own eyes forget embarrassment, forget the impulse to snatch my hand away again; to instead tighten my fingers compulsively and wrench round to follow his gaze to the glass in my doorframe. Everything exploded in the rush as something large and black and metal plunged out of a piece of undergrowth beside me.

There was a jolt through the leather seat as the brakes engaged. They gripped, only I didn't slow with the car and I slid as the wheel flung us into a swerve that sent me crashing into a parallel arc with our roaring neighbour. We took the inner turn. Brakes screamed. So did I, probably. Black metal veered and became instead the trunk of an enormous tree that had previously been on my right. The bellow of dirt and rubber and gravel smothered the frantic plea that formed around the hold I still had on his sleeve, either before, during, or shortly after we hit.

Then silence.

I think at some point during the tossing I might have raised my left arm so that it connected with the roof of the vehicle in place of my head. There was a blazing pain in my elbow. Now everything was still, even the engine, and there was a fearsome pressure on my hip too. I was crumpled horribly into the corner where my seat met the hard barrier of the door with my eyes tightly shut and half my body in the foot-well. Now I blinked and saw that my left hand was rammed against the dashboard. I remember being very glad that the hand had snatched for that and not the door handle. It was painfully easy in this sort of car to be flung out onto the road because the hinge was at the rear of the door, meaning that the opening acted as a kind of funnel in an accident. Unluckier people had been thrown out and killed.

In this instance, however, the door remained safely closed. My other hand had abandoned his sleeve to find instead the sheer leather of the seat back. Fingers unclenched. The hand moved and moved again in an adjustment of its grip and slowly I eased myself out of my painful heap.

Beside me I heard the squeak as my driver adjusted his own position in his seat. With my eyes inescapably drawn to the rough bark of the trunk barely inches away from the glass of my passenger-side window, I murmured slightly hoarsely, 'At least you needn't disbelieve me any more about the exist-ence of that man.'

I heard him give a short, dry laugh. There was a wealth of relief in it. I straightened a little more and went through the practical process of looking for that other car. It was long gone. I found it a little surprising that I was thinking so calmly instead of giving way to shock. Then I saw the way my hands were shaking and felt an overwhelming urge to be active, to get out of the car and walk about a little, perhaps under the guise of examining the tracks left by the black Ford. Only I couldn't get out because that tree was there.

The Captain had no such trouble. His door was already open and he was coming around to examine the damage that the tree might have done to his car. I took the chance to slither across and out myself. I walked a jerky little turn, feeling the cool of the shade like ice on my fingers and finding no sign even of our skid that had saved us from colliding with that man. There were the trunks of tall trees here and the mottled shade of their canopy, just as innocent as it had been before we'd seen his car. The stillness of it all made me suddenly afraid that the burglar was a master at watching from the shaded places. I found that my turn abruptly ended just behind the Captain where he was bending by the wheel arch to peer at the flank of his car.

'Any damage?' My voice was rapid.

His voice was not. He straightened beside me. I was a touch close but he didn't move away. He probably couldn't with the tree roots just behind his feet. He told me, 'I don't think so. I hope not. Presumably you've heard by now some whisper of the state of the family finances.'

He had said that quite plainly and certainly without

rancour but I flinched because it was true. It really was cold here. A turn of my head showed me the space behind scrubby undergrowth where the Ford had been concealed. I was a coward because I was protected on three sides by the car, this man's presence and that tree and yet I was still finding it a struggle to speak slowly. I asked, 'Do you think he was waiting there to do that?'

The Captain turned to me. His hand met my elbow, the one that wasn't bruised, briefly in a gesture of reassurance. His skin was warm where mine was not. The hand dropped and then he moved past me back around the nose of the car to the open driver's door. I stayed there, dithering by the tree as he said, 'If you mean to ask whether he intended to run us into a tree, then no, I don't think so. I think he was watching from afar and he got a nasty fright when our car burst out of the farmstead like that. I think we caught him at the end of a short sprint on foot and a panicked dive into his car. In a way this was my fault for driving like a fool.'

I said without thinking, 'If you'd driven like a fool, we'd have hit him.'

He was standing now with one hand resting easily upon the rim of the open car door and the other upon the frame. Then he surprised me by drumming his thumb a little impatiently upon the car roof as a worry preyed on him and he asked seriously, 'Did you get hurt back there?'

There was an intensity in his voice that shook almost more than the accident had. He was ready to feel responsible. Whereas for me, the question abruptly gave shock the excuse to work its way out of restraint and I didn't want it. I blinked rapidly and mustered a smile, only to notice suddenly, unexpectedly, that he was looking as pale as I felt. Somehow the steady competence of his examination of the car had made me think he was impervious to such things as fright after a near miss.

My heart was suddenly beating and my own hand was flat upon the warm metal of the bonnet. The touch of that solid support was the only thing that was stopping the energy that was burning within me from finding release. If I had given way to it, I didn't think I'd have ever stopped the mindless movement. 'Are *you* hurt?'

The reflection of his concern back at him startled him, I think. I suppose it was a little strong. It betrayed how truly I was shaken and just how much I had been trying to hide it. It made him straighten from his easy stance in the open doorway as he absorbed it. He already knew I wasn't particularly skilled at dealing with distress because I'd confessed it when I'd ranted about pacifism. Now I thought he was guessing that it wasn't the risk of collision that was unnerving me here, but fear from the continued presence of that man. Because I knew that this was my third encounter with that other car now and it was inescapably frightening when the common theme was me. The grim thought was followed by the twist of suspecting that the Captain was thinking that too and moving on towards considering whether I might have known the man would be here and this ongoing unsteady attempt at concealing my fear was a mark of my guilt.

I couldn't be sure what the Captain was thinking, but I could trace the thoughts running behind his eyes; the calculations and reassessments. There was certainly a glimpse of that deliberate restraint, the checking of a fuller honesty for a concealment of his own as he chose the simplest route towards managing this. He chose to diminish my part by ignoring my concern completely. He asked instead in a decidedly matter-of-fact voice, 'Will you get in or do you want to wait while I bring the car forwards?'

As an act of declaring my self-control, I waited out there alone while he eased the car onto level ground. Then I climbed in. Back in the confines of the car, it brought a fresh shock to suddenly realise the body beside me was alive with the restrained intent that had driven him to set the car at just so much speed on this trackway in the first place. The vast engine added its own impatient throb to the tension, ready for the release of motion. It made me ask on a breathless note of intense disbelief, 'Are you intending to go after him?'

My voice threatened to stray into plain revulsion. From him I got a brief flickering glance that felt like a challenge. And also amusement. 'Do you want me to?'

He knew I didn't. He was teasing me – not for the sake of argument but for the purpose of calming my alarm. He knew I wasn't prepared for this. I had the sudden doubt of considering whether that small sympathy and that alone was the extent of his effort to exclude me. Not hateful suspicion, not allied to that man or the odd insinuations of Mrs Abbey; but purely because I was, in fact, too much of a coward to handle the rest. I said rather too firmly for such a small space within a car, 'No! I think we need to go back down there and tell that woman that a known thief was spying on her.'

My fierce assertion at last of every idea I had of my own responsibility surprised him, I think. It also made the corner of his mouth curve a little again, like the amusement that went with a faint awakening of respect, only to be wiped away by the older unease that came from our recent departure from that house. And suddenly, absurdly, I was miserable. There really was guardedness here and the heavy sense of alienation.

I'd thought this had been set to be one of those moments where my unsteady but determined declaration of my mutual concern in this crisis would disperse the earlier tension – the tension where I felt trapped into worrying about the alarm this man seemed to have unleashed in that woman, and we both despised the part she seemed to be making me play in working to make this man feel his isolation. But now it was my turn to feel alone because I felt so small.

The car inched forwards, not to speed away down to the track but out into the sunshine where it settled, humming to itself, while the Captain beside me eased the gear into neutral and decided after all to broach the awful subject. He repeated himself by asking gently, 'What *did* she say to you? She obviously frightened you.'

The real guilt jerked my head around again. I couldn't bear to recount her unpleasant chatter to this man because surely it would be utterly idiotic to tell the Captain all that. And yet he was probing for something; forcing me to lurch into thinking again that he was perhaps waiting to see if I would explain my distress by confessing some connection to that man after all.

'She didn't frighten me,' I said with a shade too much denial

160

and perhaps that old irritation of injured pride. 'She told me about the theft of your accounts ledgers. She told me that you will have to visit each and every one of your tenants to warn them that this fellow might turn up at their door. And for good reason, it seems, since presumably he's lately attempted to do just that. Why didn't you tell me this was your purpose from the start? Why did you bring me along on *this?* To act the part of camouflage while you found a quiet moment in which to frighten Mrs Abbey about your ledgers?'

It came out like a justification of the idea that he really should be treating me like a child. The sense of being utterly small felt infinitely worse when the Captain was only determinedly patient.

He replied reasonably, 'It wasn't me she was afraid of.'

The implication it was me made me give a bitter laugh. But he was right, though. There had been triumph on her face when she had teased the Captain by ignoring him, whereas her greeting of me had been very different. It steadied me. It told me why I was building up to railing at him – it was that timeworn defence of being ready to hurl blame at him, blame at anyone but myself.

Only what blame here was due to any of us anyway? I said rather more calmly, 'I don't think she was really afraid of me. I just surprised her by turning up on her doorstep with you when she'd thought I'd packed my bags to run away.'

After an uncomfortable silence, I asked tentatively in that more honest version of myself that was less wracked by nerves, 'Why *did* you bring me along?'

'Why do you think?'

I confessed unhappily, 'Because you were never going to willingly leave me alone at the cottage after learning that your burglar had paid me a private visit.'

It was why he'd created a convenient excuse for both of us by asking me to come along to help. I knew he'd done it, but I'd still played along. And it was why, too, he'd kept the real purpose of his visit from me and why he'd capitalised on the chance of speaking to Mrs Abbey alone. It was because I'd made him think he had to protect me.

One of my hands had wrapped across my body, hugging myself defensively while my eyes roamed over the landscape outside the glass by my side. In this cramped, expensive car I felt my ridiculousness. The expanse out there of grassland before the distant treeline was huge and alien.

Very unexpectedly, the engine was suddenly, ominously, urged into motion. But we were only cruising gently back down the trackway into the farmyard. The wide hard-standing within that high boundary wall was empty and all the buildings were deserted. It didn't need the sudden heat of climbing out to watch while he rapped on the house door to tell me that Mrs Abbey and her children had gone. I stayed by the car while he probed the depths of the dilapidated barn. It was open-fronted at this end and I could make out the navy gleam of a battered but beloved old Austin Seven, propped up on blocks like any number of other cars up and down the country whose owners couldn't afford the petrol ration.

In the brief peace, the Captain appeared to come to a decision. He settled on direct delivery of everything that he had formerly tried to keep from me. Out of the gloom I heard him say, 'Very well, Emily. I'm sorry if this now turns into a forced confrontation with everything you hate, but since the alternative seems to be just as upsetting, I really will have to simply tell you the rest. The truth is, I recovered some of the contents of your suitcase in my father's library, where apparently they'd been tipped out to make room for the theft of the account ledgers. I have a bundle of your clothes in the boot of my car. I didn't tell you before because it was impossible to do so without telling you all this when you'd quite clearly asked me not to. I'm sorry. I was going to return them to you later, when I thought we might have safely established that your part in this was over. Unfortunately, we've now had another run-in with that man and my belief that you were irrelevant lasted just as long as it took me to notice that for a newcomer to the area, you seem to have taken remarkably quickly to having whispered conversations with Mrs Abbey.'

I baulked. His apology had just been a foil for working in this insinuation. I was mortified and I was sickened by his idea of the need for a trap. Restless energy brought me away from the car and a step or two closer to him and the heart of the yard as I retorted angrily, 'You *still* don't believe me. I don't know that man. I don't remotely know that woman.'

'Do you know,' the Captain remarked, emerging from the gloom of that barn at last and dusting off his hands. He looked absolutely nothing like I thought he did. I'd braced myself to be confronted by a soldier who was focused and determinedly seizing this chance to pursue a few painful truths. The Captain was in fact a normal man in regular city clothes who was presently saying in quite an ordinary way, 'I think it's fairer to say that *you* don't believe *me*.'

He drew off his jacket and moved past me to lay it over the hot metal roof of the car. The heat in this enclosed yard was painful after the cool of the trees. He returned to the bright blaze of the ground before me, stopping there to roll his shirtsleeves. He said, 'I'm not accusing you of anything any more. I told you that. I'm just trying to get to the bottom of what that woman said to you. What is it that you don't want to tell me?'

I saw, suddenly, the masquerade I was sustaining here. He wasn't testing my involvement with any of these people. But I was working myself into the role of the frightened and fragile female so that I might rant and storm and now claim my clothes from his boot before leaving him there just so that I didn't have to tell him any of the rest. I suppose, after all, it stemmed from protectiveness rather than defensiveness. From his point of view it must have seemed as though Mrs Abbey had said something to me that was very terrible indeed. Now all that remained for him was to gauge just how responsible he needed to feel for my welfare.

I was appalled and ashamed of myself. That and nothing else made me gasp out, 'I don't want to tell you because it's silly and embarrassing. She hasn't said anything to frighten me. She isn't threatening me. She just talked about you and your brother and it's nonsense and it doesn't have any part in this, I swear.'

'So she mentioned my brother.'

The calm observation shook me. I found that somehow I

had scurried past him to the side of his car as if my subconscious intended to make its getaway even while my conscious mind dismissed the idea of retreat as ridiculous. As I dithered to a halt near the passenger door, still a long way from speaking, I heard him add on a quietly measured tone, 'May I ask you a different question? I need an honest answer.'

I turned to face him properly. Grit crunched beneath my shoe. I was very close to the car and the black metal of its flank was radiating heat against my back.

'Do you think anything about this – the attack on Bertie; this man; Mrs Abbey's peculiar state of agitation – truly has anything to do with John?'

In the air around us was the shadow of that woman's whisper of his name. *Langton.*

I took in an unhappy breath. With it I inhaled one compelling sense of his own need here. My feet took a step backwards and my body claimed the support of the overheated side of the car. I lifted my head.

I told him plainly, 'Mrs Abbey has succeeded in bringing your brother's name into every conversation we've had. But truly, if anything she says is a clue to what is happening here, I don't believe it means John Langton's recent ... um, business activities have anything to do with the burglary of your house; or even the assault on Mr Winstone. My reason for thinking this is that I've noticed Mrs Abbey becomes strangely offensive just as soon as I attempt to ask her how she is and yet she's absolutely delighted to dissect the apparently inexhaustible topic of your brother's demise. Something *is* driving her to behave very strangely but I don't believe it has any true connection to your brother. Speaking his name to me is her sanctuary, not her threat.'

I saw the Captain's eyebrows rise a fraction. Suddenly, I suppose I'd been speaking as myself and not the frightened girl I'd tried to make him think I was.

I observed gently, 'You think I'm mistaken?'

'They were John's ledgers that were stolen. Just as they list the names and addresses of his tenants, they also list every income and expenditure he'd made on behalf of the Manor in the last few years of his life.'

Ah. I confirmed the suspicion by saying, 'Yesterday, I was supposed to agree that Mr Winstone's attacker was tall and dark with fearsomely blue eyes.'

'Like John.' He was very quick.

'Like your brother. But today she introduced the subject by telling me that I was supposed to remember that Mr Winstone's attacker was short and the opposite of athletic, like your burglar. Did you describe him to her when you told her about the accounts books?'

There was a faint tip of his head in confirmation. I drew a tentative breath. Then I confessed what had been haunting me since last night and had grown again when the Captain had irritated Mrs Abbey earlier by questioning her reasons for visiting the farthermost of two village shops at precisely the time that Mrs Winstone herself should have conveniently been near by. I told him, 'Mrs Abbey is trying to steer me into adjusting my description of Mr Winstone's attacker, but she doesn't seem to have a particularly clear idea of the direction she should take. I honestly can't quite tell if she really means to hint that our burglar today is connected to it, or connected to her, or if she's even afraid of him. I'm beginning to suspect she's actually just worried that we'll discover her part in yesterday's assault on your driver. Which, by the way, would explain her disappointment when she found I hadn't left. Because you should know that, while I certainly don't suspect her of actually doing the deed or even wishing it done, I am absolutely convinced beyond all shadow of a doubt that Mrs Abbey knew Bertie Winstone had been injured in an attack. And she cared so much that she went to extraordinary lengths to ensure that his wife was met and hurried home to find him.'

The hold his eyes had on mine was electric. I said quietly, 'Before you ask, I haven't any proof. I'm no threat to her and she will know that.'

Then I added regretfully, 'There's concealment in all of it, isn't there?'

'Yes.' In him it was a reference to that question that remained unanswered. And I knew, of course, that my reply must still involve his brother. Only I knew that it wasn't anything criminal.

The Captain moved forwards, to pass me and reclaim his car I thought, but he stopped when I clumsily put out a hand, palm towards him, as a sign of submission. I had to put his mind at rest. 'I'm sorry, Captain, you ought to know that everything else she said to me in that house was simply a variation of the usual salacious gossip. She *was* talking about your brother, but not about his business activities. Today she was distracting herself by talking about his romantic habits

... and yours ... and warning me—' I stumbled. I was too sensible to say the rest. Instead I repeated lamely, 'Sorry, Captain, but you should know I wouldn't go by what she said about you, I really wouldn't. I wouldn't presume ... I mean, I don't know you, but I know I wouldn't judge you on *that*.'

He was closer than he had been. I had the sudden absurd suspicion that he'd been approaching me and not his car. To tell me something that would lay my own unease at rest once and for all, perhaps, because he still felt responsible for my distress. Now he took the time to draw his car keys out of a pocket. Suddenly he was bemused and nothing more. My embarrassment was a relief to him. He observed dryly, 'So we come to it at last. What is this terrible slander she's made against me?'

Oh heavens, I thought. He was actually going to make me say it; every word of it. Of course he was, purely because we'd already said so much. He kept leading me into blindly telling him things and I didn't know how to stop it.

I said exasperatedly, 'Surely, you *must* know what she will have said. She told me about your brother and his ...'. The Captain's eyebrow lifted by way of encouragement. I continued stolidly, '... his efforts at courtship that tended to get a little complicated along the way. She said that you were ... well, you know, the same; only the fuss over his death had ruined your chances in good society and so I—' I took an impatient breath and had to look away. He would regret making me say this. 'She said that unless I wanted to join the ranks of the ... the idle distractions that are a temporary comfort, I—I should be careful too.'

I thought I'd offended him. I hadn't. Instead he said so easily that it was almost an insult, 'That's hardly something you need to worry about. And what did she say then?'

I risked a glance at him and then shook my head. 'Nothing. That's it.'

His silence disconcerted me. Suspicion was there in him again, more like wariness now in case a pitfall lay ahead, and I liked it even less than before. The car keys were in his hand now. They were cupped in his left hand and it was hanging free by his side. The other was loosely hooked into a trouser pocket. It was the first time I'd noticed that his hair was cut in the military style, cropped much closer at the sides than Danny's sandy mess, and dark, without the ordinary working man's flop over the brow. It might have made him look hard around the edges, but in truth it served to reinforce the peculiar experience I was having of the contradiction of what I thought he was and how he might superficially be described. I suppose I meant to observe that the cut of his hair only mattered in that it suited him.

In the same way, he defied the standard inhibition that should have made this none of my business and told me briskly and quite unnecessarily, 'You might as well know that I was set to marry a woman late last year who would have kept the scandal-mongers busy for months dissecting our comparative wealth and titles, and finding both of hers superior to mine. But I think we were neither of us as the other thought we were and so we parted company instead. It was around the time I spent my spell in a London hospital trying to remember how to walk and long before John's death, so that's another thing I really can't blame him for. I may have courted here and there, but John and I have very different tastes, and he certainly isn't responsible for ruining my 'chances'.'

It was said startlingly dryly and was more proof of the superiority of his idea of honesty over mine. I was still leaning there propped against the side of his car, almost tasting the reek of impending isolation in the air of this place, when he brought me round to the point he'd meant to make all along. He observed, 'But you aren't the sort of woman to go by rumours anyway, are you? Because, as you told me just now, you *don't judge me on that.*'

I couldn't look at him again. I said quietly in the pause he left, 'Please, Captain. I don't want to hurt you.'

I thought for a moment he had accepted my caution. But then he was adding thoughtfully, 'I think you are aware of the bar held over my head by pretty much anyone who has ever heard the name Langton – the bar that is occasionally used to give me a stern reminder of my place in this world. Mrs Abbey's recent efforts are, I think, a good example. But you tell me you don't set much store by anything she says and so, since you still patently don't believe me when I say that I'm not about to start treating you of all people as my next enemy, I can only presume that you've found your own way of measuring me. I can't help wondering what that is?'

I knew he had identified the feeling as distrust. It stung me because it was a hard enough judgement to contemplate and I thought he was probing for something deeper; something else within my feelings that I couldn't even guess at.

Suddenly the other me, the one who was shy of unpleasantness, was back in the fore. I was saying desperately, 'I do believe you. Really I do. And surely it doesn't matter anyway. It doesn't have anything to do with Mrs Abbey or that man. Can't we just leave it at that and get on?'

I believe I was ready to throw it all away, even to the extent of abandoning this trip and heading for home, all for the sake of not having to face this single thing. What I didn't expect was what my sudden plea betrayed to him. His feet shifted. Not with the design of making me flinch, although it certainly did. But to abruptly join me in my lean against the side of the car. I felt the tilt as the springs took his weight. I saw comprehension hit him almost with what looked like relief – to the point that compared to whatever else he had been dreading, this ranked as better – and then the moment that relief faded into reality and the jerk of his head as it turned aside to suppress a laugh.

I heard him say softly to the distant base of the boundary wall on a tone that must have been absolute disbelief, 'It isn't what I thought. The clue has been there all along in the way you use my name, hasn't it, and it belongs to a woman who craves peace. *Captain* ...'

My eyes drifted left to him. His head was still turned away but I could see his heartbeat racing in the turn of his throat at the point where his skin met the collar and both ran away into the line of his shoulder beneath his shirt. He was used to being called to account for his brother's choice of career, and perhaps even for his family's as a whole, but I thought this was the first time he'd ever been criticised for his own. His head turned back a little to catch me watching. I raced to explain and made it worse.

'Believe me,' I said urgently. 'Whatever else you think, I am very aware of the gift people like you have given to people like me, who never had to go abroad, never had to do anything except take your sacrifice and grow up and live.'

'I don't follow.'

'The war is over, most of the uniforms have been put away and we're meant to believe the biggest danger that persists from that time is likely to be a petty criminal touting the long-lost contents of some poor old lady's cupboards that they'd retrieved from the rubble during the Blitz.' I was watching him. I couldn't help it. He was very still. He was simply leaning there beside me with his back against the sun-warmed metal of his car while the slanting daylight cast his body into living relief, and frowning a little at the ground before our feet. I'd forgotten that any reference to looting must touch upon his brother.

It took some nerve for me to add, 'Personally, I find it remains very hard to accept this simplified summary of the way things are now, when I can't help knowing that a good number of the men I will meet in perfectly civilised surroundings will have lately taken human life.'

I felt his response to that. It conveyed itself through the metal at my back as a miniscule quiver. After a time he let out the tension in a long, measured breath. 'That,' he told me, 'is a very odd way to put it.'

'It is,' I replied, 'a very odd experience.'

And most of the men I'd met had only served as conscripts. This man had chosen do to it, and still did.

He still didn't move. I felt empowered and feeble all at the same time. If I'd ever wanted to bolster my sense of importance by proving another person's confidence in their value was a bitter sham, this was my moment.

Only if I had, I could have never forgiven myself and, in truth, with this man it probably wouldn't have worked anyway. So instead, eventually and on a painfully humble note, I added my last meagre crumb of honesty. 'I truly am sorry. If it's any consolation, you're nothing like how I expected you to be.'

His head turned at last. The depth of my apology startled him even more than the rest. Falteringly, I met his gaze. Then I dropped mine to the metalwork of the car between us. He knew I couldn't help how I felt, but he also knew that I really did care that I'd wounded him. He could read it on my face. I forced myself to bear the scrutiny of those eyes, even though doing it made my heart ache. I was conscious of the way the faintest touch of doubt was lingering at the corners of that mouth as he tried to understand what he saw. Then the puzzlement grew into the quick gleam of amusement. He'd wanted the truth from me. I didn't think he'd ever anticipated receiving anything quite as honest as this.

Affection grew there. And I, having braced myself for the shame of completing this man's alienation, suddenly found we were tipping into friendship.

And closeness. We were leaning side by side against that car once more and I was experiencing a shy thrill of comfort in this man's company; and discovering the sunlight and restfulness that for me must come from the unexpected release of finding that the workings of my mind – now that I had formulated the words to share them – were not to be argued out of existence or into humility. Right or wrong, they were being ranked equally beside those of an alert mind like his.

He was, I suppose, being protective of me again but it was in a different way and for once I didn't feel like I should resist it.

He claimed my first true smile. Then he said briskly, 'Shall we get on? I think it's safe to say neither Mrs Abbey nor that man are coming back again.'

We left a note for Mrs Abbey. It was impossible to know what her intentions were or, indeed, if we really ought to be put on guard by her repeated references to the Captain's brother, but we could hardly leave the woman unaided. The note told her that we'd seen the man on her trackway, that the police would be told and she and her children could come to the Manor if she was worried.

Chapter 11

'For someone who seems to crave a quiet life, you sound as if you envy her.'

This came from him after a particularly incoherent lecture from me on the wonderfulness of a life spent charting far-flung places on behalf of the War Office. We were making gentle conversation about something that was easy for me. We were talking about my cousin.

I ran a lazy hand over my hair. 'Do I? I suppose I do envy her in a way. Since you grew up at the Manor you probably remember that your father's old steward had seven children. My cousin is the youngest of them and the only daughter. I don't know her brothers terribly well, but she's terrifically bright. She studied geography somewhere very prestigious and later, by the time her father the steward died and his widow moved into that cottage, she had work as the assistant to someone important at the Royal Geographical Society. It was her apprenticeship to them that got her the part she was to play in the war. She became one of those fearfully invaluable people who worked right on the edge of things, gathering intelligence and surveys and so on and assembling it all into useful maps. I would have loved to have had something important like that to contribute. Imagine the places she must have seen.'

'And this from the pacifist. Anyway, they'd have never let a nice young thing like you go. Work and travel of the nature undertaken by your cousin requires a rather harder breed of person. And I don't, by the way,' he added quickly as an afterthought, 'mean that as a set-down. I'm fully aware that most people are capable of extraordinary courage when presented with a certain situation. But it doesn't mean we should recklessly put every fresh generation there just to prove the point.'

We were coasting gently into a village – the next one along on the ridgetop, which housed the shop that Mrs Abbey wouldn't use.

The change of speed prompted me suddenly to say shyly, 'You're being very kind.'

I saw his eyebrows lift. He might have pretended that he hadn't understood, but he didn't. He confided gently, 'You didn't actually do anything wrong, you know. At least no more than I.'

'No,' I said. 'But it helps that you say it.' I nearly added 'Captain' to the end of that but it was hard to use his title out loud now. Instead I gave a restful sigh as the heart of the village curled into view. It was a pretty little chequerboard of communal vegetable gardens surrounded by the most uneven square of cottages I'd encountered here yet. I said wistfully, 'I do envy her. Or perhaps it is more accurate to say that I envy you. You have this confidence that helps you act, secure in the belief that your judgement is sound, even if other people don't immediately see it that way. I don't know if it is typical of women or unique to me but either way, my confidence is always behindhand to the act. It likes to wait, to see how the event has been received before the first hint of self-belief finally, grudgingly, creeps into the scene.'

I made him laugh.

Then my exclamation made the car slow. His head turned almost at the same time as mine to see what I had seen.

The short run of houses and rough cottages that made up this village were set on a square built around rough vegetable gardens. Nestling into the wall that bounded the far corner of these gardens was the blackened hulk of what had once been a communal outhouse. There were a few village boys standing about – all limbs and tanned skin and aimlessly kicking about ashes while the smell of charred wood drifted on the warm air. The smell was familiar to me. It had drifted down the valley last night.

The boys drifted down in a similar manner too, only they came to admire the car. Their answer to my enquiry of what had happened here wasn't very pleasant. Someone had lately relieved the gardens of their vegetables and then, last night, after the agitated villagers had harvested what remained, the shed had been set alight. These gardens had not been the first to be hit like that in recent weeks, we were told, and in precisely that order. I thought it almost gathered weight for that other neglected theory about who had hit Mr Winstone; the one where he'd disturbed a passing vagrant. It was not a grateful traveller who repaid his debt of food in this time of shortages with an act of vandalism.

The other vital piece of news the boys could give us was, however, rather more beneficial for my peace of mind. This was the second car they'd seen today and the other was a black Ford 'Y' and it had taken the lane to the left at the end of the vegetable gardens towards Gloucester. We took the road to the right since the Colonel had no tenants in the other direction. It meant we didn't need to pursue the driver of that car in a race to the next name on the list in the accounts books.

'May I borrow your other great specialism?'

The Captain's voice brought me out of a deep musing on the peculiarities of responsibility; the way this man bore the responsibility of doing what he could to manage any threat to his father's tranquillity, set against the probability of bringing his family name deeper into this himself if he made a reckless choice. In my mind, the latter would have been something like going tearing down into the streets of a city after that man; which wasn't, needless to say, a decision I remotely craved. I hoped the Captain knew that. Not that there would ever have been any hope of tracing that Ford in the crowded streets of the nearby city anyway, but there was always that niggling suspicion that, given what I'd just said about confidence and my capacity for uncertainty until it was proved I'd been understood, it was possible that my sudden abstraction of thought might be taken as disappointment that we were meekly leaving that man to make his escape.

With that in mind, I turned my head and said with unnecessarily brightness, 'This sounds ominous. Which specialism is that?'

'Did you happen to notice the stack of furniture in the barn back there? At Eddington, I mean?'

The debate about whether the Captain was imagining that I was feeling disappointment or otherwise was proved irrelevant. He wasn't detecting anything in me and, quite simply, he wasn't foolhardy. He knew precisely where his responsibility lay. It lay in knowing that I was not the sort of passenger to incite a man into pursuing a dashing chase and it lay in seeking to understand the details of what we had already seen.

There was a certain sharp thrill in discovering how far his intentions mirrored mine. I asked rather more seriously, 'Did the furniture match the pieces in the house? Some of it was very good in its day.'

'In its day?'

I explained, 'Time, a family of boys and a leaking roof have taken their toll, I think. My dad is very severe upon any piece that would require extensive repairs. Unless, of course, it has been undertaken by his workshop, in which case it has been 'sensitively restored by an expert'. Why do you ask?'

I saw the brief show of a smile. 'Did Mrs Abbey happen to mention the other rumour that abounds around my brother's name? The one that says that the hoard the policemen recovered last March was only the tip of the iceberg and he's got vast troves hidden away yet?'

I shook my head. 'No. But I can assure you that even if she

had, you can certainly rest easy about her furniture. I don't think a few grubby chairs and a table with a barley twist and the veneer curling off are going to amount to much of a fortune, whether it is hers or his. If she's got your brother's wealth hidden away somewhere, it isn't in the furniture.'

'And the paintings? It doesn't take an expert to deduce that the pair in the living room were fairly shabby, but the one on the kitchen wall ...? I saw it as we passed down the hall.'

We were moving smoothly down through a sequence of hard bends. There was a sort of magnetism in the steadiness of his concentration on the road ahead. This narrow dip before the coming rise was the head of the long valley that housed my cousin.

'Was there a dark sort of landscape practically hanging in the smoke above the stove? I didn't really notice it, which means it must have been modern. Dad has coached me into being very severe upon anything less than about a hundred years old. It'll take me a lifetime to undo that training. You sound as if you've got a better eye.'

He told me plainly, 'My mother was a collector. But all that aside, it fascinates me that Mrs Abbey hasn't mentioned this particular myth in the course of her manoeuvrings. I would give quite a lot to know whether or not I should be taking that detail as reassuring.'

My silence obviously communicated rather more than it ought.

I felt his sideways glance as we reached a crossroads where the main road sliced across our little lane. It was being travelled by about five cars and a bus. He was amused.

He was grinning a little as he remarked, 'Don't concentrate so hard on looking calmly detached, Emily. You're not teetering on the brink of being dragged into a treasure hunt, I promise. I called it a myth and it is. The rest of the stories about what John did died with him and they can stay there. Sometimes I feel ...' A hesitation. 'Well, the truth is I feel that picking through the memories of this place is like meeting a stranger and even without the deep complication of managing my father's varying wishes, it would have been a perfectly valid reason for staying away. I don't want to know him like this.'

A quick intake of breath and an adjustment of the grip of his hands upon the wheel and that was it. He said in an altogether different tone, 'Ready for this?'

He tipped his head at the cluster of buildings that ranged on the other side of the crossroads. They were Nissen huts laid out in two clusters around the weed-strewn concrete emplacements where anti-aircraft guns had once stood. This was the former air-raid lookout station and if Mr Winstone's attacker was one of the local squatters, this was where he lay his head.

We weren't actually here to harass the residents into a confession. The Captain was here under another guise. This time he really was wearing the uniform of the squire's deputy and I simply hadn't noticed because the difference between this and the Captain's usual demeanour was very subtle.

The right-hand array of huts was very orderly. They even had ordinary things like a sense of community. They had collected a giant stack of rubbish and scraps of timber and I realised they were gearing up to have their own small VJ Day celebration with a bonfire. I suppose I'd been expecting the squatters' camp to look grimly prison-like and occupied by underfed men who bore the shadows of their war experiences in every gesture, but the residents had painted nameplates on their houses and planted fragrant vegetable plots, and it was all guarded by one solitary woman who had been tasked with minding the children while everyone else was out working the fields.

She was shy and I would have sworn, even without hearing her accent, that she was a displaced Londoner. Her blank stare and the habit she had of keeping a hand on her partially opened door, ready to shut it quickly, told me that she had once lived in an area where strange men who called unannounced were more often than not the louts sent to extract a little extra rent. She took the Captain's message that the residents were all encouraged to attend the Colonel's meeting in the Manor farmyard tomorrow and then she confirmed with the minimum possible words that there had been no other cars visiting today, nor – answering a quick addition from me – had their vegetable gardens been plundered. It was hard to be sure she was really hearing our questions properly and not just giving an automatic negative, but we couldn't do more.

'Rather short and to the point,' remarked the Captain as we returned to his car. 'Hard to act the part of the squire's son when only one tired-looking mother is there to hear it. I really ought to have paid more attention to the lessons of my youth and remembered that they work until dusk when they're harvesting.'

'And perhaps noticed that it's the hay they're gathering at the moment, not the barley harvest. And I think farming folk call any ripening grain "corn", just for the sake of confusion.'

'There you go, then.'

'The Colonel isn't going to tell them he's evicting them, is he?'

A grimace as the car turned left onto the main road and charged upwards through the gears. Suddenly the Captain was enjoying this car. He answered my question quite as if we weren't racing towards the brow of a hill. He said, 'Heavens, no. My father wouldn't want that on his conscience even if he did own the land, which he doesn't. No. The invitation we've just given them is to hear an announcement my father intends to make of an equally significant but less tyrannical nature about the role he's set to play in their long-term employment.'

The next junction took us back onto the narrow lane towards the village. It was the same route I'd walked with my case from the bus stop. I thought I saw a glimpse of Freddy when we passed through the little dip with the farmstead and all the horses. Then I saw a raven above a hedgeline.

I was just running on to saying something mindless about it when the man beside me abruptly said, 'You're obviously too discreet to ask, so I'll just have to tell you. The reason why my father came back today is because we Langtons are in as bad a state financially as the rumour merchants say and we're going to have to cut and run while we still can. The estate further down the valley that belonged to my uncle has gone already and we think we've got a buyer for the Manor. Father's going to explain some of this to the estate workers and tenants at his meeting tomorrow.'

The car slowed to a crawl as we took the turn down through the village triangle, past the terrace of workers' cottages and round towards the dark shadow cast by the barn that housed the machinery.

The engine died. In the silence, the Captain added, 'That much is soon going to be common knowledge, but this part isn't, so please don't let it go further. My father is selling the estate to a timber merchant.'

'Not a farmer?'

'No. No one wanted it. And even this fellow hasn't signed and sealed the deal yet, so don't go scaring the villagers. There's a scheme in place that will allow our tenants to buy their houses at a sensible price and Hannis will oversee the work to finish the harvest, so there's employment for now. But, in all honesty, I'm not sure how it's all going to change in the long run. People will say we should fight tooth and nail to meet the mortgage on this place, but the son who valued the estate and understood it as much as my father does is gone and let's just say that my salary isn't capable of keeping that many people afloat on a debt of this scale. We've got to get out for our own sake and, if we want to do it cleanly for the sake of everyone else, we've got to do it now.'

He seemed to be waiting for me to speak, so I said the first thing that came into my head. I said in a very small voice, 'You keep putting me in a very peculiar position of trust by telling me these things and I still don't quite understand why.'

'Don't you?' he asked unhelpfully. I was thinking of the concession he'd made about the cause of his slight limp on the stairs this morning, amongst other things.

Then he climbed out and came round to drag open my door. 'Six o'clock,' he commented as I joined him in the still air of the yard between this barn and the older one with the pockmarked stone that was presently shining like a buttercup.

'Teatime,' I replied, for want of anything better to say. He agreed. And then he very obviously didn't say anything else. His gaze ran over the utterly barren beds of his father's vegetable garden.

His ill-concealed hint made me smile. I said suspiciously, 'Are you waiting for me to offer to cook your dinner?'

He grinned. 'If, by asking that, you're implying that you really are willing to consider catering for the masses, give me your key and I'll walk down and fetch some of your cousin's stores.' I thought he was rather overestimating my culinary skills. Or perhaps this was a tactful way of avoiding that uncomfortable discussion about how safe I might feel at that cottage on my own this evening because he was already saying, 'Go on. I can save you that much labour, at least. You don't want to walk all the way down there and back up again after the day we've had, do you?'

'No,' I admitted. 'But I didn't begin the day by requiring the assistance of a walking stick.'

Amusement jerked his head aside and fixed his gaze on nothing. A curve plucked at the corners of his mouth as he said, 'That wasn't my cane, Emily. I thought you'd been sharp to spot my twinge and now I know. The stick belongs to my father and I was merely the porter charged with carrying it along to his room with his coat. Anyway, the real motive behind my current offer to jog down the hill is that it's the sitting down and doing nothing that's really murder. Walking doesn't hurt at all, and it helps to prove it to myself every once in a while.'

I remembered what he'd said about his hospital stay and having to remember how to walk and was sorry. His attention returned to me. He saw the question I wasn't bold enough to ask. He told me simply, 'I caught a bullet. In London of all places, after coming through the war relatively intact. Put like that it sounds rather close to your idea of unending conflict, doesn't it, but actually it was pretty undramatic and the real damage was caused by the tourniquet in the form of a belt that some helpful passer-by twisted about my right thigh. They did it to stem the flow, where a good firm wad of something and a bit of pressure would have done the job perfectly well. Unfortunately, I wasn't exactly in a state at the time to give my own instructions. But I am now and I think you really would prefer to keep my father company while I run our errands, wouldn't you?'

I really could take a hint when I heard it. 'Well ...' I began. 'Yes?'

'If it really is six o'clock – might I use your telephone to call my cousin?'

'Of course,' he said crisply. 'The telephone is ... well, you know where it is, don't you?'

And with another disorientating glimpse of understanding

that revealed just how unselfconscious I'd grown in his company, he was near enough to put out his hand to take the key from my fingers just as soon as it began to emerge from my handbag.

Chapter 12

I might have worried about letting myself into the Colonel's kitchen unannounced but I presumed – correctly as it turned out – that the old man would accept my presence as naturally as he would have acknowledged his old housekeeper or one of the women from the village coming in to clean. The Colonel shuffled in when he heard the door shut, ascertained it was me and not his son Richard, tossed a paper down on the table, and then shuffled out again. I didn't mind. I'd spent the day keeping increasingly easy company with his son, but I wasn't exactly aiming for familiarity with the man who was lord and master of these parts. A minute or so later, I discovered that there had been no real need for me to manage a tête-à-tête alone with the squire anyway while the Captain walked down to Phyllis's cottage on a quest for supplies; because Mrs Winstone had passed by and left a quite spectacular pigeon pie.

She'd left a note about it on the counter. The other note, the crumpled letter that the Colonel had lately thrown down onto the round kitchen table in a fit of temper and then forgotten, was from the housekeeper and it explained why the

Captain hadn't added her name to the list of doubts in our day. Presumably he'd unearthed this shortly after his arrival and his father had just re-read it now. In the note, Mrs Cooke wrote that she had fancied a little holiday and implied that after thirty years or so of uninterrupted service it was the sort of trip where she was going to take some time to decide whether or not to come back. The cold rejection of her closing instruction to send all communications care of her sister in Gloucester carried its own message to her employer, but for me the only part of it that could have possibly justified the feeling I had in this quiet sunlit kitchen was the brief sentence that mentioned Mrs Abbey. It wished to make the reader aware of all that lady's kindnesses over the past months.

I smoothed the creases out of the paper with my fingers and then set it neatly beneath a pepper pot on the counter, out of the way. Then I passed through the house to the stairwell and there I discovered just why the Captain was working so hard to keep his father's peace intact.

The Colonel's unfriendliness wasn't just a mark of a bullying nature. He lurched out of his library just as soon as I opened the door to the study that housed the telephone. I think he must have forgotten I was there because the click of the door had drawn him out and he spoke his son's name and then stopped at the heart of the stairwell, glowering when he saw it was only me. I suspected, in fact, that he couldn't remember who I was at all.

The structure of the man's face was impressive in its way but his cheeks were blotched with red beneath white hair that was combed but woolly. He was standing, a dark-clad man, at the point where the immaculate chequerboard floor met the curling sweep at the foot of the banister. The light cast from the expansive windows made it hard to see how old he was. Perhaps he was only in his early seventies but he looked like a broad man who had lately grown unexpectedly frail. The sharply angled sunlight was picking out the loose fit of his suit. The impression was of an older, sharper man than his son where all warmth had been etched away as a weakness, leaving behind something that this old soldier wished would bear an edge like steel but was, in truth, as insubstantial as hammered tin.

The light must have been affecting his sight too because those faded eyes could barely look at me while I explained in a clumsy fashion about my permission to use the telephone. Then I realised it wasn't me that kept making his gaze veer away. Suddenly I perceived the strength of that deep stubbornness that was keeping him tall and stern like this. My hand was out behind me on the handle of the partially opened door to his younger son's study. I softly eased it shut.

It released him to turn and lead me into the library. I followed. It was disturbingly like a question of choosing sides – and choosing in favour of the side where control had fought a brutal battle over the freedom to feel anything. Then I saw I was wrong. Emotion dwelt here and very powerfully. For a cruel, revealing moment when his gaze touched that closed study door once more, I glimpsed on the old man's face a reflection of the memory that had touched the boy Freddy, only viewed from the other side, as though he'd been in there that day too.

In the next second it was swept away. In its place, it was

possible to trace the same sense of purpose in the Colonel that gave his son Richard his energy and his presence. In this instance, unfortunately, it transpired that the old man's sense of purpose was being directed towards reclaiming a stiff drink.

The drinks trolley was, I knew, kept in the room opposite so it was clear the Colonel must have managed to venture at least once across the forbidding threshold of his son's study since his arrival. Now he was clutching a glass and staring out of a deeply elegant sash window between tall overcrowded bookcases with his bearing correct to the point of arrogance. His suit was an expensive navy wool and, it felt mad to think it, but as he stood there in the blazingly slanting light of a lowering sun between panels of darkened wood, he looked like nothing so much as a man in his funeral garb who was gazing defiantly out through prison bars onto a landscape that might well have been lit by the fires of hell.

As I say, it was mad to think it. It was one of those moments when imagination really did dramatise and find death lurking in impossible corners. But still I couldn't help interfering here. Heart beating and acting on an impulse – probably a very patronising, misguided impulse belonging to a fool stepping well out of her permitted social sphere – I reached for the bottle on his desk. It was a very expensive brandy that had become almost impossible to source since rationing. I carried it with me to the doorway. That stern face turned to watch me go.

'I'm about to set a pie to warm for your dinner, Colonel. Perhaps you would come and help me decipher the controls on your oven?'

For a moment I wondered if the Colonel were about to explode into very much the wrong kind of emotion. His grey eyes had not been made soft by drink. Then I believe it was politeness that ruled – ordinary, everyday politeness – and I heard the shuffle of his tread as he followed my footsteps through the stretch of dark passages and the dining room into the blessedly warm and well-lit kitchen.

He didn't, needless to say, help me to set the pie in the oven. I doubted that he had ever even examined the contraption and he seemed to forget that plan just as soon as he saw me set the bottle down on the tabletop. So I watched him select a tired old Windsor chair with a tall wooden bow for the back and then navigated my own way about his kitchen. This place was a combination of old and new. The oven had dials for temperature control in complete contrast to the usual old cooking range that would have a cramped cast-iron box for the fuel, but the countertop was stone and it was hollowed in places, speaking of age and memories and the years of kitchen staff who had laboured here.

It struck me that this would have been Mrs Cooke's domain. Perhaps it had been a mistake to bring him in here after all. He certainly looked out of place. Mealtimes were clearly judged a formal affair to be undertaken in the dining room. He was sitting there in his humble chair, peering about as if he'd abruptly found himself in a strange and hostile territory. It made me chatter idiotically while I found the last crust of the loaf on a board and buttered it before sliding it on a plate to the Colonel's side. I saw him blink at it for a moment or two before mustering the energy to lift his hand. Unfortunately, the hand got distracted on the way and found an easier weight to lift in the form of his half-emptied glass.

I wondered where else I could put him if not in this room. I might have lately strayed across the boundary between housekeeper and bossy equal but I could hardly pass from there to the role of mother and dispatch the old man like a child to his bed. So I rambled brainlessly on the subject of the whereabouts of the lettuce, the challenge of slicing tomatoes and the delight of a modern gas oven – bottled gas, presumably? – and I was just beginning to really warm to the part of stand-in cook and company when he interrupted me. It came with a very small voice that swept away my worries about the impact of the housekeeper's departure with such suddenness that I might as well have been fussing about the impact of a flea. He asked, in a whisper, if his son seemed damaged.

It was a frightened and frail plea. My hand hung over a partially chopped salad item of some sort while that same distant voice breathed, 'I mean his *mind* after his injury. I thought the other boy was fine but—'

He meant his other son and the injury that had lamed him. This was where the desperation came from. The Colonel broke off with a little choke. Then the whisper added, 'It's very hard to be sure any more. Richard says he's fine, but what does that prove? The other boy lied. We both lied when the blasted accident tore him apart. It ruined him and kept him from serving in the army and made him obsessive about his place here; and he hated it ... and me. And Richard had to be his usual placid self throughout, even to the point of mediating later from his hospital bed. He got nerve damage, did you know? And a raging infection. Once that had gone I stayed in London because he hadn't got the energy left to move and I had to practically force him to walk on it again and the other boy blamed me for that too. And now Richard's come back here and I can't tell any more what he's thinking. He wasn't supposed to come here today. It was supposed to just be me.'

He broke off again. The dread here was for himself and what he would learn about the condition of the surviving son's mind. The expression on his face was a very peculiar mixture of impotence and desperate fright beneath an unattractive flush of drink. It made me wonder where his own lie had lain within John's decline. And how much damage it must have done to his confidence that he couldn't tell what his eldest son was capable of; or not capable of, as the case must really be.

It also made me aware, once again, of the unbending nature of the older son's urge to protect. The Captain had known this trip might test his father's fears and I had a horrible feeling that Richard's decision to come here in person had been a careful balancing of the risks between leaving his father unsupported and adding to the old man's dread of seeing another son flounder in this damaged place. It made my heart twist at the helplessness of it. And it wasn't lost on me that his father wasn't the only person who had taken to confronting the man today with questions about the innermost workings of his mind.

While my mouth worked silently in an attempt to find some form of reply, a sudden shifty look came over the

Colonel's face, as if he didn't quite know what he had been saying but he was sure it wasn't safe. The piece of bread caught his eye again and the simple act of eating seemed to bring him round. When he next spoke, his voice was considerably stronger. 'Did Richard tell you what he does? What he did?'

'A little,' I replied, slightly clumsily.

'You understand that Richard was a Lieutenant in his first command when they were first sent abroad? But promotion was rapid, yes? Whenever a senior officer was killed or injured his post had to be filled and quickly. But promotion wasn't ratified. Not made official. My son served up to the rank of Lieutenant Colonel in one of his commands but it couldn't have stuck beyond the field of battle. It all had to be sorted out when they came home and everyone was given the real rank that was due to a man at his time in his career. I suppose you thought my son mustn't have done very much to have come through all those years of fighting and still only be a Captain now?'

'No! Of course not. I wouldn't have thought about it like that at all.'

'My son fought across North Africa in the 2nd Royal Gloucestershire Hussars. He was in the battle of Alam el Halfa.' The Colonel's voice grew grand with the precise elocution of one for whom pride lay in the details. I found that I had been fixed with a shrewd eye. He demanded suspiciously, 'Does that mean anything to you? Desert. Filthy bloody desert and hundreds of tanks and aeroplanes; Germans, Italians and our men; all sweating it out because if we could stop them there, we could work them out of Africa.'

The old man had transformed. He actually revived enough to set his nearly emptied glass to one side, the better to make room for his hands which were sketching out an imaginary plan of North Africa upon the tabletop. I stared as a crooked finger swept a line from a knot towards an ancient scorch mark. 'Rommel came from here, meaning to take our man Montgomery here. You understand me? From the southwest.' I nodded because I was supposed to. This was not, I suspected, destined to be a conversation that I could meet with equal knowledge but, to be quite frank, I was willing to indulge the old man in any subject he chose just so long as it curbed the desperate bleakness that had seemed only too devastating only a few minutes before. And this man really loved his war.

A finger was sketching a curve. 'Rommel wanted to encircle us like he'd done before and give us a sound thrashing before pushing us back into the sea. But he was funnelled north. Mines did that. And my son was here.' A swift glance at my face to confirm that I was following the lecture. 'He spent six days on the ridge pounding away with guns smaller than the enemy's while old Monty held the line firm and brought in aeroplanes to finish it. Monty was the man to see the job through. He knew what blood must be shed, what lives must be spent—'

I must have made a sound. I hadn't meant to. Sharp eyes found my face. Then he assured me kindly, 'It was all about the strategy, you see. It always is. You public, you see it like a scene on a newsreel; flickering footage of tragedy and heroes and grinning men coated in grit and filth. But Monty – and me in my time – we old campaigners perceive our cause differently. Home counts, the lives of our men count and, of course, victory counts, but at that moment – at that instant of knowing you've seen your opponent's move perfectly – you know you've got the chance to take them and then you don't need any other cause at all.'

As he spoke I couldn't help seeing the Captain as I had met him only this morning, but this time clad in sand-coloured uniform, hunkered down in the cramped airlessness of one of many tanks, working with desperation, elation and sheer strength of will to keep his men feeding that beast of a machine. Doing it knowing that the deaths of a few thousand soldiers were being coolly measured against other losses; and that by his own actions as a lesser commander of men, he was endorsing it.

I couldn't help wondering what the Captain's cause was. And doubted it would quite be the same.

The Colonel had moved on. His energy was running on now to an earnest tale of someone, something, who had been broken up. In a way his enthusiasm was infectious.

'You mean Rommel?' I had a feeling I hadn't got that right. It turned out I was correct there.

'No!' The Colonel was impatient when his pupil missed an important point. His head turned to follow me as I moved to the dresser in the far corner. The dresser stood with its back to the garden beside a long blank wall of panelled wood that ran back to frame the door into the dining room. A neatly folded pile of napkins waited there with the crockery.

The Colonel raised his voice to cover the increase of distance – which was, in fact, only a matter of two or three yards. He told me, 'I'm talking about the 2nd Royal Gloucestershire Hussars – Richard's regiment. It was disbanded. Broken up. Dispersed to other fighting units. They'd already suffered a long line of heavy losses in the run up to that battle and it had to be their last. They went into the 4th, the 8th ...' He reeled off a list of numbers that might have been armies, regiments or anything, for all I knew.

'But not,' he added, 'Richard. He came home and then he—'

Then a loud exclamation that made me spin of, *'Richard!'*

The kitchen door had opened. The Colonel said, beaming to the silhouette who still stood there with his hand on the newly opened door, 'I've just been regaling Miss, um, *Whateverhernameis* with the account of your adventures at Alam el Halfa.'

There really was pride in the old man's voice. His son was calm in reply. 'Miss Sutton. And I'm sure she doesn't want to hear about that.'

He stepped into the room. His voice was for his father, but his eyes found me in my corner and there was an undertone because he thought he knew what I would be thinking and he had mastery enough of himself now to be amused by it; only in truth, he didn't know at all. He didn't know that the vivid account his father had just given of the foreign battle and its horrific toll upon endurance was merging now with this image of a man who was here; alive. His body burned with the pure enjoyment of exercise. This was why he'd wanted to walk. His collar had been loosened and a faint sheen touched the base of his throat. It was an uninhibited reintroduction to the real man and it wasn't fair. I shouldn't have to feel like this. With my preconceptions about peacefulness and all this talk about war and soldiering that must be perfectly pitched to challenge me, it wasn't right that I should have to find a military man so appallingly attractive. But he was. He gave off this sheer human vitality and he was intelligent and kind, and he'd shaken me today with every fresh proof of it. And now he'd walked in like this in the midst of a very peculiar evening and the relief of having him here made my mind ache.

The awful thing was that I saw the split second pass while he searched my face for the expected criticism and found there something else entirely. The dresser clattered beside me as a distraction when I accidentally knocked it. I saw doubt spread like ink into the easy humour that had come in warm with his walk. I found that my mouth was mirroring the way his lips had parted in mild sort of query and instantly clamped mine firmly shut. It was idiotic and I couldn't help stiffly bustling across the room in an attempt to hide the flush that scorched my face by scurrying to the table with my napkins. But then his head turned and his gaze dropped to the old man in the chair beside him and he found the wrong interpretation for my embarrassment in the similar colour that was flooding his father's cheeks.

I believe I would have given anything to have kept him from learning why I had coaxed the Colonel into sitting with me. Now cold swept across my skin as I saw the Captain's swift intelligence take in the napkins in my hands and the brandy bottle and the evidence of my effort to soak it up with buttered bread and I saw at last the depth of the care between this father and his son. As Richard gazed down at his father's blurred features, there was, in the set of his jaw, tender understanding and an almost fierce absence of blame. This scene wasn't, I noticed, a surprise to him. But it certainly gave the Captain a hard sense of failure. And at the same time I also saw in his final, swift assessing glance to me beneath lowered brows a difficulty that might easily shift into shame, only I knew that he mustn't be allowed to feel that, not for me.

How could I possibly explain that I too could appreciate that it took a complicated, damaged man like his father to possess the kind of drive needed to push an exhausted son to recovery. Master John had struggled against the old man and I doubted that the Colonel had ever displayed much of a bedside manner, but this son's living, vibrant presence now was a mark of his father's capacity for love all the same.

I couldn't explain something like that, of course. So instead I said, with unnecessary passion, 'You needn't have ransacked Phyllis's vegetable garden after all. You and Colonel Langton have very caring neighbours. Are you ready to eat? Mrs Winstone's pie is hot, I think.'

I emptied my hands of napkins upon the tabletop and found that he was holding out my cousin's key, dangling at the end of its short chain. I obediently put out my hand and he dropped the key into my palm. Now it was my turn to be puzzled by the change in his expression. I'd caused it with my silly formal use of his father's title by way of denoting respect, and his doubt made me doubtful. I dealt with it in the only way I knew, which was to play the part of temporary housekeeper even more thoroughly than before. I went to the oven and made as much womanly clattering as I could while I extracted the pie from its depths.

I straightened and set the weighty dish upon the hob. It was hot in here all of a sudden and I had to sweep the hair back from my face with the back of a hand. The Captain hadn't yet taken his seat. I set a handful of cutlery down on the countertop for him and as I did so I gave him a truly reassuring smile. None of this needed to be difficult. I saw the surprise as my wide beam hit him and the release as he decided to accept his part in this scene. I saw him approach and collect the pieces I'd left in a stack for him. And then the jug and glasses for water. Out of the corner of my eye I saw him draw out a chair and claim it, before setting a glass down beside his place and another one for his father. There was caution in the act as though it might have been natural enough for the Captain to manage his own meals in his London home, but here tradition had always been maintained to the point of obsession. I thought he was finding it mildly disorientating to see his father taking his ease like this.

I served the pie onto two plates and set them down before the men. The Colonel approached his with boyish enthusiasm and after a moment or two more the son shrugged and lifted his fork and deliberately turned his mind to conversation that would please his father. He began by describing some improvement he'd observed on our drive about the boundary of the estate.

I took the chance to remind them of my telephone call and retreated through the passage into the house. As the Captain's gaze followed me it carried a faint question again, but he didn't act except to give a brief nod to confirm my choice was fine. But I didn't mean to use the telephone anyway. I did the only thing I thought I could do to keep from damaging the Colonel's restored mood by either forcing them into an evening of stilted conversation with an unexpected guest or, as was more likely, embarrassing us all by scuttling about after more chores like a crawling, lovesick busybody who was desperate to insinuate her way into every aspect of their life at the Manor.

I let myself quietly out of the front door and along the drive onto the lane, and then I followed it quickly down the hill.

Chapter 13

My reward for abandoning my only chance of company was a sleepless night stalked by a belief that the house was being watched and a persistent smell of burning. I stumbled downstairs sometime after one in the morning in the way a woman does when she can't tell if she is still dreaming and found a knot of matter that had smouldered for a while on the kitchen floor. The smell of smoke curled in the air beneath the narrow line of the open window. It was too small a gap for anyone to have got in from outside and, besides, the bold starlit night showed there really was no one out there. And also, just to firmly scotch my half-dreaming worries once and for all, my cousin's frustratingly difficult stove was the obvious culprit anyway.

Stumbling back to bed revived another worry though. I knew I wasn't supposed to disbelieve him any more when he said he knew I was an innocent party here, but I discovered a different interpretation for the Captain's unspoken query at dinnertime. The hint came in the form of the letter that lay on top of the cupboard just inside my bedroom door. It was my cousin's letter – the one that gave directions to her house

– and instead of being in my suitcase ready to give that strange, balding, house-invading man a good cause for coming straight to my garden gate, it had been lying here all along with the book that I'd forgotten to pack that morning. It raised the question of how that man had found me at all. And worse still, I knew that if Captain Richard Langton had happened to be puzzling over that same point himself and had thought to use his mission to collect my cousin's vegetables as an opportunity to undertake an illicit bit of snooping, in this letter he must have found just the sort of evidence he might have been looking for.

All in all, I was glad when morning came and I could take out my cousin's bicycle and make one last effort to reach her on the telephone.

The paths and trackways from the cottage door were busy today with hurrying farmhands trotting down one hillside and puffing up the other on their way to another day at the hay cut. At home in Putney the streets would have been busy with women making their purchases, going to their stations in the typing pool, women hurrying to the laundry lady to sigh over the restrictions on soap or to the butchers because word had got out that he'd received a delivery of offal. Here the traffic was entirely populated by tanned males and there was also a man who appeared to be destined for a more leisurely day, who was forging a path against the flow in ordinary clothes – and by that I mean trousers and a summer jacket rather than the rough shirt and brown trousers that made up the countryman's uniform. It wasn't the same summer jacket that had been worn by the man on Mr Winstone's path and this man's hair was fair rather than dark. After him I met Danny Hannis and his dog at the ford.

'Hullo,' I said politely. 'Are you here for me?'

He was. He had, of all things, my cousin's torch in his hands. He handed it to me and waited while I went through the tediously long task of letting myself back into the house, returned the torch to its home and then locked up again. He had hold of my bicycle now and seemed to be preparing to push the heavy frame for me up the steep hill. It must be said that I wasn't inclined to complain.

I walked beside him. He was a man who worked hard for his bread. His shirtsleeves were rolled back, showing tanned skin and roughened hands. His clothing befitted a man of work but still he made me feel decidedly shabby in that same old tired frock and a petticoat that still felt a little damp after a hasty washing last night because his style of speaking and moving only served to emphasise the impression I'd had before. The one that said that the simple routine of the life he led here was not remotely a mark of the man himself. Perhaps all farmhands were like this if one only bothered to look beyond the standard stereotype of a squire and his rustic cottagers. Or perhaps the experience of seeing the world through the eyes of a conscript had made him less fitted for the old life. It was hard to say.

It was hard to be truly sure about any view I had formed about this man. Just as he had been on that first evening in his parents' cottage, he still wasn't very readable, despite the easy way in which he was explaining his reason for meeting me. He rattled the bicycle over a rough ridge and told me,

'The Captain' – he pronounced it Cap'n – 'took the first patrol late last night. He came down after the squire had gone to bed to see that you were safely locked in. He met me on his way back up and gave me the job of doing the second tour, which in part is why I'm here now.'

The information disconcerted me and made me grateful all at the same time because now I knew the presence that had stalked me from the garden last night had been safety. I hid it by saying, 'And Mrs Abbey? When did you see her to get my torch?'

I managed to embarrass myself with my own question. I hadn't meant it to but it seemed designed to observe that eight o'clock in the morning would be a highly unusual time for bachelors to be calling on solitary widows. He made it worse when he said without hesitation, 'The Captain passed by her house last night and saw all was quiet, as it ought to be at that time of night. It was my job to repeat the exercise today, but I met her at the ford just now. She meant to return it to you herself but she was in a hurry so passed it to me.'

It had somehow the air of being too quick to impart too much information for the sake of avoiding saying something else.

Her name loomed between us all the way up the hill. It came to a head when he stopped at the last gate before the village. Behind him the farmyard was full of people and horses again and he needed to join them.

'Mr Hannis,' I began, and found that my mind was unpleasantly turning over the question of whether Mrs Abbey had addressed him with a syrupy whisper of *Hannis* just as she'd called the other man *Langton*. I forced my mind to behave itself and kept my eyes determinedly level. They strayed to his hands where they gripped the handlebars. There was a scuff on the metal beneath his fingers. There was a raw-looking nick on his thumb too.

I lifted my head and asked him, 'My cousin's fall from her bicycle *was* an accident, wasn't it? I'm not set to learn that Phyllis was the first to have an encounter with someone prone to unfortunate fits of temper, am I?'

'No, you're not.' It was said with a different kind of grit. It was a sharp reminder that the recent victim had been his stepfather. Beneath the thick mat of sun-touched hair, his eyes were a very mild blue or perhaps green. 'It was an accident, right enough. Your poor cousin landed in a heap. I was driving by and I picked her up almost the very second after it happened. She'd come off at the turn by the watershed – that plain barn on the lane above the village and the Manor. You'll find that this whole area is riddled with water houses and pump houses and the like. And make it Danny, would you, please? 'Hannis' makes me feel as though you're about to start barking orders like my old sergeant.'

It was there again; that readiness to add detail for the sake of disguising something else. This time, though, I was able to recognise the slip. Suddenly, he'd made me smile. Secrets kept sneaking in, but this one happened to have been endorsed by the Captain in my presence. Danny had been driving by in the car he was forbidden from using ...

He knew. I saw that jaw set defiantly. 'Yes,' he said. There was a trace of grudging humour there. 'And I ran her down to the hospital in it, so don't tell the squire. Pops hates driving that great hulking machine. He'd never dare admit it to the old man but he wishes the squire had sold the Lagonda and not his own car in the spring. It was a much neater vehicle, with a length of nose that could be measured before it hit a wall rather than afterwards. So now it has become my duty to stealthily take the Lagonda to the garage for its regular top-up of oil and fuel and so on. And that day I was very glad of it because there she was.'

His hands moved in their grip on the bicycle; that sort of bracing movement a person makes when they mean to get on with the next hard task but have one last thing to say first. He began by saying gravely, 'Next time you go to the shop, you should take the footpath from your cottage through the woods along the lower edge of Mrs Croft's farm. It's shorter. I only brought you this way today because your cousin would kick me in the shins if she thought I'd neglected you and I've got to ask: You are all right, aren't you? You're not frightened of staying there on your own?'

The gravity of his question made me smile. 'You're checking up on me. You said you would do as much when you wrote that note on Phyllis's letter about the eggs. Well, I'm fine as you can see and—'

He interrupted me with a grimace. My briskness only made it harder for him to break into saying what I realised now he'd meant to say all along. He repeated quite seriously, 'I really *have* got to ask. He's not dragging you into anything – anything he shouldn't – is he?'

I blinked. 'Of course he isn't.' It was rushed and slightly

appalled. The man in question was obviously the Captain and I didn't like to think too deeply about what Danny thought he was implying within the range of insinuations and warnings that had passed my way lately. And for whom he was asking them. I couldn't help thinking of Mrs Abbey again. The issue grew even more clouded when I reached the village shop and miraculously got to speak to my cousin, because, apparently, while Danny Hannis had been distracting me with questions about the Captain and the details of the unpleasant duty of picking my cousin up from the surface of the lane, he had been neglecting to include the information that the accident had only come about at all because Phyllis had run into Mrs Abbey's car.

It had been left empty in the shade beneath the watershed where people sometimes parked while they visited the church. Phyllis had struck it after spinning around a bend downhill on a bright summer's day to find that the small blue Austin Seven had been indistinguishable from the leaf pattern on the road. Speaking to me now as I stood with my ear pressed to that battered old telephone in the village shop, Phyllis must have noticed the sudden cooling of my mood.

'Emily,' she said sharply down the length of the line. 'I hope that tone in your voice doesn't mean you've been listening to idle tittle-tattle about poor Mrs Abbey?'

'Not at all.' It was a hasty assurance. I hadn't told her about any of my encounters with the woman. That was a topic to be broached later in person just as soon as I'd established whether she was being released today or if I was joining her there. 'It's just that Mr Hannis—'

'Young Danny Hannis,' remarked my cousin acerbically, 'would do well to mind his own business and refrain from adding to the gossip about a woman who has a hard enough life as it is, what with her husband currently serving a sentence for fraud.'

'Mr Abbey is in *prison?*' My voice squeaked. It was then that I noticed the postmaster was near by and listening. With an effort, I moderated my tone. 'Oh dear.'

I was frantically trying to recall whether Mrs Abbey had ever implied that she was a widow or if I had just presumed it. Only I couldn't do it because at the same time I was noticing that my cousin was now the second woman of my acquaintance to be showing a tendency for giving a single man the prefix *young*.

Young Danny Hannis and young Master John. It was the gentle condescension given to charming youths by older women who felt it essential to set themselves apart from eligible females so that they might enjoy a platonic friendship with a handsome bachelor without incurring the scrutiny of the ever-critical public. But Phyllis wasn't old – she was thirty-one and had perhaps two years' seniority over Danny – and given the fact her secret now seemed to include a powerful disagreement, I thought it pretty fair to judge that on her side at least the term disguised feelings that were anything but platonic.

How Danny felt I didn't know and I also didn't understand the nature of the hold Mrs Abbey might have over him, even while I knew she had never called *him* young. But if there were something between them and this phrase really did form an unwitting betrayal of secret intimacy, it seemed extraordinary that when Mrs Abbey used it, she should be risking the inconvenience of exposure by repeatedly mentioning the name now; when it was only her own manner of speaking that was leading me to suspect an affair at all. And, what's more, she was doing it when the former lover – either would-be or actual – was dead and she was not a widow herself but still married and she had the responsibility of three young children to bring up. And absolutely nothing to gain because young Master John, at least, was in no position to do anything for her.

And yet, that being said, I had already experienced the sense of sanctuary that Mrs Abbey found in speaking of John Langton's infamy. His name was her idea of safety while Danny lived unmentioned. It was hard to think. Phyllis was trying to fix me upon a plan of rescue from her hospital and I was blindly agreeing without really knowing what I was saying, because all the while my eyes were fixed upon the door of the shop where it had just been opened by Mrs Abbey's children.

The black Ford Y had drawn up alongside them and my heart was beating. The only time Mrs Abbey had risked letting me see that she didn't feel very safe at all was the moment she'd made me swear to watch over them; and now the driver of that car was trying to coax the three boys into the back seat.

I crashed out of the shop just as the boys were all bustling around to the far side of the car to climb in. The only satisfaction I took from meeting the black Ford again was the sight of the fresh scrape down its left wing, from where its driver had swerved into a bush to avoid the Lagonda.

My voice was shrill. 'Now boys, where are you going without your mother?'

I made them spin guiltily. This in itself was proof that I was right to act because they knew they were doing wrong. Two dark heads and one fair shuffled in the space of the open passenger door. Like the Lagonda, these doors were also hinged at the rear. Beside me, the driver smirked through his open window. 'Another time, then, boys. Looks as though this young lady has the measure of you.'

He leaned away to tug the passenger door shut. I watched him reach. He was surprisingly close to my original description; in his fifties with a thin crown and a neck that rose from his collar without bothering to define his jaw. His suit had changed; blue trousers with a cream jacket that would have made him resemble the man who had attacked Mr Winstone, except for the fact that one of the few things I could remember about that man with any certainty was that he had enjoyed a full head of hair.

I stared in through the car's open window, fiercely, I thought, although I was pretty sure its driver didn't agree. I found I was feeling fervently grateful that the occupants of the shop were within shouting distance – in fact they were probably peering at us through the glass between stacks of canned goods – and that this man knew it.

I said with as much severity as I could manage, 'I should like to know what you think you're doing, Mr ...?'

He didn't reply. His eyes were following the boys as they kicked pebbles around the front of his car and Ben, the youngest, foolishly drifted within reach and I put out a hand and snatched him away from the car's path. That made the driver smirk again. Then he completely disregarded what I had said and, with weak eyes fixed firmly on my face, continued seamlessly from where he had left off. He said in a peculiarly ponderous voice, 'Just as I've got the measure of you, haven't I, Miss Sutton? You were easy to follow this morning and you'll be easy to follow again.'

It struck me that he knew my name, just as he had meant it to. It also struck me that I had been his quarry here until the boys had sauntered into the doorway of the shop and given him room to exchange the scope of his plans for a quiet chat with them instead.

While my mind was busily tripping into impossible calculations about what exactly he had expected to learn from either of us, he added a final airy instruction that left me gaping. 'I'd like you to tell that to your new boyfriend. You do work fast, don't you, you London girls?'

This wasn't a threat for me. It was designed to mock me. And presumably involve the Captain. I was left staring in the dust of his wake as he released the handbrake and veered away downhill and around the bend, out of sight.

It took the smallest child to draw me out of my stupor by saying sternly, 'You're hurting me.'

I wasn't. It was the typical exaggeration of youth. I just had a hand on his collar so that he hadn't a hope of wriggling away into fresh trouble before I'd given him a piece of my mind. I bent down to his height and took him firmly by the shoulders. Blue eyes widened to perfect rounds as I begged, 'What were you *doing* getting into a stranger's car? Never do it again, Ben. It's—'

Fright had made my voice rise. It was brought sharply back down to a sensible level by the eldest boy interrupting to say, 'He's not a stranger.'

I turned my head. After a moment I focused my mind upon the boy's face. Brown hair, brown eyes and a mixture of tan and dirt on his skin. 'You're sure?'

'He's Daddy's friend. He found our address in the book.' It obviously didn't occur to the child to question which book. I didn't need to ask anyway. I thought it fair to guess that this was the information the man had sought to discover in the Manor ledgers.

I straightened. The middle boy added a sullen mumble with his head turned to his toes, as if he hoped he wouldn't be heard but felt he ought to take this chance of one-upmanship over his brothers. 'He's Mr Duckett. He came to see us yesterday and we asked for a run in his car just now. And,' he added with a glare for his older brother, 'we're not supposed to talk about Daddy.'

'Where is your mother?' It forced itself out of me through gritted teeth. The relief that the man had perhaps only been indulging their whim didn't do much, since it still left me as his real target.

'In there.' The oldest boy jerked his head towards the door that stood slightly uphill from the shop. There was a brass plate on the wall signifying that this was the doctor's house and it was a very effective defeat since I could hardly pursue their mother in there. It worked as blackmail too. I certainly wasn't going to leave them neglected while I pedalled home, so I took them into the shop, instructed the shopkeeper to tell Mrs Abbey about the car and handed over the sweet ration from my book as a bribe to the children to stay under guard.

I was stopped in the midst of my rush out of the door by an elderly lady customer who had apparently been eavesdropping more strenuously than the rest. There was a waft of mothballs and lavender from her as she intercepted my course and an excess of pursed lips as she mustered the nerve to whisper, 'Good for you. Mrs Abbey just waltzed in there without so much as a thought as to who had the first appointment or who would mind the boys while she was busy. Just because some fool of a man blacked her eye. And it's not even as though she can pass it off as a husband with a heavy hand either, given where he is. How that woman got Captain Langton to—'

I didn't hear what Captain Langton had done for Mrs Abbey. The elderly customer was distracted by the shopkeeper hurrying out with a parcel of goods for the Manor and a blithe confidence that I already knew I was meant to act as their delivery person. My neighbour thought it a glorious discovery and enough to supplant whatever news she had to impart about Mrs Abbey. In a blind haze I claimed my bicycle and braced for the stiff climb to the junction and then I was free and tackling the race along the two miles of lane towards home with only an anxious check every ten yards or so of the empty tarmacadam both behind and before in case

Duckett should be a man of his word and be following me still.

There was no sign, however, of the man or the car; nor room for the dread that even if it really were me he was following, he still shouldn't be let near those children; nor even of my worries about secret affairs or the realisation that the hurry that had prevented a woman from returning her borrowed torch in person had been the haste to get ahead of the old ladies in the queue to visit the doctor. My mind was filled to the point of overflowing with the way her youngest child had looked at me today. It was merging it with the embrace his mother had given him yesterday just a short while after making a show of spreading slander about a dead man's name. As I neared the village, I caught myself trying to work through the revolting process of hazarding a guess at the age at which a blue-eyed child's fair hair might be expected to begin to turn dark like John Langton's.

Chapter 14

There was a path just beyond the turn of the lane at the watershed that led down onto the cobbled yard between the house and the tithe barn. I'd intended originally to knock on the kitchen door and go in with the groceries and take the chance to tell the Captain about meeting Duckett. But Mrs Abbey skulked like a ghost through everything and it was impossible to shake her off.

To give myself a little more time to collect myself and perhaps to catch my breath after the race along lanes, I left my bicycle propped against the warm stones of the old barn and walked down towards the wider space where the second barn housed the farm machinery and the car. The Lagonda was there, gleaming in the hard rectangle of shade within the wide barn mouth, looking like it was eagerly awaiting its next outing. The space behind where the tractor passed its nights was empty, but the hulking mass of the traction engine lurked forlorn where it had been abandoned under shrouds a long time ago.

I slipped round to the boot of the Lagonda and tried its handle but it was locked.

'What are you looking for?'

The voice came from a reasonable distance away. All the same it brought me round with a start and left me flushing like a guilty thief, for all that I knew that if I'd truly meant to hide, I wouldn't have left my bicycle in plain sight of the window beside the kitchen door. In a way, that knowledge just added to my embarrassment. It felt as if this had been a ploy to lead him here on his own.

I confessed feebly, 'I was hoping to reclaim my clothes.' And watched as the Captain approached across the bare ground. He leaned past me with key in hand to unfasten the catch that secured the boot cover. He was faring better than I was. Somewhere he'd found fresh clothes that couldn't have been castoffs from his father's wardrobe. In his manner was that same natural assurance that had walked in with him last night. It was disconcerting to encounter it again so soon.

He drew out a canvas bag and handed it to me. It was pitifully small. I think he saw the swift dismay as my hope faded of finding better clothes to rival his present choice of a crisp and clean grey suit.

'I was able to get someone to go into my flat and put a packet on the first morning train for me,' he explained faintly apologetically. 'It helps.'

His ease was making me nervous. There was too much I wasn't saying and this was too much like last night in that moment when the enjoyment of his walk had still touched him and the surprise of his father's condition hadn't quite yet reached him. I wanted to treasure the cheerfulness and not be the one who surprised him into seriousness again this morning. So, by way of a solution, my mouth rushed into rivalling him for cheer. I said brightly, 'Thank you for rescuing the survivors. It's better than I'd originally feared, anyway, even if they're probably all runkled by now.' I was obviously nervous, I was using imaginary words again and it didn't help that he'd clearly noticed. I tried to draw a steadying breath. This was insane. Any second now and I'd be running out of air again as I had on the Manor staircase.

The boot lid was pressed shut. I drew another breath. Finally, I said on a rather more sensible note, 'I've got your groceries, by the way. The shopkeeper said you'd left an order earlier.'

He walked with me as I set off for the bicycle and his parcel. He told me, 'I was at the shop briefly while dropping Mrs Abbey off at the doctors before racing to meet that train. Thank you for filling the gap, although I promise it wasn't remotely expected of you, or necessary. I was going to stop there on my way into town. I was only waiting for you.'

He must have noticed my poorly disguised reaction to this mention of Mrs Abbey and misunderstood. He added by way of an explanation, 'I had thought I'd promised to take you down to visit your cousin?'

'Oh.' The sound came out as a dry note. I was walking hurriedly across the wide cobbled space between barns. There was a short rise at the corner that met the long barn and I'd never noticed it before. Now it made me breathless as I said quickly, 'Oh, well. There was no need to wait for me, actually. I finally managed to speak to her this morning.'

'So did I. Just now. She'll be ready to receive you in about an hour.'

I stopped and blinked up at him. There was nothing in his face at all, but I thought he'd noticed my sudden change of heart about seeking this conversation with him. This insistence on making steadying replies was his way of confronting it.

It was a very peculiar kind of trap. My heart was beating. I was very conscious of the bag of clothes in my hands, tying me to things I ought to say and yet hadn't. I drew breath to speak. I thought about Mr Duckett. I thought about the state of Mrs Abbey's eye and the boys and affairs and parentage, and knew it was impossible for me to tell him any of it. If anything, it felt dangerous purely because Duckett wanted me to.

So instead I found myself tripping headlong into speaking about that older, nearly forgotten difficulty that waited here. I told him about the contents of my cousin's letter, the one he might have found, as if by telling him openly it needn't be a trap for either of us any more when it turned out he knew what it said.

It was with a nervous kind of delicious daring that I told him about Phyllis's crushing judgement on my ideas of what constituted generous savings. I'd saved all of ninety pounds during my time at the chemists and had perhaps naively believed this would be plenty to fund any modest scale of future ambition. I told him about her promise to my mother to look after me and I even told him the silliest part too. I told him about her views on my father's life's work and how she said it had taught him that the things of greatest value were those that had a nice clean record of their path through life. It was just unfortunate, Phyllis thought, that my father hadn't quite realised that when he lectured me in similar terms about my own future, he was actually implying I too should be recorded and graded on the provenance of my main changes of ownership as well.

'Personally,' I added a shade darkly as I relaxed into the strange giddiness that came from the way this man stilled when I spoke truthfully like this, 'I don't think Phyllis is making much allowance for just how much Dad worries. I think, for all of Phyllis's supposed outrage and declarations of her support for my cause and so on, what she is really smarting about is the realisation that she, of all people, has been deemed the relative most suited for the role of responsible chaperone. I imagine she thinks Dad's mistaking her for her poor deceased mother. I think she's bitterly regretting staying on in the cottage for these past few months in order to conclude my aunt's affairs and I wouldn't be surprised if it turned out that she threw herself off the bicycle just to prove she was still reckless at heart.'

We'd reached my cousin's ridiculously heavy bicycle. I risked a glance up at him. It was then that I realised there was a considerable difference between knowing that the Captain had already read all this and speaking it out loud. Because I swear he *had* read the letter. I swear he knew exactly what it said, but instead of finding that my speech had undone a whole night's worth of suspicion or even concealed all those other things I so desperately didn't want to say, when I lifted my head I found that all he was doing was listening patiently to this whole ridiculous lecture, and looking a little puzzled.

It was the same air of puzzlement I'd noticed before when he looked at me sometimes. It hid itself beneath a faint trace of amusement. Usually I'd noted this feeling after I'd said or done something to work myself into a ridiculous tangle while I fought a fierce private battle between his claims on my honesty and a wish to avoid the risk of adding to his concerns. In truth, though, this peculiar tension happened whenever it seemed to strike him that I cared.

Really feeling tangled now and as though I were straying into something deeply complicated, I turned to the bicycle and set about exchanging the bag of clothes for the packet of items destined for his kitchen.

I heard him say briskly to the space above my bent head, 'Thank you for your kindness to my father last night.' It came after he'd bent to retrieve a fallen tomato, and in quite a different tone from what had gone before. Now he paused in handing it to me, hand in mid-air above my waiting palm.

It was a shock. Embarrassment was nothing. It had never occurred to me to imagine that my evasions might have been interpreted as a desperate attempt to avoid talking about *this*. It shook me into saying swiftly and seriously, 'It was nothing.'

I saw him grimace as I lifted my hand those few inches more to take that tomato straight from his fingers. I'd spoken truthfully again and this time this little piece of honesty – because of course I really didn't blame the Colonel – had only served to highlight the concealment in all the rest. At least, it seemed like that when he said sternly, 'No, it's not nothing.

222

You know it's not. I wouldn't have dreamed of leaving you to pick up the pieces if it had ever occurred to me that Mrs Cooke's resignation letter would tip him into fresh mourning. It's being there in that house. It reminds him. He's a little bit like you. Something terrible happened and it has shaken his faith in humanity.'

His words came like a bolt from nowhere. If I'd stopped before to blink at him, now I stood stock still and gaped. The implied sympathy broke the shield I'd been wielding in an effort to keep from talking about the nastier things of this morning. He'd meant it to because this man didn't want my care; that is to say, he didn't want protecting. Not by me. And certainly not when it carried a cost to myself. I had no idea where the packet of groceries had gone because I certainly wasn't holding them any more. I found that I had turned my back to the wall so that one hand was gripping the bicycle handlebar and the other was flat against the leather panel of the saddle. All were radiating the increasing morning heat. I felt frozen. Exposed. No one had ever said anything like that to me before; anything so unnervingly perceptive.

He stood before me, blue sky behind and a faint shade across his face that would have been darker had it not been for the warm glow of reflected light from the yellow stone wall. Unworried, self-assured, he claimed the responsibility for judging the severity of this untold unpleasantness for himself like it was a birthright, so that the responsibility for dealing with it might presumably rest with him too.

Cementing the effect, he claimed my heart as well. He asked gently, 'Emily, darling, what is it?'

223

And suddenly I was experiencing such a bewildering sense of his confidence in me that it nearly made me laugh. The endearment came so naturally from him. I'd thought myself alone in this. I'd almost depended on it. The question carried openness and reassurance, and no blame to imply that I had made a mistake or was inadequate; and I knew this was the last time I'd imagine I could attempt concealment with him. I began to reply, but the moment was stolen from me by a scrape of grit beneath footfalls and the inconvenience of Danny Hannis stumbling hastily down from the footpath by the watershed.

The companion from my earlier climb out of the valley was looking hot and dishevelled from a morning in the field. Judging from the lift of his hand he had come for the sole purpose of speaking to the Captain. I'd have left them to it but for the fact that I found that my right hand was inexplicably fixed in its grip upon the handlebars between the twin heats of skin and sun-warmed metal. I turned my head and found that Richard had placed his hand firmly over mine as a silent request to stay. His gaze was fixed on the approaching man. In his profile there was the expectation that I would comply and I watched as he fended off the cheerful enthusiasms of the dog and released his grip on me to take one step forwards to meet the other man.

Danny didn't share the Captain's sense of value for my company and he certainly didn't like having to speak in front of me. His eyes grazed my face and a scowl formed on his own, as if he were suddenly taking in the colour of my cheeks and learning all sorts of things there he didn't like. His gaze settled upon the Captain. He said brusquely, 'I'm glad I caught you. The tractor couldn't really be spared from the set, but I thought you should know. There's been a bit of trouble at the squatters' camp.'

'Trouble?' All gentleness left the Captain's manner now.

Danny's eyes were narrowed against the sun. 'Fire. Their bonfire went up last night and only escaped ruining half of Hardings' corn by the grace of good luck and a light breeze that was blowing the other way. And, before you ask, the main point is that they didn't light it. They also swear the stack didn't just happen to spread towards the boundary. They'd built their pyre on one of the concrete platforms for a reason.'

The Captain remarked grimly, 'If they think that's enough to stop a stray wisp from drifting in the air and catching in the standing crop, they've forgotten what life was like in a hot country with a grass fire.'

'They might have forgotten,' conceded Danny, 'for all that some of these people served in far-flung places with me. But the point is *you're* forgetting who employed them. They know precisely what fire does to a harvest because they've got the memory of your brother's voice ringing in their ears giving them a stern lecture on the rules against smoking whilst out on the strip. Whatever else anyone says, that man knew his job and he knew how to train his farmhands. That's what they reminded me of today.'

This forceful eulogy had its effect. 'They really didn't light their bonfire.'

'No.'

I was thinking that it was the first time anyone had dared

to betray their deep abiding respect for the leadership of John Langton. Other than Mrs Abbey. Then the Captain's head turned to me. 'Pardon?' I hadn't realised that I'd spoken.

I cleared my throat. 'The vegetables,' I repeated doubtfully. I wasn't entirely sure that this wasn't one of those moments when the woman was expected to remain silent. It wasn't. Both men waited so I persevered. 'The fire we saw yesterday followed in the wake of a theft of vegetables. But it didn't seem to me that the vegetable plots at the squatters' camp had been sullied at all.'

I saw the Captain's brows furrow. 'So are you implying that this is the work of this vegetable-stealing vagrant, or that it isn't? Just to be clear?'

I told him frankly, 'I have absolutely no idea. I noticed the smoke last night. It woke me up.'

That was the moment I recalled that I hadn't yet found the way to frame my thanks for the effort he'd gone to in walking down the hill yet another time last night to assure himself that my house was secure. Now I stumbled on the memory that he'd gone from there to do the same for Mrs Abbey and felt the true weight of the morning. It wasn't made any easier by the revelation that today this man had been drawn into the act of delivering her to the doctors. The concept of an injury disturbed me, naturally, not least because this might be a second assault of the kind that had befallen Mr Winstone, but I remembered Danny's advice that next time I went to the shop from my cousin's cottage I should abandon the hill and take the easier route by way of the footpath along the watercourse. And with that in mind, I couldn't help noticing the lucky chance that had led her to choose instead to take the lane at just the same time that the Captain had happened to be driving past. And then I felt wretched because this sort of cold, calculative thinking without any relief of kindness was precisely the insidious evil that I dreaded. It dwelt in precisely the same part of my mind where the idea about the boy grew, and fed on the knowledge that none of these suspicions were founded upon anything Mrs Abbey had actually said.

To my left, Danny seemed to be struggling under the weight of concerns of a different sort. He remarked sourly, 'If you're worrying about missing vegetables, Captain, you might do well to look at your own garden terraces. They're bare.'

It hadn't occurred to me to perceive the newness of their dereliction. The flowers had been long neglected but only because in a time of shortage like this Mrs Cooke as the housekeeper would have been duty-bound to concentrate her efforts upon the everyday staples such as root vegetables and other greens. I didn't think, though, that Danny was making the point to endorse my view.

Then Danny sighed under the steadiness of the other man's rather suppressive stare. 'Very well,' he conceded grudgingly, 'I'll ask the folk from the camp if anyone's passed through. And if they happen to be able to describe Miss Sutton's idea of the man who left Pops on his garden path, we'll know we're really on the trail of something.'

'You should ask about cars too. There's a man by the name of Duckett.' I suppose it wasn't the best moment to choose to introduce the information. In my head was the confusion of Duckett's parting shot *'tell that to your boyfriend'* and I cringed a little when I felt the weight of the Captain's gaze as his attention turned to me. I hadn't thought hazel eyes could be so dark. Now I think he was regretting letting me think I was remotely adequate. I tried to convey as much as I could by a single look that the encounter with Duckett hadn't actually done me any harm and it wasn't entirely Duckett who had been upsetting me before but it turned out that I needn't have attempted it anyway because Duckett wasn't the object of his concern.

The Captain demanded sharply, 'Mrs Abbey told you this man's name? You've met her today?'

And the sudden alteration of the pitch to his voice left me in absolutely no doubt of the force of his feelings at that moment. It shook me because he'd only just mentioned meeting her himself and there had been none of this tension then.

'No,' I said hastily. 'No. Duckett himself was at the shop today when I was placing my telephone call to the hospital. I haven't seen her. He's her husband's friend and I think he knows you.'

He dismissed that with a shake of his head. Something had changed here. I suddenly felt very slight standing before the two men, one crisp and ready for a day of business, the other tanned and stained from his work in the fields, but not much difference between their physiques.

'Right.' The word from the Captain was bracing; decisive and alienating. It turned out that I really needn't have worried before about finding the words to convey my thoughts, because, whatever it was about Mrs Abbey that was troubling him, it ran far deeper than a few unformed concerns of mine. Now the mention of her name carried a sharp thrill of true danger. Fierce and certain.

The Captain was saying, 'No point in standing about here. Hannis, I think I'd better go back with you to the field and ask your chaps what they remember one more time, if you can marshal them? Then Miss Sutton and I have some errands to run in Gloucester and I think I'd better hear precisely what this Duckett fellow had to say for himself at the shop.'

This at least was said more warmly for my sake. I found that the bag of groceries was being passed into my hands. Apparently I'd set it down rather roughly beside my feet. I was meant, I think, to lead the way to the house but I couldn't because Danny was still standing there, a square barrier of a man deliberately barring my path as if it were nothing and saying in a very peculiar growl, 'I hope to God you know what you're doing.'

It was meant for the Captain and the reply was a quick, dismissive, 'Yes.'

'That's not much of an answer. I saw her face—'

'I *know*, Hannis.'

It was grim, harsh, final. A brief jerk of his head said it all. He really didn't want this discussing in front of me. I couldn't help noticing the adjustment from speaking to Danny like an old friend to this curt dismissal that took on a faintly military air.

Then I was walking ahead of them into the house and taking myself to the kitchen counter to lay out the things for the Colonel's lunch while Danny reclaimed his tractor and the Captain briefly stepped in after me to make his excuses to his father. Only I found I wasn't laying out salad and tins. I was unpacking a blouse and a slip and a pale green cardigan and the Captain was by my side and quietly passing me the packet of groceries and faintly teasing again as he ducked his head to say for my ear alone, 'I think you were looking for this.' He made me jump and suppress an unsteady smile. It was as if our moods were worlds apart.

Then, while warmth still played about the corners of his mouth, he added in the same private undertone, 'We'll take lunch in town before we collect your cousin if you like? There are a few things I want to discuss with you and we might as well be fed as not while we do it. And for the sake of efficiency when we go, will you bring your bags and whatnots that you've got here with you, and I'll ferry you and your cousin and your baggage direct to your final destination later?'

His expression had settled to seriousness once more and it came closer to matching mine. He didn't make it seem as though the points to be discussed were set to be particularly pleasant. I nodded my agreement because there wasn't much else I could do and saw him note it, and then he straightened and turned away as the Colonel shuffled in through the dining-room door with Mr Winstone.

The older men seemed to have a list of things they meant to say to the Colonel's son but I didn't get to slip unobtrusively away while they did it to make that change of clothes as I was intending. The Captain had his hand out on the stone worktop still and I stood there behind him in the dead end of the kitchen counter and listened while the old driver told the Captain about the raven he'd spotted in one of the pheasant coveys, and asked for permission to get Danny to shoot it.

Chapter 15

I slunk away a little later to find a quiet bathroom in which to change my frock. Unfortunately, bathrooms proved to be in extraordinarily short supply in this peculiarly complicated house. I certainly didn't find one on the first floor. I avoided the option of changing in the Colonel's room that was set on the south-facing side of the stairs, and necessarily declined the embarrassment of making free with the room on the other side that was the son's. That left me with the challenge of passing the length of the dank gallery and the disappointment of finding first a dusty chamber that had obviously belonged to his brother and, beyond that, a last sequence of rooms that were pretty and mournful and held the long-abandoned memory of a mother's touch.

As I climbed the stairs to the attic level, still on the hopeful hunt for something that resembled modern conveniences, I couldn't help wondering how much more of this once-grand family home was waiting for its turn to be left still and dry as a memorial to the dead.

The attic floor was the contrast. There was still no bathroom, but there were no sad relics here either. I'd expected austere servants' quarters and found instead an airy passage lined on its sunny side with neat little bedrooms, stripped now of furniture, but clearly renovated in the time of John Langton's dominion here for the sake of the men employed in his daily business. And despite the idea the Colonel had of John Langton's resentment about being forced to make this estate his career after his riding accident, I thought there had been optimism here.

There was one final room at the end above the Colonel's rooms that must have been the housekeeper's domain. It too had been left orderly and empty and the only thing that remained of Mrs Cooke's presence was a worthy print in a frame on the wall and a humble dresser. Since there was still, inexplicably, no room for washing, I chose her room as my dressing room. Her mirror showed the sad state of my frock and the uneven flush to my skin that spoke of a strained morning and a hard bicycle ride.

I remedied the first problem easily. Along with the blouse and slip, the bag yielded a blue jacket, a frock and a pair of grey slacks and it was the latter of these that I now dragged on. It was as I was completing the restoration with the judicious application of powder and a much-treasured lipstick that I noticed him in the doorway.

Or rather, I sensed the subtle shrinking of this room that came from realising that someone was creeping around the edge of the doorframe behind me.

I whirled. The lipstick fell with a crack upon the floor-boards. I heard the tinny roll as it took itself off to hide under the dresser. There was no one in the doorway. There was no one in the passage either and nothing to confirm that heart-stopping impression I'd had of a brief encounter with an electric-blue gaze. The noise that met my dash along the length of it was nothing more than the thump of my own stockinged feet on uncarpeted floorboards. All of the doors into the little bedrooms were open and empty and, besides, there was no telltale snap of a door shutting. I slithered down the tight turn of the narrow attic stairs and stopped at the limit of the long gallery with all its closed doors. There was no one there.

A dry whisper of voices murmured against the panelled wood behind me. This gallery ended roughly at the wall that divided the dining room below from the kitchen in the space beyond. It seemed the Colonel was finding himself more and more at home in that place. I could distinguish his distant voice and Mr Winstone's, seemingly chatting easily. I had the sound of my own rapid breath and also the sinister rustlings of a handful of sparrows feeding in the Virginia creeper that robbed the windows in this gallery of their light. Nothing else stirred except my own uneasy imagination.

I felt like I was the imposter when I descended the stairs fully dressed with the addition of blouse and shoes now, some five hurried, guarded minutes later. The library door was open where I thought it had been shut and I tiptoed in to complete my search. The murmur of the Colonel's speech ran down the passage like a ghostly echo. I heard Mr Winstone laugh. Their noise was a muted undertone set against the discovery I made on the green baize of the desk of some of the survivors of Duckett's raid. There was a stack of old accounts books there and, resting in the open drawer to one side, a new record had been begun by someone, either the Colonel or more probably his son. A regular, clear hand listed each property within the care of the estate and the rents owed and repairs ordered since their arrival only a day ago. I thought the author must have had a very long session of hard work last night after his dinner.

The set of older record books was missing the volumes that would have spanned the past two years. They proved that my guess was right and Duckett had come here to trace the present whereabouts of his friend's wife. He had taken the newer books that clearly recorded her name as the tenant of Eddington, so he must have either discarded or overlooked the mention of her name in the older volume that covered the end of the war. There was a note dated May '44 within its pages. *Eddington: Paint, roof repairs and chimney swept. Approached by new tenant: Mrs Paul Abbey presently of Berwick House, Parliament Street.* The author of these books wrote carelessly, as though he were always in a tearing hurry, and the energetic script had tacked on as an afterthought the comment, *'Approved 15th May'.*

It was strange to be handling the dry unemotional words of the dead man. I found myself examining them as if they were a formal introduction. I noted too the simplicity with which he recorded the application from this new tenant and found myself measuring its date against certain suspicions that lingered around that tenant's insinuations. But more than that, I found that I was drawing all sorts of conclusions about the author's personality and independence based solely on the inattention he had paid to the curl of his Fs. I found my fingers tracing the lines in a sort of greeting and heard myself whisper a plea to the secrets trapped within these pages. *Please don't haunt me.*

The Captain hadn't yet returned when I finally slunk into the kitchen like a guilty spy and the Colonel was leaving by the kitchen door. Today was the day the old man was set to announce the sale of the estate and if imagination really had been ruling in me at this moment, I might have believed that the debilitating distress I'd encountered in him last night had been an invention of mine too. Today, control was back in force in the man, only without the red-faced temper. He still looked undersized for his clothes and slightly unsteady on his feet but alert and formidable in a way that gave his old frame power and decision. He was looking, in fact, like the prospect of marshalling worried workers and tenants into doing what he wanted had revived an old thrill of bygone glory. I only went out with them because Bertie Winstone was going too and he had something vital he thought he had to tell me about the disposal of the goat.

First I had to learn that the goat was the last remaining member of the young Master's stable, by which I understood that John had used the goat as companion for the young stock in training until he'd died and the horses had been sold, leaving the goat alone to grow steadily fatter on the feed that remained. We were picking our way through the fierce darkness of the machine barn. As we emerged abruptly into the farmyard through a hatch within vast wooden doors that were so crusted with tar that they would never open again, I was allowed to understand precisely why Bertie Winstone should be happily talking about the dead son in such terms beside the old man. It was because here was the prospect of a good dinner and the Colonel's return had brought the authority to pass judgement on the beast at last. And the part I was supposed to care about was the news that the task of contacting the butcher had been delegated to the Colonel's other son, and therefore everyone else here considered it perfectly natural that the job would ultimately fall to me.

A crowd of people were waiting for their squire and just before he faced them, the Colonel had another, more immediate request to make. Luckily, it turned out to be one that I was more likely to fulfil. He had forgotten his walking stick and I was happy to run back to the house for it. As I left them, the old Colonel and his shrunken driver revealed themselves to be, for the first time, just what they were. A pair of time-worn gentlemen braced and eager for a last dance with the old world of landowners and cottagers in the sunshine.

The cane was in his bedroom. It had been hooked over the foot of the bed frame with yesterday's trousers, shirt and a very tangled tie while the overflowing case stood upon the floor. After witnessing the man's abiding passion for the military life, I'd expected rigid order and neatly folded stacks on shelves. But this small sign of disarray was proof of the reality of the scene I'd found last night. It was a mark of a gnawing sense of rejection following his housekeeper's departure. It contributed to the sense of homelessness in this place. The Colonel had no one to lay out his things for him and while this could easily be dismissed as the laziness of rank, I thought that this sort of little gesture would have been taken as a

237

mark of friendship rather than servitude. And by leaving in the manner she had, the housekeeper had made it only too clear how little she thought he deserved that friendship now.

Perhaps, therefore, I'd attempt later to set things in a better balance. The chores that had seemed last night too close to the play-acting of an ingratiating female might simply be ordinary usefulness by then. But not now. Now I turned in this room that had as glorious a view as the sun-shot study that housed the telephone, and found myself being watched again.

Chapter 16

He fled as I turned. This was no ghost. He was flesh and blood and his feet made a racket on the gallery as he raced away. I remember that he had dark hair. I remember that there was something about his hasty turn that set his physique against the fragile memory of that scene on Mr Winstone's path, and found them to be a match. His eyes were blue, as Mrs Abbey had promised, but more muted than the electrifying glare I had been trained to anticipate.

I thought he was heading for the attic. I reached the point where the cluster of bedrooms met the mouth of the long line of the gallery as he reached the turn onto the narrow attic stairs. Only he didn't race upwards. He put out a hand onto the dark wooden panelling on the end wall and passed silently through it.

The door swung a little on its hinges, back and forth, but it was still by the time I reached it. I had the Colonel's cane in my hand. I don't know why but I used it rather than my hand to prod the concealed door ajar.

It swung smoothly and no violent hand snatched from the other side. My heartbeat was a dull roar in my ears. So was my breathing. There was no one inside. I was stepping into a plain and ordinary landing lit by a window at the far end and housing a collection of various closed doors and a smell of dry dusty wood. There was also a narrow enclosed stairs that led steeply downwards to the bright rectangle of an open door. This was not the moment to marvel at the discovery that at last I'd found where the Colonel kept his bathrooms. Clattering downwards, I found myself bursting abruptly into the kitchen in the space beside the dresser through what I'd taken to be a plain, uninteresting wood-panelled wall. It was disorientating. I didn't really know what I was doing, except that somehow there was a vital lure in the hope of snatching a closer look at this stray man. I had to choose between racing into the yard outside or back through the house into the darkened dining room. Both doorways were open and empty. He'd moved quickly to escape me.

I opted for the less intimidating space of outdoors. There was relief in the idea of air and light. I couldn't see any sign of him. But the goat muttered something, a tentative question, and drew me to that small knotted door in the old tithe barn wall.

The cane was again my door lever. Inside was cool and dark like a cave, and quiet except for the clatter as the goat stood up at his door to peer at me down the length of the row of stables. I took a horribly reluctant step towards him along the line. There was the silence of the steps up to the hayloft at the end.

I didn't have to steel myself for the insanity of climbing into the unknown. I was swept painfully into the rough stone wall when the nearest stable door swung open and the man crashed out and past me into the sunshine once more. I still hadn't seen him properly. He'd designed his ambush to blind me with the swing of the heavy wooden door. The crush of it hurt. I called out to him but he didn't wait. I thrust the door back with a bang and lurched out into the sunshine after him, squinting and following instinct rather than his trail down the length of this barn and across the wide yard to the vast gaping maw of the machine barn.

I was snatched back there on the edge of the dark by a thud of feet from behind and a hard hand that caught at my arm.

It yanked me round in a spinning turn. Now my mind had the chance to shrink from the idea that this man might take steps to stop me from pursuing. He didn't know I only had the idiotic idea of asking his name and I should have guessed from Mr Winstone's injuries what he might be prepared to do to stop me. I cringed and flung out my free hand to block myself from colliding with his chest and perhaps to fend him off. Only I found that the cane was in my hand and it tangled with him and in the flurry, as I stumbled and a squeak escaped, his hands thrust me onwards almost absentmindedly into the grip of another. As we passed I caught a blur of an averted profile beneath lighter-coloured hair and then Danny left, intent on continuing the hunt. The new set of hands adjusted their grip to take a firm hold of my upper arm and bore me away before I'd even really identified him.

He was marching me across the yard towards the tithe barn once more. Away from that man and away from the noise and bustle of his father's meeting in the farmyard. Now he merely had a hand out, ushering me along. As we went, I heard him say in a voice that was inexplicably close to being torn by a laugh, 'Emily, you need to tell me what you thought you were doing.'

The sense of urgency eased. We were heading to the house, I think. He knew I would go with him. He'd released me completely. I was turning my head to ask him something when he abruptly stopped with a sound like a sharp intake of breath and made an impulsive snatch to reclaim my hand and require me to stop also.

We were at the corner of the tithe barn. He was close to me and his hand still had mine. Laughter wasn't in evidence anywhere now. His attention had passed over my head, captivated by something deeply serious beyond. I twisted round to follow his gaze and saw Mrs Abbey.

Mrs Abbey was standing near the place where my bicycle still rested, watching us with a speculative tilt to her head. She was late for the Colonel's meeting and she had her children with her. She had been hurrying down the length of the tithe barn but she'd stopped at almost the same moment as we had and with the same air of guilty discovery that wracked us. It was as though we'd all been caught sneaking and now she was standing there, watching us, or rather watching me first and then the man beside me and she was waiting for the friendly fuss and sympathy to explode from one or other of us, as was her due. This was because it turned out the old lady at the shop had slightly underplayed the truth when she'd told me that someone had blacked Mrs Abbey's eye. They'd blacked the entire left side of her lower jaw.

I think I made an impulsive movement towards her. His hand still held mine, resting now behind my left hip and deliberately, I thought, out of her sight. A faint tightening of his grip begged me to check the impulse to leave him. It worked. And made her eyebrows lift a fraction because she saw my change of heart. My glance over my shoulder up at Richard was no help. The fine line of his jaw was set as he stared past me at her. I bit my lip. Uncertain, while all the guilty suppositions I'd been harbouring about her evaporated in the discovery of the full horror of that assault. She must have needed the doctor to check her cheekbone wasn't cracked. In my head I had the grim echo of Danny's admonishment, *'I saw her face'* and I didn't like to imagine what it should mean.

Now I couldn't quite read the expression beneath that bruise. It had eased to something like curiosity. I thought that in Mrs Abbey there was a growing interest in my inexplicable stillness, only she couldn't have known that for me the stillness was contradicted by the pulse I could feel pounding through the contact I had with Richard. Still he had his fingers entwined with mine; not for comfort or kindness but as a security to keep me on his side. I don't know what he would have done if I had resisted it. I felt that I alone was being asked to choose and I suspected that, in all honour, I ought to be standing with her.

Still Mrs Abbey said nothing. We all said nothing. I turned my head. A few long seconds passed before the Captain withdrew his gaze from her to find I was looking up at him too. He tipped his head almost imperceptibly towards his car, where it waited before the machine barn. His mouth formed a very muted but urgent shape of, 'Please?'

It went through me like an arrow. He specifically didn't want me to speak to her. His hand dropped from mine. Under his scrutiny I chose to betray a beaten woman and broke every commitment I'd ever made to consideration and care. I should have been reacting to the inexcusable violence of the awful bruise that coloured her skin, but instead I turned and marched before him towards his car. I went in near-perfect silence. Mrs Abbey made no move or sound to stop us. Halfway to the car I stopped myself when I remembered the cane. The Captain was there beside me.

'The Colonel,' I told him in a race, meaning, I think, to find the old man myself but I wasn't remotely surprised to find that my hand was met and encouraged after only the slightest resistance to surrender the stick to his grip. I reached the passenger door to the car. It was opened for me and I slid in. The cane flashed overhead as Danny appeared in the doorway from the barn and put out his hand to catch it. I saw the shake of his head and the way he mouthed the word *gone*.

The car door was pressed shut on me and then the Captain was around the other side and in beside me and we were away, taking the turn past the cottages and up onto the lane from the village towards the main road. As we went, I knew I still had absolutely no justification for the choice I had made except one small excuse and it was this. It was the way Mrs

Abbey's expression had changed as she reached the corner of the tithe barn in time to observe the moment that the Captain dropped into his seat beside me. It was the way the ugly lopsided tug of the bruise upon her mouth had changed as she had smiled. Her mood had been lightened by our flight; her eyes were alive with fascination where they ought to have been delivering a glare of condemnation. I'd dreaded that my parting view would have been of a frightened woman and beneath the interest she *was* frightened; at least her eyes had been fixed and wide as she had watched us. But now my head was echoing with the memory of Mrs Abbey's only words spoken through the open window as the car had curved past. She'd made a point of thanking him quite seriously for driving her to the doctor's house earlier, and her children had waved.

Chapter 17

The brief bare ground of the squatters' camp between all the fields of grain had flown by long ago. It had been possible to discern the scorch mark where the flames had consumed a small outhouse and crept painfully close to the line of tin houses. No wonder the residents had been alarmed.

It made me ask a little tentatively, 'Did the men from the camp have anything to add when you spoke to them in the field?'

The reason why my question was posed awkwardly was that he hadn't yet said anything. I suppose I'd been expecting quick reassurances now that we were in the car and that he would say something, anything, to restore our peace after that odd encounter. But he hadn't. He'd done nothing except set this car at the freedom of the main road to Gloucester and turn those alert eyes to the task of negotiating the thin traffic ahead, as if I wasn't even here. I felt as if I'd done something terrible in leaving her and that in the process I'd somehow betrayed him too.

Finally he spoke and his answer to my question about the source of the bonfire was a sharp sideways glance followed by a swift shake of his head and then, 'They didn't say much, no. They were thinking about getting down to my father's meeting.' The car checked with a hard touch of brakes for a turn before accelerating again. We'd passed beyond my knowledge of this area. Our speed wasn't even close to reckless but beneath his hands the car – his brother's car – was loving this chance to prove its power.

Unnervingly, I wasn't entirely sure that the thought wasn't uppermost in his mind too because he chose that moment to ask, 'Do you drive?'

'I can drive. My brother's friend taught me in his Sunbeam coupé. It was a dream.'

My tone betrayed my unease. I wasn't quite sure whether the question had been designed to permit me to introduce the awful subject of Mrs Abbey's last words. But I wasn't brave enough to do it blind. The car abruptly dropped like stone over a deep wooded escarpment so that the wide fields of the Severn Valley spread in a patchwork from the white pillar of a cathedral tower that must have been Gloucester.

'Runkled.' Again my driver broke the silence and this time it really didn't make any sense at all. After a swift sideways glance to catch my stare as I waited for him to give a better cue, he added, 'You said your change of outfit would be runkled. A combination of wrinkled and rumpled, I presume?'

Oh. It was as if he'd forgotten that we'd had a minor disagreement about a point of vocabulary once before. I'd thought, at the very least, he'd wish to ease the peculiar shame that had run through that confrontation with Mrs Abbey, but I was carrying it with me. I suppose I felt a little like I'd been sullied by the choice I'd had to make and I was waiting for him to say something that would smooth the thoughts away. Instead I was being made to revisit a subject that couldn't help but make me feel just a fraction smaller.

It took considerable effort to sound normal as I said, 'I noticed my use of *runkled* myself and, actually, I've thought about it and I'm pretty sure it's a valid term. I swear I learned that one from someone else.'

'I've never heard it.'

'In which case,' I retorted slightly less patiently, 'it's a legacy of war.'

His eyebrows rose. 'Really. And how, may I ask?'

High hedges streaked by and the occasional cottage gleamed grey in the gaps. We were racing along a road that led like a spear straight towards the distant prospect of the heart of the city.

Suddenly energy awoke within me. I fidgeted in my seat so that the leather squeaked. I told him, 'I believe you'll find that my grasp of the English language lies abandoned somewhere in an underground station that was doubling as an improvised schoolroom in an air raid. It was accidentally left there after a particularly disrupted – and final – grammar lesson at the age of thirteen and fifty-one weeks. I never went back to claim it.'

The tartness of my reply made a brief touch of what presumably was amusement show at the corners of his mouth. Probably because he could tell it blatantly wasn't true. The occasional entanglement of my word use was a weakness that was a part of me and stalked me as a faithful reminder of just how endlessly difficult I found it to voice precisely what was in my thoughts. Impatience made me try a little harder.

I asked, 'Did you see much of my pursuit of that man? Did you come back with Danny from the field in time to see me follow him through your house?'

'What man?'

It must be said that I really didn't expect this bland reply. I was, in fact, utterly stupefied. It wasn't just the absolute denial of what we had shared but the manner of it. His profile was relaxed, calm and conveyed mild curiosity. He steered the car around a bus. Blindly, I clung stubbornly to the thought I had that I was supposed to tell him this. 'I met that man today in your house when I was looking for your father's cane. He ran when I spotted him so I followed him out, only you held me back and left Danny to run onwards on his own. Why did you do that?'

'Why do you think?'

I watched him as I said slowly, 'I haven't the faintest idea.'

In truth I hadn't the faintest idea about any of it. Houses closed in; the vast hangars of an airfield retreated beyond our wing and I barely saw any of them. This wasn't merely the old confusion of reaching for the right words to convey precisely what I meant. In my mind was the memory of the way he'd steered me as he'd led me quietly back to the house for a chat just so long as he'd thought we were only dealing with imposters and itinerant arsonists. But then Mrs Abbey had appeared on the scene and he'd practically bustled me into his car. I believed I never would quite escape the chill that had possessed the way he had said the word *please*.

I said carefully, 'I believe you meant to prevent me from speaking to her, or rather stop her from speaking to me and I thought that was why you brought me along. I thought you meant to explain.'

He didn't explain though. He negotiated a junction and then, as the first houses of the city closed in, I found that I was suddenly in the midst of a long lecture about the people hereabouts and the River Severn. He paid particular attention to its tidal bore and the local adoration of jellied eels.

It was so mundane, it felt like an insult. As he did it, the man beside me was looking the way he always did and yet also completely unlike himself. He was calm, concentrated and unnervingly attractive, which didn't seem right at all because it wasn't like him to capitalise on it. It was as if he'd decided I was a stranger and was tactically evicting me from this scene by any means possible, even to the point of using charm; quite as if I hadn't myself just been party to the abandonment of a woman with an awful bruise on her face to a lonely and unguarded walk back to her isolated farmstead. He was making absolutely no allowance for my own raging guilt.

It made me say loudly into a pause, 'Do you know, I'm increasingly concerned that despite everything, Mrs Abbey might be the victim of this thing, not the perpetrator of it.'

That got though. 'Fine,' he said at last in a tone that implied we might have been bickering about the availability of eggs. 'Since you clearly are determined to make a point here, I really ought to let you get it over and done with. Do you want to ask me if I hit her?'

He knew I didn't. He'd just said it for effect. My exclamation came out as though I'd received an act of violence myself. 'No!'

Then I added gingerly, doubtfully, 'Did Danny?'

The question provoked a short, hard laugh. 'You don't like Hannis much, do you?'

'I feel as if I can't get to know him. But *you* should; he's your old childhood friend and yet you call him Hannis when you could call him Danny and he doesn't like it.'

'Emily, I call him Hannis because, given our respective positions in this place now that we're grown men, to call him Danny would be to risk dismissing him to the level of old-time Manor servant. Particularly as situations must inevitably still arise when he would have to address me as "sir". Elsewhere we could forget it. Here the use of surnames is the best balance we have. And, anyway, he calls me Cap'n. I doubt you'll find he means to imply much respect by that.'

While the brief flare of better humour faded, the real question hung unanswered. He finally said firmly, 'No. I do not believe Danny Hannis struck Mrs Abbey. For the sake of curiosity, whatever would make you ask?'

'Because there's something between them—'

'*Between* them?'

The way he repeated my words made me flush. I was fighting an increasingly desperate battle to assert some control over what I said and how he took it, and finding it all systematically eroded. It touched a nerve. I'd experienced this before and not from him. I said in a hard little voice, 'Yes. And when he spoke to you in the yard this morning, he said very specifically – as a warning, I thought – that he'd seen her face.' And in my head was the Captain's awful reply; grim and resigned. *I know.*

Unexpectedly, my question seemed to shake him. I mean it shook him out of the concealment I now knew he was trying to exert here. I saw his mouth suddenly lose its air of disinterest. He took a shallow breath and then another and with an urgency which was quite unlike the rest of his carefully unhelpful answers, he told me briskly, 'That was something else. Nothing. It doesn't have anything to do with Mrs Abbey. You needn't concern yourself with that.' It was for the first time an honest plea.

I saw his hands shift on the wheel. An almost angry narrowing of his gaze as he searched out some guiding landmark on the road ahead, and used it to avoid meeting my stare. There was something here that could wound, that was somehow more unpleasant to him than his strange decision to make a secret of his hunt for the man who had invaded his house.

After some time while the buildings around us grew from stained brick terraces into warehouses and grand company frontages, he risked a glance at me. He caught me watching and what he read in my expression he didn't like. And that was the moment I realised that Danny Hannis hadn't been warning this man about the marks on Mrs Abbey's face. Danny had been commenting on the emotion he'd read on mine. It was my face that had raised comment and my feelings that had caused him alarm. And now this man beside me had attempted to make a hasty deceit of it. And it was both touchingly protective and humiliating at the same time. I've never known mortification like it.

I'd already been feeling unnerved by all these things I couldn't quite comprehend. This was a crushing, burning shame. It made me feel like the delicious conflict between what I kept presuming he must be and what I was repeatedly discovering he was – and the confusing power of the latter – must have been drooping from my lips like the simpering of a dewy-eyed schoolgirl. Suddenly I had no control whatsoever over how my mouth shaped itself. My face felt bloated like a gargoyle's. I couldn't settle to any particular expression and I couldn't look at him because then I'd have to test how he himself had perceived the rushing in my heart and watch him struggle to tactfully meet whatever awful contortions were marking my face now. It made me lurch into speech purely for the purpose of refuting the idea that there had ever been any warmth inside me at all.

I turned my gaze fiercely to the dirty terraces passing outside my window and said with such airiness that it betrayed my disgust, 'Do you know, after our misunderstanding yesterday I've realised I don't know how to address you any more. "Captain" seems a touch pointed now.'

The car had slowed to wait at a junction. 'Well, make it Richard, then.'

There was unease in the way he said that. He knew that I'd guessed this particular secret. It also made me suspect that I might have called him by his name from the start. The use of my first name by him hadn't been a mark of my inferior status but an assumption that there was no distinction to enforce between us at all. It was horribly disarming, but I was already sweeping on with all the blind bitterness of a woman who had thought she was playing a part of quiet usefulness, only to learn that she had cast herself in the role of a slavish fool who was almost certainly becoming an ever-increasing liability. I said in that same brittle tone, 'So I wondered if, instead, I should take the other tack. I wondered if I should call you *Langton* …'

He concealed his flinch well. It was a terrible thing to say. It was the kind of cruelty that was born from the sheer dumbfounding agony of finding myself exposed here, and I had no right to do it. I suppose he might have taken it as a clumsy demonstration that he wasn't alone and I had at least guessed something of what had disturbed him in that encounter with Mrs Abbey, but he didn't. It still didn't suit him to shed these secrets. They bubbled away in that house and multiplied with loneliness and his father had been right to worry because now they were working to claim this man's decency too.

I knew they were because while I rushed headlong into a genuine and heartfelt apology for the appalling barb, my eyes took in the shabby frontage of the building that was looming alongside our slowing car.

I found my pulse settling back into cold reaction. He could read any emotion he liked in my eyes now. They were all there, plain to see. I forced out the words in an unnatural snarl. 'The railway station? *This* is where you've been taking me all this time?'

He didn't have a reply. The car slid to a stop with a hiss of brakes and after a few painfully speechless seconds, his hand moved to set the handbrake and silence the engine. Without the roar of the motor, I could hear the distant cry of the announcer and one sharp blow of a conductor's whistle.

In that same altered voice, I said, 'You're packing me off back to parents and London and you didn't even leave me time to collect my clothes, or a jacket and handbag ... or money.' My breath caught on the shock of comprehension. I said slowly, 'That's why you wanted me to bring my bags with me on our outing today. You never were going to carry me and my cousin back to her cottage. You were merely intending to soften the blow by breaking it to me over lunch first.'

I've never known revulsion like it. The feeling in itself scorched every nerve. 'Did you ...?' I had to stop and begin again. 'Did you have this in mind all morning?' I meant from the awful moment that I'd been rattling on about my cousin's letter as if honesty mattered. My mind shied from the rest of that conversation. I continued in that same voice ripped to roughness by disgust. 'Or did it come about when I first mentioned Duckett by name and you thought I'd been speaking to Mrs Abbey?'

I saw his head tip in the only brief, uncontrolled gesture that betrayed his frustration at being brought back yet again to the subject of Mrs Abbey. For me it was inescapable. For him it was rapidly suppressed to the level of an inconvenience. With his gaze fixed on the people milling outside, he conceded carefully, 'I was going to ask you about it over lunch. But time's slipped away from me and circumstances have ... changed.'

'Yes,' I agreed. 'You and I both know you meant to prevent me from speaking to that woman, or rather stop her from speaking to me and yet you still won't admit it. You're just going to send me off without so much as a nod towards the confidences that you've been working out of me endlessly for the past two days.'

He actually turned his head and looked at me then. Very briefly. Then he added this last point as if it answered everything; as in a way it did. He said gently, 'You might simply choose to trust me.'

The awful validity of the appeal shattered my resolve. It deflated me. It made me sit back in my seat and blink fiercely at the glass.

After a time, while a few more passengers dashed in and out of the station, I finally managed to say, 'No.'

I took a breath before adding, 'Please don't do it like this. You know I can't compete on this footing. You know what you're doing here and this isn't about trust. You have this wonderful decisiveness that overwhelms – don't deny it; you know you have – it runs through everything you do. But when you use it now, like this, as a weapon, just so that you can steer me into doing what you want when you know full well you could simply explain and I'd probably agree to almost anything anyway ... It makes me afraid that there's danger here and it isn't just from those people.' It wasn't much of an explanation. I took an unsteady breath before adding the rest. I felt the intensity of his attention. Finally, I managed to articulate what was making me resist so much and my voice grew stronger as I added at last, 'I can't stop you from buying my ticket and I expect I'll let you put me on the train, since it clearly matters to you and I suppose I can guess why. But I don't think you realise what damage it's doing. When you *could just ask.*'

He didn't reply. I sensed the sudden frown, though I didn't see it. I felt the temporary dip of his confidence. I'd thought it would help to put my agitation in terms of my desolation. I'd thought it was right that he should understand what this manner of inflicting his decisions upon me was costing me in terms of hope and that fragile independence that I'd been working so hard to nurture. I'd thought it vital to give a hint, too, of what I thought he was risking in terms of his own nature. But I hadn't quite anticipated how close this came to comparing his kind of instinctive action in the face of a threat to the first hard choices that must have set his brother on his long slide into dereliction. It was an unforgiveable repetition of the cruel misuse I'd just made of his name purely for the sake of reasserting my own bit of control. In its way I thought it was as shamefully manipulative as any of the manoeuvrings of the Mrs Abbeys, the Ducketts and the visiting vagrants of these parts.

So I'd go. And peaceably. But first I found I was speaking again; fighting to remedy the mistake; confessing that I knew he was a man who depended on his power to identify a complication and then to act upon it, and working to cancel out the authenticity of the feelings I'd betrayed by forming some kind of ridiculous excuse for my resistance based around the fate of the goat and the raven.

I heard the springs in his seat squeak as he moved restlessly. His voice was clouded with frank incomprehension. 'Pardon?

Did you say a *raven?* What on earth am I supposed to have done wrong now?'

There was resignation there rather than the same dip in certainty that had frightened me a moment ago. I worked to reduce my dignity a little bit further by taking a shaky breath and saying in a bitter rush, 'You're going to ask Danny to shoot it. Poor thing. I presume its mistake was to take up residency in a set of trees that you've just happened to determine are vital for your darling young pheasants.'

I heard his breath go out. With relief, I thought. His manner was suddenly softer. I found I was bracing myself to meet a laugh and further humiliation but he didn't find it amusing at all. He said seriously, 'So *this* is what has been upsetting you? Emily, I'll just issue a decree that the raven is to be left in peace. There must be at least one permitted use of authority here, don't you think? And actually, for your information, I don't care to go blasting pheasants or carrion birds or any other kind of fowl out of existence either. I told you I wasn't ready to step into my brother's shoes. He enjoyed the sport. *I* like to keep it very clear in my mind precisely what weapons are actually for.'

Now, suddenly, this was more like the man I thought I knew. There was humour there. I found myself replying in a stronger voice, 'I know that you're trying to tell me that you don't think death and sport belong together, but actually that's not quite as reassuring to hear as you might suppose, given that it only serves to reinforce the idea I have of just how much you personally must know about the proper use of a gun.'

I heard the creak of leather as he relaxed. He'd seen the brief show of a wry smile on my lips. I sensed the answering warmth in him. Outside, a train must have been due because a steady stream of cabs was flowing past us and drawing up outside the entrance to the station. People and suitcases and office workers were all clambering out and racing in.

After the rush had passed, I too was calm at last. I broke the silence that had stretched for some minutes. 'This is an evacuation, isn't it?'

I felt his hesitation. Then he accepted the term. 'Why not? Yes. That's as good an explanation as any. After all, as you just remarked yourself, there is a ferocious bruise on a woman's jaw and even I can tell no swelling of that kind was ever applied with make-up. So if she's vulnerable, I really don't want you to be next. I feel responsible enough as it is, and I am, I suppose, your employer of sorts—'

Exasperation made me interrupt, despite all my good intentions. I said hotly, 'No, you're not. You're the one who keeps mentioning renumeration – remuneration, thank you – and I think you'll find that I haven't asked for it once. I had thought I was only being neighbourly. I thought I was being useful.' My voice caught on that last word and I snatched it back with a sharp intake of breath. 'You asked me to help. You wanted me to do what I could to make things easier for your father. I've been trying to help *him*.'

'Well,' he replied with his gaze firmly fixed on a passing pigeon. 'Now I'm telling you that you can help us both by going home.'

He shifted in his seat to face me. Here was rejection again, firm and final. The body of the car tilted slightly as he moved. He said reasonably, 'You told me you don't like violence. You don't like distress. What else am I supposed to do?'

'*Ask* me.'

I hadn't meant to repeat that one unresolved argument, but the validity of the point was inescapable. At last he could gauge how far I believed I was fighting here for more than just myself. I might just as well have been asking why he might not simply choose to trust *me*. It drew an impatient jerk of his head. He really hadn't expected this. He hadn't expected to encounter any other reasonable point of view. The adjustment of his thoughts didn't sit easily in his mind. I might have supposed that he was experiencing the surprise of meeting me as I really was for the first time. But this wasn't one of those moments when a fearfully domineering male was forced to confront the news that a woman had her own capacity for independent thought. This was more tender than that. I thought instead that in this small moment I was confirming suspicions that he'd long held about my nature but hadn't before glimpsed the proof.

It was then that I heard him say on a very odd note. 'Very well. Let's talk about this. You mentioned my brother's name. Emily, will you tell me—?'

Then, before I could even begin to grasp that he was beginning to confide the truth, he cut the sentence short and I heard what might have been a mutter under his breath of 'Oh, hell!' before, significantly more clearly, he turned instead to the relief of accepting that capitulation I'd offered shortly before.

He said in a very different voice, 'Look, let's not do this. You know I meant to talk this through with you properly before you left. There isn't enough time now. I've got a meeting in about half an hour that I can't miss, not even for this. I'll come and see you when I'm back in London. Won't that do?'

My heart gave an uncomfortable jolt that told me that I still felt rather more for him than could possibly be healthy or perhaps even deserved. I was painfully unsure that the feeling wasn't betraying itself all over again on my cheeks. But this was one concession I wouldn't submit to. I couldn't bear the idea of going home and meekly waiting there for the next in his line of rescues, as if there was truly anything for him to actually come for. Miserable pride made me shake that future away and say coldly to the hands clasped in my lap, 'I don't think that's very wise, do you? If you're worrying about reclaiming the cost of my fare, you needn't. My father will send it back to you tomorrow.'

I heard an intake of breath. 'Emily, sweetheart, come on ...'

The gentle reprimand brought my head round. In his expression, I actually discovered a trace of amusement of the sort that grows from exasperation purely because he hadn't meant to let this argument lead me into that kind of rejection. Not quite, anyway.

Suddenly I was wading through a different kind of shame. All along I'd been battling my own insecurities – my sneaking hatred of being made to acknowledge I was still an inconvenient tag-along when I'd hoped the little help I had to offer a person these days would be enough to make me fit to play a part even if I wouldn't bear arms. But while there was certainly a threat here that had motivated him to act with such unswerving purpose on my behalf, I discovered within the sudden honesty in that reproof that his decision to fling me away wasn't noble. It wasn't heroic and it certainly wasn't because he was trying to shelter a delicate young thing. It was a hard and uncompromisingly desperate act of self-defence.

He was trying to protect himself and, knowing him as I thought I was beginning to, the threat to him had to be something substantial or else he wouldn't bother to do it at all.

Suddenly I was wishing passionately that I'd let this man talk more about the car and other harmless pleasantries such as the passage of elvers up the River Severn. I swallowed my pride. I managed to look him straight in the eye. I had the sudden disconcerting experience of discovering that he in his turn had been assessing me. It was safe to say that the results of his scrutiny hadn't been very happy.

Outside the car, newly arrived passengers were flowing from the station and we were the only still people in a sea of motion. I knew I had to do something to make amends; to restore his confidence that his decision about me had been sound if I could; just so, at the very least, he wouldn't think that the threat came from me.

In the midst of that flood of people, I told him urgently, 'I'm sorry. Of course I'll go. I didn't understand what you were trying to do. I wish I didn't always get things so wrong; or at least that I could say the right thing more easily.' His left hand was moving. Not towards me but the little compartment on the dashboard before me, where presumably he'd put his wallet and the funds to purchase my ticket. It paused when I added in a flushing rush, 'Only, before I relieve you of the cost of my ticket and perhaps beg you for a small loan to cover my lunch too ...'

'Yes?'

I finished in a smaller voice than I intended, 'I think it's important you know that I never did want anything real from you. I wasn't meaning to pry. It's simply that, for what it's worth, I wanted you to know that I'm on your side.'

After a moment, his hand resumed its path. But it wasn't heading to the catch on the storage compartment. I wasn't entirely sure it ever had. It went to the heart of the dashboard where the starter button lay.

I wasn't sure his confidence had ever needed my meagre restorative efforts either. He wasn't me, after all. His self-assurance didn't ebb and flow with every word of mine. The engine growled into life. Without a word, while a train steamed its way messily out of the station, the car was sent forwards gracefully into a wide loop down the slope once more. It hesitated at the junction. Then the traffic eased and we moved gently on towards the town. It didn't escape my notice that with the same precision with which he had previously decided I wouldn't stay, he had now decided to ignore my resolution to go.

I was brave enough to ask him about it when we parked the car at the point where a busy shopping street gave way to offices and workshops. It was reasonably near the hospital, he'd told me, and we were to meet back at the car in about an hour. It was all done in a very friendly fashion. Politeness reigned between us. He seemed as much a capable man as he ever did and I, for once, felt more like a woman than a naïve girl when I climbed out onto a sun-scorched pavement made deafening by the flow of city traffic. Petrol rationing didn't appear to hold much sway here and noise shrouded me as I stood to one side while he came round to lock my door. While he did it, I risked unseating our renewed truce by asking tentatively, 'Why *did* you let me stay? I mean, thank you very much and all that. But why did you?'

He paused in the midst of reaching into an inside breast pocket for his wallet and a note that would buy my lunch. His head turned to me. 'I thought you'd decided that one for yourself?'

I raised an eyebrow at him. It said everything that needed to be said.

He handed me my loan and then returned the wallet to its place. His eyes were grave, but there was also a flicker of a lighter feeling playing there. I didn't know what the difference was in my voice now, but he'd noticed it too.

'Very well,' he said, putting out a hand to my sleeve to warn me that someone meant to pass us from behind and to keep me from straying into their path. He let them go past and then dropped his grip. We were standing in the space between the car and the soot-stained stone of an office of some sort. Heat blazed off every surface.

He returned his attention to me. 'It's because you lied yesterday when you let me believe your greatest terror is that the peace means nothing and it's your turn now to face something dreadful. I wondered at the time about it, but let it pass.

I can't let it pass again today. You gave yourself away just now when you made your sudden about-turn to tell me about that unfortunate raven. You did it just at the very moment that I was about to have to acknowledge how badly I was behaving, and I realised just how much you are in the habit of making endless calculations about what other people want, and then modifying your own wishes just so you don't harm them.'

He cast a swift glance over his shoulder to be sure that no one else was coming past. No one was. The only bustle at this end of town came from the rumbling traffic as he confided gently, 'I think I would even go so far as to suspect that yesterday the impulse led you to play to my own preconceptions when you let me believe you needed to be shielded from the distress of a violent scene. I suppose you *were* honest in as far as it goes, but I've also noticed that you've been regretting leaning on me ever since ... Haven't you?'

He was doing it again; this was like that instant by the bicycle outside the tithe barn. It was a disorientating swoop into a fuller empathy presented as a shatteringly perceptive portrait of myself. And again, just like the other time, I wasn't sure he knew how close his judgement was cutting to the bone.

It felt as though someone else's body were moving when I conceded the point with a faint tilt of my head. Then he added, 'I think your real terror is the act of being sheltered itself. In part it's just as you said: you're afraid because the fact someone would even think you needed help must mean that aggression is close by. But I'm beginning to suspect that the real issue is that you believe that when nastiness does finally break, it won't matter what you've decided you're prepared to do. Other people will always set the rules for what counts as a valid intervention, and any effort of yours is, and will remain, perpetually below par.'

Suddenly I was smiling and shaking my head. Not because it wasn't true but because he really wasn't saying this to wound. This wasn't quite as perceptive as I'd feared either. He wasn't making me confront anything I wasn't ready to admit and the discovery left me room to feel a powerful and disabling appreciation of the exact worth of this man who would act to save a person, even from an emotional hazard. Because this was what he was doing here. He was undoing all those parts of the argument that had worked upon my sense of being small and useless. He was letting me know that he would find a role for me if I wanted it.

Suddenly I was a step closer and my hand was on his sleeve. And, trying hard to avoid the agonised tones of our last conversation, I was telling him very earnestly, 'This is going to sound terribly crass after the fuss and guilt I've just inflicted upon you about staying, and I'm certainly glad I'm here now so I'm not trying to turn this into yet another discussion on the state of my self-esteem. But please, I mean what I say. I don't want my name to be added to your list of responsibilities. Your perception of this part of me is wholly accurate. I refuse to be made the object of any more grand gestures when I know full well it is impossible that I'll ever be able to reciprocate and—'

'Any more grand gestures?' He queried the count as well as the term.

'I won't be indebted.'

I stalled there. He didn't understand and I was straying into an explanation of those things I didn't mean to lay bare. I shook it away and found my eyes had settled upon the grey fabric of his suit jacket where it ran smoothly beneath my fingers. My body was still feeling like it was something distant from me. Without really thinking that I ought to drop that hand, I lifted my head properly. I told him boldly, 'To be perfectly frank, Richard, I think you've got quite enough to deal with as it is, without adding my silly insecurities to the list; what with your father and that house, and the very real antics of everyone else too.'

I expected him to smile in return.

I'd thought a man like him would value the way I was alluding to my sympathy without trespassing into barefaced commentary, after all that had been left unsaid in the car. I'd thought it would amuse him because it would make sense to him. I wasn't expecting him to react as he did.

He was suddenly looking blank. The set of his mouth was a deeper mark of the puzzlement that had steadied him in the past; a sudden intensity of concentration that came horribly close to looking like I'd hurt him.

Then I was suddenly aware of how close I was to him and was thinking I ought to step away, and I was belatedly snatching my hand from his sleeve and touching my fingertips to my temple instead as if to hide my confusion. But his stillness broke like it had been an ache in the mind. He moved to stem that retreat. He took hold of me. He hesitated just long enough to read the sudden adjustment of my thoughts as I better understood his intentions. Then he bent his head and kissed me.

The touch of his lips was a very brief blaze. The merest scorching run of seconds or more of contact with the core of him before he drew away. It rocked me when he told me on an undertone, 'I think, Emily, you woefully underestimate the contribution you make.'

There was a whisper of a laugh beneath that roughened edge. It mingled with the uncontrolled awareness of knowing that it had been my last little statement of care that had unwittingly laid bare something deep within this man; and that for him it went beyond trust that he'd let me see.

For me, I thought that sometimes it was wonderful to be so lacking in confidence. Nervousness was followed by the intensity of perceiving that he meant to kiss me again.

Then, in the next moment, someone was coming along the pavement and it wasn't the done thing to give way to public displays of affection and Richard was straightening to watch them pass behind. I was dragging my mind back into some kind of order while I discovered at the moment I attempted it that I'd been leaning into him. His grip steadied me as I stirred. When his hand moved to my upper arm and settled there with a brief contraction of his fingers, the gesture was like a question; a first real greeting, perhaps.

His gaze dropped to me. The attractive line of his jaw was perfectly defined in this summer's afternoon. So was the brief smile that showed in his eyes. It hit me like a bolt. But he grew reluctantly businesslike as he told me, 'I'd better go if I'm going to make this meeting. Are you happy that you know how to find the hospital?'

I mustered a nod as he stepped away; a busy man in a

neatly tailored suit on a city street. I was in control of myself again too by now, but my cheeks burned. And so did my lips with the memory of his touch. I put an unsteady hand up to them. I thought I finally understood the feeling that had followed me from the car. It was the consciousness that in the midst of blundering through an attempt to explain my distress at being sent away, I'd actually been daring to assert who I was a little more clearly before him.

'By the way,' he added as his hand lifted to sketch a farewell, 'it's nice to hear you call me by my name.'

It was then that I noticed that I'd called him Richard and realised that he'd been Richard in my head for a rather longer time.

Chapter 18

I had, in the brief window between feeling belittled and unnervingly bold, thought to ask him if he had the time to spare five minutes to snatch a meal. He hadn't. So my lunch had consisted of a solitary walk uphill to a tired crossroads and a table at a hotel that was one of a number of sagging medieval buildings feeling very sorely the present shortages of paint. The decay of age was, I realised, the main burden in this city and it was as I stepped downhill again bearing the additional prize of a small packet of sandwiches that it dawned on me that barely anywhere here was the dereliction of bombed-out buildings. It was a long time since I'd last passed along a shopping street in London and not been greeted by bare ground and defiant signs pasted up by the survivors declaring 'businesses open as usual' ...

My destination lay downhill, beyond the place where we had left the car. The hospital was near the docks. I could just make out the tall rooftops of various warehouses glinting through the smog that oozed from the enormous chimney of an electricity station. The imposing spread of the hospital consisted of a vast spread of wards and extensions, all

270

constructed in imposing brickwork and stained black by coal dust. It was also built on the corner of a junction with a little side street named Parliament Street. It was the name logged as Mrs Abbey's former address in John Langton's book of accounts.

Quite without any thought for my cousin, I abandoned any immediate idea of rescuing her and turned left instead.

Everything here was brick too. Beneath the settling fug of coal smoke, low workmen's houses occupied every space not given over to either warehousing or health and recovery. Then, with a suddenness that rivalled the contrast between the Manor and Mr Winstone's cottage, the cramped two-storey terraces with their small barren gardens abruptly terminated beside a significantly grander rank of merchants' houses. These houses had no garden at all and stepped straight down onto the street from smart porticos. I was able to identify Mrs Abbey's former home based solely on the fact that all the others were numbered and I remembered hers had a name. It was called Berwick House, which suggested nothing particularly significant to me, and it was a well-tended Victorian property, but no one was home.

Now that I was here, I had absolutely no idea what I was expecting to find, but the one thought that pushed through all the rest was to marvel at how determined she must have been to achieve a move if she had willingly exchanged this crisp style of dwelling for the soggy plasterwork of Eddington.

I didn't have the chance to think about it for long. A woman's voice accosted me as I dithered on the pavement.

She called me 'missus' and she wasn't terribly polite, as I suppose no one would be after discovering a person prying through their neighbour's window.

She was short and sturdy with shrewd black eyes and she was wearing a knee-length housecoat of the style that renders a woman strangely rectangular. She was also brandishing a broom, which looked as though it frequently gave service as a fire iron and just occasionally, as it was doing now, weighed in her hands as a suitable weapon for repelling burglars.

I beamed and immediately transformed from burglar into something else – a person collecting charitable donations, perhaps – and remained equally unwelcome. 'Good afternoon,' I trilled and made it all so much worse. 'I was hoping to find the owner at home. Are they away?'

I received a pair of blank stares in reply because now the lady's friend or sister had emerged from the gloom within and had joined her upon her front step. The two yards of untended garden and the rotten little gate was no protection from their total absence of friendliness. In fact, I wasn't even entirely sure they'd understood. I tried again and sounded even more stilted. 'I was wondering who lives there now. I suppose you know?'

The women exchanged glances. Not sly and knowing ones, nor even hostile. But blank glances, where each silently asked the other if she had made out what the stranger had said. I might have thought they were doing it deliberately, except that I could hear my own accent and it sounded painfully stuffy even to me.

Very briefly, I considered the idea that I should offer them money, only I didn't know how. They were losing patience and interest. The woman with the broom was considering her unfinished task of sweeping her front step. The other lady found something she didn't like about the cut of my trousers. At least, I think that was what held her stare. Perhaps it was simply that her thoughts had given up and retreated elsewhere.

I drew myself up a little straighter and tried a fresh tack: a little honesty. 'I'm a neighbour of Mrs Abbey where she's living now.' A waft of my hand to indicate somewhere above the distant escarpment that marked the edge of the Cotswold Hills. 'Up on the hill. I believe she used to live next door to you, with her husband Mr Abbey?'

I don't know that they'd caught any more of my words now than they had before, but one thing crossed the divide. The lady without a broom turned to her friend and whispered, 'Him from the docks?'

She got a nod in reply from her stern friend and it prompted her to ask again eagerly, 'The one who was in prison?'

'*Was?*'

They understood my accent that time well enough.

This time the lady with the broom was the spokesperson. Disapproval formed on thin lips; hard, tough and entirely unforgiving. 'Eight years he got for stealing the food out of our mouths and let off after three, for all that. And barely a murmur raised by anyone about the fact that someone must have sent that warehouse blazing up like a torch with three good men inside.'

I found that I was suddenly at the limit of her garden gate.

The woman's lips pursed, released and pursed again. She told me sourly, 'The firemen didn't get out again, missus.'

Her friend added, 'They called it an unlucky accident and just sent him down for the fraud, but I said at the time and I'll say it again now – that man is a fiend. What else do you call a man who ran one of the grain warehouses and instead of feeding a nation at war he fed his pockets and the black market, and then burnt down the lot the same week his little racket got discovered? Treason I call it, in a time of war.'

She took a little breath before confiding in a voice that took a certain malicious delight in the horror of it, 'I say it wasn't an accident. I say he thought he'd pass off the whole conflagration as an unlucky hit from a bomb. I remember the sirens going off and the ack-ack guns starting up and he must have known it was always them sorry folk by the railway that took the brunt of our Blitz and never the docks. But still he took his little light and climbed six flights of stairs into the warehouse attic. The lot went up like a matchstick and he must have heard the auxiliaries raise the alarm and go in, but he didn't stop them. He just laid himself sagging in a stairwell for the main rescue to come with the fireboat, while three poor old men went clambering up with nothing between them but blue bands on their sleeves and a hand-pump with a hosepipe to die suffocating in the smoke.'

I was repulsed. I blinked when the broom-laden woman spoke loudly into the silence.

She demanded sharply, 'Why do you ask? You with the paper?'

'Actually, no.' I had no idea where people kept getting this impression. 'I really am just a neighbour. Has he been back since, do you know? Mr Abbey, since he got out, I mean. He does still own this house, I presume?'

Suddenly, I was sensing a cause for Mrs Abbey's exhaustion if this was the man she had married, and if I'd ever felt sympathy for her before I certainly felt it now. But it got all so much more tangled when the woman with the broom replied roundly, 'It's not *his* house. It was his wife's and her mother's before her and I'll bet she thanks the heavens the law doesn't give a man all his woman's inheritances these days, eh? So she sold it and now it belongs to that other chap. The one she must have run to from up the hill.'

I caught a shrewd glance as she recalled that I was from that place too. She spoke slowly, while watching me like a hawk. 'There was a terrible fuss about him. She doesn't have much luck, that girl, does she?'

I think she was testing to see whether I was a love rival. Which, luckily of course, I wasn't. And then, in the midst of my silent attempt to decipher just how possible it would be to probe this woman's knowledge of when they'd met, the bustling friend lit up to contradict her gleefully, 'No, it wasn't him. He died. It was the other fellow that bought it; the soldier from that same place, who pitched up here in the spring. He came with a great band of demob boys to save people's houses by stacking sandbags against the floodwaters. Mrs Blake next door was talking about him only the other day; about how she'd had to put up him and half a dozen others in her son's room, with wet boots everywhere. Only,' she added, just as I was squinting through the numbing unlikelihood of thinking does she mean Richard? 'I don't think he can still be a soldier now; he's a farmer.'

She meant Danny.

Chapter 19

It was the water that intimidated me here. I'd come to the docks almost blindly, automatically undertaking a hunt for that warehouse. I suppose, in a way, it was a means of repeating the unthinking method of my discovery of Mrs Abbey's former home and through it refocusing the distaste of what I had learned there. On my way to this place from the hospital I'd passed a sign pointing between the prison and an employment exchange to the barracks for the Royal Gloucestershire Hussars. That was Richard's regiment and I had no idea whether Danny had served within it too but, like the punchline to a bad joke, the significance of all my doubts about his part in Mrs Abbey's present life were stalking me now, just as I stalked the woman's past.

Rail tracks ran everywhere here. They were embedded into the roadways at just the perfect depth to turn an ankle and on the far side of the main basin there was the incongruous sight of a big black steam train rolling tamely along in a queue of lorries and horse-drawn wagons. Just to my left, a fearsome crane was hoisting goods overhead from a heavily laden barge, supervised by coarsely spoken men. I ought to have been used to the noise and bustle, having grown up in the territory of barrow boys and cockney markets, but I didn't remember ever being made to feel quite so clumsy at home. I think it was the water that finished the job. It oozed inkily between the rows of tightly moored barges. It cast rainbow reflections upon the bright flagstone kerb of the wharf and puddled too close for comfort when I had to move between hard-working people who were in the habit of shouldering aside anyone who had the stupidity to get in the way.

The Abbey warehouse loomed at the lower end of the largest basin. The channel of water narrowed again here between lines of waiting vehicles in smart liveries. Here I found Duckett too. His name joined the criminal's under the title *Abbey, Mole & Duckett Ltd.* and even without the tall lettering emblazoned upon the brickwork, I might have identified the second warehouse as theirs because the upper five storeys had been demolished, leaving the building a stunted, shrunken version of its undamaged twin.

The office building was even smaller. It squatted with dwarfed dignity before its nearest warehouse – the undamaged one – and when I stepped in, I found myself at a smart reception desk staffed by two very busy young women. I'd forgotten this was a Friday afternoon. So much of my approach to this moment had been guided by nothing but a general sense of curiosity. Now my wide eyes took in the vision of two harassed office girls who were furiously hammering at their typewriters, presumably on a mission to get the week's invoices out. There was a man in shirt and tie and overalls who looked like the foreman, flirting unsuccessfully with the prettier of the two while ostensibly trying to check his hours for the coming week. The other girl was scowling into a telephone receiver, saying nothing and not appearing to be listening to anything either, typing all the while and looking as though she would have preferred it if the foreman had chosen to hint about the Saturday dance to her instead. A pair of private offices – almost everything seemed to be done in pairs in this company – stood at the back and were empty; or, at least, I could see no sign of movement through the partially frosted glass.

'Yes?' The girl who wasn't batting aside compliments had looked up. The telephone receiver was still held loosely against one ear, so presumably she was waiting to hear from someone on the other end of the line. Neatly rouged lips moved. 'May I help?'

I smiled haplessly. 'I'm looking for Mr Abbey. Is he in?'

I knew he wasn't. I was hoping for more good fortune of the sort that had come from my encounter with the woman with her broom, if good fortune it could be called. But this young woman delivered the company line on Mr Abbey's fall from grace very smoothly. I also had a feeling that she, in her turn, was noticing my age and my looks and was decidedly disinclined to imagine I was anything impressive like a prying journalist. I found myself wishing abstractedly for my handbag and a hairbrush.

She told me in crisp tones, 'I'm afraid Mr Abbey doesn't have an office here any more. He hasn't been here for quite some time. Mr Duckett handles his side of the business now. Perhaps I can take a message. Unless ...'

The poor woman gave me a flustered stare when the

earpiece beside her suddenly stuttered and she had to tear her mind between me and her counterpart on the other end of the line. 'Yes? Hello? Is this about the—?' She was suddenly speaking very seriously about pelleted animal feeds. It made me aware that Mrs Abbey's husband had lost something else in the course of his misdemeanours. His business was clearly no longer in a position to sell rationed foodstuffs to anyone, whether legitimate customers or black-market dealers if it now had been relegated to the business of processing the waste into animal feeds.

I turned my head to the foreman, who was eavesdropping near my side. 'What were you making before the fire?'

He told me easily, 'Toasted cereal. We—'

'Excuse me, what about the fire?' The girl before me had her hand over the mouthpiece to her telephone and was suddenly looking at me as though I were something poisonous. She told me huffily, 'I told you, Mr Abbey's business is being handled by Mr Duckett. You'll have to direct your questions to him. He's just coming in now. Someone to see you, sir. It's concerning Mr Abbey. Yes, I'm here! Don't go away again!' This last was to the telephone as the receiver chattered crossly.

Behind, the volume from outside briefly rushed in as the door was opened and then silenced again as it clicked shut. I turned. The middle-aged man who had stolen my suitcase stood there staring at me as I stared at him. I was suddenly truly feeling the lack of my handbag when my hands clasped tightly upon a packet of sandwiches and found it didn't give quite the same sense of something secure to hang on to. Duckett pulled himself together rather swifter than I. He lifted

off his grey-banded hat – a must for any gentleman of business – in vague salute and dropped it on a convenient stand
just inside the front door. It emphasised for me that he was
there, between me and the outside world, and I was here in
his office asking questions about his discredited business
associate, who was the husband of the woman he'd been so
determined to trace that he'd committed burglary. I'd said to
Richard that I always seemed to get things so very wrong.
The idea that I'd come blindly to the place of one criminal
without a thought for the fact it was also the place of the
other was one of those moments, I felt.

Duckett didn't fling me out. He opened his hand wide in
an exaggerated gesture of welcome and ushered me through
into his office. I went, feeling like a fool walking to the gibbet,
and took the proffered seat as he turned and shut the door.
I half feared he might lock it and even went so far as to muster
a breath to call out if he did, but of course he didn't.

So I waited, feet crossed at the ankles beneath my chair
and hands gripping the arms rather too tightly with a packet
of sandwiches resting in my lap, while the man who had stolen
nearly all my clothes in the world walked round to his place
behind his desk and settled himself there amongst the files
and shelves, a Great War medallion and the photographs that
ranged like a stage-set across the wall. My heart was beating.
I blinked at him mutely, in a manner that appeared to make
him think I was meaning to convey, heaven help me, something
of a challenge.

I had no idea I had it in me to look forbidding. It prompted
him to begin by treating this meeting as a difficult session

with the board. When he leaned in to prop his elbows upon the tabletop and joined his fingertips before his mouth, it occurred to me that neither of us was quite sure at that moment who was in charge of this. I could judge that he intended to establish pretty swiftly it would be him.

He spoke through the point of his joined hands in a voice that told me he was tense to the extent of breaking. 'I must say I'm impressed. I didn't think you were the sort for this kind of heroism. Unless you've got something particular you want to tell me? A message from the man himself, perhaps?'

My nerves were equally sharp. So was my tongue. 'Actually, I *have* got something to tell you: I don't like the way you're trailing about my neighbourhood or Richard's—' I spoke determinedly over his pointedly raising eyebrows, which presumably meant to remind me that currently I was guilty of invading his neighbourhood. 'And I should like my suitcase back, please.'

'I haven't got it.' His gaze was expressionless now behind the screen of his fingers. Then something flickered and he amended his reply to say coolly, 'Anyway, what suitcase? I have no idea what you're talking about.'

He was proud of his parry. His right hand dropped to the tabletop where it thumbed idly through a few papers while his eyes never left my face. I, in my turn, could finally establish that he was of average height for a man – an inch or so taller than me – so not quite the stunted male I'd described before. The thin belt of hair that rested above his ears was the colour of flecked steel and he had mercifully resisted the impulse that drove some to grow the top long and sweep it over. 'So,' he said crisply in the manner of one who was calling a meeting to order. 'What is your plan here? Do you want me to make idle small-talk while you get round to asking me whatever it is you came here to say? How did you find your walk through the docks? You should be careful where you step out there. Sometimes I think the dockside machines take a tithe of life as their due. They'd certainly relish fresh prey like you.' A brief glimmer of a smile came and went on his face as if to imply this was a joke and I shouldn't take it seriously.

'Really,' I remarked flatly.

Amusement quirked again. 'I first met your man ten years ago, you know.'

This was a surprise. 'Really?' This time I meant it as a question, quick and doubtful.

'Yes. He seemed a weasel-ish sort of fellow, but she liked him so I let friendship overrule back then ...' He wafted a hand to emphasise that circumstances had changed now. He watched me to make sure I'd got the point – which I hadn't – and then he dropped his attention to the disordered pencils on his desk. He had neatly filed fingernails, each very clean, and a gold signet ring on the little finger of his left hand. He was twisting it now.

I stared at him nonplussed. '*Mrs Abbey* introduced you?'

He swept on without acknowledging my question. 'I knew roughly where Florence was living since her move away from Parliament Street, of course, but she took off just as soon as the judge passed sentence three years ago and at the time I thought it best to let her alone. But then he got out and started leaving a messy trail of dirty lairs and thieved gardens straight to that valley and I thought I'd better show my face. All in the spirit of friendship, you understand?' His left hand strayed towards a waiting ashtray, but then changed its mind and resumed fiddling with a pencil instead. He peered at me from beneath lowered brows. He asked me quite calmly, 'Have you encountered betrayal before, Miss Sutton?'

I was left wondering why he was saying it like that. Why he was saying the word *betrayal* as if it deserved time and consideration. It had struck me with a kick already that he was talking about Mr Abbey; he'd always been talking about Mr Abbey. Of course he was. This was the man Mrs Abbey had introduced as her lover ten years ago, and presumably introduced him to the business too, not Richard. It was ever so slightly absurd, really, that I should have ever thought otherwise. I moved to correct the mistake. 'I don't know—'

I might as well have not spoken. Duckett merely raised his voice a little to cover mine as he barked, 'Has he told you what he did? Has he told you he's a fraud and a hypocrite? Have you even bothered to wonder why a man who has barely had his liberty back for a month should prefer a life of hopping about from hut to shed to hovel over leaving us all alone and starting afresh elsewhere? It's because he's planning a far greater betrayal this time. He's got that poor woman frightened out of her wits. He's got her cowering in that filthy farmhouse where she thought she'd be safe enough from his attentions when he got out. But he won't let her alone and I think he's made it pretty clear that he's got no intention of letting things rest between him and me.'

There was, in the midst of that authoritative torrent, that word again. Betrayal.

This time it was concluded by a slap of his hand upon the tabletop. It made me flinch and drew the attention of the busy ladies outside his door. For their sake, he leaned in and beamed at me as though the strike of his hand had merely been a loud substitute for applause. He pretended that I'd made a witty joke and lowered his voice to a confidential growl. 'He spent his war earning merit as an ARP by night, while by day he used the business – *my* business; her brother's business – to defraud the Ministry. The press had it that he was only siphoning off a few sacks of grain here and there like a jolly sort of black-market trickster, but that's just because they couldn't report on the kind of treacherous, conniving crookedness that the propaganda machine was teaching us to believe was the reserve of the enemy. The truth is you could let your imagination run riot and still you wouldn't come close to grasping the truth of that man's total disregard for common decency.'

I retorted hotly, 'I think I could grasp it. His fire killed some people.'

Duckett choked. The acid in my response stunned him. So much so, his only solution was to ignore it. His hand strayed to the ashtray again and this time his fingers started jiggling a matchbook up and down so that it made a rapid little tapping upon the desk. He said roughly, 'Paul Abbey nearly died too. He *ought* to have died. Did you know that? The fire started in the attic where we housed our records – supposedly it was an accident – but he was there. He got caught by the flames when he tried to make a run for it. The heat sucked all of the air out of his lungs so that he could barely speak for weeks. And the last punishment of all came from the fact that I had some of his decidedly ambiguous papers in my office, so he didn't even have the luck of knowing the fire had succeed in destroying the evidence. When the police started talking about possible charges of arson and began telling the world it had been an insurance job, I did the only thing I could do. I handed over the lot.'

As Abbey's supposed friend, I was supposed to be outraged by that I think. Like Duckett's act of good-citizenship was a different kind of betrayal. But I wasn't. I was mesmerised by the photograph that hung on the wall just behind his head. Duckett twisted to follow my gaze just as I said in a tone of absolute disbelief, '*Who is that man?*'

'Who?'

The photograph was a large hand-coloured scene populated by stakeholders and directors at a gathering of some sort. I judged it to be a picture dating from later in the war since a number of the figures were clad in the single-breasted suits that belonged to the era of rationing and clothing shortages. It was this detail, and this alone, that had alerted me to the presence of the man beside Duckett. He was a man with a pleasant face and a supple smile that rivalled Mrs Abbey's. A man she'd claimed as her husband but couldn't possibly be, because by the time the people were assembling for this photograph, he'd have been either in prison or on his way to it.

Duckett himself was surprisingly hirsute in this portrait,

to the extent that I wondered if he regularly sported a wig. The living, balding man before me looked perplexed. 'What man? The man beside me? That's our backer; the son of the fellow who founded this outfit. He's Toby Mole, Florence's brother. Has Paul mentioned him to you? Toby looks virile enough there, doesn't he, but believe me, he coughed and spluttered when the Ministry had their revenge for the embarrassment we caused and downgraded us to animal feed. That fire nearly ruined Toby. He wasn't terribly nice to his sister about it, either, so I doubt she's told him about the threat Paul's posing to her remaining tranquillity.'

His head swivelled back to me. I got the impression that if anyone dared tell Toby Mole about this, it wouldn't be him. He climbed to his feet and as he did so, he suggested thoughtfully, 'Perhaps you should warn Paul. Tell him to clear off while he still can and leave us all in peace.'

I found my hands were gripping the armrests of my chair so firmly that the strain was running up my arms. I made to rise and found Duckett in my way. I subsided and sat there, looking up at him as he stood over me. I told him with what felt like remarkable steadiness, 'I would do if I knew him. But I don't. I don't know him at all. When you mentioned a friend ... I thought you meant someone else.'

I sat there flushing slightly and I wasn't remotely sure what I expected Duckett to do. I knew if he took hold of me I'd react, and loudly. He didn't look particularly close to risking it, but then I wasn't entirely sure what such a man would look like. Duckett was glaring at me, a mildly overweight businessman with a tie done up too tightly about his neck, sweating slightly because the room was hot and chewing a little on the inside of a lip.

After a breathless moment he wondered quietly, 'I can't help asking myself what's in this for you?'

'Nothing,' I replied. 'Nothing at all. Because I don't know him. Now I'd really better get on, if you don't mind. I only stopped in because I saw your name on the sign and I wanted to ask you about my case.'

It wasn't a terribly good idea to remind him of his lie, but it was the only excuse I had. His jaw tightened. For a moment I thought he really was going to act upon it. Then, suddenly, he stepped back, nodding vigorously, and made a gracious gesture that invited me to rise. 'Absolutely,' he said. 'I quite understand. Nothing more to be said, is there? Let me show you out.'

And then I was bustling through the office and past the curious women, still clutching my packet of sandwiches, and he was opening the door for me onto the deafening roar of a busy docklands. The wide flagstones were shining silver. I was about ten yards away when he called my name.

He made me turn while every instinct told me to keep walking, to run, even, if that got me away from him. Instead, ludicrous civility made me dither, retreating more slowly with each backwards step while he strode out of his office building in the manner of one who was just meaning to share a private aside. Reaching me and bending closer as if anyone was likely to even see, let alone overhear, he said on a conspiratorial undertone, 'I know Abbey is lurking up there and I know now that you're the woman to help me find him.'

I baulked. He came with me. We were yards from the rank of three or so reclaimed army wagons that were now doing service as delivery vehicles to the local feed merchants. They bore the company name *Abbey, Mole & Duckett Ltd.* and positively oozed resentment for the enforced reduction in the scale of their business. They were parked with their noses towards the sheer drop of the kerb into the basin. The towering hulk of the nearer, undamaged warehouse behind him and the crowd of decaying boats behind me waiting for their turn in a dry dock made this feel, suddenly, like a very private spot. He'd planned this. I really was a fool for coming here.

Duckett's temper was suddenly quivering. He seemed powerful out here. Braced beneath the padding of too many boardroom lunches. 'I know he's up there. I know he is because he's acted with his usual tomfoolery and thought nothing of harvesting food from honest folks' gardens and thereby repeated his mistakes that got us all into this mess in the first place. He can't live off stolen beans. He's done it because he knows a few robbed potatoes will save his hostess from having to betray her dinner guest by suddenly trying to buy double her usual rations. I presumed at first that Florence herself was that woman – Don't do it.' This was as it occurred to me that I might just walk away. It was a mistake. I couldn't. I hadn't got the confidence when I knew it would only escalate this scene to the point where he would feel obliged to lay a hand upon me purely for the sake of forcing me to listen while he said his piece.

Instead, his sharp command jolted me into taking an involuntary step the other way into the shade of the last delivery lorry. He continued as if nothing had happened. 'I know I was mistaken about poor Florence. I realised it as soon as I saw her face, poor woman. She's worn and wretched and she wouldn't have him back now and she wouldn't betray me. But you ...? Did you really think no one would notice the uncanny timing in your sudden enthusiasm for the company of his wife? Or the fact that your little cottage garden has conveniently escaped the ravages of thievery? Or your recent interest in the condition of his old house?'

A smile came and went on his thin lips when he saw the shock run through me and settle in the grip my hands had on that poor packet of sandwiches. He admitted, 'I saw you when you were choosing the hotel for your lunch. You're young. You're at that impressionable age when any man who can spin a tale of injustice is going to win your heart. Did you know him before you came here or did he befriend you on your first day?'

'He didn't,' I gasped. 'You've got it all wrong. Someone else did. I mean—'

'Keep your voice down. And step back out of the lee of the lorry here and tell me what you see.'

The slight movement of his hand towards me made my feet do what my mind couldn't. And I saw the span of his warehouses, the malthouse that toasted the grains and the damaged warehouse beyond. I swallowed my nerves, found my courage and suggested hoarsely, 'Your business.'

I think the defiant lift of my chin amused him. I was an ordinary woman standing before him in slacks and a blouse and to anyone passing this would have looked like a swift meeting between an authoritative company director and his junior secretary away from the wagging ears of her superiors. He laughed. 'Clever girl. My business. And I suppose Florence's business and you can tell your man I intend to keep it that way. It's her name on the wall now, not Paul's. I only allowed that man onto the board when she married him as a grudging favour to an old friend. He lost his stake when he went to prison. She bought a small portion back through her brother just as soon as she could and we intend to keep it that way. The dividend pays a kind of pension to her and I haven't spent all this time rebuilding my good name, only to have him destroy it a second time. So when you see Paul later – and I know you will – you're going to tell your man of our meeting today and then you'll—'

That amusement deepened when I flinched after he shifted a fraction closer. Eyebrows lifted. 'What are you frightened of, Miss Sutton?' he asked silkily. 'No one's touching you.'

He was enjoying this.

He thought I deserved this for launching into a sordid affair with a corrupt married man. It burned my pride. Unexpectedly, I felt my resolve rise. I stood a little taller so that there was only an inch's difference between our heights. I demanded icily, 'You know my name and I should like to know how you learned it. Did you bully it out of that poor woman yesterday before you pitched up at my cottage, only to have the misfortune of finding a policeman already there? Or did you have to go back later and beat her into telling you, since you didn't find any clues in my suitcase? Doesn't it even occur to you to wonder why my case was there in the

Manor? I was going away again, until you took my things and made it impossible.'

Suddenly, he was looking at me strangely. As if I repulsed him. His tone demolished mine as he snarled nastily, 'I haven't bullied anyone. Florence is a good friend and she's as angry as I am. When you met me on the stairs yesterday, I thought I'd just had a brush with some little woman of all work. But Florence told me who you were. You were probably hiding him there. And now I'm treating this nonsense about your suitcase as a sign he sent you here today to pursue a pathetic attempt to incriminate me in some imaginary crime. Is this the best shot he has? Really?'

His anger wasn't the part that made me press the heel of my hand against my brow. The sense of his words was working like needles in my mind. My thoughts were jarring. I had to fix myself to something sure and solid by putting out my other hand against the wing of the nearby lorry. Finally I formulated the language to make sense out of what had shaken me. 'She *told* you to come after me?'

Duckett was smiling at the sudden strain on my lips. He didn't quite understand how deep it ran, but it was enough for him. I watched him smirk as he tasted victory and then heard him add, 'You clearly don't know what you're doing, but I do. You can tell your man from me that he can leave that woman alone. I mentioned betrayal and this is it. It's yours. You're going to find him for me and when you do, before you tell him anything, you're going to look into his eyes and remind yourself that any man who has taken human life is never quite the same again.'

I was shaking my head as though that would be enough to fend off his obsession. He didn't care. His gaze passed beyond me. I saw him give a slight nod of encouragement for me to do the same. I turned my head.

And jerked sharply back against the solid anchorage of the vehicle. The pale line that marked the point where the wharf dropped away into oily water was no more than half a yard from my heel. He'd been steering me to this all along. My fingers clutched at the rim of the windscreen. The heel of my right hand, which was still grasping its silly little parcel, rammed itself against the arch of the front wheel. Beside me, something bobbed on the filthy surface. A piece of rubbish, some jetsam, it didn't matter what. It wallowed nauseatingly in a rainbow of grease.

Duckett spoke from a clearance of a yard or two, his voice oily like the water and very precisely devoid of any specific threat. He left nothing to chance, this man. 'Do be careful. I told you the docklands were dangerous. If you fell in now, you'd be under without anyone even hearing the splash.'

I knew he was doing it to frighten me. I knew he hadn't made so much as a move to touch me. The problem for me lay in the fact that my knowing this didn't make the blindest bit of difference to my dread of it.

The wheel arch held me secure on solid ground, away from the water's edge. The fragile handhold on that metal rim gave me strength. With my eyes fixed upon the nasty floating debris, I asked with cold curiosity, 'What precisely is it that you expect me to do for you?'

He laughed. 'Nothing.' He really wasn't intending to leave

me with anything I might repeat as a quotation. 'You're the one who walked into my office and since I presume you've finished here, you'll now scurry off to your man. Who knows if I'll happen to follow along, for your safety, you know? Now off you go.'

He stepped around me in an arc with his arm outstretched as though he were manfully shielding an excitable woman from an unfortunate dip. With an effort, I released my grip on the lorry. Later I would find score lines cut by edged metal on the insides of my fingers.

He said, 'Go on. I've got work to do.'

When I took a few unsteady steps, I faltered, stopping before I lost my bearings and veered either into the lorry or the inky depths all of my own volition. I heard him behind adding a cheerful prompt of, 'Shoo.'

I turned my head and saw him give a little waggle of his hands as if he were herding a stray pigeon. He was smiling again.

I went.

Chapter 20

As I passed the last warehouse at the other end of the basin I believe a hoist slipped its load barely ten yards away but I didn't really notice. It was proof that Duckett hadn't been lying about the dangers of the docks, but the ensuing swearing and rushing hardly registered. I was quite preoccupied enough by the shadow I had gained that followed me step for step from a distance of about half a warehouse away. And the hope of one thing and one thing only. That the lateness of my return wouldn't cost me the sanctuary of the car.

It wouldn't. There he was. Richard was much closer than the distant parked car, which was still two streets and a junction away. I thought he must have just emerged from the passage between the employment exchange and the prison because he seemed to be hesitating on the corner there, getting his bearings. I half-lifted my hand but he didn't see me with a steady line of traffic between us. Now he was walking inland towards the turn onto that shopping street where his car waited. He was going at a leisurely pace, completely at his ease, and there was no sign of a limp or stiffness or anything. I hadn't noticed before but he had added the staple urban gentleman's accessory; a stylishly brimmed hat. He wore it tilted low over his eyes and the combination of it and his clothes suited his frame so well they looked like camouflage – a screen of conventional good looks for the real man, with all the restrained physicality I thought he kept in hand. I couldn't have been more relieved to see him and yet, for a moment, one insanely complicated moment tied up in the rush of needing his help, I almost turned the other way.

But I didn't. I scurried across the road with barely a pause for a gap in the traffic and, before I knew it, had my hand under his arm at the elbow. It was selfish and weak and, after all my stern words about independence and responsibility, I hated myself for it, but I did it anyway.

His voice showed mild surprise. 'Why hullo. Were you waiting for me?' My smile must have faltered and strayed a little because he followed my gaze to look back between us. The brim of his hat was casting a line of shade across his eyes and over the bridge of his nose, but I didn't think that he saw my tail on the far side of the road as it ducked out of sight behind some other pedestrians. Instead his eyes passed back to mine and onwards to the street ahead with perfect indifference. Then we were walking past a water-bottling plant through still air that was thick with vehicle fumes and I was saying something about seeing the sign to the barracks at the same time that his free hand was closing over my nerveless fingers and he was saying with that tone of his that bordered on a laugh, 'You truly haven't grasped the full ugly truth about the family you've been fraternising with lately, have you? I wasn't visiting the barracks and even if I were required to present myself at my old regimental HQ, it wouldn't be here. My official base was always Bristol. No,' he added. 'I was visiting my uncle at the prison.'

He let his good-humoured frankness shock me – because, despite all his earlier determination to keep me at an arm's length, he had never tried to make a secret of simple things like the wholesale ruination of his family – then he was saying quietly, 'Your hand is cold.' And I was thinking that it was more than cold; it was shaking, and I was gently withdrawing my fingers from beneath his because I still needed to practise concealment after all, albeit temporarily, and I was pressing the packet of sandwiches into his hands instead.

While he was distracted by investigating what I had given him, which by his expression he must have been presuming was something deeply strange, I confessed in a tone impressively devoid of melodrama, 'I haven't paid my visit to the hospital yet. I'm afraid I've just done something very silly, but I'll tell you the details later if I may.' And then, belatedly, added doubtfully, 'Did you really just say *prison?*'

I didn't get a response immediately. I had automatically turned to check that I still had a shadow, which indeed I had. Duckett was currently skipping across the road on the heels of a delivery man pushing a handcart. Whereas Richard was entirely absorbed by the surprise of my parcel. His eyebrows rose a fraction as he established the nature of the contents, then he wrapped the whole lot up again, cast a brief glance down at my face that was hard to read and then finally continued in that same relaxed manner to say, 'I did. I think I told you that my uncle's estate had been sold well ahead of the recent decision about ours. Well, this is why. He's presently enjoying a nice tidy prison term for blithely committing fraud and handling stolen goods with the additional offence of trying, with touching optimism, to get himself and his wife out of the country and holed up in a clinic in Switzerland. The hasty sale of his estate was meant to pay for it all, but all it did was alert the police to his plan of escape and give weight to that enchantingly romantic myth that John left behind a hoard of unclaimed spoils. The gossip-mongers think that Uncle William was making off with lost riches and they won't give up the hunt for them now. You'll have noticed,' he confided a shade less lightly, 'that I didn't tell my father where I was going today.'

He waited for me to give a faint nod, then he added soberly, 'Father last saw his brother four weeks ago when my uncle was finally sent down and, to be honest, I think it'll be a while before my father's ready to face it. It was for my uncle's sake that we've been observing a kind of voluntary exile since March anyway. I'm sure you've heard the usual slurs about my father shirking his duties in the estate, but in this case it truly was a ... necessity that we both should have stayed away from the Manor. It was the only way to ensure a seamless trial.'

I thought he was referring to its proximity to the home of Matthew Croft, who must, I realised now, have been one of the main witnesses for his uncle's prosecution. No wonder Richard had reacted as he had when one small slip from me had dragged him back, after all that effort to keep clear and all the plans he must have made for his father's quiet return.

Then he was adding with unnecessary carelessness, 'Anyway, I suppose I'm just grateful that my father *could* come back and they dropped the charges for my uncle that would have carried a more brutal penalty. There were others that were harder to digest, believe me, to do with the loss of life from that time.'

For all his plain manner of telling me this, it was impossible to ignore how close this ran to the concerns I'd levied earlier about his proximity as a brother to the madness of John's choices and the shadows this return home might be leaving upon him now. And he'd only come back at all because of that one selfish impulse of mine to reach out for the familiar comfort of that ringing telephone.

I had to say, 'I'm sorry, Richard. I had no idea your uncle was involved too. I suppose it must become a bitter kind of legacy – like a stain on your genetic heritage – to learn that your blood has done things that don't bear scrutiny in the light of day. But you know it isn't true. You share their name but this isn't a debt you have to shoulder. I don't believe a person can inherit a relative's wrong-doings any more than you could inherit their greatness of mind. You'd still be you even if the infamy ran the other way and your uncle were a great inventor or something.'

In the midst of saying that, I turned my head to check behind and, seeing nothing, turned back to catch another of those startlingly intense glances that he couldn't quite smother quickly enough. I faltered, choked back some fresh nonsense and instead said in a sheepish rush, 'I'm so sorry. That sounded like I was labelling you an idiot, didn't it? I do seem to be very good at saying the wrong thing. I'm just glad that for once I stopped before I managed to run on into saying something truly unforgiveable such as somehow making you personally liable for every act of violence ever conceived by anyone – Langton or otherwise – purely because of your profession. That's the sort of thing you're coming to expect from me, isn't it?'

He was suppressing a smile. 'I should say,' he confided gently, 'that you're actually very good at saying exactly the right thing. More than you know.'

We were at the junction with the shopping street but we weren't turning left to reclaim the car. Richard was resuming my aborted attempt to visit my cousin. He stopped at the tip of the pavement and scanned left and right and behind for traffic. I felt sure he must see Duckett dodging just out of sight into a doorway but he didn't. Richard was stepping out with me across the road and telling me, 'But speaking of my profession, you should know that, actually, there is something of a debt to pay, albeit of a lighter kind. My father told you, I think, that my regiment was disbanded in North Africa and that other officers got sent to new commands while I was recalled to undertake work of a different nature. The simple truth is that my father's name carries its own weight at Whitehall, and did so long before my brother's activities became known. It seems to amuse the powers that be to have someone on the books who isn't tied to any particular regiment, and at the moment that man is me. It's my purgatory and my escape. You might say I'm surplus to requirements; an odd-job man, if you like. And, notwithstanding the brief hiatus of my injury, you might slightly less jokingly call me a free agent. Which admittedly has its advantages at times like this when I've had to drop everything and hightail it to the country.'

I abandoned my effort to find Duckett again and looked up at him. 'You're a spy?'

'No, sorry, I didn't mean to imply that kind of agent.'

'An assassin?'

'For all your brave words, you're not entirely convinced that I'm not a shadow of my kin, are you?' He was mocking me. 'But in this instance, I promise, it's really not the case. Admittedly the work is hands-on enough to warrant the term 'grisly' every once in a while, but in the main it is only nice and safely – and utterly tediously – administrative. My last job involved chasing down stores that had been looted during the decommissioning of the old pier at Weston-super-Mare. They turned out to be crates of boots. You get the idea.'

I did get the idea. I had the idea that purgatory was the word. I thought his idea of responsibility must go a very long way and it made my clumsy mutterings about the sort of man who would choose such a life all the more cruel, suspecting as I did now that soldiering was for him the single balance through which he could restore the burden of his brother's guilt and his uncle's, and perhaps even his father's. I thought he underestimated the simple power of his own nature as the point from which everything about him was measured. And I doubted very much that the reality of his work matched the easy way he'd described it. I suspected that in truth this man must be deeply respected by his superiors since they'd chosen to retain him when they might have easily forced him into retirement after his hospital stay. And it was testament to his tenacity that he hadn't simply asked for it.

I couldn't see Duckett and we were crossing Parliament Street to where the imposing frontage of the hospital waited on the other side. I couldn't see the lady with the broom any more either but her revelations about Danny and that house hung unhealthily in the air. So did John Langton's name once again.

Richard must have noticed my hesitation. 'What is it?'

I shook my head. Then I saw that his eyes had found the name sign for the street and saw that it meant something to him too. I saw his mouth tighten. We were already walking in through the hospital gates towards the open-sided porch that ensured ambulances could unload straight into the hospital in the dry. It was quite pretty in a utilitarian sort of way, with rounded arches above brick pillars and hard shadows cast by the fierce afternoon light. A nurse was smoking in the far corner on a rest between rounds on her ward. The hunger with which she was drawing on her stubby cigarette did not inspire confidence.

'Stay a minute, would you?' His voice brought me to a halt beneath the pillars. I turned back to find that Richard had propped his shoulder against the second in the line and was in the process of opening his sandwiches. I allowed him the peace in which to enjoy his first bite. I turned away as the nurse stamped on her cigarette butt and went back inside, braced and ready for the next round. A small herd of people ambled across the car park and past us. A cab disgorged its passengers and departed again. Another member of the hospital staff was lighting a cigarette at the far end of the porch. The scent was sharp and the first faint plume drifted past me into the sunlight. The match went spinning to the ground.

It was then that I heard Richard say gently behind, 'Tell me, has that very silly thing you've done happened to run to the discovery that Abbey is out?'

It drew me round to face him as he had intended. He read the answer in my parted lips. Amusement touched the corners of his. 'Don't look so guilty. My uncle told me. Apparently the man is an excellent chess player and helped Uncle William while away the hours between sessions in court.'

I was wondering if this was the moment I was supposed to tell him about Duckett. Only I didn't quite dare to because although that man was nowhere to be seen, I couldn't quite believe that we'd lost him and I didn't remotely want to put Richard in the position of thinking he was required to do something about it. I was afraid he'd think I wanted find out what that something might be and I really didn't want to learn I was the sort of woman who would spend long hours telling a man just how much she detested violence, only to enjoy the first opportunity that came along to incite it. And I didn't expect it from him anyway. I expected it from Duckett. It was all very tangled and still I couldn't find Duckett; not on the road behind, not in the line of parked cars before the hospital and certainly not in the gloom within the double doors inside.

Richard's voice brought my attention sharply back again.

He had finished his sandwiches and remarked, 'You know, I've noticed something else about you just now that I've been suspecting for some little time.'

He had apparently been observing me with the same intensity that I'd been reserving for my hunt for Duckett. In my head was the painful impulse to wonder what my face had betrayed now, but I managed a creditably nonchalant, 'Oh yes?'

'Yes.' Then Richard was standing up from his lean against the wall and patting his pockets. 'Have you a pen to hand, by the way?'

I showed him empty hands. 'No handbag.'

He ignored that. He produced a small stub of a pencil from the inside pocket of his suit jacket. Then he propped himself against his pillar again, smoothed the brown paper wrapping from his lunch against the palm of his hand and finally wrote a few lines. Then he paused and lifted his head a little so that the brim of his hat wasn't screening his eyes. He continued what he'd begun to say before. 'For example,' he said, 'you've told me how you came to be sent here, but you haven't told me what you were intending to do before your father changed your plans.'

I hid my gaze by turning my head to the small area of shrubbery beyond the last pillar, where the nurses took the air between rounds. The greenery was presently occupied by a quantity of sparrows who seemed to have plenty to chat about. I told them, 'That's because I'll feel foolish.'

Richard's voice brought my gaze firmly back to his face. By contrast to me, he was utterly at ease and, it seemed, just passing the time while he wrote his letter. 'Humour me,' he said.

I found I'd folded my arms defensively across my chest and made myself slide my hands into trouser pockets instead. This was only the truth, after all.

I confessed, 'I thought I might find a job as an assistant, or something. Or perhaps find work as a mannequin if that's not setting too much store on what amounts to a very ordinary figure.'

I smiled in a tight-lipped sort of way to show I didn't require him to deliver instant compliments upon my figure and reclined against my own pillar with my hands still thrust into deep trouser pockets in an attempt to find my own degree of ease. He didn't compliment me. He only asked, 'You like clothes?'

My answer was a question for him. 'Do you know that during the early days of the war they tried to dress everyone in uniform? We all needed something that would plug the gap in the clothing shortages and they thought it would give the women and the men in non-fighting roles a sense of their importance. Then they realised that it would be terrible for morale because it was steadily turning all the streets of London into a vision of utilitarian hell. It was, in its own small way, I think, a close-run thing, like the war itself. They nearly smothered the very idea of British colour that people like you were fighting for. But just in the nick of time they lurched into the other direction and started dressing women in bright, garish prints instead. Clothes fascinate me.' My eyes were narrowed against the glare that was being cast from the windscreens in the car park.

'That explains why you were so upset when your suitcase was taken from you.'

'Yes,' I agreed before adding dryly, 'and also the fact that it left me without the power to even change my petticoat.'

'Where would you have worked?'

His question was rather precise. A wasp drifted near my nose and I steered it away with a lazy hand.

'Emily ...?' The prompt was made on a cautionary note.

I gave in. This point clearly mattered. I conceded, 'Very well, although why I should have to say it when I'm pretty certain you've guessed already. I wanted to work abroad. In Paris, in fact, where the fashion houses are, even though I know the city itself is still recovering after the Occupation and I knew it was beyond me to go there alone. So, in a way, I was relieved when Dad started ranting and my mother mentioned Phyllis. Dad latched upon aged spinsters and improving trips to the country and I thought, why not? I had the idea that I might be able to persuade Phyllis to take me along on her next trip, now that the embargo on foreign travel has been lifted. That's what my savings were going to be for – to pay my way. Pathetic, isn't it?'

'Not really.' He was surveying me beneath the brim of his hat. Then he added, 'And I notice you said there that you *were going* rather than *are*. You *were* going to pay your way. But we'll talk about why that should be later. For now I could bear to hear more about this man of yours.'

This, suddenly, was rather too close to the conversation with Duckett. The doubt must have shown on my face or in the sharp movement of my body. He only tilted his head so that his face was cast into shade as he carefully read through what he had written, considered it for a moment and then added a few extra words. He lifted his eyes to mine. 'I mean, this man your father is convinced you're running away from.'

I laughed in a nervous sort of away and turned my head aside again. 'You do pay rather too much attention for comfort, don't you?'

He waited for me to brave meeting his gaze once more. It took me a while. My arms were wrapped about me again, but this time less defensively and more for comfort. I told him, 'He's that friend of my brother's with the Sunbeam; the one who taught me to drive. He was in the RAF so liked to live life to the full, naturally. I was barely seventeen and he was only a few years older. He was charismatic and had been plucked from his quiet life in Hereford to face terrors that belonged to another world. You know how the RAF boys lived. The pressure of it all. He told me how unprepared he was and inexperienced and utterly, bewilderingly petrified, but he was determined to do his duty anyway.'

'*Was?*' It was said quickly. A sharpening of concentration, as if I'd finally explained every single one of my oddities.

'No,' I corrected him hastily. 'No, I mean after four weeks of dancing and gentle courting, I caught him spinning the same tale of woe to the girl who lived two doors down from my aunt's house. She was more immediately expressive with her sympathy than I was willing to be.'

I stopped. This was even more embarrassing than I'd thought.

'Oh?' Relief made him laugh. And then he said it again,

rather more soberly, when he realised what I meant. 'Oh, I see. You mean it was a *line?*'

'It's not quite the tragic history I ought to have, is it,' I confirmed wryly, 'given the fuss I make about grieving for the war? I was too young to serve; I abandoned the only material act of heroism I ever had to make because I didn't care for lessons when they proved to be nothing more than a daily study of the ways and means of providing a distraction to the younger children whenever the sirens went off. I didn't lose a family member to either the Blitz or the fighting; and finally the man I courted was merely a little overly keen to proceed to bed ...'

He didn't reply and after a moment I returned my gaze to the tiny stone I was turning beneath my toe. Feeling a certain amount of bemusement at the ease with which this was slipping out, I told him, 'The truth is, the worst that happened to me is that I had a brush with that easy tale about needing to snatch happiness today because the world might be gone tomorrow. And the poor man did actually have to fly and every single thing he said was absolutely true, and given the average lifespan of the RAF boys I can see why there was a sense of urgency for him and serious courting wasn't really part of his plan. But anyway,' I suddenly grew bold. I lifted my head. 'The point where Dad decided that I needed a bit of a stern lesson on maturity was this: apparently my brother's friend's plan does now incorporate scope for serious courting and I'm supposed to be devastated that she isn't me. Dad, of course, doesn't entirely know that marriage wasn't the man's intention before – he just thinks it fizzled out because

I was too young, with the net result that Dad remains stead-fast in his complacent hope that this visit here will give me a swift reminder that it's time I gave up mooning over a childish love and knuckled down to the real nitty-gritty of life as a grown woman.'

Exasperation was making me smile. Richard was watching me with his hand poised in the midst of putting away his pencil. 'To be honest,' I told him plainly, 'The only part I'm devastated about is the part where everyone thinks that a man's marriage is why I wanted to come away. I'm glad that he's getting married. He was young before and at war. It's right that everything should be different for him now. Why does it need to have anything to do with me?'

Richard wasn't sharing my amusement. Suddenly this conversation wasn't cringingly embarrassing. It was too excru-ciatingly probing to be borne. I'd never have told anyone else this. Because I'd never have really wanted them to know. They'd have only contradicted me and told me that I'll see my way out of this tangle of irritation and sympathetic understanding once I'd learned a little more about the ways of the world. But I knew all about the ways of the world. I might not have fought or lost or had great sacrifices snatched from me by the life-altering horrors of the war, but I had watched while all that awfulness dropped from the skies overhead and crawled insidiously through the rubble beneath. I knew precisely what war was. I turned away at random.

And caught the sudden sharp blur as the person at the end of the row pitched away their cigarette and moved to light another one. It wasn't a nurse and it made a mockery of the watch I'd been keeping on the road. It was Duckett and he was scowling at me from barely three yards away.

I span on my heel back to Richard to find my heart beating high in my chest and that my movement had brought me very close to him. My eyes were already straying back over my shoulder at that figure at the end of the row when I framed my fright around a whisper of Richard's name. His proper name, that is. The one he wanted me to use.

But he was already speaking over me. I thought, in fact, that he was oblivious. He was absorbed by the task of carefully folding his note into a very neat square. With his eyes and hands thoroughly occupied, he asked, 'Do you want to know what I think? I think I know now what you meant when you said earlier that you always seem to get things so wrong. I think your father and this man and various other people have taught you that. They've somehow got the absurd idea that you need to be told you are this fragile, impressionable young thing ready to be swayed by every fresh, impulsive bit of nonsense unless someone more experienced directs you onto a firmer path. And yet you don't really believe it, do you? Your personality is fully formed. You keep giving me glimpses of the real determination that lies within. This is the discovery I mentioned just now. You give the impression of being in the habit of finding compromise wherever your wishes run the risk of directly offending someone else's. But I've also noticed that you'll only compromise so far. Your decisions about leaving school, coming here and the lunch you made yesterday are perfect cases in point.'

I stopped worrying about Duckett for a moment and

blinked a shade doubtfully. 'The lunch I made for you yesterday?'

'Absolutely. After I'd demanded silence from you and all but joined the ranks of the people who will persist in goading you into a sense of guilt when you haven't actually done anything wrong, you would have been fully within your rights to have been appallingly rude to me. In fact, if you'd told anyone about it, I have absolutely no doubt that they would have given you a lecture on standing up for yourself more. But why should you and what would it have achieved anyway? Personally, as one of those people who has seen quite enough strutting and posturing for the sake of pride on the stage of war and in that particular instance truly, truly appreciated the simple kindness of an easy lunch ...' He lifted his hand to add today's sandwich wrapper to the list. 'I cannot comprehend why anyone would wish to teach you that empathy is the weakness of a malleable mind and you'll only be improved once you've been hardened into our rather more jaded worldliness.'

I was gaping at him.

'And,' he added on a rougher note, quite as if this debate angered him, 'to return to the point at hand, you couldn't love a man like your brother's friend anyway, because whilst his actions were perfectly comprehensible, they weren't exactly right, were they? And coming from you that's about as severe a judgement as they come because I think you're willing to do anything for pretty much everyone, just so long as they're nice.'

The shock of discovering that Duckett was barely yards

away became almost nothing while my mind shattered and reformed on a nonsensical irritation at the sudden compliment. Particularly when it came at the end of an intensive study of the balance of strength and weakness concealed within my character. Strain and helplessness, and perhaps an underlying sense of how the threat of that other man was still making me crowd against Richard, made me rush to contradict.

I snapped crossly, 'I don't love everyone. I think I might love you. And what's your story, anyway?' Then, before it had even really dawned on me how I'd jumbled his words in my head and what I'd accidentally confessed, the presence of Duckett reasserted itself and I straightened and shook my head hastily. 'No, sorry, don't answer that. Richard—'

I was instinctively craving the security of contact again. My right shoulder was brushing against the warmth of him while my head turned, seeking Duckett once more. I was distracted from my search by the shock of finding that Richard's hand – his right hand – had lifted to find mine and closed upon it. I hadn't realised that my fingers were gripping his suit. His touch drew my unsteady gaze because his hand was gently but firmly detaching mine from the safe anchorage of his lapel.

While he did so, his voice told me with quiet simplicity, 'I've mentioned my story before. And like your RAF man's tale of woe, it doesn't really deserve your sympathy either. I met Lady Sarah at a London parade and about six months later the affair naturally progressed to an engagement. Then I was suddenly injured in a maddeningly unnecessary little spat on the Strand. It was a brush with a crooked youth who'd decided he didn't like the questions I'd been asking his employer and confronted me about it five miles or so later across town. I suppose the drama of it made me more interesting; heaven knows, I appreciated the idea of her support at that time. But then the fever passed and, as it turned out, our idea of what we wanted from each other didn't survive the treatment either. For reasons I'll tell you about some other time, I think she got carried away by the idea of playing the elegant socialite tending to the wounded veteran. She might have found the act easier if I had been more willing to retain a limp.'

I was spellbound by the grip he still had on my hand. I also wasn't sure I liked very much to be told he'd been set to marry a titled heiress. Daughters of retiring antiques dealers didn't tend to compare. And I didn't know either why he should get to retain certain parts of himself when I'd been required to share my whole embarrassment and have it cripplingly dissected. I found I was gnawing on my lower lip. I forced myself to release it and discovered that the subject had already been dismissed and he was moving on to the next question at hand.

It began by changing his hold on me. It had felt for a moment like rejection again, but now it adjusted to become something rather more certain. My hand was laid palm to palm in his grip and quite naturally turned to rest with its back against his chest. It meant I was very close to him. Then he bent his head towards my ear and said in quite a different tone of voice, 'Now, what do you say – shall we do what we came here for and try our hand at springing your cousin? If you can begin the arduous process of enacting her rescue, I'll go and fetch the car. Can you hold your own for about ten minutes?'

His manner was easier now, brisk, as though some brutal pitfall had proved to be shallower than he had thought and had been overcome. Whereas the one set by Duckett was yawning wide before me. I was about to give an urgent shake of my head, only suddenly I had the surprise of realising a coarse edge of something crisp had long been pressed between our hands and now its presence was being compounded by the crush as his fingers closed mine over it. It checked me. I couldn't open my hand to see because he still held me, but beneath the steadiness of his grip, my skin was able to deduce the texture was of stiff, folded paper. At the moment that I lifted my head to convey a query with a look, his free arm closed very briefly about me to draw me tighter against him.

The shock of his sudden gift of reassurance stilled my heart. Then he said clearly, 'Give this note to Duckett for me, would you? I think he's danced about behind that pillar eavesdropping on a gentle summary of our credentials for long enough.'

Then he let me go. He left me. I twisted tottering, abandoned, desolate and bewildered to meet Duckett as he raced forwards to take Richard's place.

I let the smaller man snatch the note from my unresisting fingers.

Duckett read the note for a moment, red-rimmed eyes scanning a few short lines and then again as he had to check he'd understood their meaning. He was sweating. A clammy sheen greased his neck and his forehead. His gaze snapped to my face. 'I suppose you thought it clever to let me think you were on your own. He was there at the waterside, was he, listening? And where does Abbey fit in to all this, eh?'

I saw the pallor set in as he worked it out for himself. A spasm passed across his face. 'Fine,' he said. 'That's fine.'

I put frozen, trembling fingers up to my mouth. I found I was laughing through my hand when it finally dawned on me what Richard had done.

This was because my distress in the car earlier had been a product of my hardest past. I'd lived through the time when unilateral decisions really had been made for me and people like me for the sake of managing a danger that ran far beyond the scope of my usual misunderstandings. Powerlessness had been one of the most fundamental symptoms of war and Richard's attempt to put me on the train had felt like that. But this wasn't the same. Here, his quiet insistence as he'd led me into talking about myself; the careful drawing of my gaze perpetually away from that threatening presence; the gentle use of my feelings for him to break down my reserve enough to let me speak. These were all the weapons he had needed to nudge me carefully, methodically into demolishing every single falsehood Duckett had formed about me. Richard must have seen me as I'd passed the prison wall on my way to the docks. He must have followed me and overheard our scene by the liveried vehicles, and later he must have engineered the opportunity to intercept me. This was a rescue without pride, without wading in like an avenging warrior. I'd fretted about drawing him into interceding, as if there would be a danger of falling into an excess of aggression, but there had never been any danger to either of us here. It wasn't in his nature to stand aside when he might act, but he had tried very hard to give me room to save myself. It was peace and it was a mark of kindness, and, perhaps, a mark of what he thought of me too.

I was still laughing when Duckett barged past in a fury and stormed away.

Chapter 21

Phyllis looked dreadful. Her right wrist was clad in plaster of Paris, she had a crutch under her left arm because her ankle was unbearably swollen and she'd apparently had to use her chin as a brake on the surface of the lane. She would never have been able to cope at home on her own, but her gratitude for our rescue did not remotely lead her to overlook the fact she was being cast as my sensible chaperone again so that we could spend the night at the Manor. Nor did it prevent her from remarking fussily that whilst she had expected me to help myself to the contents of her garden during the two days of my stay, she hadn't quite expected me to deplete her future harvest quite so much.

But the garden wasn't actually the victim of my greed or Richard's pillaging expedition. We'd been hit by the vegetable thief. And that wasn't the only jolt that waited for me there, nor was it the last addition to the long list of reasons why I should be feeling so glad we'd decided she and I wouldn't be spending tonight at the cottage. The real concern was that the steady and wearying fussing from my usually indomitable cousin didn't stop at the garden. It followed us over the threshold and up the stairs. Then she opened the door to the bedroom that had formerly been her mother's, and my concern bloomed into full-blown alarm.

I had never really thought before to notice how strange it was that while my recently deceased aunt had given over so much space in her house to treasures and relics from the past, she hadn't seen fit to also make room for family photographs. As it turned out, she hadn't needed to make space for them. Because they were all amassed in her bedroom. People and faces crowded about on every wall and surface, watching and judging every move.

Phyllis seemed oblivious. She was rummaging in drawers supervised by sixty or so ancestors who glowered stiffly beneath Victorian headgear in artful soft focus. It was probable that my aunt had enjoyed the company of these men and women in the same way that she had collected oriental vases, but for Phyllis I thought it a dangerous shrine to time. It made me afraid that a part of Phyllis – the part of her that was a single woman of an age where she already felt it necessary to dub a man 'young' just so that she could secretly like him – was only waiting for the time to come when a stereotype of age and spinsterhood could truly be assumed as her identity and she could begin to add her own collection to the rooms of this house. She was trying it on for size now in this bedroom and I thought vehemently that she shouldn't be because she had always been my inspiring heroine and age had no business defining any woman, unmarried or not; but now I saw she had already added the portraits of her wartime friends to this company of bygone faces and I wondered what had happened to her. And how much it had to do with Danny.

On that basis it was hardly surprising that I practically galloped her through the process of selecting clothes and hurried away with her case down the stairs and back to the glorious, vibrant present. Richard had left us in peace and I found him outside by his car, where the late afternoon shadow was creeping down from the high valley ridge. He lifted his head as I tripped carelessly out of the garden gate. He rose from his lean against his car and turned to meet me. He was looking relaxed in that way people have when the warmth in every memory passes electrifyingly across the space between you, and yet from the expression of his mouth no one would think anything had changed. It was the first time I'd had the chance to look at him properly since he had returned after collecting his car. I faltered with a hand on the scorching metal bonnet and murmured something nonsensical. His reply was similarly ordinary. For the moment nothing else needed to be said.

Then Phyllis crashed out of her house, looking for all the world like a thirty-year-old playing a mad old hermit delivering curses and I hurried away to wrestle with the heavy bolts on her door. It was quite laughable, really, that when we finally left the insanity of her house and arrived at that great cavernous mausoleum, the Manor, I found it to be the gloriously living embodiment of homely comfort.

The Colonel was glowing pink and thoroughly at his ease at the kitchen table and chatting with Mr and Mrs Winstone over a small brandy and apparently delighted to be told he had two guests for the night, particularly when I was able to take over Mrs Winstone's role of rattling about in his oven. She passed over command to me like it was the changing of the guard and when she bustled her husband into his coat and away some fifteen minutes later I learned that the feeling was true in more ways than one. The salute and witticism Mr Winstone sketched at the kitchen door as he left proved that he had previously served in the military as the Colonel's driver and it was the Colonel who had retained him afterwards and brought him into the sphere of the woman who became his wife. And also into the part of stepfather to that woman's boy.

Richard had long since taken himself quietly off on an errand into the Colonel's library, but the old man was telling Phyllis that she must remember how wayward young Danny had been in those early days, since she must have been cast as his nursemaid and given the responsibility of pulling him out of trouble. 'And Richard too, as I recall.' The Colonel said it quite proudly.

'Yes,' agreed Phyllis sharply while she adjusted her choice of chair at the kitchen table and selected another as a stool for her swollen foot. 'And they weren't terribly polite about it either. They always managed to make me feel that the two years' advantage I had on them put me in the category of being as old as the hills.'

Richard had reappeared in the kitchen doorway in time to catch his father's laugh. The brief sound came out brashly, as if the old man wasn't quite sure mirth was something he was putting in its right place. I thought this was the release of having done his duty by speaking to his tenants.

His son was saying mildly, 'I hope at least we've learned better manners now?'

It wasn't the most tactful of things to say when he ought to have been making some comment about the insignificance of the gap between their ages these days. Particularly when I turned from one counter to the next in time to catch the movement on Phyllis's face as she noticed that Danny had just passed along the tip of the garden terrace with his dog on his heels, without, it must be said, once sparing a glance for the house. She'd seen him through the window that was set into the wall beside that large dresser. I thought Danny's manner implied an unwillingness to be trapped in conversation. The Colonel thought it stemmed from the urgency of feeding the goat.

The old man turned to me and asked quite severely, 'Have you spoken to the butcher yet?'

It was a demonstration of his best strident tone – strong and dictatorial – and not a tone he had ever needed to use on me before. The roughness of it completely robbed me of an easy reply. I was just beginning to frame a clumsy excuse when Richard answered for me more smoothly. 'Of course she hasn't. She's been dancing about at my beck and call all day. I'll speak to the man myself tomorrow. How was your day, Father?'

It was a perfectly pleasant question but, instead of replying, the Colonel's eyes strayed next to the brandy bottle on the table. I believed for a moment it was a guilty confession that he had spent his afternoon retreating into companionable drunkenness with his old driver after the hard work of speaking to his tenants. But it couldn't have been because he wasn't drunk. He wasn't even close to being drunk. And he didn't look shrunken today or beaten. In this bright warm room, the old white-haired man looked just as he had when I'd left him in the sunshine that morning, and perhaps how he had hoped to be last night, only the drink had robbed him of his control. He looked now fully in command. And because of it, gave me the novel experience of thinking that this sudden loss of concentration and his earlier laughter might both be another masquerade.

Then I realised I was worrying about the wrong person. The Colonel swept this particular concern away as nonsense when he began telling Phyllis something else about Danny Hannis. He spoke smoothly and calmly and he continued telling her about it while Richard left the room again on some other duty. The Colonel told her about his patronage during the war to ensure Danny's lowly status as a farmhand hadn't sentenced him to the wastefulness of life as a swell-the-ranks kind of soldier. I had a feeling she already knew all this and didn't want to hear it now. I saw her reach for the brandy bottle, only to abandon the effort when it was just too far.

Richard hadn't left us after all. He moved quietly into the room for the sake of reaching a few more glasses down from the dresser that stood in the corner – beside the blank panels that I now knew concealed the servants' door – and poured into each a small measure of something more appropriate than brandy to serve as an aperitif. He set the bottle down and slid a glass across the counter to me, then one to Phyllis and, finally, after the briefest of hesitations, another towards his father. He carried his own back to the dresser and rested there.

Instead of conveying thanks, Phyllis twisted awkwardly in her seat to deliver an absurdly forthright beam and to observe, 'When I last saw you, Captain, you were a fresh-faced youth in your first officer's uniform. I wasn't yet established here when you came back briefly in the spring, so I didn't see you then. I was still wading about in flood water in Gloucester.'

I saw her falter as her reference to her unhappy hospital vigil over her dying mother strayed into an accidental reference to the incident behind Richard's own abrupt return home at that time. We all knew John shouldn't be mentioned here before the Colonel. And I was unhappily certain that the urgency that had driven Richard's desperate race across country to this beleaguered house must have stemmed from a stark idea of rescue far beyond the vital care that belonged to a parent grieving for the loss of a son. I'd seen a glimpse of its legacy last night in Richard's eyes when he'd had the surprise of finding his father in this kitchen with me.

I didn't know whether my cousin knew that part too but I certainly thought her slip had irritated her. She lurched into saying something else that was just as badly placed. And this time it was rather more deliberate. She remarked with an acidic edge to Richard, 'You were so optimistic when you first took your uniform. I've wondered since how it is that you should know now what soldiering is, and yet you continue to make it your career.'

'Phyllis!' The exclamation came out of me uncontrollably. I knew what she was doing. My role-model had re-emerged, and with a vengeance. She'd noticed the quiet sympathy between us. She couldn't help but notice, if Danny's opinion of my capacity for disguise was anything to go by. And on that score, I knew she had been made uncomfortable by the Colonel's insistence on talking about Danny and I thought this was her deflection of it. So, while I accepted that she believed she was acting here as a kind of spokesperson for my welfare, I was wishing passionately that she wouldn't do it in this state of mind. Particularly not when she was trespassing so horribly close on doubts I had similarly expressed myself and not yet had the chance to soften.

Richard, at least, was undisturbed. He was leaning against the robust prop of the kitchen dresser with his arms lightly folded and the glass shining in his hand. His clothing had relaxed a little since his formal appearance in Gloucester; that is to say the jacket had been shed and the rest had eased a little at the neck, so that I was half expecting to learn that he had lately taken himself off for another strenuous walk. He asked Phyllis, 'Is that a serious question?'

'It might be. The gruelling years behind us would be enough to put anyone off. And you were shot.'

'*After* I came home.'

'How?' Quickfire, her question was tart.

An eyebrow quirked. 'Oh, didn't you know? You're not supposed to ask. No soldier wants to talk about the past any more, least of all a brush with death. We're trying to put the war behind us.'

'And yet, unlike all the conscripts who really are home for

324

good, you aren't putting it behind you, are you? You continue to choose to do it.'

I've never known jealousy before. There was something in her slanting looks and Richard's steadiness that shamed me. Whereas I'd forgotten that for the Colonel, the subject of war was one of his most comfortable topics. He was lounging in his creaking wooden chair with his hand out upon the tabletop, idly toying with his sherry glass. Heavy white eyebrows twitched above sharp eyes as he roused himself to say grandly, 'Of course Richard has stayed in the army. My son fought in the vital conflict of North Africa. He was part of the force that ultimately gave us the chance to turn the Axis out of the entire continent. His courage there was what got him his post as Captain when he came home again. He was mentioned in dispatches. And now he's practically Whitehall's right-hand man.'

The Colonel was actually happy. He really believed in the doctrine of war as a force for salvation, but I wasn't quite sure Richard liked being cast as the hero of the day. The son really was being honest when he said he didn't want to revisit his part in the war and, really, I thought I oughtn't to be the only person in this room capable of guessing why. Richard's experiences had been such that nearly two years after he'd come home, he'd still been so utterly exhausted by it all that when he'd been abruptly consigned to hospital by a violent scene on a London street, he'd found that he hadn't the reserves left to fight for recovery.

That time, his father had pushed him through it with his

bullying support. Now, roughly another year on, I thought things must be generally better. But still it was no wonder to me that Richard didn't want to talk about his past duties or hear them catalogued over a kitchen table as either triumphs or tragedies.

It was very clear, however, that his father hadn't noticed. Across the room, Richard was standing up a little taller in his place by the dresser while the Colonel told Phyllis proudly, 'My son is set now for a part in what I suppose must be classed as the reconstruction work. The business he faces these days is the task we all face of re-establishing this life on the model we wish it to be. And, with that in mind, you're chasing a lead off to Greece next, aren't you, boy?'

Phyllis wasn't impressed. I caught her lifting one sardonic eyebrow that was at once defiant and supremely elegant. 'And do you often work abroad these days, Captain? Really? And are you destined to fight on this next trip? I quite fancy the idea of paying a second visit to Greece myself, but isn't the country currently sinking in the mire of a bloody civil war?'

'I'll be in Athens. Where the government is. The fighting is further north.'

'So you're going to undertake – how did the Colonel here put it? – reconstruction work there? Because you know full well our government ditched its responsibilities to the Greeks earlier this year and left them to fight it out amongst themselves, and I'm trying to establish whether we should worry about you or not.'

All of a sudden I saw that I'd been mistaken about her

motives here. This wasn't an excruciating repetition of my attack on Richard's nature or his choice of career. This probing was personal to me and it was because of that old correspondence that had made her familiar with all my childhood woes. It was a reference to my experience with the RAF man and she was testing to see whether Richard had a better grasp of truth and kindness than my brother's friend had shown. She was doing it because she thought that I was naïve enough to let that little bit of bother about a first romance with a charming man repeat itself now. It was a repetition of that age-old slander against Richard's name. She had, of course, no idea whatsoever that Richard would understand her opinion of my past history as well as I.

My intense restlessness wasn't remotely relieved when Richard added with mock formality, 'You know I can't tell you the details of the job.'

He was amused rather than offended and I didn't like the way his reply was making Phyllis smirk. I hoped he'd seen that her sharp humour tonight was not entirely her own. Now she was retorting in a contrary sort of fashion, 'No? Do you enjoy the secrecy?'

'No.'

He had seen. On a sudden very definite note, he stood up and crossed the room to set his glass down with a click upon the counter beside me. He turned to her. 'And,' he added, 'to finally answer your real questions, at least in part, this next job will mean I will be briefly away, yes. After a few more weeks or so of preparation. And then I'll be home again. My work is varied, Miss Jones, but not excessively gruelling. And, believe it or not, the principal reason why I chose to be a soldier – and still do – is not because I enjoy the fight.'

He was near me but looking at her as he added, 'The truth is, I like the fact that my training has established my physical competence. It has given me confidence in the power of my actions, if you will, so that a significant vocabulary of alternatives is laid out before me. I accept that I'll always have a part to play in future conflicts and I imagine I'll always be given the task of responding to something insane that someone else has done, either in the manoeuvring of nations or, as it is these days, the criminal underhand dealings that run like a fraying seam through the aftermath of war. But I know just how hard-pressed things need to be before violence is the proportionate response. And for me the hope always remains that when I look back, the balance of my own actions will be on the side of reason.'

This, suddenly, was meant for me rather than her and marked the end of it for him. This was the close of the debate, whether resolved to her satisfaction or not. And it was then that I realised that while my cousin was trying all too hard to make me aware of an impending conflict between my perspective on life and Richard's, it was all rather more a case that she was teasing him into acknowledging questions that she thought I ought to be worrying about rather than those I was actually asking. I mean, secrecy really wasn't a difficulty for us. He had already told me the details that had prompted that other jibe of hers. He'd told me a little of the history of his injury. He'd offered it quietly, inconspicuously, outside the hospital because he'd wanted me to know and it rather proved the point he'd made to Phyllis about the impoliteness of asking, if it was only for the sake of defining a man.

Now Richard turned his head. 'Father, I—'

The Colonel's response made me certain now that he was determined to limit his son's opportunities to speak directly to him. The old man pretended that he hadn't quite heard and rushed in to say pompously, 'Of course, if you ask Danny Hannis about his ideas for the future, he'll just give you a long list of all the machines he's worked on so far. He's got a wonderful mind for mechanics, that boy. He looks after my car for me too. He thinks I don't know, but I do.' He tilted his glass in a toast to the absent man. 'That's why I was glad to stand as his guarantor when he bought that house.'

'*House*? What house?' Phyllis's head snapped round.

The Colonel replied genially, 'Mrs Abbey's old house. He bought it in the spring. Won't live in it, though. Amazing that he could afford it at all. He's saved every penny he could since he was a boy working in the fields, more when he was fighting and now he's applied that same determination to the purchase of a property that must have paid excellent rent. But this one's not quite right for him and as it turns out he's got to sell up again now because he needs the money to buy his parents' cottage when we go. He takes tremendous care of them, you know. They didn't even know he owned a house.'

Phyllis hadn't known either. I was sure of it. And Richard must have made the mistake of seeming like he might speak again at the same time that my face must have been mirroring a suspicion of Phyllis's feelings because suddenly the Colonel was using me as a distraction and growling, 'What's the matter? Why are you looking like that?'

He was glaring at me and then he was blustering in a bullying tone, 'You've seen the man. You've had a chance to compare. Are you gossips forever going to tar Danny's achievements with that slur everyone casts against his mother just because she was the pretty young widow who worked alongside Mrs Cooke in this house and I've done the best I can for the woman by leaning on a few old army friends for the sake of her boy? An introduction from me got the boy enlisted into a role that used his real skills and trained them, too. And because I cared enough to do it, are you now carefully examining the colour of his hair, his build, the colour of his eyes and comparing them to *mine*? Are you? *He is not my child.* His father was a belligerent fool who died falling off a hay wain and I had a wife and two sons, and two sons only, and now—'

I gaped. It was too close to the slur I'd lately been forming about Mrs Abbey's son and I knew, too, how the Colonel's last sentence had been supposed to finish. He meant that his wife and child were dead. And it flustered him, mainly because he knew it carried a great weight and it might have seemed as if he meant to tip us all into outpourings of sympathy. He stumbled and the moment might have passed into deeper confusion except that Richard remarked calmly, 'Emily isn't remotely insinuating that, sir. Knowing her, she won't have even heard that particular rumour until just this moment.'

And the mildness of his intervention seemed to restore the Colonel and, unexpectedly, the old man was settling into wafting a hand while saying, 'All right, all right. You don't need to come over all courteous to me, boy. The girl knows I didn't mean it.'

There was fondness there, beneath the bombast. And then Phyllis was adding to the salvation by remarking for the benefit of both men, but perhaps not for mine, 'You were in London during the war, I believe, Colonel, in an advisory role? My cousin once described the sound made by wave after wave of our planes as they passed overhead there as terrific. But I think she meant it was terrific in the truest sense of the word, as in full of terror.'

This was rapidly turning into the oddest evening of my life. She naturally had an aversion to any more revelations about Danny and she thought this was the surest way of ensuring it. Whereas I was burning the dinner.

I wrestled with the oven and muttered, 'I wasn't in London when I was describing that. Mother and I were staying with my aunt in Norfolk.' I had a crushing suspicion that Richard would be piecing together the details to guess that this was yet another reference to the era in which I'd learnt to drive a Sunbeam.

'Brave heroes those RAF boys, the lot of them,' the Colonel murmured into his glass.

'Emily would tell you that it wasn't heroic,' countered Phyllis, woodenly ignoring my second desperate plea around her name. She was looking heated, almost feverish after seeing Danny passing this time along the length of the tithe barn and still not coming in. He'd walked uphill towards the lane and out of sight and I sympathised but I couldn't stop her.

Phyllis was adding cheerfully, 'She'd tell you that it was a terrifying thing to be lying there each night counting out the planes one by one and hoping against hope that the same number would count back in again. She'd call it barbaric, desperate and even essential, but never heroic. My cousin,' she added as a confidential aside to the Colonel, 'believes those who didn't have to fight are all experiencing a legacy of secondary guilt. She'll tell you that the sheer weight of accepting that people acted as heroes to save her life and the lives of helpless people like her means having to shoulder the responsibility of deserving the generosity that inspired it. The pressure to be perfect exacts a toll upon the soul and she can't bear it. So instead she denies the lot.'

'You were young,' the Colonel observed kindly to me. 'It must have been very frightening.'

I was horribly conscious of Richard standing somewhere near me. I was also thinking that I really shouldn't have written Phyllis so many letters if she was going to persist in quoting from them.

'That's not what I meant at all,' I said rather more heatedly than I intended. 'My cousin is paraphrasing, and badly at that. I believe what I said was that I was witness daily to the sheer hunger for German death; heavens, I probably shared it because losing was too terrific – there's that word again – to contemplate. A short time ago I was waving young men off into the skies, knowing that they were frightened out of their wits, but that they would do it anyway. And knowing that they would bring death to people I'd never even met, who were almost certainly doing the exact same thing on the other side. But, all the same, I was wishing our men to be successful because that meant they came home again. I knew that what they were doing was a gift. I'm fully ready to call anyone you like a hero. But the term itself isn't healthy. What we took from them was alien and cruel and any goodness that came out of the war came from hate. There's my piece of your guilt, Phyllis. It's the strain of being made to feel involuntary gratitude for a gift so horrific I can't even comprehend the sacrifice. It's the responsibility of having to grow up being the helpless figure these people were laying down their lives to protect and yet never having the power to refuse the part or even ease the debt just a little. And it's the unforgivable shame of knowing that all the time they were fighting I'd already lost sight of my basic humanity to such an extent that I too was wishing a stranger's family dead for no better reason than that she and her German children stood between me and some hazy idea of kinship. I betrayed *everyone*.'

Silence.

It was suddenly hard to catch my breath. My voice had risen at the last. I hadn't meant to say any of that. I'd only meant to suppress this line that was leading inexorably back to mentions of the supposed injury to my heart caused by some foolish young airman. I should have left well alone. As I'd said, Richard's secrets weren't anything to worry me. Now this one vital secret of my own was unleashed and rattling about in this room with everyone else's peculiar agitation – with Phyllis's and the Colonel's, I mean – and still it was impossible to catch my breath. My hand quivered when I felt the merest whisper of contact as Richard put out his fingers to briefly touch mine. It drew my eyes and I focused with slightly desperate exasperation for the few seconds of contact before his hand returned to his side again and at last my lungs steadied a little. There had been an answer in that speech of mine to the observation he'd made this morning about my loss of faith in humanity; here was the explanation for my absolute refusal to accept any more grand gestures. This was why I had begged him not to turn me into another one of his responsibilities. I didn't know if he'd noticed before that the aversion was in reference to men like him who'd given their soul for people like me. My powerlessness during the war to either accept or deny their sacrifice had been unbearable. Now the war was over, the decision to depend on another person had to be mine. It had to be, otherwise I would never be able to keep any hope for a more equal future at all.

This guilt was the true force behind that sense I had of always being in the wrong. He hadn't understood before that the blame was something I'd inflicted upon myself. It was the sort of thing that didn't normally form into words, and probably for good reason. Through that brief, private touch to my hand, Richard had been making it clear that he certainly didn't think it warranted being wrenched out of a person to serve as an idle distraction like this. Any second now, the Colonel was going to finish the job and ask me quite seriously if I had been 'Blitzed'.

But he didn't. After an excruciatingly intense moment, the old man laughed. And I mean to say, he really laughed. His head fell back with a roar and sometime afterwards he had to wipe away a tear. Still snatching for breath, he lifted his head once more and managed to gasp out, 'Did you hear that, Richard? Your young friend has concluded, after due consideration, that war is *unhealthy.*'

The Colonel made his chair creak as he sagged in his seat. 'Refreshing honesty,' he said, fighting and failing to contain himself. 'Summed it up in a nutshell. Put her finger right on it. I want to know what she thinks about famine.'

I hadn't thought the Colonel had it in him to laugh like that. I didn't believe his son had thought so either. Then Richard risked undoing it all by cutting straight through all the minutes of disguise by at last asking plainly, 'Father, who was here earlier? What is it that you don't want to tell me? Because someone *was* here. There are teacups all over the desk in the library and I know it can't have been for Bertie Winstone because you've never willingly served him tea in your life if a good spirit happened to be near to hand.'

It was said boldly and delivered with a consideration that was inescapably wry. It had its effect. I had been certain that the answer would involve yet another mention of Mrs Abbey. But when the Colonel collected himself and brought his eyes to his son's face, I thought Richard had been bracing himself to meet something else. Something more desperately personal, like this old man's agonised shame whenever he felt the urge to shield his remaining son from any more injuries in the Langton name, and in the process achieved nothing but the drawing of further care from that son for himself.

In the event, however, the Colonel's expression was somewhere on the edge of failure instead of consumed by it. Agonised, but clumsy, as though a difficulty dwelled here that was awkward rather than tragic. And perhaps a sense that it was further complicated by the presence of two guests. I watched the Colonel's face as he shot a little glance at me and then confessed quite pathetically, 'A man from one of the newspapers called by. I let him in. I'm sorry. He mentioned something about PC Rathbone and I didn't guess what he was until we'd been all over the house. He was looking at the traces Mrs Cooke left behind and he seemed rather too interested in that old print of your mother's that is hanging on the woman's bedroom wall. I deduced he was sniffing out a new story about John's ridiculous treasure hoard and I'm sorry.'

It was, unexpectedly, the first time I'd ever heard him mention John by name and in some ways it was wonderful, but still it was all wrong because instead of the usual pattern of the father seeming beaten down by a reference to the younger son's death, this shamefaced confession seemed centred on the mention of the journalist. It seemed to me that here the Colonel was making an awkward demonstration of his idea of what constituted a father's defence of his living son. It was less practised than Richard's endless efforts to shield his father from the layer upon layer of grief that dwelt here. It was gingerly done. Gestures of parental concern did not come remotely naturally to the old man. But, above all, it told me that the Colonel believed very seriously that the distress of a newspaper story was a symptom of Richard's history rather than his own.

As it was, it appeared that concern really wasn't required here anyway. Richard drew breath, with relief, it seemed to me, and said with quite extraordinary affection, 'Is that *all?* Heavens, Father, you had me expecting ... I don't know what. But this was bound to happen eventually, wasn't it? And I find that these days the sort of stories the rags pick up don't quite matter as much as they did.'

The Colonel was taken aback. 'They don't?'

'No.'

'Oh.'

Grey eyes widened upon his son's face. They seemed to read something in Richard's words that I couldn't see before retreating to the empty glass as if he didn't quite dare look anywhere else. Then he repeated himself on a stilted note of realisation and from the faintly impatient movement of Richard beside me, it was clear his father thought he had stumbled into proof of something else that was equally personal, although it wasn't clear that the discovery was either expected or easily digestible. Or that Richard had necessarily intended to lay whatever it was quite so bare before his father like this.

'*Oh.* Well, anyway,' the Colonel declared with a flickering glance at me that made me flush without quite knowing why, before the old man suddenly returned to action as if he'd decided the safest course was to simply ignore the lot and take the reassurance as it was intended. He lurched bull-like onto a new path. 'Anyway, Bertie came in at the end and set this fellow scampering onto a wholly different scent. Bertie made a point of declaring that his recollections of his assault are hazy at best. So now this newspaperman is going to have a fine old time making up nonsense about that story instead.

Bertie told him that the first person he remembers seeing with any clarity that evening is our new young friend.'

The Colonel was beaming triumphantly. I stood there letting the dinner burn a little more, trying not to look at Richard, and thinking: I'd understood why Phyllis might have wanted to direct our conversation away from the endless talk about Danny and I believe I had guessed something about the Colonel's frailties that had made war his safest topic. But I wished I could understand where everyone had got the idea that it was acceptable to keep using my name to divert attention from the more unpleasant things, when it could only end with Bertie Winstone telling a journalist a particularly silly thing like that.

Chapter 22

Iwas woken by the smell of burning again. My cousin and I were in John's room since it was one of the few chambers that had a decent bed suitable for an invalid and enough space on the floor to make up a mattress of sorts for me. It had, believe it or not, been the Colonel's suggestion. After the peculiarity of our pre-dinner conversation, Phyllis and the Colonel had enjoyed themselves immensely during the meal by arguing about the correct course for our nation's behaviour to Greece and the miners' strikes and other worthy issues. For me this had only served to prove that I'd been wildly naïve in ever imagining that I might tag along on Phyllis's next trip. Her brand of splendid femininity and worldly cynicism was rather out of my league.

John's room had an enormous Georgian linen cupboard that spanned the space between the bedroom door and the window. It towered in the gloom of night. It also gave off a faint smell as though something unpleasant had been left to dry in a corner in a way that even penetrated the pervading scent of mothballs. But all of it was overcome at about two o'clock in the morning when this eerie room became tinged with the odour of fire.

My mattress was practically beneath the heavy green curtains that screened the window anyway so it was easy enough for me to twist onto my knees behind them and peer out. The moon was a miniscule fingernail sinking behind distant trees. The garden terraces stood as dark bands beneath my window. They ran smoothly, line by line, downwards past the severe dark of the machine barn and the farmyard until they met the rougher blur of sheep pasture on the valley hillside below. The valley bottom was screened by the tall evergreen plantation, but I could make out the faint profiles of the rooftops from the settlement opposite. And far to the right, before the valley was obscured by the tall stand of trees that surrounded the steward's ponds, a distant window light marked where Eddington must be. It was too steady and small to be a fire and was probably a small lamp set to act as a nightlight for the children. Apart from that there was nothing. Nothing but a faint haze in the valley bottom as if there would be a heavy dew in the morning, only there couldn't be because the ground had been dry for weeks.

On an impulse I eased myself to my feet and claimed my cousin's long cream housecoat from the back of a chair. Its silken lines were a long way removed from the box-like house-coat worn by that sweeper of steps in Gloucester; this was on the scale of borrowing the floor-length sophistication of a London socialite and it showed how little Phyllis was really suited to the strange, dithering character she had assumed in her cottage.

I was stopped at the door by murmur so faint that it barely took the form of sound.

'Emily? Is that you?'

I opened the door a fraction and slipped out, making no more sound myself than a rustle of skirts. His eyebrows rose a fraction as he took in my borrowed glamour, but he said nothing. The unbrushed hair and the fine-drawn face was me. The long line of the gallery stretched behind him, dimly lit by a distant oil lamp. He didn't even bother to mention the smell of smoke.

He merely said softly, 'Will you come?'

I nodded and slipped back into my room. He was more properly dressed than I was. He was wearing trousers and a woollen jumper and this time he really was braced for walking because the jumper was also dark. I wished it wasn't. Firstly it suited him and it was distracting when I ought to be serious. And secondly, the idea of stealth gave the urgency of our errand a different edge of tension.

He was waiting for me at the head of the servants' stairs when I re-emerged some five minutes later, clad once more in my rather more ordinary slacks and blouse. He collected a torch from a broom cupboard in the dark of the stairwell and it was as he reached down a thin navy gardening coat from a hook by the kitchen door that I realised it wasn't actually so warm on this summer night that I shouldn't have thought of bringing a jacket. As it was, the coat was for me anyway. He hung it around my shoulders, hesitated for a moment in the act of straightening the collar to explain in an undertone, 'Your present outfit isn't quite as blindingly bright as your previous elegant getup, but it wouldn't hurt to at least have the power of running to ground, even if we don't intend to use it.'

He turned his attention to the search for a spare key with which to lock the kitchen door – leaving the original neatly on the neighbouring window ledge for the remaining occupants – and I dutifully slipped my hands into the overly long sleeves. This was the moment I realised just how much I had to learn about night-time adventuring.

Then we were outside and he was drawing the kitchen door closed behind us with an awful lot of concentration on not letting it rattle. As we passed lightly along the length of the cobbled yard, he asked quietly, 'Where precisely were you off to just now, anyway, looking like an angel of ... I don't know what?'

'It was only my cousin's housecoat. I think my aunt made it for her.'

'Don't you ever answer a question at the first time of asking?'

The question bore a touch of exasperation. He was leading the way to the corner of the tithe barn. Following close behind, I gave in. Outside the smoke was merely a faint scent on the air. This was feeling more and more like a needlessly cautious hunt for something that might be miles away. Or perhaps that was just wishful thinking.

I said baldly, 'I was thinking about my cousin's garden and the usual sequel to a visitation from the vegetable thief. And then I was thinking about cans of petrol being stored for future use in your barn and how sensible that might be for similar reasons.'

'I—see.' Then he said in an odd voice, 'You really do pay attention, don't you?'

It wasn't fully dark because there were an awful lot of stars, but this wasn't exactly my idea of a glorious walk in the romantic moonlight. Ahead, the machine barn loomed. Bleak and singularly unappealing. It was no place for me.

He sensed my hesitation. Amusement drifted on the night air as he whispered, 'What is it?'

I wasn't going to admit I was afraid. Instead, I betrayed it by saying rather too sharply, 'I'm being realistic. I'm wondering why you wanted me to come along.'

Something metallic was put into my hands. It was the torch and I thought it was designed to give me a sense of control. He stepped ahead of me into the gloom, tracing his way along the edge of his car with a guiding fingertip while his eyes worked to adjust. He told me on a hushed note, 'I asked for your help because if I'm to go wandering about where an arsonist has lately been at work, I judge he'll find it considerably more difficult to catch me off guard if there are two of us. And less likely to try, too. It is a wise soldier and a long-lived one who tries to find the path of least conflict if he can ... Careful. What did I say? I suppose it is more uneven than it looks in this light.'

This last part was as a jolt went through me and made me take a clumsy step. I rejected the impulse to steady myself with a sudden clutch at his sleeve and retorted dryly, 'You know precisely what you said. I don't want to contemplate the various ways your longevity might be curtailed. And besides all that, we might simply use the torch.'

'And spoil the fun?' That amusement was there again. 'Look, cautious or not, only a fool would go alone and although I have, out of necessity, already told my father the bare bones of what might be at loose in our neighbourhood, I couldn't rouse him for this because he'd feel obliged to crash about falling into things. I'm afraid I thought it would be easier for you. Do you really mind?'

I shook my head, which Richard probably didn't see because he was running his gaze past me to the deep shade of the yard and the house front and its gardens. He was looking for signs of movement behind us. I suppose it was easier to be sure without the concentrated intensity of a torch that would inevitably leave us blind to all else. He answered my nervousness anyway with a brief murmur of comfort. 'I promise I won't let you be frightened.'

Then he led me deeper into the machine barn between the sleek line of the car and the towering menace of the slumbering steam engine. The tractor was there too, eyeing us as a suspicious extension of Danny's disapproval. It was possible to feel a sense of the history that might have inspired Danny to give Richard his warning about me. It was as though we were following the ghostly memory this place had of all the times John had slunk out of the house this way without telling his father, perhaps at a more reasonable hour of the evening but always following a similar course down the hill to the ford near my cousin's house. I thought John Langton's walk might have taken him onwards up the path that wove its way through hawthorn and trees to Eddington. Danny, on the other hand, presumably preferred to do his visiting in daylight and under the guise of propriety. It was impossible to judge how hard a debate Danny might have had after his footsteps had carried him to the valley bottom and left him there to choose between his odd bond with Mrs Abbey to the right, and the short walk the other way downstream to the place where my cousin's cottage stood.

Richard obviously wasn't imagining romantic walks of any sort. He was focused and efficient. He established that the pair of fuel cans was still propped in the boot of his car – where presumably he'd had the foresight to secure them earlier – and then got me to dare a brief flash with the torch into the corners. Nothing loitered here except the antiquated teeth of abandoned haymaking implements. I turned out the torch and, while we waited for our eyes to remember how to see, Richard told me what he planned to do with the cans now that he'd escaped the embarrassment of giving an arsonist his fuel.

He said briskly, 'I'm going to pay an early call tomorrow to the man in charge of the wireless station and get the cans safely locked away in his compound. I've no doubt he'll be happy to keep them in return for a small percentage and I may even end up giving them to him, for all that it's illegal to pass on rationed petrol.' A movement in the air beside me as his eyes located the faint shape of the stunted hatch that was set in the great sealed doors of the barn. 'So brace yourself, dear Emily, for this proof of the full extent of my criminal dealings. Anyway, what else am I going to do with them? I don't want this car in London and after tomorrow my father thinks he may well decamp back to his flat in Richmond.'

'After tomorrow?' My enquiry was given blandly.

It hid nothing. Understanding gleamed briefly in the dark. 'Yes, I'll be going with him on Sunday. Now that I've had time to think about things, it seems ...' A hesitation. '... the safest course.'

'Oh,' I said clumsily, because a whole tumult of questions were instantly racing through my head in an embarrassing tangle that grew from a sense of all the promises I'd made earlier about not prying. Privacy wasn't really the issue any more, but here was a void that loomed of wishing to go with him only at the same time being fully conscious of the possibility that it wasn't so much that he hadn't asked but rather that he couldn't without thrusting us into a harder discussion about the danger here. His tone as he side-stepped the subject was different now; because we both knew I was here with him when he might have left me safely inside and he had, after all, promised that he wouldn't frighten me. It wasn't the most comfortable of thoughts.

So instead of broaching that grim line, I asked idiotically, 'What's going to happen tomorrow?'

He laughed at my question, necessarily very quietly, but it was a laugh all the same. 'Good question, Emily. No, I'm not mocking you.'

Now we were passing deeper into the blank depths of the barn, towards the vague form of the small access door into the farmyard. Carthorses stirred in their stables as we slipped out into the starlight but nothing else moved. Richard's voice was soft but relatively ordinary and it seemed to me he was more concerned about not making a noise that woke the villagers than any particular threat from a waiting vegetable thief as he led me through the yard gate.

'Tomorrow, Father is having his customary dinner with his

old army friends. And I'm afraid he's naturally assumed you'll be on hand and eager to help. I'm sorry.' His voice was a touch of warmth in the night. 'It's preying all too heavily on that neighbourly kindness you offered, isn't it?'

We had joined the trackway where it passed down the hill. The scent of smoke was so thin now that I half expected to be met by half a dozen men from the village puffing their way back up after putting out the fire. But no one moved. Richard seemed to feel it too; a sudden charge in the intensity of the silence like static electricity building for a storm. Perhaps it belonged to Richard himself. I was right about his hesitation before. He seemed suddenly very conscious of the risk, a hazard; which couldn't be violence because I knew he'd never have asked me to help him now, but danger lurked here all the same and this was the cusp of it. He gave it away when he stopped with his hand on the final gate. 'Emily?'

I didn't know why but his doubt made me look back. The house was obscured and the village was dark, of course, but something about the quality of the night made me realise something I'd missed before. The lamp that had illuminated the gallery had been an oil lamp, which meant that the electricity was off. And this meant that it was the turbine house that had been selected as the vegetable thief's latest victim.

Paul Abbey. It was high time I started using the fellow's name.

And I knew now, because Duckett had told me, that those outhouses hadn't been burned as a cruel thanks to the owners of a crop of purloined vegetables. It had been a systematic destruction of Abbey's lairs.

It made me shake off Richard's concern in the only way I could. I opened the gate myself and stepped through, and as I went I said irritably, 'He's been hopping in and out of your house for days. We're lucky it's the turbine house he's targeted and not the Manor. I should have caught up with him today when I had the chance.'

A smile briefly ran through the dark. Richard eased the gate shut on its catch. 'You shouldn't. What would you have done if you had?'

'I mean that I could have seen enough to identify him properly to the police. That might have helped, I think.'

Richard was leading again now. He went cautiously, assessing the rough ground on the path ahead. The patch of valley where the turbine house stood must have been somewhere in this gloomy view but no telltale gleam betrayed its location. There were no flames, nor even smouldering ashes. Smoke clung to the undersides of the trees that marked the limit of the steward's ponds but that was all. In a way the absence of fire made this descent more reckless rather than less. Now that the thrill of tracing the smoke to its source was passing, it felt as if we were walking blind into a dark wilderness where harsher things must wait.

Richard led me off the trackway onto close-cropped pasture that smelled strongly of sheep rather than smoke. His voice was still level despite the tension. 'The police already have Abbey's name. Danny Hannis was given the task of relaying what he'd learned from the farmhands and from that brief chase through the Manor to PC Rathbone today. When you saw Hannis scurrying past the kitchen window earlier he'd just finished making his report to me in the library. I telephoned our policeman after dinner to give him what little else we've gleaned since. Constable Rathbone has got Abbey's name from me and he's going to relay it to his man from the Gloucester station once he's caught up with him. Apparently this detective is proving elusive too, just like everyone else.'

'*Danny* told the police?'

I must have stopped. Richard turned to wait for me. I didn't quite know how to frame my concerns. I didn't know how to ask if Danny's information would be considered helpful for Mrs Abbey or a hazard because I didn't quite know what I was looking for in the account of a man who might yet prove to be bound to her by more than just the ownership of her old house. Then it struck me. 'Of course he would tell them. Paul Abbey attacked his step-father.' Then, more urgently as a harder thought hit, 'Richard, the turbine house was where Mr Winstone met his injury.'

It was there ahead of us. Richard was negotiating the tricky climb down from the rough ground that marked the last descent of the pipe and also the rough gravel of an old streambed. The turbine house was just a little way to our right. Silent and hulking in its damp footings.

The drift of Richard's reply on the night air was calm. 'It seems to me that we need only worry about Abbey if we should happen to catch him unawares. He did, after all, run from you earlier when he might have done otherwise and we mustn't forget that he brought poor injured Bertie home. Which is why we're talking as we go. I doubt very much this is a lure designed to claim me as Abbey's next victim – how could he know that we'd come tonight and not tomorrow with an army of villagers? And if we give him fair warning that we're coming, it'll rather lessen the impression we mean to trap *him*. That's PC Rathbone's job. But I'm sorry, *are* you—?'

There was a crunch as a fragment of earth broke away beneath his foot and a slither as he caught himself. In the dark there was a low, 'Blast.' And then, entirely cheerfully, 'And if that isn't proof of why an attempt at stealth is absolutely a waste of time, I don't know what is. That being said—'

He waited while I caught up with him. He put out a hand to restrain me. 'Stay behind me, would you, for this last part? For all my confident assurances, there is always that tricky moment when you have to put your head around a door and hope against hope it isn't answered by the report of a gun.'

I was suddenly clasping the hand he'd put out to hold me between both of mine. But we weren't met by a gun. There wasn't anybody there at all.

The fire in the turbine house was thoroughly out and had been for some time. The door was sagging from its hinges with its lock almost wrenched clean from its housing by the force of Abbey's entry. Inside, the single room was in a filthy state. Torchlight picked out a bank of enormous lead batteries and the metal bulk of the turbine itself, all swimming in a lake of greasy water. The fire had a heart. Its charred remains lay directly upon the squat metalwork that looked, to my eyes, like a large painted bobbin about the size of a drawing-room table. Water was still shushing its way vigorously through its innards until Richard's hand reached for the heavy metal wheel and stemmed its flow. It seemed perverse to me that whoever had been here before us to put out the flames should have been reduced to bucketing in water from outside when here was a carefully organised supply on tap, so to speak.

I asked in a voice made harsh by awe, 'Did Abbey put it out?'

The fire had been set using a bundle of rags and paper before whippy twists of green hazel had been stacked on top. Flames had shot up to the apex of the roof and done considerable damage to the tiling and the metalwork. We were lucky that the roof had been set upon girders rather than timber. If the fire had taken hold there nothing would have stopped it, not when the bank of batteries waited like an explosive charge in a neat row against one wall.

They hadn't escaped unscathed as it was. The heat had warped their housings and they were giving off an unhealthy chemical smell. The impulse that had driven the arsonist to save this place had fortunately included the wisdom to throw the switch that isolated the house from this power source so that the additional strain of circuitry hadn't made matters worse.

Richard had the torch and it flicked back from the batteries to assist me in my examination of the matter on the turbine. 'What do you think?' His voice was still hushed but cooler now where the cheerfulness had gone out of it.

There was a small knot of rags by my foot that had tumbled to the floor. I bent to take a closer look. As I did so I remarked with unnecessary impatience, 'Richard, the house fires in my neighbourhood were in the main lit by something rather larger than a match.'

'Well?'

I was still struggling to achieve a more normal tone. Something was making my heart beat uncomfortably quickly and it wasn't all in the ashes of this fire. I straightened. 'Very well,' I said shortly. 'Since you're really asking me because you want the opinion of a novice but are too polite to phrase it quite like that, I'll say that I think it's odd that a man as experienced as Abbey in the art of destroyed sheds and outhouses should have stacked his kindling on top of the metal casing of an entirely non-combustible water turbine. It's as if he didn't want the place to go up.'

The torchlight touched the batteries again. They swam in the inky water that had been flung over everything. My voice was hollow in the tinny acoustics of this small brick chamber. 'Do you think he believed the foliage and twigs and things would make smoke rather than flames? Did it catch him by surprise and go up like a tinderbox because it's been so dry of late? Where on earth did he get the bucket to put it out again? There isn't one here.'

'Bravo.' The admiration was serious, but then so was his tone. The relaxed man who had led me down the hill was entirely grim now. 'But it wasn't Abbey.'

His hand reached out to take the matter from my fingertips. The light caught the fragment of cloth that lay singed and curling in his flattened palm. It was a small portion of blouse with the button still attached, reading CC41 – the date and the assertion of Crown Copyright over the design. The fabric was patterned with a large repeating design in orange and white in a manner that confirmed the substance of the comments I'd made earlier about the wartime enthusiasm for dressing women in cheerful clothing. This blouse had belonged to the 'Utility' branded range, which always featured robust fabrics because they were supposed to last a person for years before wearing out. Now I might have wished they had been made just a shade more flimsy, because I had every reason to believe that this fragment and all the survivors of this fire like it had once been part of my own treasured collection.

Duckett. I was shaken. I barely needed to say his name aloud. Richard said absolutely nothing. He simply returned the fragment to the pile on the surface of the turbine and turned his attention to the scorched remains of paper that oozed soggily over the rim. I knew what they would be. They'd suffered more from the effects of the water than my clothes had, but if even a tiny fragment had retained its legibility, I knew it would reveal a note written in John's extravagant hand, recording rents accrued and expenses made by the estate for the comfort of his tenants.

My whisper was lamentably hoarse. 'Duckett set this fire. That's why it's different. There's no vegetable garden here. And this place was locked. This isn't Abbey's usual dramatic attempt to expunge all traces of his lair.' Then, more edged, 'Was this left by Duckett as a warning for *me?* Because of what I did today? I thought he'd understood that I wasn't involved in the game Abbey's playing with the nerves of his wife.' The remaining debris in my hand was wiped away as if it were poison.

Suddenly Richard's arm was around me and as quietly

secure as it had been under the arches of the hospital porch. This time he didn't let me go again. 'No, Emily. I—'

I swept on in a whisper of disbelief, 'Is this supposed to embarrass me? Is this meant to capitalise on Mr Winstone's silly joke about my face being the only features he can remember from that evening of the attack? Is Duckett trying to prove I did it by forcing my connection to this site? Because how can Duckett have possibly heard enough of Mr Winstone's comments to think this would work? I mean, I can accept Duckett might have heard of the attack on Mr Winstone, but if he knows where it happened and he knows to use me here ...' I stopped on a shiver of doubt. I didn't like where these thoughts were going. Because even on the hope that Duckett might discredit my witness statements with this fire to the extent that no word of mine would ever be believed again, all he was really doing here was risking incrimination himself. Particularly when I'd seen the culprit that evening on Mr Winstone's path and he wasn't Duckett. He'd been tall and dark-haired.

I asked, without really believing it myself, 'Is this supposed to make Abbey culpable for the theft from the Manor as well as all the rest?'

Richard turned me with him as the torchlight played one last time over the building around us. I watched what he watched. There was nothing else here but the remains of a fire that had been deliberately set and then decisively extinguished supposedly for the purpose of leaving a perfect reminder of the connection between me and the violence in this place.

Richard's reply was rough with the hush of night-time, deliberation in every word now. 'No. He must know it just won't stick. You saw Duckett take your case. He must at least suspect that I've deduced he took those ledgers at the same time. He certainly saw the policeman visit you at the cottage that day. And if we hadn't told PC Rathbone then, Duckett must presume that after his little effort down by the docks today we'd take a pretty dim view of any further threat to your welfare.'

'So he *is* hoping to discredit me and incriminate Abbey.'

Richard just held me and said nothing.

'Richard,' I began. My hand was gripping his clothing again, only this time, since there wasn't a convenient lapel to clasp, my fingers had twisted themselves into a knot with the woollen jumper somewhere about his middle. My hand adjusted its grip restlessly. It came with a sudden reluctant concession to the doubt that had been building in Richard all the way through this madcap night-time excursion. I finally said what he needed me to say. 'You don't think this has been left here for me or Abbey at all, do you?'

'I don't believe it has, no.'

He left me the silence in which to accept that and the first of its unhappy implications. Then, bewilderingly, he reverted to talking about Abbey. He told me swiftly and quietly, 'Danny Hannis found two of Abbey's lairs today. After the funny little incident this morning where you chased Abbey through the house, it occurred to Hannis to take a good look at all our buildings and outbuildings for signs we've been harbouring this man. After all, our – or I should say Mrs Cooke's –

vegetable garden has been obliterated. And as predicted, Hannis found signs of a style of living room in the darkest corner of the watershed.'

'No bed?'

'Quick again, Emily. No, there was no sign of a bed. And he hasn't slept in the hayloft above the stables either, where Hannis found similar signs of a little lair at the very back where Abbey's been lounging away his days amongst the old musty hay. He hasn't been sleeping in the house so wherever his night-time haunt is, it isn't the Manor. When I saw the electricity go out tonight and then the smell of smoke followed it, I don't know what I expected, but I certainly thought I knew enough of Abbey's habits to discount the expectation that this would be just another fire in the style of the blazes set in other outhouses. Those have been the beacon trail left by a hunter who is drawing closer to his quarry and making a very bold statement about destruction. This blaze, I can see now, was a token gesture. Desperate, ill-thought-out and amateur at that.'

He was discounting the arsonist from this act. But all the same, Abbey's name rang on and on.

My gaze was fixed fiercely on absolutely nothing except the memory of how reluctantly Mrs Abbey had been named between us this morning in the car. I remarked grimly, 'I ought to be asking how Duckett even heard enough of the details of Mr Winstone's assault to know what it would mean to leave this kind of mess, oughtn't I? You heard Duckett tell me how he knew to find me at the cottage, didn't you? And in just the same way, she must have told him about Mr Winstone's assault. Duckett told me today that she's a very old friend. He called her Florence.'

'You're reading this as a battleground between an old love and the new?'

I conceded, 'I really do want to presume Mrs Abbey must have persuaded Duckett to do this, just as she told him I was harbouring her husband. It's possible that she enlisted Duckett's help and that she brought him to set this fire.'

'But?'

'But I can't stop thinking how that man – Duckett – was a bully to me earlier.'

I felt his hand tighten its grip fractionally. I turned my head. His profile was being thrown into exciting shadows by the torchlight. I told him in a clearer voice, 'Duckett is obsessed with the idea of betrayal, Richard. It begins with the treachery that led Abbey to thieve rationed goods and it ends with a new kind of treachery of the sort that leads a former prison inmate to haunt his wife and children. Duckett says it is all being done for little purpose other than revenge for the fact that Abbey lost his stake in the business, and then he lost his wife. Duckett is terrified that Abbey is going to target him next. You saw how Duckett handled his conversation with me because he perceives me as a part of the threat. Perhaps Mrs Abbey had to tell Duckett that I was harbouring her husband because otherwise Duckett would have decided she was betraying him too. Perhaps he wanted to leave a little challenge for you after your intervention today. It's possible, isn't it, that she told him about Mr Winstone's attack here and said that this place belonged to the Manor and now he's used my clothes to leave a warning for you because he hates that you intervened earlier and he suspects you're helping Abbey too?'

'No.'

'Perhaps we should ask Danny Hannis.' It burst out of me almost angrily. All these perfectly viable suggestions and Richard was contradicting every single one. 'You have to consider it a possibility that Danny knows more about her feelings than he's willing to admit. It's very convenient that he's been using that hay loft for months now while he feeds that poor blighted goat and now, today, he's miraculously made the sudden discovery that Abbey has been using it as his daytime lair.'

I was thinking about the way Danny had kept his connection to Mrs Abbey secret. I was thinking about all the furtive exchanges the pair of them had made in Mr Winstone's house on my first night here. And lastly I was remembering how my cousin had looked as she'd watched him walk past the kitchen window. And I was adding to the effect the information that he had been in the library with Richard only a few minutes before and had learned Phyllis was there, and had still emphatically decided to avoid her.

Richard's voice was very gentle. 'Emily, when I spoke to Hannis earlier, he said something to me that I think you should know. As well as giving me a sound ticking off for keeping you here and lecturing me, not unreasonably, on the Langton history when it comes to ruining innocent peoples' lives, he growled something along the lines of 'and you had to embroil her too, didn't you?' He was referring to your cousin Phyllis.'

It was a new small rescue.

Richard was firmly drawing my mind back from constructing its own horrible list of betrayals. I gave an involuntary shiver against the warmth of his body, not because it displeased me to hear Danny was angry that we'd rescued Phyllis from her hospital bed, but because if I'd been wrong and Danny wasn't another man who belonged to Mrs Abbey, it meant nothing else could stand between me and a return to the wretched knowledge of what this really meant. I was back in that awful conversation in the car and the discovery that this man beside me was highly conscious that something was building around him and himself specifically. Only this time, instead of feeling alienated and confused, I could feel the full force of his arm around me and he didn't want to let me go.

I felt Richard's jaw brush against my hair as he led me to what must be said. 'This was meant for others to find tomorrow. I was supposed to learn about it after the wide-eyed public and the police had waded in, as they inevitably will when the sun comes up and the farmhands start their walk to work. Instead, I've managed to come and see what they've left and I don't like that it seems designed to work around your name.'

A fresh chill ran beneath my skin. That last part didn't matter – surely no policeman worth their salt could possibly read this as proof that I had anything to hide, and I wasn't prepared to worry about what that journalist might say about me before this particular well ran dry. But the rest was unshakeable. Richard wasn't going to remove what we'd found, but all the same this was why he'd brought me along on this night-time trip and it was why he'd hesitated too, at that last gateway by the farmyard. It was an extension of the impulse that had driven him to attempt to put me on the train earlier. Now he'd committed himself to letting me understand the truth before the world rushed in and, knowing him, the decision wasn't selfish at all.

I drew an unhappy breath. Proceeding very cautiously so that he should have full room to silence me if he wished, I asked in an oddly flat little voice, while my heart beat in strong painful strokes, 'Richard? What *did* she say to you when you drove her to the doctors?'

I felt him stiffen. Then with deliberate steadiness, he told me, 'You said before that you thought Mrs Abbey might be the victim here. For what it's worth, in some ways I agree even now.'

There was no sound but the distant rushing of the stream, no feeling but the warmth of his arms and his body and the touch of his cheek to my hair in the pause before he added, 'In the car this morning, I asked her frankly what had happened to leave that bruise. I thought it might give her the idea of not being left alone to face Abbey or Duckett or whoever struck her. Her reply was to tell me about the snow last March because she thought I would be interested to know that the harvest will be poorer than usual. Apparently, the awful weather meant that they had to put the seed in late.'

That last part had come with the wry delivery that would normally belong to the punch line of a bad joke. I was bewildered. I'd expected some lurid demand or a slander, or something. 'You think she was protecting the ears of her children?'

'On the contrary, I think she was keen to draw my attention to them and with John's name ringing in my ears. I believe the mention of the bad spring was as close as she dared come to another mention of my brother, given the audience.'

'Oh.'

Suddenly I was away from him and breaking through the battered doorway. Outside was better. The air was free of unhealthy fumes and there were stars and the hard glare of the torch could be put out. He'd followed me. I hadn't been running from him. I stopped as my feet met the rougher terrain of the sheep-grazed hillside. He was with me. I could see his profile just slightly above me but the dark meant he couldn't read my expression as I listened to him observe without a trace of accusation, 'You've known about her claims of an affair for some time, haven't you?'

We were standing at the point where the rough hillside met the track. The light at Eddington was out now. I wasn't looking at him, but I could feel his gaze burning upon my face. We'd come to it all of a sudden and I hated it. 'Yes. Yes, I have,' I confessed bitterly, 'because she's been taking pains to mention his name to me too. And today I learned that she tried to sell her house to him.'

I heard his sharp intake of breath as he moved to ask a question. I raced to fill the gap. 'She didn't tell me about it. I heard it from her old neighbours on my ill-advised walk through Gloucester today. Only they didn't say anyone's name. They merely talked about Mrs Abbey's 'friend from up the hill', which I took to mean your brother, and then a soldier turned farmer, who I guessed must be Danny. Did you know that he tried to buy her house?'

He might have deliberately misunderstood, but he didn't. 'John? Yes.'

I kept my gaze fixed fiercely on the grey form of the opposing hillside. Barely half a yard away to my right, Richard's voice merged with the dark. He told me crisply, 'The truth is, John was in the throes of thrashing out an agreement when he died. I only learned about it because the solicitor forwarded the papers with his will. Delightfully, it fell to me to write to her and inform her that the sale would not be proceeding, though I doubt that the news came as a surprise to her.'

He took another carefully regulated breath. 'The popular explanation for the attempted purchase – had it ever been made public – would have inevitably been that he was intending to furnish it with his stolen riches, or something along those lines. The timeline certainly matches the culmination of his efforts in that department, but it doesn't remotely make sense to me. As I understand it, he was meaning to profit from his activities, not fit out a house with them like a mad museum to crime. And yet, without all that nonsense, I still can't quite fathom how he ever dreamed he might have managed the debt. You know the Manor is under an all-consuming mortgage. After his death, when it became my job to negotiate a stay of judgement from the bank on our payments, it would have made it a whole lot closer to impossible if John had managed to tack on the Parliament Street property too. So lately I've had to start wondering if the whole disaster – the attempt to sell his soul for looted goods – came about because he needed to pay a bribe. The sudden interest in her house certainly smacks of an attempt to pay her off, doesn't it? A nice honest transaction over a private property to conceal a greater exchange of funds. But in truth I can't believe for a moment any woman had such a hold over him as that.'

'Why?'

'*Why?* I should have thought it was obvious.' This, suddenly, was said roughly. 'My brother was a murderer. He'd found his own way of dealing with people he didn't like.'

Ah.

Then he followed this bruising show of temper with a swift apology that I, in my turn, dismissed by turning to face him so that I could say quickly, 'Richard?'

The meagre light was making it very hard to make out the features of his face. I could feel the watchfulness of his eyes, though, and knew this was hurting him. I added cautiously, 'It makes you uneasy that the neighbours didn't explicitly state that the friend was John, doesn't it?'

Unexpectedly, I heard the breath go out of him with a little easing of tension. It was because we'd reached the core of what was troubling him and I was brave enough to face it – this something that was more painful for him than the small discomfort of having to embrace the idea that a brother who had willingly crossed so many other moral lines should have apparently indulged in a spot of adultery.

For me, this little nudge nearer to the grim truth made the space between us seem just a fraction wider. I think I'd spent so long teaching myself to believe that this existed only in my mind that it felt like a fresh betrayal to be mentioning it now. And this betrayal was of myself. Because it unleashed a dread that was horribly like loneliness.

Richard prompted, 'Tell me what you know. Please.'

'All right,' I agreed with determined crispness, 'But you should know that I think the part where her little boy might be John's child doesn't quite stand up to scrutiny. The boy is roughly three years old, yes?'

A tip of his head in confirmation.

'But she moved here herself three years ago, and only *after* her husband was imprisoned? So by her timeframe she was either heavily pregnant when she moved into Eddington or had a very young baby. It would be easy enough to check, I think, if it matters. What certainly does matter, and I'm sure you must have realised, is that for your brother to be responsible, he must have known her when she lived in Gloucester, when her husband was still free and at home, long before she applied to become John's tenant and years before he even conceived of buying her house.' Something in his stillness made me stop. 'I'm sorry,' I said. 'This isn't very nice.'

Richard's manner was very gentle. 'I can't at this stage tell you which I should be more ashamed of. The fact that I'm leading you into dissecting the begetting of a young boy as if he were a badly bred calf, or the fact that I knew when I brought you down here that we'd end up discussing this and I swore I wouldn't let anything upset you.'

I beat aside the chill that ran through me. It was a feeling very like anger. I told him firmly, 'Mrs Cooke's sister.'

Blankly, he confirmed, 'Mrs Blake. Yes?'

The name scorched my mind. This was the second time today I'd heard the name and it sharpened my nerve. I'd only been about to observe that Mrs Cooke's letter had mentioned a sister who was living in Gloucester and to ask Richard if he could remember the address. Now I said with a hard kind of impatience, 'According to the rather fearsome ladies I met on that street earlier, Mrs Blake is their neighbour. And three years ago, Mrs Abbey was another. Surely if Mrs Abbey had been seeking to move and she'd mentioned it to her neighbours, the most helpful of them, Mrs Blake, might have happened to mention that the estate her sister worked for sometimes had vacant tenancies.'

I thought he must have sensed my determination. But his response was only a cautious, 'She might.'

'So it is perfectly probable that Mrs Cooke was the connection that brought Mrs Abbey to Eddington. Not John.'

His reply swept the thought away. 'Don't you find it a little odd that of all the rumours which abound about John, this is the first time that this one has come to light? Haven't you wondered why Mrs Abbey has chosen this moment, this precise moment when her supposed lover is dead and her husband is released from prison – her violent, bruising husband, mind, who is stalking the neighbourhood – to risk some unverifiable scandal that might just jeopardise everything she holds dear?'

He was suddenly taking control over this discussion and it rocked me. This wasn't quite about unpicking Mrs Abbey's idea of truth any more. I watched with a kind of horror as he added with quiet force, 'If she were claiming that the child was John's and her purpose was to get the family to release funds for the boy's care, wouldn't you think that surely the swiftest way to reach that end must be an approach to the bereaved grandfather? For the sake of the dead son's long-lost love child, she could be confident that the old man would fund a place at school, at the very least, even if he didn't believe her. And yet my father doesn't even know.'

This was for Richard. Again, the focus of this threat always came back to Richard. It hit me with a bolt.

'No.' The word was wrenched from me on a deep note of protest.

All of a sudden, I couldn't look at him. The hillside around us was mottled black with grey patches where ant hills rose. Beside me, his presence was how I shall always remember him. Standing near by while I worked it through to its natural conclusion. Steady but not savage. He hadn't wanted to tell me this, and for obvious reasons. There was a divide here; a severance of innocence; an acknowledgement that if I'd gone away on the train as he'd asked, I need never have known.

At the same time, though, I wasn't entirely sure that he wasn't relieved to be telling me now. That artificial idea of the purity of my innocence would have left a taint of a different kind; a divide with an alternative beginning but the same ending. Because knowing his character as I did, he would never have let me claim him while the secret of what he had tackled here – and presumably had been concluded – waited as a second trap to prove later that there was a world of difference between his experience of life and mine. Because somehow, and I knew this now without remotely understanding how, the secret must surely involve me.

I heard him draw in a sharp breath. Richard needed to admit it now. He led me to it. 'You're perfectly right – Mrs Abbey's connection to my brother isn't watertight. There is no real proof that he might ever have met her before her move from Gloucester, regardless of what developed between them afterwards. But—'

Suddenly I couldn't bear it. 'No.'

'The evidence is there that I might.'

'No!'

The cry silenced him. He waited there, a capable man with every muscle unspeakably braced. He looked, in fact, as he had that first day in the car when he'd first given me a glimpse of how much he was used to standing alone.

My breath snatched in my throat while I mustered the words to form my protest. They came in a desperate rush. 'Your regiment might be the Royal Gloucestershire Hussars, but you said you were based in Bristol, not Gloucester. And besides, you were away at war!'

Now there really was a powerful force in his stillness. My protest held every sinew in him chained. I truly believe he'd anticipated recriminations; that my cry had been a forerunner to turning away, to refusing to bear this, to delivering blame. Not, perhaps, to the point of admitting that I believed the charge – I think that last part was reserved for his nightmares rather than waking sense – but there was still, for him, the perfectly reasonable likelihood that the accusation in itself was too great a burden for me. I'd said all along that I couldn't bear the darkness of conflict. If I had an ounce of self-preservation, I should refuse it now. Even the admission of Mrs Abbey's insinuation had the power to run nastiness through every single vein. I could feel it working there; staining me with disgust, and impotent, disbelieving rage.

But not directed at him. The part I couldn't bear wasn't what he thought. In him, resolve was settling to a softer kind of certainty that belonged to a sense of my care for him, and his subtle acceptance of it caused a wrench in me that hurt almost as much as rejection.

'I know,' he conceded gently. 'But still I think she's levelling the charge.'

I was shaking my head. I couldn't give it the substance of being spoken, so he said it for me. 'You are going to have to believe me when I say that although she hasn't levied her actual demands yet, the suggestion is there and I'm expecting them any day.'

'Blackmail.' It was said scathingly. In a sneer. Angry resistance, even though I'd suspected this was her end for long enough myself. 'And for what?'

'You've seen the state my father is in. If her threat to me is to expose me and mine to the attentions of the world, don't you think it's reasonable to imagine I'd work to shield him from further public humiliation? Or myself?'

Or me now. I supplied the addition in my head and felt its strain while he added swiftly, 'She doesn't want money. She doesn't want any help of the kind that would be within my power to offer willingly because if she did she would have asked me openly in the car. This is about snaring me, and me specifically, because I have the skills she needs.'

'Because you're a soldier.'

I was standing with fingers tugging at one fraying cuff of the gardening coat and staring blindly at the darkened streambed below. Beside me, I sensed the way the shadow of his mouth twisted into a brief show of a bitter smile. 'I think, Emily dear, you'll find that's your prejudice. I can't imagine my choice of career even ranks with her.'

It was a poor attempt at humour. 'No,' he continued, 'she's chosen me because she believes I'm a true brother to John. This is her other motive for continually mentioning him, I think. I imagine she has a pretty shrewd idea of what he was capable of and she must imagine the same blood runs through my veins. She means to harness it.'

There was one grim second before he added, 'I suppose it proves at least that one part of this madness is true. The danger this arsonist poses to her must be real. What other insanity would lead a person to resort to spinning lie upon lie to tame a man she barely knows and make him her servant, when she could simply tell us all the truth and report her husband's activities to the police and ask for official help?'

I offered quietly, 'Unless she's already tried, you mean, and got nowhere?'

It was there again. An echo of the debate he'd shared with Phyllis, where the actions within a conflict were either rational or not. Cold and distant, the weight of what Mrs Abbey was expecting of him finally hit me. To me the woman was seeming considerably less like a helpless victim facing unspeakable revenge at the hands of a violent husband and more like this was her final word in the bitter scheming of an acrimonious divorce, where all parties saw betrayal as the currency for everything. And all the time I was coming back to the one simple truth that coursed through it all. That even if she were the victim – to choose this route, to enlist a man against his will to undertake this work when there must be other, gentler ways to save her … It was barbaric.

My voice was not my own. 'She's treating this like a debt you have to pay. Because of who you are.'

Richard had said nothing. He was standing there watching me as I watched the blank and dormant turbine house.

I thought I almost surprised him into reaching out a hand towards me when at last I added on a completely bewildered note, 'She *really* doesn't know you, does she? I mean, if she's so alone and Duckett isn't enough of a friend to truly help her and she wants you to intercede between her and this husband who seems to think it is a good idea to hedge her in with little fires, why doesn't she just *ask?*'

I found I had made him smile at last. When he returned to the self-imposed distance after that one impulsive movement towards me and nothing else moved in the valley bottom, he said on a wry note, 'Why not, indeed.'

I thought I'd actually made him laugh. He confirmed it with a sudden return to that brisker tone I knew. 'Anyway, let's not forget that it doesn't really matter what she has in mind here – regardless of whether I'm supposed to lay a little trap for Abbey and lure him out into the open, or hunt him down where he sleeps. I am my own man here. This isn't war.

There are no orders, and the lines between right and wrong remain perfectly clear.'

He drew a little breath, gathering his thoughts before lifting his jaw with a grace that actually verged upon arrogance. 'To be frank,' he added, 'we can guess all we like at the depths of her predicament, but we both know she's put it out of my power to do anything about it by her own actions.' I could feel the anger there, licking like fire beneath the resolve.

He told me, 'And I haven't brought you here, either, for the sake of frightening you with the responsibility of understanding her choices. I've brought you here because it is right to tell you the truth of mine. I don't intend to serve up my conscience on a platter to her as a bargaining chip for the sake of anyone's reputation – not John's, not mine, nor my father's 'and not even yours – come what may. My going away on Sunday should put me out of the way of being called to immediate action while I calculate what can be done for her through more safely regulated channels such as PC Rathbone's man from the Gloucester station. But I can't stop her from following her part of the threat to its end. If even a fraction of what she's engineered here gets out, the gossips'll feed on me for months and they won't care who else gets dragged into the crossfire. Do you mind?'

Abruptly, the charged, intimidating sense of this night's isolation broke into relief. This had been my dread; the part I wouldn't bear. It had dwelt in the impossibility of imagining how he could both deal with this threat and keep his integrity intact. But this was how he would do it. And in amongst all that, there was also a glimpse of an assumption he was making about my future.

Suddenly it was easy to lift my head and smile quite genuinely. 'You ask me that?'

My question was answered in the steadiness of those eyes, but the feeling didn't quite reach his mouth. Grit turned under foot as he took a step closer. He shook his head before his gaze dropped its hold on mine and cast something very grim out into the gloom. 'No,' he said. 'Not really. I think you've made your position on the principle of sacrifice very clear at last, haven't you? And you still have absolutely no idea what part you really play here.'

His gaze returned to me. I found I couldn't quite understand what he meant by that. My mouth fractured to reveal the brittle self-doubt beneath. I knew he was confronting me with something about myself; the part of me that had made the unwilling confession earlier about refusing any new surrender of another person's welfare for the sake of mine. For a moment I'd thought I ought to be happy because surely that was what I'd done just now – I'd wielded that power. But the hard evening spent debating conflict and salvation and the dreadful strain of being part of the world that called for both was suddenly taking its toll. And even if I didn't yet fully understand what he had meant there, I knew full well what had been troubling him because it occupied the part that carried that note of temper. His doubt was in his sense of how my stubbornness would bear upon me, both now upon my happiness, and in the future as a person drawn in by my proximity to him. And for me even the thought of the debate that must be running through his mind about whether we would regret this decision to let me stay close – it made me angrier in a way that must leave permanent traces between us. It was all so desperately bleak.

'Emily?' My name came as a whisper on the air.

'Yes?'

He hadn't really meant the murmur of my name as a question. It was more a statement of fact. A simple assertion that I was still myself and unaltered and, like a ripple of the memory of the way he had looked earlier when I'd dared at last to call him by his name, I realised I must have gifted him this same sense of being valued.

It was probably the only word he could have used that was capable of sweeping all this hopelessness aside, as though he were wielding a little brush of light. The distance between us was nothing. He'd never been far away at all. The realisation was followed by a real whisper of his hand as it lifted to my cheek. With the lightest of pressure, he tilted my chin so that the features of my face were touched just a little by starlight. My body instinctively moved to follow the turn of his hand. I went to him with relief. My own hands found his chest and clung to his jumper there while his other arm closed about me, drawing me against him. I could feel his heartbeat beneath my fingertips. I thought he was going to finish this sudden relief of contact by enfolding me completely within the crush of his arms. But then his body stilled and his touch was held lightly against my jaw so that I had to look at him, and when he spoke, his voice was grave.

'Ought I to have told you all this?'

He was reading every trace of every cruel second of my time in this place upon my face, waiting for a response to a question that had no happy answer. My reply was the faintest turn of my cheek against the warmth of his hand in place of a small nod.

Then I grew embarrassed and asked foolishly, 'What do you think?'

I suspected there wasn't a happy answer to that question either. The force of his life-blood beat beneath my palm, steadying and regular. Then he remarked on a quiet note, 'I think you care for me.'

I could sense again that hint of doubt within the decisiveness that ran through every corner of his mind and, very faintly beneath it all, a disorientating confession of his need for me. But, suddenly, there was a shadow of a smile on that mouth. There was no need then for the strong rhythm of his heartbeat to set the pattern for mine. Because my pulse was hurrying, lifting into a lighter race really, and there was a wry twist of amusement in the darkness of this night.

He made my breath catch when he confided cheerfully, 'I just wish I knew whether it was a reflection of who I am, or simply that you're really, really kind.'

Chapter 23

The night didn't end there. It didn't neatly fade to black on an endnote of intimacy. Instead there was a sudden intensity of disbelief as we were climbing our way back up through the faint aroma of smoke because it struck me then that throughout all of this we'd been ignoring the detail that Mrs Abbey's car was presently up on blocks, looking as though it had been there for years. Yet only a week ago it had been bearing wheels and parked outside her husband's daytime haunt of the watershed, ready to meet Phyllis and her bicycle. Mrs Abbey might have been visiting him there. Or perhaps it was a coincidence. Or perhaps the husband himself had demanded the use of it. Whichever way it was, there was the sudden muddle of stopping Richard in the lee of the kitchen door with the urgency of saying, 'You have considered that Abbey mightn't be her enemy at all, haven't you? But that this is wholly a trap for you?'

Then the Colonel snatched open the kitchen door. He'd been waiting there in the dark and I didn't like to imagine what he thought he saw in a scene that had a young woman gripping his son's sleeve and that man's hand firmly over hers.

The Colonel didn't acknowledge me at all. He must have heard our exit, or at least discovered it later, because he had been waiting in the dark behind the locked door like a ship's guard ready to repel all boarders. There was tension in his posture as he watched us step in through the door that made me think this was a welcome that had been enacted before; perhaps when the other son had returned from a night out with some girl.

Only in those days presumably the lights would have been blazing because the electricity would have been working and the old man wouldn't have been required to sit in the dark so that he could watch undetected for the approach of an arsonist.

In the slow rise of light after the door was locked and an oil lamp was lit, the old man's head was high and jutting from his neck. This was the old soldier preparing to fight a difficult battle and this one, I thought, was something of a rearguard action in the midst of a messy retreat. Survival was depending very heavily on standing guard here so that he could snatch the first possibility of speaking to his son. It was also immediately made very clear that whatever it was that he had to say so urgently, it couldn't be said in front of me.

I couldn't help looking back as I slid quietly through the door to the servant's stairs. Richard's father was red-faced and impatient to begin. Richard himself was possessed by that watchfulness that showed he wasn't quite sure what to expect, but was going to meet it anyway. He spared one small glance for me. A tip of his head in gratitude for my discreet withdrawal was followed by a single bright flare of care.

My return to the bedroom was only temporary. Phyllis was snoring when I slipped back into bed, but she was awake and bouncing when I drifted groggily back into consciousness about three and a half hours later to find the room full of sunlight. My sense of befuddlement wasn't improved by the fact that the first thing I had to say was, 'Phyllis? Why have you stolen Danny's dog?'

She was lounging on the bed with the dog, which had adopted a kind of boneless lean with his forelimbs sprawled across her lap. It was an arrangement they'd obviously enjoyed before on other days and in other houses on other pieces of furniture, and I was expecting, I think, another one of those conversations where strategic wordplay tried to disguise that the dog's presence was real at all. Only he was there and Phyllis had stolen him from Danny's parents' house after she'd taken the trouble of hobbling all the way round there, only to find that Danny had gone out with Richard in the car.

She also informed me that Danny Hannis was arrogant, childish, infuriating, pedantic and an idiot. The only thing she didn't include was that he was young.

Then she added while I blinked and tried to battle my way into stockings, 'He's the sort of man who will happily ignore the fact that you've told him you never want to speak to him again when it suits him, such as when he happens to arrive first at the scene of a crisis to find you in a state. Then, he was the sort of man who could willingly set aside every injunction for the sake of wading in and acting all caring and dependable just because I'd come off my bicycle and was suddenly in such a blasted mess. On that day he even managed to work in a few calming words while he handed me a hand-kerchief because I was sobbing a bit and bleeding all over the leather seats of that ridiculous car. It suited him perfectly to set aside my wishes then, presumably because it allowed him to demonstrate what I was missing. But now, just as soon as I've managed to get out of hospital and I've decided it might be a good idea to clear up a few misunderstandings, he's immediately decided that my former wishes are set in stone and he's sticking to them so bloody rigidly that I can't get within twenty yards of him. He's a pig. And this poor little dog here is the leverage I need to force his master's hand.'

The dog didn't seem particularly concerned by his fate. He was very hairy and had wonderfully mobile eyebrows. He'd raised them quizzically at her and she was smiling down at him as she said, 'Would you believe Danny and I actually rowed about the hanging of some new curtains?'

As the dog wasn't the one who was supposed to answer, I stopped fighting with the cake of mascara that was stubbornly refusing to soften and asked kindly, 'Well, what sort were they? I suppose you were trying to choose a design that would go with all the ceramic ducks, or the commemorative plates or something?'

'*Not* the ducks, you nit. The curtains were symbolic. I was trying to let him know how I felt … I was trying to hint that he should tell me what he thought about the idea of living with me.'

'Oh. Oh, dear.'

I wasn't sure that sympathy was the right thing to give. Phyllis shot me a wild-eyed look. 'Don't say it like that. Please. I know it was a clumsy way of giving him the idea he might make a home at the cottage, but what was I meant to do? He's been living in his mother's attic ever since he was demobbed and it amazes me that he even fits. It makes him feel hemmed in when he's perfectly capable of setting up his own home somewhere and, lately, he's been talking about moving away, emigrating even. Perhaps Australia. So I thought I should at least *try* to have that conversation with him. But women like me aren't meant to have company. It seems we had a choice back at the beginning of our careers. Either we could opt for the life of an intellectual female and abide in splendid but respectable isolation forever more, or give way to an aggressive kind of femininity and work up to becoming one of those wildly confident women who will perpetually lust after the young man who comes in to fix the plumbing ... It seems romance isn't meant for the academics. It isn't for the women who grew up thinking they could contribute in this way and still rank as a female. And it seems you certainly don't get it by making an offer to a man to join you in a mad little cottage. Particularly,' she added bitterly, 'when all along the man in question has had his own house and gone to great lengths to avoid mentioning it.'

'Dear Phyllis, I am so sorry.' I didn't really know what to say.

'And,' she added more soberly, 'it's his fault I was horrible last night. I wasn't myself. I didn't mean to be rude.'

There was a rather weighty pause and I felt compelled to say, 'I thought you were impressive last night. Your style of debating with the Colonel after dinner was a vital distraction. *Is* vital.'

'I prefer to use the term terrific.'

She made me smile. And then she undid it again by remarking carelessly, 'Anyway, it isn't my chatter about India and politics that's making all the difference to the old man's comfort in this house. But you can think that, 'my young friend', if it makes it easier. You do know, don't you, what sort of hard life a woman will lead as a soldier's wife?'

I choked. And managed to mumble, 'I don't know that I'm afraid of *that*. That'd be the easy part.'

Then, in the wake of that embarrassingly revealing nonsense, I said rather more strongly, 'Quite honestly, Phyllis, at this moment my very real fear is that the world and all its nastiness isn't prepared to leave either of us alone long enough to find our own course beyond these first few days of knowing each other; or even let us have a future at all.'

And then, having forced a confession like that from me, before I could so much as recover to the point of making a more coherent explanation, perhaps even to the point of confiding a selected portion of what had happened last night, she was already assuming I meant it as a reprimand to her and was hurrying on to say, 'Don't listen to me. What do I know? I'm beginning to suspect I really am the giddy eccentric your mother wanted me to be. And do you know, I haven't seen our Captain since my father's funeral, which would have been about ten years ago and around the time that the portrait of him was taken that hangs on the gallery wall just outside this room. Have you seen it? It's the photograph hidden in the midst of all those very intimidating ones of the Colonel. I can't imagine why John had to choose that one for the family record. As I recall, it wasn't long before Mrs Langton's death and that was why he was home. Their mother developed some awful complaint of the kidneys, poor woman. It was a complication of the scarlet fever she'd had years before. She wasted away no matter how many times the Colonel whisked her off to see one of the Harley Street physicians. That photograph must mark the time her illness reached the point beyond hope. So, actually, I *can* calculate perfectly well why John insisted on using it. There's no sign of our Captain's uniform since he was on leave, it was taken on one of his rare visits home at a time that must have painful connotations for him and I suppose John thought he was subtly underlining his own claim upon this house.' A sharp glance at me. 'And that, my dear cousin, is why I am thoroughly expunging that man's presence in this bedroom by spreading about my clothes.'

She cast a scathing glance about the monumental formality of the room. 'Although,' she added, 'it doesn't exactly scream of John's personality in here, does it? Do you think anyone has ever thought to make this place a home? Except perhaps his poor deceased mother whose personal tastes are still to be found everywhere in the wallpaper and paintings.'

Phyllis was looking magnificent as she sat there, enthroned on the vast oak bed-frame with the dog worshipping her. The fussy woman of yesterday who had been seeking retirement in a museum of a cottage had been left there, hopefully never to be reclaimed. Then another doubt struck me. I asked carefully, 'Phyllis? Did you really say that my mother *asked* you to play the worthy chaperone?'

My cousin looked first disconcerted, then guilty. Finally

she looked reproving and informed me, 'I wouldn't say your mother exactly came up with the idea, but she must have guessed my motives when she told me in a letter that you'd caused a row by saying you wanted to go away and I suggested you came here instead. If we hadn't planted the idea into your father's head of sending you to me for a display of drab spinsterhood, he'd never have let you go anywhere, would he?'

I must have still been half asleep. I still hadn't quite managed to work myself into my frock. I did so and then discovered that Phyllis was suddenly eyeing me austerely. She scrutinised my appearance, nodded her approval and then remarked thoughtfully, 'Do you know, the Colonel was right last night when he remarked that we're in this peculiar state of trying to reconstruct the sort of life we want to live now. But the problem is that everyone's got their own ideas of the form that reconstruction should take, and it was wrong of me to harass the Captain into explaining his part in it. If he's anything like the other men who fought and came home, his main wish will be to embed some semblance of calm order into each day. And this isn't a fresh criticism, by the way. It's right that he should have it. But for me, order means a return to how things were before and that means the past is a trap.'

'Is it?' I asked, thinking rather too closely about her strange relationship with the gallery of dead portraits in her mother's bedroom.

'I don't want to go back to how things were before the war. Given my expertise and the credibility I've won in these past years, I could take work now lecturing at my old college. But because I am a woman of a reasonable social standing and because of how things were before ...' She was speaking slowly, as if she were almost tasting the insult. 'Normal order dictates I should only keep the work if I never marry. If I marry, my husband ought to keep me on his income and direct me to make way for others who would be in greater need of the work. But I am permitted to keep myself, if I remain a *spinster.*'

The word was cast between us to land on the bedspread and linger there positively, simmering with revulsion. She told me, 'I suppose it's a bit of a moot point now after all that nonsense about curtains, and anyway, I don't think I actually *want* to lecture. But I don't think people should be allowed to call a woman a spinster. It's an awful way to dismiss all that a woman is and all that she does and recast her in the image of a dithering old fusspot whose words needn't be listened to. Unless she's a forthright intellectual, in which case she's permitted, grudgingly, to be an eccentric old battleaxe instead. It's a ridiculous kind of straightjacket to put upon any person and it's making me flounder. It's been hard enough to reconstruct an ordinary life for myself after all those years of living to someone else's orders. I wanted to move forwards. I wanted things to be different now. But exciting still. And you—'

She made me jump with the force of the sudden focus of her attention upon me. She told me curtly, 'I thought you were caught in the other end of the same trap. Your parents' description of a war-befuddled, rudderless girl destined for marriage to some smothering boy made me think I only had to get you here to give you room to say what you really wanted. I thought I would draw out the young woman I believed I knew from your letters and teach you to make tougher choices. But I don't think you need anyone to do that.'

She surveyed me with another of those peculiarly shrewd glances. But then, when she finished, it was on an unnervingly uncertain note.

'As I say,' she added, 'I thought this was a rescue ... But now I'm not sure what this is.'

I might have thought that she meant to gratify me with the suggestion that she didn't quite know who was rescuing whom here, whether in fact I was aiding her, or even the Colonel or Richard. Then it occurred to me that she had detected at last some of the larger complications that were tugging at my hand, and this was her caution. It was a deeply unsettling way to be launched into a new day.

Chapter 24

The feeling had grown worse when I had arrived downstairs and found an old man in a state of urgent bustle about the condition of his dining room. He was worrying about his dinner-party plans and this was tension, not temper. Whatever parental concerns had motivated his late-night discussion with Richard, it hadn't translated into rudeness to me today. Instead, I got the impression that he was clutching at tradition because he didn't know what else to do. So now I was at the village shop on his behalf again with his list of ingredients for his dinner party because it seemed to be what he needed most.

I had travelled by bicycle for the sake of avoiding the easier but rather more isolated walk through the lonely woodland as Danny had once suggested, but I did, however, take the precaution of going by the little green lane that ran just beyond the farmyard with the ponies in it. It had seemed to me that I would be unlikely to run into Duckett by going that way, since he couldn't have taken his car.

As it was, I didn't run into anyone. And it turned out that nine o'clock on a Saturday morning at the shop was a scene of happy activity. It was full of women, men and boys with empty baskets who all, it seemed, had picked up the idea that I had taken employment at the Manor. It was a repeat of the conversation I'd had with Mrs Abbey, except without the undertone of accusation, and it was then that I noticed the woman at the counter with the three lively children. I couldn't help observing how much she had been transformed by the change out of her usual threadbare work-a-day housecoat into a vivid green day dress.

She was the beaten-down slum survivor from the squatters' camp and she was shyly dismissing compliments by drawing attention to the tightness of the waist and enjoying the unexpected gift of clothes and marvelling that such a frock had ever fitted a woman of Mrs Abbey's stature at all.

I was thinking it was no wonder it looked as if it had never been made to fit Mrs Abbey's tall figure, because the frock was mine and the fabric that had made it had previously belonged to my mother's treasured floor-length evening gown, only because of wartime thriftiness my mother had passed it to me to make up anew into a skirt, a hair wrap and this one particularly splendid frock. It had been in my suitcase when Duckett had taken it and until now I'd imagined it had burned with the rest.

As it turned out, very few of my clothes had burned last night. The arsonist had wasted just enough to leave a lasting trace of my presence. The rest had gone to this woman as a gift, yesterday, while I had been in Gloucester tackling Duckett about the return of my case.

Mrs Abbey had been generous enough to make a present of three frocks, a skirt – the twin to this dress – and also a couple of blouses, which the woman from the squatters' camp was intending to alter for her eldest son, ready for his new term at school. I hadn't the grit to tell her that the clothes were mine. I let the gift stand and then, I'm afraid, I queued with ridiculous meekness for my turn at the counter to collect the Colonel's order, and then I left.

But not before a man who I had barely noticed detached himself from the gossiping clutches of the postmaster and followed me outside.

He was not Duckett and he was not Abbey. He was a man I would have said I had never seen in my life, only I had a feeling he was the man I'd passed near the turbine house on the morning after the assault. He'd been eating his sandwiches then and would have passed for any ordinary gentleman on a scenic walk in the midst of his holiday. Yesterday he must have been the man who had tricked the Colonel into giving him a tour of the house. Today the man was broad-shouldered, about Matthew Croft's age, nearly as tall, and distinctly over-dressed for a warm day in the countryside. Wearing that long cotton raincoat, he might have been taken for an office clerk or a travelling salesman, but his stare gave him away. I'd met that kind of intensity in a look before. I'd encountered it on the street outside my chemist's shop in Knightsbridge whenever a rumour had circulated that the royal princesses had been put to work in the Lancaster bomber factory which had occupied the great department store next door. All the journalists had got for their trouble on those days were blank screens of boarded-up windows and a depressed air of frustrated greed. This fellow was, I hoped, set to have a similar experience now.

He had learned my name. 'Miss Sutton?'

I was already loading my purchases into the basket on my bicycle. Somehow the Colonel's menu had managed to fill quite a package and all without trespassing heavily on items that were rationed. I turned, hands ready on the handlebars. My left foot was on the nearside pedal, ready for the push from my right that would send the bicycle downhill to that tight bend beneath the shop and allow me to do that hop across the bar people do to claim the seat at speed. The journalist saw I had recognised him and seemed to take it as his cue.

'Might I have a word? I'm meant to have a quick chat with Captain Langton this morning, but I missed him.'

'Oh?' I believe my response conveyed perfectly my disinclination to answer any of his questions.

The journalist wasn't going to be easily put off though. 'Yes, he was here asking after PC Rathbone about twenty minutes ago, but he was disappointed because the constable's not at home. The constable's been called out to examine a fire.'

I caught the flash of a swift smile. He was a good-looking man and I thought he knew it. I was trying very hard not to show that the news meant anything to me. Then he added, 'Over at a place called Miserden. Apparently an outhouse got burnt to the ground last night. Did you know about it?'

'*Miserden?*' Suddenly I could speak. Because an outhouse in one of the neighbouring villages certainly couldn't be mistaken for the turbine house near Washbrook. Then I was shaking my head and giving a hasty answer to his question.

388

It was an honest answer as they go. 'No,' I said. 'I've never even heard of it.'

The man was eyeing me with disconcerting boldness. Now his expression didn't quite fit my memory of the hungry look worn by the newspapermen who had clamoured after a story – any story. This look was rather more calculating. He was seeking something very specific and I felt, with a sudden jolt, he was reasonably certain that he'd found it in me.

While I struggled my way through tangled doubts about multiple arsonists and different fires on the same night, the man before me was flashing me another disarming smile. 'Actually,' he said. 'The Captain was chatting to the man in charge of the wireless station. The fellow buys his lunch in this shop, just like everyone else. They were discussing something about sheds and outhouses and where the station gets its water ...?'

I didn't reply. I moved my hands on the handlebars and allowed the bicycle to roll forwards a fraction. He put out a hand, not to touch me but as a restraining gesture and said swiftly, 'I wanted to talk to you anyway, Miss Sutton. About how you happened to come by this work for Colonel Langton? Might I ask—?'

I shot him a look that might freeze. I said stiffly, 'I don't work for Colonel Langton. This shopping trip was done in the spirit of friendship. And I'm sorry, but who do you report to exactly?'

I stopped there. A door had opened behind me just uphill from the shop and both of us turned to see. It was the doctor's house and Mrs Abbey was emerging, blinking in the sunlight with her children at her heels and bearing a bruise on her jaw that was now reduced to an awful mottled sepia. The improvement, if that was what it should be called, was owing to a heavy application of face powder. And the expression on her face, when she saw me today with this man, was different from the way she had looked yesterday as I'd left her at the tithe barn for the sake of climbing into Richard's car. This time there was no triumph and there was no requirement to choose sides. Her children were smiling shyly again, whereas she looked, in fact, just as she had that day when she'd found me on the doorstep at Eddington after she'd thought I'd gone away. Beneath the crisp styling of a coordinated skirt and blouse and jacket that conveyed a gritty readiness to meet any difficulty alone, she looked exhausted.

Mrs Abbey barely mustered a good morning before she had stepped out of the door, shut it and was hurrying her children away up the short rise to the junction at the top. She opted for the alternative route home along the rough trackway that I had used earlier. To get to it, she first had to turn left around the curve of a house and pass out of sight along the lane through the village.

I took advantage of the silence she left behind to say shortly to the man near my side without turning my head, 'Actually, never mind about your newspaper. I don't have anything to say to you.'

Then I dodged his automatic exclamation and pushed off with my foot and let the momentum of the bicycle carry me onwards down the hill and around the turn.

That part was easy. It was a far harder push up the next

hill to rejoin the lane and find Mrs Abbey. When I reached the junction, she was nowhere in sight. I traced the lane back through the village and found her about halfway along in the process of making her children climb through one of those footpath stiles that form a narrow 'v' between slabs of upright stone. It was a shortcut on the route homewards that was closed to me due to the handicap of my bicycle. She must have been very nervous because instinct carried her just as soon as she heard my approach in one leap through the stile onto the other side. The reaction was a touch extreme, but it fuelled me as I launched into the first of the frustrations and accusations left from last night. 'Mrs Abbey. Why did you set the fire in the turbine house?'

She wasn't afraid of me. She also wasn't concerned by anything I had to say. She turned there behind her stile and smiled one of those disbelieving smiles made by a person who had been braced for a shock and reacted accordingly, only to find the threat had only been me. I wasn't even sure she was listening. She was blinking at me and the space around us and it was then that it occurred to me that she too was taking the route home that avoided exposed lengths of road accessible by car.

It was in the following second that I noticed the fresh strapping about her wrist.

With my gaze inescapably fixed on the bandage, I persisted somewhat more distractedly, 'Please, Mrs Abbey, I found some of my clothes there and don't pretend it isn't you who has had custody of them for the past day or so because I met one of my frocks in the shop just now and I wasn't the person wearing it.'

I looked up and found the colour had ebbed back into her cheeks. Her children weren't worried at all. They were hunting crawling things further along the hedgerow and she didn't think to call them back. She wasn't behaving remotely as I thought she should. She was, in fact, making me increasingly convinced that I'd made a mistake by beginning this confrontation because the more I said, the more I was frightening myself. I mean to say that I was suddenly discovering that I was frightened of her; actually physically afraid and I didn't fully know why. I just know that I kept back, just out of arm's reach.

I heard myself add, 'We know it wasn't Duckett who set the fire in the turbine house. Because the arsonist burnt some of my clothes and I understand at last that Duckett was being perfectly honest when he said that he didn't have my suitcase. I didn't realise what he meant at the time but now I know. He was telling me that he'd given you the accounts books and my bag. And,' I finished on a colder note as I suddenly grasped the full implication of what I had learned, 'I believe that two days ago, when I came visiting with Captain Langton and you very seriously offered me the loan of some clothes, you had my suitcase in your house all along. Didn't you?'

Now her stare really was frightening me. She was watching me with the sort of ambivalence that belongs to a person who is so emotionally removed from a scene that all empathy is dead. Whereas, for me, the whole truth was sliding, reluctantly, step by step into concern. I felt the moment I recalled just how hard Duckett had worked to find her. And the memory burned when I realised that, for an old friend, she had been awfully quick to use my name to send him away again. It wasn't fear for myself any more that made my voice tight when I asked quickly, 'Duckett is setting the fires in the outhouses, isn't he?'

I'd leaned closer while my hands remained secure on my handlebars. I expected her to shake free of this stupor and ridicule me. I certainly expected her to demur, based on the way she'd evaded every other opportunity she'd had to share the truth. But something had changed. I have never seen a woman so close to breaking. A vital and urgent eagerness transformed her features and she confessed in a voice made shrill by the race to speak, 'He's flushing out my husband. He's all that stands between me and Paul. He's here. Close by. It's a nightmare born out of that disaster at the warehouse. Neither of them will let it rest. And it's—' A swift glance behind to assure herself that her children were still safely close at hand in a way that was at last painfully authentic. Then she confided in a whisper, 'It's *unbearable.*'

The hand she lifted was the one with the bandage. If I'd wondered what had changed to loosen her controls enough to speak to me now, this new injury was the clue.

It made me ask urgently, 'Who did that? Your husband or Duckett?'

She didn't think of the bandage. She thought of the bruise on her face. Fingers lightly reached to cover the mark, as if she'd forgotten it was there. She admitted, 'Paul took Mrs Cooke's keys from me.'

'*You* had them?'

'Of course I did. And yesterday I gave them back after the

Colonel's little speech to his tenants in the farmyard. Mrs Cooke was my friend and she gave them to me for safekeeping. But Paul wanted the food she'd left behind, so he took them. Then your Captain pitched up on my doorstep with the news that the squire had come home, so I went in the daytime to retrieve them before anyone could think to ask for them back. *This* was my reward. A nice return for a bit of kindness for that foolish Colonel when I could have quite easily feigned complete ignorance.' The hand dropped from her cheek.

'Why?'

I saw Mrs Abbey's face cloud into puzzlement. She asked blankly, 'Why did she give the keys to me? Because when she left, she left quickly, of course. She packed her bags almost as soon as she got the old man's note telling her to get a bed ready just in case he came. She'd dedicated her life to tending to that man's wishes and I think she was a little bit in love with him, for all that he and his son both always treated her like a fussy, servile fool. But she couldn't bear to stay when she heard the old man was thinking of coming back. Sometimes I think Mrs Cooke and I have rather too much in common. We neither of us can forgive the old man for what he did to John.'

Her mouth twisted. And so did my mind. It was a jolt to suddenly pass from concern about Abbey and Duckett into hearing about John Langton. It was with a considerably cooler tone that I remarked, 'Actually, I'm still trying to establish who is frightening you. In my question just now I meant to ask *why* was your husband in a position to ask you for the keys in the first place? I thought he was hunting you – taking his revenge because you ran away after he was sentenced or because he's trying to claim his share of the money from the sale of your house in Gloucester, or something. I didn't expect to hear he has been pitching up on your doorstep in time for tea. Do you mean to say he's been sleeping at Eddington?'

Then I realised. 'The light that shines from the back of your house at night isn't coming from a window as I'd thought. It can't be, because there aren't any on the side that forms the high boundary wall. It's a signal put out by your children to tell their father that the way is clear. And he was waiting that evening when he collided with Mr Winstone, who was hurrying home for his tea. Are you trying to tell me that you *want* to shelter Paul Abbey in your house?'

Wide eyes jerked upwards to mine. I was thinking that all this detection might have been made so much easier had Richard only taken his last night-time walk a little earlier on his first night here. If he had come at dusk to assure himself that I'd made it safely home after leaving him and his father to their dinner, he might have been in time to see Abbey moving around in the company of his children in the lamp-light of Eddington.

Her voice was hollow as she admitted, 'Selling my house in Gloucester was a mistake. I thought I'd never get the chance to go back. I was safe here and I could manage the rent. But last winter my husband had the chance of a new legal case. He needed money. He needed it to get out. He's my husband. I didn't have a choice.'

There was a bitter edge to her voice as she leaned over her stone stile again to confide in a last whisper, 'He's out, but

I'm still trapped by everyone. We all lost money in that warehouse fire and now we're poor when I want to be free to live again.'

She straightened once more, but left behind that crucial word. Free. It was a word that might mean everything to a person hedged in by threats and violence. From the way her eyes were still searching the vacant lane to left and right from her place behind the barrier of the stone stile, I believed it meant everything to her.

And yet, in the back of my mind was the impossibility of believing her at all. Because this simple justification of all her actions was all too much like freedom for me too. I asked doubtfully while my pulse beat strongly, '*That's* what this is about? This really is about reclaiming your house because you sold it and now John Langton's dead, you knew the estate would be made bankrupt and you wouldn't be able to stay here for much longer. So you want his brother's help, after all, to return there? Is that *all?*'

She wouldn't hear me. She was already saying, 'Everyone has a hold on my soul. Do you know Paul never even stayed at that squatters' camp? I had to give away the clothes as an apology. I knew he might go there and I couldn't even tell Brian he'd made a mistake, because if I had, Brian would have known that I'd lied when I'd said I didn't know where Paul was.'

'Brian is the man I call Duckett?'

'Yes.'

'And this is why you told Duckett I was helping your husband and engineered all the rest. Because you don't dare to be caught out on that single lie? Is the truth really so dangerous?'

She was saying quietly, 'They mustn't meet. If they do, Paul will try to stop him. But he's deranged. Quite deranged. He wants revenge for the money he lost in the business. We're so afraid.'

My heart slowed to a hard, clear rhythm. It was heavy with the burden of realising that she'd told no one this and yet here she was telling me now and I mustn't break this chance by a clumsy misstep. Mrs Abbey was putting out that hand towards me again. In supplication, I thought, hesitantly, doubt-fully because she was aware the shift of power here was oddly in my favour and for the first time since meeting me I thought she perceived my resolve. My own eyes were drawn inescapably to that bandage and this time I was torn between feeling the cruelty of it and a repulsive suspicion it was merely a burn from last night's fire.

'Who helped you to set the fire at the turbine house last night? Duckett or Abbey?'

'My husband. Paul thought it would leave irrefutable evidence for the police that the fires were being set by Brian. That's why we used your clothes and the books. To tie him to it.'

'*Really?* Just that? You had no other purpose?'

She nodded a confirmation blankly, as if my sudden eager-ness to clarify that single point was impossibly strange because there was nothing else it could be.

Relief swept over me. And guilt. We'd been wrong. This woman really was trapped. Relief nearly made me rush to offer my help. Only I heard myself ask instead, 'Why are you letting him get so close? Now that your husband is out, why don't you simply pack your bags and leave? Couldn't your brother help?'

'Why I—' I saw it hit her that we'd uncovered the lie about the photograph on her mantelpiece.

A movement dragged my attention from her face. It wasn't the children who were shredding seed-heads from tall grasses beside the footpath. It was the man from the shop, approaching around the bend in the lane and not bothering to hide the fact that he was watching us. Then Mrs Abbey gave her reply and it snatched my mind with almost painful swiftness back to her face.

Her voice was raw with strain, but still defiant. She told me with a brave little lift of her jaw, 'My brother doesn't even know Paul's out. He isn't well and if he learned any of the deeper details here, he'd be dragged in too and that would be worse. I can't go anywhere because wherever I go, my husband goes and Brian will always follow. And my children—'

She checked, then eyed me with cold determination. 'This is the only way to prove it was him all along. He just ... he just can't know I'm betraying him until it's over.'

I knew we couldn't stay here, not with that newspaperman sidling closer. I said quickly, 'We should tell Richard this. Now. He and Danny Hannis have gone looking for your husband, I think.'

'Now?' she repeated blankly.

'Paul Abbey's at the pump house, isn't he? By day, I mean? Richard was asking the man at the wireless station about huts and where they get their water. And that means he was asking about places that are like the turbine house, doesn't it?'

She was staring again.

I rushed on. 'So I think it's fair to guess that this wireless station's pump house is where the Captain and Danny will be. You know where it is, presumably, so we'll go now and find them, and then we can help your husband to explain all this.'

I thought she was angry that I meant to get her husband to confirm her story. I thought I'd just caught her out on another lie after all. But the transformation in her face wasn't anger or pride or defiance. It was a repulsively urgent version of the way Duckett had driven me away from his warehouse yesterday.

She shrieked out, 'Stop him, Emily. For heaven's sake, stop him. He'll kill him. You'll get him hurt.'

I was practically forced backwards by the power of her conviction. Before I really knew it, she had flung out instructions on how to find this pump house and then, without any thought for the suggestion that we ought to go there together, she had me turning the bicycle around and astride it. And then I was racing away with pounding pedals through the quick serpentine bends of the village, as if every wasted second was yet another act of betrayal.

The lane passed a line of dirty cottages and a smithy and then onwards past the rough trackway that had carried me here and onto a route that I had formerly only loosely pieced together in my head. This lane coursed its way down yet another steep hillside to meet the bottom-most limit of the gated lane from the Manor. It ran from there into the trees beyond my cousin's house and rose again to the ridgetop and Eddington.

Trees lined this lane too. Dense broadleaf woodland that turned the air thick and still as I spotted Richard's car standing empty in a passing place. It was the only feature I noticed. There was no room for anything else in my head. I'd been so convinced that she'd been exposing her fear of Duckett as she explained her husband's plans to betray him. Now it was utterly contradicted by a recurring echo of the core details of what she had really said. Her bruise was the reward ... he wants revenge ... he's deranged ...

She'd been speaking about Paul Abbey. And I'd said that Richard would find him.

Chapter 25

*H*e's *quite deranged.* Those few devastating minutes after that frantic discussion with Mrs Abbey were summarised in a few hateful words.

I left the lane for a track that led into the woodland from the spot where Richard had parked his car. I crossed the footpath that Danny had promised would lead to the shop and rattled down many twists and turns before engaging in a brief battle with a hawthorn, where the smothering trees gave way to grass. I was at the foot of a long field occupied by a couple of horses and three goats and marked out at one end for the villagers to use as potato plots. The rest was meadow. I rolled through long grasses that clutched at my pedals onto a sunlit bank and found myself on a short rise above the pump house. But this is the simplified version of that frantic bicycle ride.

In truth, this dry description of trees and trackways belongs to the run of events that I assembled later, once logic could place everything that came after my interview with Mrs Abbey in their correct order. In the interests of accuracy it seems honest and fair to record what happened after I left that woman in the manner in which I truly remember it.

My first memory is that I knew quite clearly that I was confused. Touch was present and so was sight, in a particularly restricted form where the peripheries might not have existed for all the attention my senses were paying them.

I knew I had lately been travelling rapidly. Now I wasn't. I appeared to have exchanged the heat of a sweating tarmacadam road in a village for this violent brightness of open sky and the crisp tang of fresh grass. I had swapped the sensation of racing downhill on a bicycle for an unyielding mat that pressed hard against my side. It felt upside down for a moment, like it was pressing on me from above. Then gravity swirled itself back into its correct alignment and my head hurt and I could hear the faint ticking as a bicycle wheel span slowly towards a halt near by.

I lifted my face from the hard-baked ground. Blades of grass stuck to my skin. It appeared that the weighty bicycle had succeeded in unseating another female rider. I was sprawling any old how on the side of a gentle slope. Every limb hurt. It was as if the force of gravity were stronger than normal, making the pressure of lying here agony. I wasn't alone, either. There was a shuffle about two yards behind and a rustle of footsteps drawing close. There was the faint glint of something small and metallic being lifted from the grass not far from where my right hand was helping me to ease myself upwards, followed by further footfalls beating an uneven retreat to silence. My head was sounding a final verse of that old refrain. *He's deranged.*

I knew who he was. And I knew why I thought the object

he had lifted had been metal. It was because I had seen the blade flash from his hand only moments before, to miss me by a cat's whisker as I plunged recklessly down the slope on a collision course. It had been one of those insane split-second choices. Injury from a weapon or to act for self-preservation. The choice had been immediate.

I turned my head and found the other one. The man who had inspired this mad dash. Richard was a few yards away, suit jacket unbuttoned and closer to getting up than I was. He said something to me, but I didn't catch it. I concentrated on beginning to push myself up into something closer to a sitting position and regretted it. Everything hurt, or at least I knew there was pain without quite being able to decipher the feeling. This, I told myself quite sternly, was all a matter of choice. One had, quite simply, only to decide to set it aside and everything would relax and ease back into its normal balance. I sat up a little straighter. No, I had to concede, it really did hurt. And not surprising, either, given the pace of my descent on that final slope to collide deliberately with Paul Abbey and drag him and his knife away from Richard. That had been my choice between injury and self-preservation; Richard's injury or my comfort. The bicycle lay on its side about a yard away, one wheel still spinning because only seconds had passed since I had last noted it.

Something moved. It was close by. Abbey hadn't gone. I turned my head, leadenly it seemed to me. Then Richard was moving. Perhaps it was him who had caught my eye in the first place. He was saying something to me, and then again more strongly, and he was up on one knee and his mouth was twisting as he shouted at me violently, and I was recoiling, disbelieving, cringing as he lunged across the grass as if to strike. He was on me with a thump before I could do more than cower away and this time there was absolutely no doubt whether my mind was capable of deciphering pain.

He had hold of me. My cry meant nothing. He was dragging me round, using his body to lever me against him into an excruciating curve so that my view was no longer the pump house and a pretty little streambed but uphill, through long grasses to where thistles stood high on the skyline. His hands had turned me face down beneath him, yanked me there, really. For a moment he only had one hand clamped about me. The other was reaching up behind him against the sky, palm uppermost and open as if in the act of fending something off, or in supplication. Only there was nothing there and I couldn't see very much anyway because of the sun. I could feel the way his arm was flung wide through the twist of his upper body as he shouted, and I felt that because of the way his lungs moved. I still couldn't hear a thing. Or at least I could, but I couldn't register it long enough to remember it.

It occurred to me then to wonder if perhaps Abbey really hadn't gone. I only had the briefest, cringing fraction of a second to consider this and to anticipate fresh pain before the upraised hand changed its mind about its plea and dropped down beside me. Then his head dropped as well and his weight crushed me and smothered me until the only part of me that wasn't covered by him was the part that was being pressed into the cruel, unyielding ground.

There was a single jolt. It ran through every one of his muscles and into mine. Just as I was beginning to believe I might never have the chance to breathe again, I felt the pressure ease slightly and the twist as his torso turned once more to trace again that run of the stream bed downhill. Then my ribs ground against a stone as he turned to look the other way. I could feel his chest moving in short, hurried snatches for air, but the renewed pressure of his weight on mine was almost suffocating. His right hand was the only bit of him I could see. It had landed palm down against the rough, dry stalks beside me. It had shifted slightly as he'd twisted to look the other away. There was blood on it. A raw graze like a burn that was running red just beside my face.

Abruptly the weight lifted. The hand helped to thrust him to his feet. I was barely stirring beside his dust-stained shoes when his other hand reached across his body to tug me to my feet in my turn. I was standing very close against his left side. I couldn't help it since his left arm firmly clamped me there. He had turned again to look downhill. I followed the line of his eyes that were narrowed against the glare and I could see the shocking contrast between the dark green foliage of a redwood that rivalled the one near my cousin's cottage and the lichens that coated the corrugated roof of the pump house. If that was the way Abbey had left, he was long gone.

Richard's gaze moved back again, deliberately passing just above mine, and then swiftly travelled onwards to the rise with all the thistles. I watched him as he watched the landscape. His expression was that of a mind performing endless, very rapid calculations. I could feel the tremor where his hand had tightly closed upon my upper arm, pinning me against him. The other hand was flexing into a fist and then releasing again; trying to ease the pain, I thought. He twisted back towards the pump house. And was finally ready to intercept my gaze on the return.

He was like himself, but not quite. His mouth moved. I could hear after all. He remarked, 'That entrance of yours was a touch dramatic, don't you think? You could have just said hello. Or rung your bicycle bell.'

'He had a knife.' My mouth was dry. And something was wrong with that statement, only I couldn't think what. I couldn't understand why Richard should be looking like he was torn between reading a threat in every blade of grass and frantic about it, and trying not to laugh.

His eyes moved on again. That hazel gaze resumed its search once more, only this time the pattern changed and his attention finally settled upon his wounded hand. He was staring at it, serious now, turning his hand this way and that as though he were expecting the blood, and yet surprised to find it there.

I found myself staring too and shrinking slightly as I said blankly, 'He was moving in. You hadn't seen it and he was going to – I don't know what. But I had to do something.'

'So you ran him down with your bicycle.' There was something rather dry in the way he said that and his arm was wrapped like iron about me, but I didn't believe he'd even noticed. His attention was fixed on something high on the hillside now, as though preoccupied and his mouth was only going through the motions of speaking to me.

Suddenly, though, his mind sharpened. His voice broke into the roughness of a reprimand and he told me with some force, 'You should have stayed back. What the hell is the point of me being as I am if someone like you ends up being called on to do it too?'

The abruptness of the change stung. Jolted me back into life, really. I'd thought we were making light of it. That was what one did, wasn't it, whenever something had happened that was starkly frightening, only it was easier to pretend that it had all been a bit of a close shave? None of this was quite what I'd thought. Every nerve ending was suddenly fully alert and I felt it when his head turned to check behind through the twist in the grip that was clamped hard around me. As his gaze turned back, that all too brutal honesty added sternly, 'You should have trusted ... you should have left me to do what needed to be done.'

Then I felt the sharpening of his concentration on the hillside beyond me as a fresh tightening of muscle that ran all the way through my veins to my heart. It came at the moment that I found my hands were bracing in a probably futile attempt to ease myself out of the curve of his arm and he said with a quick concession into ordinary reassurance, 'Hush now. I know.'

And any idea I had that I had returned to full awareness of my surroundings was first corrected by the bloodied right hand that moved across to touch mine – for a brief moment I'd been able to forget it, but not now – and then I realised someone was coming downhill at speed when Richard raised his voice to speak clearly over my head. It was done with a considerably brighter tone than the one he had lately used on me. 'Good morning. A timely arrival, I think.'

Despite his tone, I felt the impulse to put himself between me and this new threat course through the iron grip of his arm, and then the sharp suppression as he checked the feeling as absurd. I soon knew why. Because it wasn't Abbey who had arrived slithering at the end of a descent from that thistle-topped ridge. It was Matthew Croft, with Freddy just behind. This was their land and Richard must have been watching their approach all the time we'd been talking. It came to me abruptly that this was the first time these two men had met in a very long while.

And Richard, at least, had been expecting Danny to be part of this new arrival and come ready to perform the introductions. I thought Matthew Croft had noticed it and was determined to get through this meeting on his own good manners because he explained mildly, 'Danny couldn't stay. He came up to the house to tell us that you'd found signs of occupation in our pump house and to ask Eleanor to telephone PC Rathbone, and then he thought it best to get on to the Manor to see that things were as they ought to be there. He sent us down here not a moment too soon, it seems. That fellow's gone now, I think. Was this man actually living at the pump house? Danny wasn't clear. And did he attack you? I mean, I assume you didn't initiate that?'

'I didn't initiate that,' Richard confirmed. Something tugged at his voice as he sidestepped the presumably unintentional implication that, as far as history was concerned, people mightn't always be too sure who was the aggressor when talking about disputes involving a Langton. Richard tipped his head towards the pump house. 'Abbey emerged from beneath a shrub shortly after Hannis disappeared on his errand to your farmhouse. He was brandishing a log at me and, from the way he hefted it, I suspect the same kind of impulsive, panicked idea of ambush must have come to that man's mind once before as he cowered by a different brick hut.'

He meant when the passer-by had been poor Bertie Winstone. I silently added to the list the name of Abbey's wife on her quest to reclaim the Colonel's keys.

Matthew Croft's eyes were performing the same intense survey of the silent landscape that had occupied Richard a few minutes before. Richard's grip on me eased at last as he turned to look as well. I thought Richard might have been concerned that the other man would have something to say about his own trespass here, rather than merely Abbey's, but Matthew was determinedly ignoring it. I took the opportunity to step away and retrieve my fallen bicycle.

Richard intercepted me just as I was dragging it off the ground – everything really did hurt. His voice had the faintest trace of his old self in it when he asked in genuine surprise, 'Where on earth do you think you're off to?'

I gave a guilty start when his hand met the saddle to ease its journey into being upright and in the process restrained it. And I must have nearly dropped the impossibly heavy bicycle because his other hand – the injured one – had reached for the handlebars. Suddenly I was recoiling; this was too much. I intended to take the bicycle to that neat little gate cut into a hedge on the far side of the pump house and go away because I was wise enough to recognise that real incidents like this were hard, brutal things that required room to breathe and I'd made a mistake. I shouldn't even be here. Richard had remarked himself that I didn't want to be called on to test just how far I would go for someone I cared about. And Duckett himself had observed that taking a life changed a person. I hadn't quite taken it that far, of course, but I certainly hadn't played the part of bystander just now. I'd acted whether I believed I'd been right to do it or not, and, in all honesty, I wasn't sure I wouldn't do it again.

And something *had* changed in a way that felt like a continuation of the wretched bewilderment I'd experienced as Richard had plunged towards me. Richard had told me once that it was impossible to be prepared for nastiness, but I couldn't even put a term to the kind of blind incomprehension I'd felt as he'd shouted at me. In truth, it had felt like an echo of my terrible urge to stop Abbey; a kind of justified retribution, as if my own actions had thrown Richard's out of all normal balance and I was the enemy here. I think I'd felt, for a terrible moment, that the violence that must truly dwell within my world had finally been unmasked. Now I was calm enough to see that the fear had been the irrational dread of panic, but the memory of that momentary sense of finding everything utterly altered by my own actions was inescapable. It was a match for the present disquiet of knowing that shock was fading, but still something felt terribly awry.

So I wanted to leave this place, all of these disorientating contradictions of what I believed and how the danger to

Richard had required me to act, only all the while he was holding the bicycle and that hand was near mine and I couldn't change that without surrendering the bicycle, which I had a peculiar idea was a symbol of control. The feeling was compounded by the way all my groceries were scattered on the ground around my feet in a giddying arc.

That hand moved, just once. It made me flinch and I managed to say through a snarl with my head turned very firmly now towards that gap in the hedge, 'I'm leaving now. You don't need me here. And anyway, I've got to get home—' I stumbled over that telling word, because it was the Manor that had fixed itself in my mind as home. 'I mean, I've got to get back because your father wants his shopping and don't think I don't know what you were saying back there. You're just the same as everyone else. All along everyone's been making me feel small and cowardly for refusing to intervene. Only I've done it now. I saved you and *still* you're ready to explain all the reasons why I've got it wrong. But you know that this time it's you who's wrong because, actually, I didn't get involved for your sake just now. You're the man who makes a career out of violence. I was trying to save Paul Abbey from *you.*'

I didn't quite know where that had come from. Nastiness was the only alternative I had to crying. In a way I was impressed that no imaginary words had slipped in. Because all of it was made up. All the same, for a moment triumph reigned in a burning throat. Then Richard stirred. He didn't argue. He didn't even sound annoyed. He didn't touch me, either. He adjusted the nature of the stillness that possessed

411

him as he stood there holding the bicycle so that it couldn't topple and take me with it, and I felt the rise of his protectiveness once more as he said on a note of realisation, 'That's all fine. But you should know you're trying to run off in the wrong direction. Emily, did you hit your head?'

The truth dragged my head round. 'Yes, but—'

Beyond Richard's shoulder, Matthew Croft took a small step forwards. He remarked idly for the benefit of no one in particular, 'The first time I met Miss Sutton, she was standing in a crowd like this and Bertie Winstone had just bled all over her arm. I took care to spend a not inconsiderable length of time talking about nothing very much before inventing a few usefully distracting errands into the kitchen.'

That grisly hand retreated out of sight.

Then I lurched away from the idiotic blundering of shock. I forgot all about the bicycle, so it was a good job Richard had a hand on it still because I was running shaking hands over my face and through my hair as if to wipe away the shadow of bewilderment and exclaiming, aghast, *'Richard!'*

This was because my eyes had regained their sense of scale and distance and I remembered now the real mistake I'd made.

Now my mind was lurching back into working properly again, I could make out the distant point far to the left where I had emerged from the woodland beside a vicious hawthorn. It was quite a different part of the field from the small gap in the hedge I had lately been rushing for. This field stood at the end of the well-trodden deer track that led from the gateway where Richard had parked his car. Slightly nearer was the rise where I had first made sense of the disturbance that was distracting the horses. And there, at that point beyond the scattered debris of my shopping, where anthills crowned a little knoll, was the spot where I had set my bicycle at the slope and careered down the last few yards into the middle of a fight in which I should have had no part.

There had been no hesitation in Abbey as far as I could recall. They'd broken apart and Abbey had stepped back and was in the process of stepping in again. At the time I think my plan may well have been to reach out a hand at speed in the hope of dragging danger away from Richard. Now I could see that I'd made the error of not quite allowing for the fact that in the three seconds it took me to close in, it was quite enough time for Abbey to not be quite where he'd been when I'd started. In fact, he'd been in quite a different place, such as directly beneath my front wheel. And Richard had stepped blind into me to take his share of the collision when we all went crashing down. No wonder he thought I'd overstepped the mark.

Particularly when the weapon Abbey had retrieved as he had clambered to his feet had not been a knife. It had been a gun. And Richard's wound had come as he had enfolded me within the safety of his body and Abbey had opened fire.

Freddy was taking the bicycle from Richard and I hadn't remembered quite as much as I'd thought. I was asking rapidly, 'What sort of gun was it? I mean, I realise now I saw it was a handgun. I just forgot.'

My manner of speaking made a brief glimmer of that old warmth appear on Richard's mouth but his reply came without any humour at all. 'A Webley, perhaps.'

Freddy was wheeling the bicycle into the shade of a great beech tree and we were following him and the boy was saying on a note of marvel, 'It was a bit close, wasn't it? What I don't understand is why he hesitated like that. It was like he was trying to make up his mind.' Freddy looked young today. At first, he'd been keen to hang nervously behind Matthew's heels. Now he looked delighted as he abandoned the bicycle and hurried about retrieving my fallen groceries.

'Freddy.' This was a caution from Matthew. The youth turned to look and got a quick suppressive shake of the head.

'Oh,' the boy said with a sheepish glance at Richard and then at me. 'Yes. Sorry.'

It didn't matter. I wasn't worrying about what Freddy had said. I still couldn't really absorb words unless I concentrated hard. I was thinking that I knew why Richard's reply had been brief. It had been for me. I knew he'd guessed I would know what a Webley was. It was a revolver and the sort of beast from the Great War that always turned up in some old veteran's effects and made my father curse because members of the public shouldn't have them at all. Richard meant me to know that this was something more – something to be discussed in a quieter moment when Freddy wasn't forgetting Matthew's caution all over again and telling me with an eager kind of horror, 'He wasn't aiming at Captain Langton anyway, Miss. I saw him as we were finding a way down from the hilltop. He was standing over you with that gun hanging from his hand. It felt like he was there for ages.'

Freddy was thrusting food items back into their wrappings as he told me all the rest of the ugly details. 'It was like he was weighing options in his head; as if he wanted to have revenge on you for knocking him over with the bicycle but knew it was mad to do it. He looked hungry enough, anyway. Only then *he* was there – Captain Langton, I mean – and we thought he was enough to persuade that man to think again. We saw the man dither between letting you go and taking aim. His hand dipped. But then he just shrugged, raised his hand again and pulled the trigger. When he saw us yelling from the top of the ridge, he ran. I think Captain Langton was really brave, don't you?'

It was clear that whatever forbidding weight the Langton name had carried for this boy, it had all been supplanted now. Whereas I barely knew what I thought; only that I was cold, even in the sunlight, and I really had tipped this thing into violence and I knew Richard would be noticing the way the line of my lips grew taut again with Freddy's heroic summary. It wasn't enough that I'd forced Richard into the path of injury for the sake of saving me. I knew now that Richard's rough-ness before had been from the shock of nearly losing me.

He was beside me now and taking the clean handkerchief from my fingers that I hadn't even noticed I'd drawn out of the depths of my handbag for him. He pressed it over his hand before telling me in a hard, serious voice, 'I should say thank you. As it was, Abbey wasn't going to shoot me. He didn't mean to get me at all. I believe he'd pulled out the gun as a kind of display of bravado before his strategic exit rather than with any intention of using it. And even if he wasn't, I probably could have managed him. But then you appeared and ...' He stopped. Some second thought prevented him from adding anything more. He was as conscious as I was of the others here. But it wasn't that he cared whether it might seem to them that this was rather too close to apportioning the blame that was due. I thought he had probably been about to attempt to reassure me. It was what he always did. Only something checked him and I didn't want reassurance anyway. Like him I was feeling grim and hard and braced, and everything still felt strange here and it wasn't the blood any more or the brief effects of a light concussion or even the sense that Abbey had taken my intervention badly because I was fine, really, and it was impossible to explain this restless energy I was feeling.

It wasn't even the strain of knowing that in one simple act I'd abandoned all my ideas of standing firm in that way that had always been half hope and half dread for me – I'd always been capable of acting, just like most people given the right threat of loss. And as I've said before, I've seen war. I've known what it is for a very long time and I was still myself then. But all the same, there was suddenly some increasing sense that something had irretrievably changed here – it wasn't exactly the culmination of that fear I'd confessed this morning to my cousin of being alienated in the end from Richard by everyone's cruel interferences, because we were still very much united, but now everything was altered, colder. Perhaps the difference was in Richard's blunt manner of dealing out his honesty to me; but more probably the change was inside me. And it was almost certainly owing to the sense that Richard had put himself in the way of harm for me.

This was never going to be an easy thing to discuss. So I

helped Richard to put off the awful conversation for a moment when I might be able to muster some better self-control than this grimly restrained revulsion, and then we all went down to look at the pump house. There wasn't much to see behind the greasy pump machinery except a small mess of fresh rubbish belonging to a brief period of daytime occupation and a truly disgusting aroma of urine. There wasn't much room, either, so I stepped back outside to hug myself in the sunshine without going so far that anyone needed to worry that I was giving way to that old urge to flee the things that frighten me. I went no further than the corner of the pump house where the windows were.

I found that Freddy had come with me anyway. I knew he'd heard the way Richard had addressed his friend as 'Mr Croft' as we'd stepped out of the door rather than merely *Croft*, as perhaps Richard's status as the squire's son might have traditionally required him to do. There was a furtive keenness in the boy's face that did not sit well there. Hero worship was fading and the old distrust was lurking, waiting to be revived.

I said gently, 'It'll be all right, you know. They're both decent people.'

'I thought,' remarked the boy, replacing watchfulness with a grin, 'that I was supposed to be looking after you?' Then one of the horses, a great dark bay beast, loomed beside my bicycle and he moved to fend it off while a woman joined us.

She was a slight woman with a shy smile who wore slacks and a shirt like this landscape was where true happiness lay, and she was presumably Eleanor Croft. She also had that over-dressed journalist in tow, only he wasn't a journalist; he was a man by the name of Detective Constable James Fleece and he'd charted his own course here after overhearing the last of my conversation with Mrs Abbey. He already knew both Mr and Mrs Croft quite well. He had a wry quip for Matthew as he caught a greeting from where that man and Richard were now examining the shaded places beside stone troughs that marked the springhead. Richard was tied there by seriousness and the necessity of nodding his agreement to whatever was said to him, but when I moved once, I saw his head lift. Richard was leaving me room in which to breathe, but it seemed to me that he'd let down his guard only so much.

The policeman was speaking to me. He didn't seem to mind that I'd been particularly rude to him before. Now he heard my description of what had happened here and then he left me too so that he and Mrs Croft could take their own turn at muttering over the mess inside the pump house. Then, finally, Richard was able to return to me.

I saw his brief exchange with Mrs Croft as they passed. I distracted myself from seeming to watch too closely by noticing that her horse was grazing again now and the goats were there as well. I found myself recalling someone's remarks that Mrs Croft would normally be seen out riding, but this intimidating animal looked thoroughly on holiday and I thought there was probably a correlation between that and the few months since her marriage, if only the happy gossip in me was alert enough to see it.

Richard approached me. His presence made me ready to unfold my arms and muster a smile when he came to a halt by me. He was standing by my side. I hadn't realised how tightly my arms had still been clasped protectively about me before. And I made a corner of his mouth quirk when I tipped my head at the space between the pump house and the spring-head and said, 'Do you think Freddy believes he's looking for John's treasure?'

Freddy was doing what no one else had. The boy was lifting the manhole cover on the vast underground cistern that was buried beside the pump house and was peering inside.

The sense of cold that had accompanied my full under-standing of the way that Richard had shielded me had eased a little now and become a little more reasonable. He was looking fit enough but tired. The fall had hurt him too. He had removed his jacket and folded it over his arm. It was the arm with the bloodied hand. He was close beside me and I was conscious of his stealthy examination of my face as I watched the policeman join the boy. Richard had noticed that calm good sense was fully in charge of me now and it seemed he approved. At least, I thought he did.

Then, while Richard was nodding in reply to my comment and likewise watching the unnecessary inspection of the underground cistern and drawing breath to begin what really needed to be said and what would presumably become that very bruising discussion about my actions and his, my self-control slipped a bit. This was because I was still myself, really, and not terribly practised at speaking what I felt.

The slip didn't take me into pride. I wasn't distancing myself here. I was turning my eyes suddenly to meet his and lurching headlong into saying rather too desperately, 'I'm sorry. I didn't mean what I said back there. I don't know what came over me to make me speak to you like that. It was reaction, I suppose. And I'm sorry because now you're hiding your hand from me as if I've got a real phobia, but I haven't. It isn't anything like it. It's not really the sight of blood that affects me. I can't really explain. I'm sorry.'

I stopped. This much-needed apology was too naked and too close to concealment as well, because I realised I could explain how the sight of blood affected me, I just really didn't think I should. He probably knew anyway. I'd told him enough about my feelings to make him capable of guessing that the difficulty arose as much from my mind's deep, instinctive aversion to the evidence of a person's cruel intent as it did from any real fear of the blood itself. But if I repeated that claim now, he might grow to believe I really had been shying away from him as though he and his profession were tied up in the core of my fears. Only they weren't, and to say something like that would only cause pain when the instinct didn't obey any conscious rules anyway.

I shook it away and began to say something else that was better but equally earnest, only to stop when I realised that I needn't have been worrying about what he thought at all because I wasn't actually sure Richard was listening. He was watching Matthew Croft as that man cheerfully debated something with Freddy and the policeman. The boy was probably being teased about his disappointed search. Then Richard's eyes slid left to catch me watching him. He caught me as I was biting my lip a shade doubtfully and I quickly released it for the sake of a brief uncertain smile, expecting to draw a smile in return. It would have been a simple way of dismissing anxiety and, with it, establish relief in that usual pattern where I borrowed a little bit of his assurance.

Instead, Richard's brows lowered. I heard his breathing check. Then his left hand – the unbloodied one – reached to gently take hold of mine. Even that simple act surprised me with its suddenness, but he seemed to pause a while to weigh it in his palm, as if considering the details. We were very near. It was instinctive to watch the way my hand lay in his as closely as he did. Then his fingers tightened and he turned my wrist as he had once before, so that my hand was held between the warmth of his grip and the soft texture of his clothing. Only this time, instead of completing the act by closing my fingers over a neatly folded note, he briefly raised the back of my hand to his lips.

His gaze lifted to meet mine across the grip he had upon my hand. It was like being touched with a bolt of pure energy. Every nerve focused on the intensity of the few inches of space between us, on the glimpse of the mind behind those eyes. He was grave, as though he'd been abruptly startled yet again with a mark of my care, only I knew I hadn't done anything of the sort at all. The bewildering stillness was released a moment later by a brush of his thumb across the back of my hand, which left its own trail of sensation.

Then a noise from those other people beyond his shoulder drew his head round. They were about to rejoin us. Richard let his hand fall into the space between us, but he didn't let me go. His grip was firm. I still didn't know what I thought I'd done. He didn't wish to explain here. I might have believed this brief expression of his need for me had been a swift means of settling my unease without openly acknowledging the disturbing truth that something really had been altered by my arrival in this place. But this wasn't about me, at least not in that way. This was something strong and immediate that was contained within his own feelings. This was disconcertingly like an impulsive gesture of respect.

It was the steadiness of his attention on the people by the pump house that gave me the clue that something might have happened in the space of those minutes alone with Matthew Croft. I had the peculiar moment of thinking that this feeling might relate to the simple fact that I was here and by his side, amongst all these people who might have every reason to distrust him.

'Richard, I—'

I'd been about to gravely break that other rule of mine – the one about not claiming a little bit more of his strength by adding to his list of responsibilities. I'd been about to admit just how much I needed him to be on my side too. But it was a raw thing to confess in this hurry of speaking before we were swept up in the bustle of meeting the others. I'd only have said it wrong. Then the policeman appeared before us and it was too late anyway.

Detective Fleece gave stern instructions about going to the doctor and getting Richard's wound properly recorded. Then he hurried us through the woods in a crowd to the Lagonda with the bag of groceries but without the bicycle. They all stood there to watch us get in. Then they watched us get out again when it became clear that Richard couldn't comfortably handle the car.

Now I was turning the great machine – I really could drive, it hadn't been a reckless boast in the midst of an argument – and I was setting it sedately at the climb out of the woodland, and Richard was finally asking in the peace of being alone together, 'Emily? What are you thinking?'

He surprised me into speaking the truth and for once it wasn't any worry about Abbey or powerlessness or the weight of realising just how much every ounce of me ached for this man beside me.

In this instance, amazingly, I was able to observe, 'That horse was John's, wasn't it?'

We were passing the first of the rough cottages into the village and I'd surprised him. My comment drew a laugh. He remarked, 'Dark thoughts indeed. What has led you to conclude that it was John's?'

'Freddy was trying to lead it away before you could notice, but had to give it up as a bad job.'

'Ah.'

There was a pause while Richard gave every appearance of being one who was watching for the brass sign that marked the doctor's house. But then he confided to the window beside him, 'If the horse was John's, it's probably valuable and probably still ours, officially. I believe Mrs Croft offered to buy the beast when John died, but since my father couldn't exactly engage in business with her or her husband without risking accusations of trying to influence the witness, I imagine he just denied the horse was ever ours. It was a solution of sorts, I suppose. And yet,' he added after a slight hesitation, 'the truth is, I still can't help thinking that this discreet way of settling an exchange was rather too similar to a gesture of thanks.'

'You think your father was *grateful* to them?' I didn't understand.

He told me, 'The whole world delights in dissecting the horrors of what my brother did and the lies he spread and yet they've never quite turned upon my father. The way the Crofts tell it, my father did nothing more serious than believe my brother's tomfoolery and allow himself to be led into attempting the arrest of the wrong man for various crimes at a very wrong time.'

I steered the enormous car to a halt outside the shop. I knew Richard had always been clear about his family's past, but this ran deeper than any necessary honesty. It felt like the sort of thing that should never be voiced. It was for Richard's sake and his alone that I asked quietly, 'You think there's more to it?'

Richard waited while I silenced the engine before he turned his head. 'The way Father is now? I just don't know. But knowing the aversion he has to hearing Matthew Croft's name and the sentence my uncle is serving these days, I think it must take a harsh toll upon the spirit of a man like my father, who for all his faults has a strong sense of honour, if he even partially owes his freedom to the generosity of a man he once tried to have hanged for murder.'

This was the lie the Colonel had given me a glimpse of on

his first wretched day home. Now Richard let me absorb the full scale of its hold on the old man and the hard trust Richard had in my fitness to share his secrets. And then we went into the doctor's surgery.

Chapter 26

'I've got to tell you something, even though I know you don't want me to, and I'm sorry.'

We were in the car again. We'd spent a long time with the doctor. My own session with the man had been brief on account of the fact my concussion wasn't interesting enough to require me to sit for a week in a darkened room, but Richard's session had been longer. When he had finally emerged it had been with a hand that had been recorded in every conceivable way and was now smothered in bandages and dressings to the point of madness. Just the very tips of his fingers were protruding. Needless to say, I drove us home and now Richard was directing me to draw the car to a halt outside the kitchen door rather than its usual place in the shade of the machine barn.

I thought he was reducing the distance we would have to travel without shelter. He was thinking of Abbey and the range of that gun. And in a way I was glad of it. Even the sudden hush as the engine died revived the cringing sensation I got in the nerves at the back of my head whenever I remembered that all the while I had been lying on the ground blinking dumbly at Richard as he shouted out his warning, Abbey had been standing behind me, contemplating the pros and cons of taking my life.

Richard was waiting for my gaze to find his face. My eyes got distracted on the way by the outrageous bandage on his hand. I said, 'Would you like me to rebind that?'

He thought I was evading this again. But I wasn't. Now I braved his gaze. I even mustered a vaguely reassuring smile. 'You'll only have to do it later yourself.'

He gave a single nod and allowed me to take his hand. 'But,' he cautioned, 'leave the gauze in place, would you? For your sake and mine.'

While an obscenely unnecessary yardage of bandage unravelled into my lap and I took great care not to hurt him, he spoke again and this time I didn't interrupt. He said in a hard, decisive tone, 'I believe you've already guessed some of this and since you can't remotely expect me to leave you on your own while you piece together the rest, try not to blame me. Please.' An enormous volume of wadding joined the bandage in my lap. Beneath that was the fine gauze dressing and I left that alone. As I worked, he added, 'I have reason to believe that the gun Abbey was brandishing belongs to my father.'

I flinched. This was why he'd told me about his father's guilt. I had to understand that the loss of the gun was another mistake that would be working its terrible shame upon the Colonel. And I had to appreciate the responsibility Richard must be feeling to support him.

I set my hands to work methodically winding the bandage into a roll. Richard continued, 'Father kept his old service revolver – a Webley – in his desk in the library and I know I don't need to describe to you the highly illegal habit old soldiers have of keeping a firearm as a memento. He even concealed it from the police during their search of the house in March. He did at least keep it securely locked away, until, that is, his business brought him back here two days ago. Unfortunately, as I understand it – and he's a little vague about this point – at that time he reunited it with the handful of ammunition he kept locked away elsewhere and shut them both in the drawer of his desk.'

I could feel Richard watching me. My hands were making a business out of stripping the wadding into a smaller square. My mind was tiptoeing gingerly through the memory of that first evening at the Manor; the battle I'd interrupted in the library between the old man and a furious melancholy. I was remembering the close chance that had inspired my decision to carry off his brandy bottle while I prepared his dinner. No wonder the old man had taken anchorage with me in the sudden comfort of the warmer, friendlier space of the kitchen. The room had been, and remained, a vital sanctuary from the whisperings of grief and the evil lure of a tool the Colonel had clearly been fighting desperately to ignore, but was inescapably designed only to bring death.

I wasn't sure I should tell Richard. Or perhaps it was something he already knew. He'd raced for the train, after all, just as soon as I'd mentioned the name of a man most likely to remind the Colonel of what he had lost.

Briskly, Richard said now, 'Father discovered the lot had gone last night while you and I were off on our little sortie to the turbine house. That's what he had to tell me after you slipped away to reclaim your bed. I think we can safely say that we know who has the gun now.'

My hands were in my lap, gripping the shreds of discarded wadding. I heard myself ask in a dry, flat little voice, 'Have you told Detective Fleece about the theft?'

'I have, and I left a note for PC Rathbone earlier this morning when I couldn't find him. My father and I agreed it was for the best. We think Abbey took it yesterday, just before you chased him from the house.'

I lifted my head. I'd been crashing about in the doorway of the tithe barn with a man bearing a gun and Abbey hadn't thought to use it on me then. I said hoarsely, 'He must have taken it yesterday if it was in the drawer. I saw that drawer myself at that time and it was open and empty of weapons. But what was Abbey doing prowling around your house yesterday in the first place? He can't have known the Webley was in the Colonel's desk waiting for him, conveniently liberated after all this time. It must have been an opportune discovery, so what else did he take?'

Richard stirred restlessly beside me. 'I don't know.'

It wasn't a happy concession. Then he added, 'Detective Fleece is set to come to the house shortly for the sake of going through the motions of trying to find out. It'll be strange to meet him in there. Did you know the detective was part of the investigation into my brother? No? Fleece was a uniformed constable then. Which would be why my father didn't recognise him. Apparently this detective has been keeping a light eye on the place ever since, in case anything should turn up that might be relevant to the unclosed threads left by my brother. I'd resent the insinuation that those of us who remain at large are still under suspicion, except that I think the man means to find the line of my brother's criminal contacts rather than evidence that we're guiltily guarding any more hoards. And I got the impression today that he was as displeased as I was that he will now have to interview my father about that gun. The good news, if we can call it that, is that we can be certain the gun itself is just an innocuous legacy of my father's career. The Webley ties my father to Abbey's actions today, but it carries no significant link to my brother. Which brings us back, yet again, to the question of Abbey and what he really thought he was doing today.'

There was a peculiar steadiness there to the way he'd phrased that. Like a drawing in of breath before he explained just precisely how things were even more dangerous than I thought they were. I took a firm hold of his hand once more. I was winding the bandage laboriously over the much-reduced piece of wadding, beginning with a neat fold by his thumb.

Richard's voice was firmly level as he said, 'You should understand, here and now, that I do not believe Abbey meant to catch me with that bullet. I believe he meant me to know he had the gun and to recognise it for my father's, and to take it as a warning. Specifically me. You understand?'

I thought I understood. He was deliberately echoing his words from last night and the snare Mrs Abbey was laying for him.

I said uneasily, 'You think this is her blackmail. Still. Even though her husband really is behind those bruises. There was another mark on her today, you know.'

'I didn't know. But yes.' It was a rough agreement. 'Even so.'

He watched me bind a little more of the bandage onto his wrist before he remarked thoughtfully, 'And I notice that you're not berating me for letting it fall to Detective Fleece to go over to Eddington just as soon as he's marshalled some uniformed men when, by all moral duty, I ought to be personally leading the race over there myself. We can guess that's where Abbey fled to after all, and we can't abandon an isolated woman and her three young children to this wretch.'

I briefly lifted my head. I wasn't blaming him. Every part of me was dreading that when the search finally did reach Eddington they'd discover something terrible had happened, but I wasn't foolish enough to believe my part there or Richard's would be the one we thought it should be. Instead, the anger that had licked though my veins last night was burning again now. Because her fear as she'd sent me racing after Richard today had seemed so real and we hadn't even got to the part yet where Richard explained just how much my blundering arrival at the pump house had made matters worse.

And, besides all that, there was also the larger problem of knowing, that just as I wasn't blaming him, I was sure I ought to know by now that Richard was likewise not the sort of man to lead me through this difficult subject purely for the purpose of berating me. I was just wishing he would, because the sense of being at fault would have followed a nice, safe, normal pattern and I wouldn't have had to be feeling quite so afraid.

He was telling me with absolute certainty, 'Abbey must have been watching today when I arrived with Danny Hannis. He must have watched from the bushes as Hannis left to give the Crofts due notice that we'd found another lair on their land. And Abbey must have waited while his nerves frayed to the limit before attacking with that branch. If he'd wanted to use the gun, he'd have shot me then. But he didn't. He panicked and tried to disable me with the branch first. I imagine he found himself in the midst of a fight before he'd even really thought about it and then, once he was there, that was the moment he remembered that it would suit him to give me a good look at the weapon he'd stolen.'

I'd finished my bandaging. Richard reclaimed his hand from me and was running the tip of a finger under the end of the bandage, testing its tension. The injured hand dropped to his lap. He told me, 'You arrived only moments after he'd pulled the Webley out of a jacket pocket. Which, by the way, makes me wonder who on earth taught him his idea of the safe way to handle a loaded gun. I'd barely seen the thing when you pitched into the scene. And I know you thought you had to act – and truly, in a way, I'm grateful. But I honestly don't believe that he had any intention of using it until that moment. Not really. Not if I can trust my interpretation of the wild gesticulations of a man who had lately been grappling at my throat.'

I was sitting very still now, watching Richard's profile. It was hurting him to acknowledge the moment when Abbey's harmless posturing had changed to willingness and become focused upon me.

His voice was deeper. 'I think the power of the thing took over his mind when he saw you. I watched his face as it contorted into a mask of daring temptation. I'm certain his plan must have originally been to give me a sense that I should tread carefully or else this weapon might find its way into a public scene. I'm sure, then, that their blackmail had hinged upon the idea that the gun could become the tool that would truly distress my father. But your arrival changed it. I thought when I put myself between you and him, it would be enough to remind him of the madness of what he was doing. I thought he'd feel he'd made his point about possessing the weapon well enough. But he treated my shouted cautions of *no* and *don't do it* like a challenge. I think he saw the opportunity to ram his point home, and then he took it.'

Richard took a breath. The palpable reluctance to continue touched my core to ice. He was only telling me this because he hadn't the right not to. And because this really had nothing to do with the sort of harm I might do with a bicycle and very little, even, to do with Abbey's power. This was a confession of Richard's own sense of wrong.

Richard's determination carried him through. 'We've known for a while, haven't we, you and I, that they've been groping about to find some leverage to work their claim on me. This theft of my father's gun was opportunistic and probably their most effective threat yet because while I don't fully know what the penalties are for possessing an old service weapon, I *do* believe they thought I'd act pretty decisively to shield my father from something hard and legal like a threat to leave the weapon at a crime scene. I'm sure they thought that just showing it to me would be enough to enlist me for their schemes regarding Duckett. And it is clear to me that whether they meant use the weapon to finish Duckett and then force me to cover it up again, or to use the threat of the whole to force me into acting decisively myself; either way, it remains grimly clear that they mean Duckett to die and Abbey intends to ensure it happens without risking detection and the gallows himself.'

He was speaking as if there was a path ahead where Richard might be coerced into performing the sort of second-hand evil that, once begun, would run on and on into our future, weaving new lies and new dangers into every little aspect of life until every part of our souls corrupted and more violence would have to follow just to avert betrayal.

The path wasn't real. Richard would never do it. The betrayal lay elsewhere. It lay in Richard's honesty as he told me, 'But, anyway, none of those plans remotely take into account the fact I keep making mistakes that involve you.'

I really was cold now. Ashen, frozen, while everything burned; my eyes, my lips, where they pressed into a tight line, and my fingers curled into balls in my lap. He was already saying, 'Yesterday I think Mrs Abbey guessed what I felt for you when I took you away from her in my car. Last night we entertained the brief but pointless worry that they meant to incriminate you. But when you arrived today and I reached for you and shielded you, I think I taught that man to think of the value of your life and yours alone. Properly; not just a few idle threats strewn about here and there. And I don't need to guess now what he'll think of doing with my father's gun.'

'I—see.'

I really did see too. I'd always thought it would be the memory of his brother that did the real damage. Until now, I'd believed in an obscure way that I was helping to shield him from it. But this thing Richard was describing here wasn't the threat of an old family tie, nor was it the inconvenient impulsiveness of the rescue and counter-rescue that he and I had shared this morning on the slopes above the pump house. This was layer upon layer of guilt – *his* guilt, and capitalised upon by these people. And while they did it, they were proving that all my fears about daily life being indistinguishable from war were for naught.

Because this wasn't war. This unconscionable inhumanity didn't deserve that excuse. Like an intake of cold air, my voice grew strangely calm. I heard myself observe, 'It's happening again, isn't it? Someone is made to make the sacrifice while I do nothing.'

There was a bite in those last words. But I wasn't sneering at the mistake that had made me a target or what Abbey might do now to truly force Richard's hand. There was no suggestion here that Richard would cede to the blackmail and tamely proceed to do their work for them. Richard knew neither of us would allow that. Instead, the injury Richard was reluctantly committing here was the harm he was causing by ranking his decisions above mine, because my own judge-ment was inescapably clouded by the fear I had of the protectiveness that had stalked through the nightmare of my adolescence.

It was no wonder I'd felt altered by the aftermath of the morning's shocks. I must have perceived the change in his thoughts of me. This was the caution that had curbed my willingness to admit I needed him; this sense that speaking honestly only added to the burden of my claims upon his conscience.

I ought to have gone to meet the bus on that first day. I ought to run now, except that I didn't know there was time to run from this. And, besides, they might simply adapt and pick another target such as the Colonel or someone else even more unprepared, and that would be worse.

I turned to him. 'Am I supposed to just accept that this ... this *helplessness* is still my part, just because you think you should assume responsibility for this? Because you do know, don't you, that while you're deciding these things for me, it matters that you try to stay unharmed and untainted by this thing yourself?'

I noticed that brief flicker of a frown. This wasn't another row, but I had surprised him. He'd expected panicked distress but was getting cold, determined argument instead. Now he was saying rather too forcefully, 'No. But you can't control the Abbeys' actions and you can't control mine. You're not responsible for any of them, either. Everyone has all sorts of external excuses and motivations for doing what they do. But it is still up to each of us to make our own choices.'

There was a brutal sense he was cautioning me here to avoid thinking too deeply about what he might be preparing to do now, because he *would* act. The rest was debateable, but that part was certain. In a way he was as powerless as I was.

But he did have some choices. And amongst them was the knowledge that while I was stubborn enough where I knew I was right, he certainly had enough power over my care to shame me into accepting almost any point of view just so that I didn't hurt him. The cringing agony that dwelt behind the acidic rage was because I thought he was preparing to test it.

But this idea I had that love was just another means of applying manipulation was proof, at last, that I really hadn't emerged unscathed from that bruising romance with my brother's friend.

Because, while my head shook out an urgent rejection, the world swung onto a different kilter that was almost as disorientating.

Richard was saying on a steadier note, 'You already know, I think, that I held various ranks during the conflict in North Africa?'

I interrupted on a bitter note of caution, 'If you're building up to telling me that your training as a soldier makes you better fitted to decide my path through this cruelty than I am ...'

He persevered patiently. 'I held various ranks during the North Africa campaign. When you find yourself abruptly promoted into another man's newly vacated boots, you suddenly have a very serious job to do and an awful lot of death comes very quickly at close hand to the people under your authority. There are many ways to describe what I witnessed in that last great battle which everyone seemed so determined to talk about last night. But the truth is that my abiding memory is of the sound. It's the roar of the guns and the shells, and the shouting that was indistinguishable over the volume of all the rest. It was a maddening saturation. It remains so inescapable that somehow it still whines away, even in my dreams. For my father, though, the part that has lodged in his memory is that, as it turns out, it seems I am a good leader of men. For better or for worse, far wiser, older soldiers than I followed me during those days. In the main.'

This, unexpectedly, was that moment Phyllis had tried to invoke before dinner last night. This was the moment he gave me the gift of understanding a very little of his war experiences. I saw him grimace. Then he continued, 'What I mean to say here is that we're the same, you and I. Someone always seems to be trying to turn our actions to prove a harder point, whether for glory or for shame. But my actions are my own. And yours ...?'

His eyes were on me. This was being said sternly beneath lowered brows. 'You still seem to think that you're considered a bystander in this. But to give you an idea of the contribution I think you've already been making, I'm going to tell you that Matthew Croft asked a favour of me today while we were peering at rubbish behind the generator at the pump house. He was very civil and left me plenty of room to pretend I hadn't heard. It was all done very smoothly. He asked me to step into the squire's shoes and do for Freddy what Father did for Hannis when he enlisted.'

I asked in quiet bewilderment, 'And will you?' My question

was given automatically because he required it, not because I understood even a shred of what he was saying or how it related to me.

Richard's attention was drawn past me to the glass in the driver's side door by a movement at the house beyond me. It was Danny peering through one of the kitchen windows to see whether we were still inside the car. The man lifted his hand in a silent communication and then, satisfied that Richard knew fresh business was waiting for him, turned back to the gloom of the kitchen.

And all the time that this mimed exchange had been passing back and forth across me, Richard had been saying, 'I understand that Freddy's set his heart on doing his National Service, on the assumption it is still required a few years from now and the boy persists in refusing to claim a reserved occupation for his work on the various farms hereabouts. And although Matthew Croft and I didn't get as far as outpourings of emotion or gushing confessions, I think I grasped enough of his thoughts on the matter to judge that he is desperate to keep the boy from blundering into a violent scene. Desperate enough, in fact, to set aside his own judgement of me long enough to gamble on what he thinks he's seen of yours. I don't know how you acted to that man and his people during the evening of Bertie's scene on his garden path – although I can hazard a guess based solely on my own two ridiculously busy days of knowing you – but anyway, today, clearly your opinion holds sway.'

He took a breath. Then he added gravely, 'So Matthew Croft asked his question, and I told him I would write to a friend of mine in the Royal Army Veterinary Corps, for all the good it might do, but that I had a price.'

'Ah.'

He sat back to settle more easily in his seat once more and made the springs creak as they adjusted. 'That's what he said too, but with rather less bewilderment. It's hard to be surprised when you already think the worst of a man.'

He caught my eye. There was, inexplicably, the faintest of teasing notes there. Then Richard added, 'I told him that he could have his letter on the condition that he gave a home to that blessed goat.'

Silence.

Then a creak of my own seat as I found my position uncomfortable and moved, only to find discomfort everywhere. Suddenly I knew I was going to cry. After such a morning, it was this news that was going to do it.

'Oh dear,' I said, fiercely examining the wadding that still lay in my lap. I fidgeted again and finally gave in and covered my eyes with a hand. And then dropped it again because I wasn't going to do it. I gave a funny little choking laugh instead. The hand that dropped to my lap was the one he had taken earlier and it flexed involuntarily at the sensitivity of the memory. This was his gift to me; this explanation of what had prompted him to make that one intensely speechless gesture of taking my hand after his time in the pump house. He had been compelled then, just as he was doing now, to show me the part I had played in giving a vital introduction on rather different terms from the one he had been used to.

And for a man who bore the burden of blame in every

recent memory, for whom a simple thing like his family name was an unbreakable shackle on his life and career, this little deviation from an old hostility was a wonderful lesson for the man on how he was really perceived. I thought the experience was so rare it was almost painful for him. It could be a liberation for me too. Richard was more confident than I; he didn't allow other people to set the standard by which he measured himself, regardless of which way their judgement fell. But, in a way, none of that mattered here anyway because no one would dare define his kindness in telling me this now as a mark of weakness. And that meant whatever kindness dwelt in me couldn't be dismissed as such, either.

It was a very beautiful way of showing me that my actions had a little more significance than I often believed. It addressed, too, my fear that he would wish to control me now.

Richard allowed me a moment to wrestle with myself, then he asked gently, 'Why does that goat matter to you so much? It's not as if you have spent every spare second since your arrival idly crooning over the creature's stable door.'

I lifted my head from the fragments of fluff my fingers were shredding in my lap. I felt my determination build as it began to take on a surer form. It made my heart work in powerful, steady beats. 'It's because he belonged to your brother.' For all the force of my restored sense of purpose, I made the confession in an unsteady jumble. 'Your brother kept him and named him and gave him a job keeping company with flighty young horses. Now your brother is gone, the house and car he loved are being sold and this creature is the only living legacy of his left and after all the awfulness of

441

what he did, it has seemed to me to be very close to revenge on the man to turn his poor goat over to the butcher. Believe me, I know you wouldn't do it in that spirit, but all the same, given the way everyone talks about him, it's as though, piece by piece, the real living John Langton is being expunged from memory. Eventually all that will remain will be the part of him that was a figment of horror. And, whilst I can't say it's wrong that it should be that way, since his victims must have respect, I don't think either you or your father have considered just how damaging it would be for you both if this final piece of destruction is how you end your relationship with John too.'

I thought I'd surprised him. Stunned him, really. The amusement switched off like a light. I dropped my gaze to the mess in my lap again. After that brief respite, it wasn't so easy to be happy. There was too much at risk here, even when fear was firmly held in check.

After a brief silence, I heard him draw a little breath. He said carefully, 'In so far as my memories of John go, my most recent ones are that my hospitalisation last year made things difficult for him. He had many ferocious rows with our father about the cost of it all and I believe it coincided with his first real steps along the path of devastation. And yet, in the midst of all that, John paid many sly visits to London to do nothing more than sit for a day in the stark tedium of a hospital room with a sibling who wanted to talk about nothing of any importance at all. I don't hate him, Emily, or wish to remove him from my memory. I miss him.'

When finally I dared to look, I found that I was sitting

beside a man who was calm, relaxed and utterly serious. I let out a breath like a sigh. 'Oh Richard,' I said more steadily than I'd felt for some time. 'How do we defeat this?'

I meant, I think, how do we defeat these people without losing ourselves in the process?

Richard extended his left hand across his body to accept some of the matter I was tidying from my lap. I shouldn't have shredded it. White fibres were drifting everywhere. He closed his hand over the mass as I passed him the last of it, so that my fingers briefly covered the loose fist he'd made. His hand was warm and steady and it was such an ordinary, comforting gesture. If I hadn't known, I would never have thought that there was an all-consuming anger burning beneath.

There was no sign of it in his reply when he said, 'First you're going to do what you've always done – you're going to surprise me with that beautifully unshakeable courage of yours and then you're going to help me unpick whatever it is that we've missed. It's just as you say; just because these people are determined to work the dark corners to get their way, why on earth should they get to dictate that we have to share the shadows with them? So, with that in mind, we're going to begin by breaking the news to Father that his dinner will have to be cancelled. Then I'm going to beg you to keep up his morale by making him an early lunch.' He glanced at his watch and his eyebrows lifted. 'Very well, a late lunch, while I go over the house with the police to ensure we've secured every corner, every window and every possible entrance and exit that doesn't have a policeman next to it. And then you and I ... well, what do you think we should do?'

'I imagine you're going to ask me to help you find whatever it was that Abbey was doing in the Manor yesterday before he stole the Webley.'

'Precisely.' The agreement was accompanied by a flicker of amusement. Perhaps it was the release from surprise, because I thought I really had surprised him. I believe he had truly been bracing himself, all this time, for recrimination just as soon I had the room to understand what he had brought me to. And not because he'd meant to inflict his authority upon me. But because, in this instance, he'd thought the fear of the Abbeys would be enough to leave me clinging to him for shelter. He'd thought they would override every other idea I had of freedom that had only lately begun to find hope after the war.

It was a relief for both of us when he added, 'And you'll generally keep an eye on my father for me, won't you?'

For the first time I smiled. I remarked dryly, 'I believe that is a technique for giving the less-experienced members of your party a sense of purpose. You'll be asking the same thing of him about me, won't you?'

He grinned. I felt again then the full, humbling force of his care for me. And, more doubtingly, the hard resolve of a man used to battle. Suddenly, I was very conscious of what he had said; we'd only known each other for two short days, and it had been a brief enough time that my determination had still been unexpected and only served to unwittingly reaffirm the value of who I really was for him. But, with that in mind, and all that I, in my turn, thought he was, I couldn't shake the fiercely chilling suspicion that while he'd been carefully supporting whichever choice I made, he somehow hadn't quite filled the ambiguous void of just how far he was still preparing to act himself.

For the moment, though, his determination to shield me was dedicated to letting me see that he really did need me here. I sensed, with the sort of emerging confidence that hurt, that my fierce commitment to bearing equal responsibility was making him stronger, purely from the novelty of not being required to meet this particular battle alone.

'Absolutely I will,' he said decisively, with a fresh glance for the window beside me, where Danny was hovering again. 'We're going to do everything in a nice orderly fashion, and then we're going to put a stop to this nonsense about enslaving me or bringing you face to face with my father's gun. And we're going to do it all with full benefit of good sense, law and policemen.'

Now the temper showed. Put like that, though, it all sounded perfectly calm and manageable. But then we entered the kitchen and found Phyllis sitting at the table with the dog on a string and looking as pale and magnificent as ever. The detective was there and he was able to tell us that they hadn't neatly apprehended Abbey and they hadn't found Mrs Abbey either, because her house was devoid of people and evidence. He also told us that the call was out in Gloucester to find our true arsonist Duckett. And then, in the wake of all those empty reports, we learned just how little control any of us had.

Chapter 27

It began with the discovery that while our time in the car outside the kitchen door had been comparatively peaceful, the rest of the house had been filling with policemen. The main drive beyond the library window was strewn with four or so liveried police cars because Detective Fleece had enlisted a number of additional hands from the county force. They absorbed Richard into their ranks just as soon as we stepped in through the door. I could hear them clattering about upstairs as I took my customary place at the kitchen counter.

Only two people seemed oblivious to the chaos. Phyllis and Danny were in the same room, at last, and Phyllis had the high colour that had alarmed me last night. After all her determination to snatch a chance to talk to Danny, she didn't seem to be particularly keen to take advantage of the opportunity now. I suppose it didn't suit her to play the helpless damsel any more than it did me, and that was, after all, presumably why Danny had abandoned Richard to the encounter with Matthew Croft. He'd come back to stand guard until Richard's return and it was the sort of chivalry that went hand in hand with picking tearful invalids up from their bicycle accidents. It also, apparently, went hand in hand with showing no interest in wretched curtains and leaving an intelligent woman trapped in an odd purgatory, where neither marriage nor spinsterhood seemed to be remotely empowering.

That being said, it wasn't exactly his fault that he'd helped her after her accident because he was hardly the sort of man to have driven blindly by, and it wasn't his fault either that his presence here now had come at a time when she was painfully aware of the handicap of her well-strapped ankle and her wrist when she would have preferred towering elegance. Her mouth had set into a determined line as she looked at anything but him.

Danny was leaning in to rest his forearms on the tabletop beside her. He looked tanned and vigorous in his well-worn working clothes, like a capable man determined to say his piece, but also braced for the moment that someone – not Phyllis – barked out his name and dismissed him to his tractor.

He was saying in a persuasive undertone, 'What does it matter if we talk here or in another room. Better to get this over with, wouldn't you say?'

I was sorting through the battered contents of my shopping, but I saw Phyllis move in her seat. That stung, I think. There was an emphasis on the part that said it was over.

'Fine,' she snapped in a whisper. 'I really didn't want to do this with all the local constabulary listening in and my cousin over there looking like a cross between a cook and an avenging warrior after a bad scrap, but have it your way. Please explain.'

'Which part?'

I thought that Danny was conscious of the way that Phyllis didn't seem remotely out of place in the grandeur of this Manor kitchen – she would have mixed in some pretty cultivated circles after her studies and, besides, in the days of her early life here her father the steward had been ranked in this place as second only to the squire. But personally, at this moment, above any other, I was suddenly able to see why the Colonel should have been quite so defensive about rumours of this man's parentage. And why, in defiance of the rumours, the Colonel persisted in encouraging Danny's skills and ambition, even to the point of supporting his purchase of Mrs Abbey's matrimonial home.

The same thought must have been in my cousin's mind. She hissed, 'That house!' It was raw and angry and very lonely. 'You let me think last week that you didn't want to come and live in my cottage and I assumed it was because you didn't want to stay here. Only now I know that you fixed yourself in this area months ago when you bought your own house in Gloucester. You kept it from me while you went on pretending that you had to live in that tiny little attic above your parents' bedroom and I know now that all along it wasn't because you were waiting to build a new life. You'd already got one and the simple truth was that you were just waiting for the right moment to explain that you didn't want to share it with me.'

'Nonsense,' Danny retorted. 'Don't reduce the ultimatum you gave me last week to an argument about that house. You gave me my marching orders long before you knew about it.'

'But the point is *you* knew about it—'

The curt manner with which Danny spoke over her made me think sharply of the concealment that had stalked my understanding of his relationship with Mrs Abbey. He demanded, 'Why have you suddenly decided that now is the moment to talk to me? I tried to give my side of things last week and you stopped your ears and told me in very incoherent terms to leave you alone for good. So what's changed?'

As I say, I had thought he was angry because she was tackling him about the secret of the house. I knew now my suspicions had been a mistake; I knew there was no affair to be discovered there. And that meant that if it wasn't concealment that was driving his behaviour now, I thought it must be self-defence.

I saw it suddenly. She had the power to hurt him and she didn't even know.

She was saying briskly, 'Nothing's changed at all.'

'Yes it has. You stole my dog and you haven't done anything so decisive in months.'

'I keep saying what it is and you're just not listening. That house—'

'— is just the perfect excuse for you. For ages now you've been entirely content to keep me at a nice, safe, friendly distance; ever since you moved into that cottage, in fact. And I think, today, the difference is that you're here in the Manor instead of your cottage, and instead of being deaf to everything I say you've decided to seize upon this business about the house and you're going to use it to slide unpleasantly into an end to our little affair.'

'Am I?' Phyllis's eyebrows arched. 'I suppose I might if it

wasn't the case that I don't actually need to end anything at all, do I? Because it's already over. You made that clear yourself last week when I mentioned curtains and you started going on about stagnation and retirement and your thoughts on moving away. So, if the lie about the house is irrelevant and I'm too stuffy and you're still absolutely dead-set on plying your trade elsewhere, why on earth should it matter to you if I'm here now and not at home?'

I noticed the change that came with this last part. It was as if it had suddenly been voiced on a revealing note, rather than with the blinding mask of temper. I noticed the change in the way she was looking at his averted profile, and the way she was suddenly feeling again that path ahead where she truly assumed the label my father had given her. I also noticed the small adjustment in the way Danny was leaning beside her upon the tabletop as something she'd said made his sense of purpose subtly lighten from survival into something equally intense but rather less closely guarded from her.

Movement in the doorway from the dining room drew both their minds raggedly away from this debate. The rooms upstairs had been deemed secure. Richard was passing through the kitchen with PC Rathbone, who was clutching an enormous bunch of keys in his fist – the housekeeper's set, I thought. They were accompanied by a few other men who were keen to examine Abbey's lairs in the tithe barn and the watershed. I believe the constable thought Danny ought to be leading them there rather than Richard, but one sharp encounter with Danny's gaze as he lifted his head told us all what he thought of that idea.

Richard passed my space behind the kitchen counter. There was a moment when he reached out a hand to me. My hand answered and he touched his fingers to mine. A gesture of reassurance and an acknowledgement of my own tasks. Then he was out of the door and walking with five or so uniformed policemen, all looking very correct and straight and determined behind the young and wiry-haired PC Rathbone.

It was hard to return from that light touch to the tangled mood of my companions. Phyllis was glowering at Detective Fleece, who had passed through the other way with a warning that he would soon be requiring this room for his interview with the Colonel. I wondered if someone had mentioned to the detective that the old man was more at home in this part of the house than any other. I wondered, too, if this was the real, unspoken, purpose of the meal I was preparing – an excuse to bring the Colonel in here without injuring his precarious dignity. Phyllis only glared at the man who would dismiss her own important conversation as the inconvenience of a minor domestic disaster. Danny returned his attention to Phyllis – I thought his own manner had grown more gentle. He was still leaning in to rest his forearms on the tabletop beside her and he had his fingers intertwined in an easier grip now. His gaze rested upon them as he told her quietly, 'We've been friends our whole lives, you and I. I've known you while the forthright girl of my childhood marched off to pursue her studies and university, and waved you off when you took up your role in the war just days before I assumed mine. It seemed to me that it was perfectly fitting that I should have to meet you again in Gloucester this spring, paddling about in the floodwaters with your suitcase held over your head and barking out instructions to anyone who needed them as though we were merely the grubby farm boys of your youth. To be frank, it was nothing short of a relief to me, since I was one of about thirty tired soldiers who were desperate to be demobbed, but cursed with one more hard duty of battling a flood with sandbags whilst ducking the sort of opportunistic idiots who always seem to emerge from the brickwork in a crisis.'

I'd never heard him run so many words together. It was clear this wasn't easy for him. It was also clear just how well these two people must truly know each other. They'd grown up together and if I felt war had changed my childhood, I could only imagine the void it had left where their first years of adulthood ought to have been. She must have been roughly twenty-three at the outbreak of war and he only a couple of years younger. I thought it must have been odd for them to meet again, both thoroughly ill-fitted now for the habits and limitations of their old lives and yet still recognisably the same people, really.

He said in a rougher voice, 'Then your mother died. It isolated you in the way that only grief can. You retreated to the cottage to sort through her things at the same time that I was learning that all hell had broken loose here. I hadn't exactly reckoned on coming back to find all those in charge either dead or gone and the running of the Manor farm left to me. And, besides all that, it's been hard enough for any of us to adjust to the shock of meeting normal life at the end of our war service, hasn't it? I bought my house in the weeks that you were learning that your mother's will had left you her cottage. I know she only left it to you because your brothers are all married and you aren't, and she wanted to give you your independence. Only I think she must have also left you her mad old life of retirement, because I'd always thought your identity was the most robust thing about you until you came home weary and disorientated and found another person's idea of living as a single woman laid out on the doorstep to meet you.'

The Colonel shuffled in, handed me a sherry as if I wanted one, and shuffled out again. I suspected that this was his idea of a strong cup of sugary tea and it told me that he must have heard something of the account of the disaster at the pump house and my part in Richard's injury. I thought it a very touching mark of solidarity.

Across the room, while I was laying out the last few ingredients for the Colonel's cold lunch, Danny was adding, 'I didn't dare tell you about my house at that time because then we'd have had to discuss why I was still here and staying with my parents. You knew I didn't intend to go on labouring on the farm here any more, whether I counted as the last man standing or not – and if I'd mentioned the house in Gloucester, it would have been very hard to deny that its rent would have given me the security to set up work elsewhere.'

Phyllis's brows were puckering. 'What's wrong with my identity? And, more to the point, why *did* you stay?'

For a moment there was a flicker of exasperation on Danny's mouth that came very close to amusement. 'There's absolutely nothing wrong with you at all. Nothing, except the trap of that blasted cottage.'

Then, just as suddenly, amusement evaporated. His voice grew very hard. Those clasped hands were gripping each other tightly now. 'Do you honestly think that my tiny corner in my mother's squalid attic might ever have been quite so appealing if you hadn't been here? This clearly is going to come as a surprise, but the truth is I only bought that house because I could afford it and I'd been advised that the rent it would bring would be a useful income when I first moved away. Patently, however, it was a ridiculous mistake because it has become a lie I don't need and now I'm frantically trying to sell it back to its original owner after I spoke to the woman about it last week and she said she wanted it. I want to be free of it and it's a damned good job we settled that she does want it because, as it turns out, I'm not going to be funding my future life. I'm going to need the money now to ensure my parents can stay in the home they've loved all their lives.'

His frustration burst from him like a whip. It hadn't really occurred to me to consider before that anything that had been done here for the upkeep of the estate during the Colonel's absence had been done by him. This was a man who felt the different calls of his life very deeply, and performed them without anyone giving him much credit for the struggle he had to lay his thoughts before others in the form of plain speech. Phyllis sat up rather straighter.

Danny swept on. 'I hate that cottage of yours. It has worked its way into your brain. It suffocates your thoughts just as mine get turned to sullenness by the effort of juggling all that work.' Now he was ducking his head closer to hers and lowering his voice to a rather more private level as two uniformed policemen came in to find the detective. 'Oh, I'll admit that our rare days out with the car have been companionable enough, but there's always been the grim threat of having to return you to that place stuffed with all those interminable trinkets, reminding you to cling to old things instead of thinking about the future. I couldn't even guess what you wanted from me when you were there. Occasionally you'd give me a glimpse of your usual decisiveness. But in that cottage you grieve and you're docile, or at least I thought you were until last week. That was the moment when I realised I was going to sell my house. I thought it was perhaps time we talked so I brought up the age-old discussion of my plans but, instead of listening, you started screaming at me about curtains. Suddenly you had an opinion after all. You made me think that all these months of waiting while you sorted through your mother's bits and pieces had been a deliberate delay, because it turned out you actually wanted the life she'd left for you. It looked as if you'd finally fallen into the trap of that place and I'd scared you by suggesting we went away because suddenly you started lecturing me about becoming the tame companion of your life in your cottage. And then you told me to get out. I wasn't entirely sure you hadn't staged the whole thing. You knew I didn't want to stay here, hoping to curry favour with the new owner of this estate, trying to be the next steward to march in the footsteps of your father. Good as the job might be, that man can't be me. And it's taken me until now to realise that the woman in your mother's kitchen isn't you either.'

'What do you mean?'

His reply was touchingly simple. 'Because this is who you are. This woman before me now. She looks the same, but she has a very different energy. When you asked me just now why it should matter that you're here and not in that cottage, it's this. Until this moment it hasn't so much been that you wouldn't listen to my questions, but that you couldn't. Honestly, this is the first time I've thought you've been able to hear me. When I asked you just now what had suddenly changed for you, I was wondering about the fact that this is the first time you've let me know that you'd taken my talk about my plans as a kind of punishment. It explains an awful lot if you thought I was hinting that I intended to leave you behind. I meant them as an invitation. For you to tell me about your own plans, I mean, and say what you truly wanted, and we could work out everything from there. Except, I really, really hope you aren't now going to repeat your offer to redecorate that cottage ...?'

There was a blankness on her face that looked like a memory of heartbreak.

'And,' he added after leaving a silence that she hadn't filled, 'I hope I'm right for telling you this because the simple fact of it is I've been missing you for years and these past months have been making me miss you even when I'm beside you. Now I don't know whether we've got to thank your brief stay in hospital or your cousin, or whoever for this sudden piece of liberation, but this is the first time in months that we've been free to act like our old selves again.'

At last, with an effort, my cousin found her voice. She asked him on a cracked note, 'How can you tell?'

He turned his head and studied her. Gently, he said for the second time, 'Phyl, love, you stole my dog.'

I thought he meant it as a good thing. He definitely did. I thought that this morning, when he'd realised what she'd done to force him to speak to her, he must have taken it as the first real glimpse of hope that she knew her mind and he was wanted after all. It turned out that there had been rejection on the other side of that argument about curtains too, and the pain hadn't just been hers.

But I'm afraid the single point that registered through this lesson on the benefits of trying to understand another person's point of view wasn't the relief of finally understanding the true nature of Mrs Abbey's hold on him. It didn't matter to me that his worry had been the burden of maintaining this secret while he negotiated his way through the complication of selling the house back again. It was the fact that Mrs Abbey was able to contemplate buying it at all.

I knew she was poor. She'd said so, and that much I could believe. I believed too that she'd sold the house to pay for the legal work that had led to her husband's release. So, if she was buying the house back again now, she had to be buying it on the expectation of future money, and with an idea of gain that long pre-dated Richard's arrival in this place.

The only other source of wealth I could think of beyond blackmail was Duckett's share in the business. She was a stakeholder, after all, beside her brother, so the power was there to take it, and Richard and I had guessed already that her plans for Duckett were very final indeed. But, actually, it came as a surprise to find the woman conforming to this blandly mercenary turn.

Or rather, to be truly accurate, it left me with the worry of trying to calculate what other older, baser ambitions might be lying concealed beneath the present ruthlessness with which she and her husband were pursuing Richard.

Chapter 28

I walked through the house to find the Colonel and to tell him that his lunch was ready and then I followed a trail of policemen up the stairs. I'd never been in the Captain's room before. It was neat and orderly and quietly papered in soft greens and blues, so that the affected grandeur that made his brother's room oppressive was eased here. It made me realise that, in a way, these rooms did reflect the tastes of their occupants after all. But I wasn't here to pry. I was doing my job and seeking anything that Abbey might have left awry.

In John's room, I found that Phyllis had completed her mission to expunge that man's ownership of this place and had, slightly foolishly, hung my few rather grubby clothes alongside hers in that vast wardrobe. I reached to pull them out and found John's jacket in the way. It was filthy, like my slacks had been after last night's excursion, and possibly the source of the faintly sickly smell that had met me on my first visit to this room. Because the jacket's collar and left sleeve were rancid with dried blood.

It was the light summer coat Abbey had worn during his encounter with Mr Winstone. It explained precisely how the man's wife had been inspired to tell me that I must have met John's angry shade on the garden path. It surprised me that she hadn't simply chosen to destroy this piece of proof that her husband was in the habit of borrowing clothes, just as he thieved other people's food, but perhaps they'd hoped that the myth of John's wrath would be a useful disguise.

With the knowledge of how she had spoken of John that night in my cousin's kitchen, I thought that Abbey must have come here to shed his borrowed clothes after he had left me on Mr Winstone's path. He might have been lurking up here while I had been speaking to Richard on the telephone. This was what had kept Mrs Abbey from her home so late that night. She'd come here herself for the purpose of consulting with the man about what might be done about me. Then she'd come knocking on my cousin's door, eager to get me, the only witness to her husband's crime, to walk her home to Eddington.

I remembered her sudden change of heart when she had spied my suitcase on the stairs and informed me that I was planning to continue my holiday elsewhere. There must have been a moment before that, when she'd intended to take me out there into the darkened woods between her house and mine, and introduce me properly to her husband.

But she hadn't done it. And the return of this jacket to its hanger represented the time when the plan had still been merely to escape the consequences of the assault on Mr Winstone. But yesterday Abbey had come again for something else. He'd been drawn here for the sake of something that must have grown from their inspiration to use Richard and to think of him as the surviving replica of John. And Abbey had run from me because he hadn't yet had time to tell his wife about the discovery of the Colonel's gun.

I found his secret concealed in the jacket's sleeve. The left sleeve – the one coated in blood – was stuffed with green silk. It was a skirt of mine and it hadn't been given to the squatter woman with the frock after all.

The skirt the squatter woman had listed had been merely an old rough skirt for menial work and was a different kind of green. This skirt was the other portion of my mother's old evening gown and it was soft and pliable beneath my fingers. Mine and yet alien to me and hated now too because they'd corrupted it, adulterated it with splatters of blood so that it pretended to belong to the attack on Mr Winstone.

Well, this at least was the harmless part – apart from my natural recoil that slung both jacket and skirt hastily back onto their hanger and into the wardrobe, and the dubious worry about where Paul Abbey had sourced the blood. Because this was all Abbey had been doing here yesterday. He'd been secreting this trace of me, which was part and parcel of their plan to leave the scorched remains of my other clothes in the turbine house. He had meant to ensure that Duckett really could be tied to the attack on Mr Winstone as well as all the fires. Unless Mrs Abbey had lied earlier about that part too and this had all been meant as a warning to Richard. But even if it was, it was still harmless because that particular threat was obsolete.

Footsteps tramped along the gallery and drew me to the

door. And a silken whisper drew me back again as the skirt slid a little on its hanger.

I was reaching to draw the wardrobe door open as the front door slammed downstairs. A car engine was idling in the drive. Then it crawled away again and after that brief flurry of thinking I ought to gather the policemen in here, I was glad that my private search had found peace again. There was a paper in the skirt and it rustled and tumbled as I fumbled for it. I reached gingerly between bloodied fabrics to retrieve it.

The sheet was written on both sides and the first was penned in that same neat style that had lately been working late into the night filling out the new records for the Manor accounts. It was a letter from Richard dated September 1946 and written to his brother from his London hospital bed in a rather dry humour. It said:

Thank you for your sympathetic note. It is such a relief to know that your long train journey home was improved by the chance to read that particularly saccharine article published in a certain women's magazine. I'm glad you enjoyed Lady Sarah's account of her tragic cares for the crippled war hero. I had no idea she'd been so much on hand to assist my first faltering steps out of bed. Nor did I know it was vital that she should tell the world in such syrupy terms about the bittersweet honour of being loved by a man who'd been 'damaged in the cause of the national interest'. It's alarming how many people have read the thing. Even the man who mops the floors in this benighted place, would you believe?

I suppose I should be glad to have been able to lend a bit of cheer to all my fellow invalids, but you know … well, I won't call it betrayal because I know she saw this story as an act of leadership for all the real women whose husbands have come home damaged from war. She also thought she'd found the ideal means of fixing herself firmly in the public eye if I might shortly be pensioned out of the army. But I'm like you. Lamed or not, I won't slide into meek complacency and I certainly won't buy a new career by seeing my recent deeds dressed up as the stuff of glory.

Truly, I can't help wondering what glory she imagined would be found anyway, in trading on the actions of an angry youth from Battersea who will now have to spend a portion of his life behind bars?

I'm sorry about this mess, though, for Father's sake. I won't mention wealth or social standing because I know that for all the lectures he and Uncle William have given us over the years, that won't be the part he'll be disappointed about. He liked her, I know.

I found that I was sitting on the edge of the bed, clutching the disgusting skirt – which I dropped just as soon as I realised – and staring at the letter. I was thinking that I understood now why the Colonel should have believed that his encounter with a journalist would hurt Richard more than him. And I was thinking that I shouldn't be surprised any more that

Richard had always seemed faintly uncertain as he accepted each quiet proof of my care from me.

This Lady Sarah, who was like Mrs Abbey and the dead brother and sometimes even the father, despite his better intentions; they all tried to claim whatever Richard had to give, as if it were debt he should pay purely because he was strong enough to bear it.

But not me. I wanted to burn this letter. Ruin it, so that it couldn't hurt him again. This ought to have been his own past and his own story to tell if he had wished to, not a weapon for Mrs Abbey to use in a fresh assault in a bad battle. I didn't burn the letter, though. I read the part that came afterwards that was like an introduction to the real, living John Langton and proved his core to be possessed by a horrible, selfish man.

The last of the paragraphs that had been penned by Richard indicated the true purpose of his letter. It revealed that a request had been made in the course of John's visit – and forgotten until a note from John had prompted him. Now Richard detailed, as promised, the name of a local family contact who had helped to source some of their mother's choice artworks. There was a hope this person would prove useful to John in the disposal of a painting. I thought for a moment this was going to turn into an astounding declaration that the myth about a missing treasure was true after all, but it didn't.

The scrawl on the reverse was the part that was written by John and it told the reader that he was forwarding the long-awaited details now that Richard had *'finally recovered his wits enough after that ruinous conquest to remember to send the name'*. It also offered his services if the reader wanted some support during the ensuing negotiations over the sale of their particularly foul and muddy painting and that was that. It didn't even bear John's name.

I could identify the man's hand by his flamboyant way of handling his Fs. That initial, taking the form of a 'Dear F', was all there was on this note to indicate that this had been addressed to Mrs Florence Abbey. It occurred to me to wonder if this letter was supposed to incriminate Duckett – based solely on the fact that it had been Duckett himself who had given me Mrs Abbey's full name. But a simple handwriting test would eliminate that theory and on that same principle, I barely spared even a moment to worry that Abbey might have thought the untidiness of the scrawl would allow the 'Dear F' to be mistaken for a 'Dear E'. No one would believe I'd ever met John. And no one would imagine I would stain my own clothes with blood and then thrust them here with an old letter, as if to hide them.

The alternative was that this note had been placed here as a final attempt to add weight to the rumour of a love affair between John Langton and his neighbour Florence Abbey, but even that wasn't particularly successful. John's cruel, unsympathetic handling of Richard's letter wasn't lightened by expressions of undying love for the reader, or mild affection or even dignified friendship. The abbreviation of her name to an F as an introduction was as intimate as it came. And there were certainly no messages from a doting father to his beloved little boy.

It was a very peculiar piece of the bribe. It left me tense, trapped. Particularly when the whole experience evaporated into a sudden and horrible sensation of being watched again.

I twisted sharply to the door. There was no one there. Of course there wasn't. The house was muted and empty. In a way, that was probably why this place was feeling quietly hostile again, as it had on that very first walk through to the telephone. Because it made me very aware of the distant whisper of conversation that was drifting up the stairs from the front door. I believe there were two or three bored policemen outside by the cars who were acting as a kind of guard. They were probably smoking because after these past few days of worrying about fire, my nose was sensitive enough to detect the faint tinge of sulphur from a match.

Disputing my idea of quiet isolation, their voices were rivalled by the equally distant rumble of the Colonel's interview with Detective Fleece. The brief rattle of temper that drifted along the gallery from the other direction seemed to me to belong to the bullying squire that the old man might have been had John not died. Presumably they had got to the part where the Colonel was learning precisely how Richard had come by his injury at the pump house.

It wasn't the most encouraging note on which to turn my footsteps to the door that concealed the servants' stairs. But the discovery of this letter had to be shared, whether I loathed the idea of Richard knowing how his brother had handled his private cares or not, so I eased my way through into the landing with all the bathrooms and downwards into the gloom. I knocked lightly on the servants' door into the kitchen for the sake of politeness, and put my hand on the panel.

And then stopped because something about the pitch of the Colonel's voice in that room had me turning on the spot and hurrying back up the steps again.

Instinct had me thinking very clearly about those idle policemen standing on the front step. It also had me thinking about how the Colonel's temper was strangely constrained when he had never thought to moderate his tone before.

I was already running back up through the gloom – already thinking of raising the alarm – when the door was snatched open behind. Comprehension had come too late for me. A sweaty hand reached. It claimed my right arm at the elbow. It wrenched me off the stairs and into daylight. Excruciatingly. Vision was confused, but I heard the clatter and felt the collision when I met the dresser. It was used as a prison and I was jammed there without a thought for the pain of it. My left side must have struck because it was agony, but at least it was the opposite side from the hip that had met the sun-baked ground above the pump house. The paper in my hand met the smooth wood of the dresser with a crisp clack. It all occurred at the same moment that I saw that the Colonel was on his feet by the table near the policeman. Duckett stood quite a long way beyond them. He threw out a lazy order. 'Don't let her scream.'

And then, while the hand took a better hold to keep me from getting into a position where I might fight him and in the process rattled my teeth, a breathy instruction was hissed into my ear. This was a voice I barely recognised from the single time I had it heard before and he didn't issue a curse or a threat or anything to match the grip he had on my upper arm.

Abbey said in a desperate undertone while he shut the door, 'Help me.'

Chapter 29

Of the two instructions, I obeyed Duckett's first. I didn't make a sound. Duckett was standing with his back to the window by the kitchen door, besuited and wearing that ugly yellow tie. The gun was in his hand this time. I thought he must have taken it. And perhaps, for our sake, it was a good thing. He was probably better trusted with it. He was wearing neat black driving gloves while Abbey was bare-fisted and his hands had the job of bustling me into a vacant chair by the kitchen table. He flung me there, really, for all that I was relatively willing to go. And even without Duckett's caution, grim sense would have kept me silent had those hands not tried to ensure it as Abbey thrust me into my chair by giving me a short, sharp slap across the cheek. The shock of the blow dragged a cry from me as the seat caught me and kept me from falling. It also made willingness evaporate. It made the other two men start forwards as Abbey's grip righted me in my chair and hovered on the cusp of hitting me again, this time with real force. The detective's voice was loud. He was checked by Duckett's command. We all were.

I had my hand up to fend off another strike. As I lowered

my guard and shaking fingertips moved instead to lightly probe the heat that consumed my left cheek, I saw the detective subside grudgingly into his chair on the far side of the table. Abbey released his grip on my clothes and settled for taking the letter from me as he stepped away. He was watching me as though I fascinated him. I suppose he saw me as his salvation. His posture was that of a man unhinged, but that brief hushed break of his voice had told a different story. It wasn't madness, or recklessness, or pure coincidence that had brought him to a house occupied by the policemen who hunted him. He'd come here knowing he would find them. And just now he'd tried to trip me into sound for the sake of calling Richard.

But it hadn't been enough. Later I would be desperately grateful that my cry really hadn't been enough.

Duckett was staring too. He was gazing at me from across the room like I was a gift; a surprise and his own dear prize. I thought I knew now in what form the two men were here together – captor and hostage – but this emphasis on silence told me what my mind didn't want to imagine. For Duckett, at least, there was no thought for Richard except to keep away from his attention. He had no intention of using me to bend Richard to his will. I was Duckett's target here.

That hungry stare made me feel sick. I wasn't badly hurt. Just shaken in my chair and feeling that brief relief of burgeoning anger slipping helplessly away. Because, in all the time that I'd been fighting against being the Abbeys' lure as they drove Richard to act, it had never really occurred to me to consider the depth of the enmity that was motivating them to behave like this in the first place.

I was unimaginably relieved when finally the policeman gave me the excuse to break away from that gaze.

When Detective Fleece spoke, he was sitting quietly but braced in his chair about two yards from me on the other side of the round kitchen table. I hadn't quite appreciated before what a big man the detective was. He had an elbow resting upon the tabletop, which was inexplicably cluttered with household objects that someone had placed there and his hand was idly rearranging a collection of pepper pots into various alignments. It meant nothing. It was just a symptom of his mind's preoccupation. His glance towards me behind the screen of this lazy act was designed to assure himself, through an unspoken question, that I was unharmed. It also told me what he wished me to do, which was nothing. I knew why. It was because, while one of us might take the initiative of raising the alarm, there was absolutely no way of ensuring that it might not fall upon another to bear the wrath of Duckett's instinctive response with that gun. In a way, our united caution gave a sense of control; it underlined the normal civilised concern that each of us felt for the lives of everyone else in this room. But, in truth, Duckett was leaving us with only the power of doing nothing to hasten the inevitable, which was no control at all.

Apparently we were permitted to speak though. I expected Duckett to demand silence but the detective was calmly telling me, 'You've found us like this because the man who was recording my interview with Colonel Langton was called out to take a message from the other team. They'd sent the driver back to us to carry the news that Mr Duckett's battered old

Ford has been found by your cousin's cottage. Unfortunately, having taken that message, my man hasn't come back. I expect he's gone to relay the information to the men at the tithe barn. It goes without saying that we hadn't any real idea that the Ford's owner would calmly walk in through the kitchen door.'

'The tithe barn is empty, policeman.' It was Abbey speaking. His voice was high and scolding. 'Your man's at that barn higher up on the lane. The watershed. And it's your man's fault we had to step inside here. Brian brought me here to clean up my little roost in the tithe barn – with more fire, you know? And the girl—'

He was interrupted by Brian Duckett. The man holding the weapon explained on a considerably less confrontational note, 'Paul wanted to leave a clearer mark that he'd been here. We thought the place was its usual deserted self. Only that stray man popped into view around the corner of the house and we had to dive for the first cover we found, which was this great cavern of a kitchen. We weren't expecting the place to be overrun with men and policemen.'

Duckett was thoroughly unruffled. Which was odd because he'd never been relaxed before, even when quietly enjoying the opportunity to bully me. He was also turning to lift an oil lamp from the window ledge beside him. It was one of a pair set out in anticipation of the Colonel's dinner party tonight. And it was as Duckett returned it to its place again that Abbey retreated abruptly to the dresser in the corner. I caught the change in Abbey's face. He'd been glowering furtively while Duckett examined the lamp. Now white-rimmed eyes swam in a gaunt face. He didn't look very much

472

like John Langton's ghost. He was tall and dark-haired, true, and his eyes were blue, but they lacked the steel of the Langton gaze and he was older too. He was perhaps in his forties and had the nervous energy of a man who hadn't slept well in years. I suppose that was what prison did. He was certainly tense now. He was fidgeting restlessly, fingers toying with a jacket pocket. I thought it was the pocket that until recently had held the gun.

The probability that the jacket was another item of clothing that had once been John's made me find the temper to turn my head and say tartly to Duckett, 'You might not have thought the police would be here, but I should have thought Abbey might. After this morning, he would have known that they'd either be here or at Eddington, and he would never have dared take you to his wife's home. Richard wouldn't have been neatly within earshot and what would be the use of presenting you to the policemen there as the arsonist who has been destroying a few outhouses? They'd be far more interested in arresting *him*.'

Abbey's sudden move towards me silenced me sharply. He didn't want me to mention the pump house nor his wife. Nor the idea of calling Richard. And perhaps not even the chain of fires by Duckett's hand.

Then my chair creaked. The Colonel had been on his feet all along. He had moved to fix a hand on the back of my chair. Now he was standing guard as if it would be a deterrent if Abbey really did mean to hit me again. He looked awful and I could hear his breathing. A greasy film stood out upon his skin. Beneath the ruddy tinge, he was desperately pale and I wondered if anyone had ever thought to check the state of his heart.

It was a surprise when from his place some way to my right, the policeman's voice calmly directed a question to Duckett. 'Am I to understand that you brought Mr Abbey here to set alight to the last of his lairs? Did you intend to leave Mr Abbey stranded for Captain Langton to catch him in the act?'

Abbey was snatching his eyes from me to peer almost owlishly at Duckett's face. It was the reference to the fire that was bothering him now.

I added in a voice that was a distracted whisper, 'And why not? After all, everyone here is trying to incriminate someone.'

And it was that last statement that tightened my hands upon the rim of my seat on either side of my skirt. Because everyone really was trying to incriminate someone here and, for all the madness of the act, it was suddenly occurring to me to wonder if I had just discovered that Abbey had deliberately given Duckett the gun.

After all, a few burned outhouses really were nothing compared to Abbey's own crimes so far. And what trap might Abbey be trying to weave into this scene now that it was Duckett's fist that was clenched around the butt of that Webley?

My heart was beating. My fingers were adjusting their grip on the chair when the policeman cast me a questioning look. I knew I was looking disbelieving. I couldn't explain. I didn't really know myself beyond the doubt of how far Abbey could still be depending now upon the concept of harnessing

Richard, when surely Abbey must know, as the rest of us did, how little even a soldier could do against the pure uncompromising speed of a bullet.

I found that Abbey had returned to his dresser and was reading my face in a way that wasn't quite so ready to provoke me into a fight any more. He was looking, in fact, like he was reading my thoughts, almost enjoying them, and that, in itself, was deeply unnerving. Because, on Abbey's face was a shadow of the same kind of daring that Richard had described facing in the aftermath of my intervention at the pump house.

It made every nerve scream caution when the policeman remarked to Duckett, 'I suppose you *do* know you're already free from Abbey, don't you? You do know a man was lately shot with that stolen Webley?'

I hoped the policeman had understood my alarm; that he was taking charge. But my chair creaked again. The Colonel was leaning heavily. His own mistake had armed this scene after all. And with his ebbing pride, the rest of my meagre hope failed too. Duckett didn't seem at all relieved by the news that the revolver in his hand had a different history from the one he had imagined. I had believed Detective Fleece's comments might render this entire exercise redundant now that Duckett knew that the weapon was actually already part of a police investigation. Instead, Duckett was blindingly, humblingly, indifferent. And no words from a policeman could remove the bullets from that gun.

All Detective Fleece had succeeded in doing, if anything, was remind Duckett of his control. Duckett was barking at

Abbey, 'Get back to your job, Paul. Stop looking like you're about to harass the girl. Bring me that paper in your hand. Show me what she had.'

The girl bridled at being mentioned in that order of diminishing status as a human – men, policemen and womenfolk. I was also terribly aware of the shift towards obedience in Abbey's manner as he sidled across the room. Anticipation stalked with him as he let the other man snatch the paper from his hand and returned with him as he reclaimed his place by the dresser, and it was frightening because I began to see that some of Abbey's attempts to stem my words hadn't been from dismay that I was exposing him. The mark on my cheek burned like a memory. He'd begged me to help him, but from the first he'd been in danger of steering this scene into a harder depth of tension. With his little lurches across the room, he might have frightened me into calling out for a second time. But not necessarily, I thought, for the sake of calling Richard.

Certainly, he'd given the impression that the risks of antagonising Duckett had been working as powerfully upon his own nerves as they had upon mine. Once his initial excitement from plucking me off the stairs had passed, I had grown deeply conscious of the caution that had kept him back from me just far enough to let me feel some of my own determination. I thought his restraint might have grown from a very ugly instinct that he didn't want to be near me when Duckett reacted to my next cry for help. But the true weight of his actions was more sinister than that.

I understood now that, above it all, he'd tried to turn every little drift in concentration back to me, by word or by deed. He'd been frustrated when Duckett had persisted in remaining so calm. But now he thought that Duckett was beginning to notice me.

Chapter 30

It was the brief stray of Abbey's eyes across the room that gave me the clue about the rest. His glance wasn't for me. It was for the person who had been standing, unmoving and unnoticed, in the space where the broom cupboard met the wall bearing the kitchen door.

Mrs Abbey drew my head round so quickly to the distant corner beyond the policeman that it hurt my neck. Or, at least, reminded me of an ache that had been put there by one of my many falls today. She was still wearing that neatly tailored skirt and jacket in navy of the sort that gave a woman like her a formidable kind of style. She didn't look like a prisoner but she didn't exactly look free, either.

Mrs Abbey didn't notice my shocked dismay. She was staring at her husband. She was exchanging a silent question with him of the sort that only ever occurs between two people who understand each other perfectly. His answer was the faintest of shrugs. I was remembering the way she'd screamed her command to hurry to Richard's side because he was deranged and he'd kill and I knew then that it had been Richard's violence she had desperately tried to prevent at the pump house. She'd been afraid that the living Langton would hurt her helpless, defenceless man. And I thought it answered too a little of the question of what she really felt for Richard's younger brother John. For all her protestations of a deep and abiding friendship with the young master of this estate, she must have had no real faith in the blood that had coursed through John's veins if she could have instinctively believed the surviving brother capable of acting with that same want of reason today.

Now she was noticing her husband's desire to draw sound from me, and digesting it. Whatever he was doing here hadn't formerly been part of any plan of hers.

I thought she was conveying disapproval when she allowed her eyes to drift to me. She told me as if I'd even thought to ask the question, 'I came in a few minutes before you did. I was looking for you. Or that Captain of yours.'

My lips were dry. It was hard to ask, 'You were looking for me?'

'Yes. No one could tell me that Paul was unharmed and still free. I hadn't any choice. I was going to have to ask you to tell me plainly what had happened. My only other option was to just go home to wait endlessly in that desolate, empty house and it was hardly fair when I did warn you to be quick, didn't I?'

'Yes,' I agreed very cautiously. 'Yes, yes you did.'

Her lipstick was a garish smudge in a pinched but elegant face as I floundered in the effort of trying to calculate how thoroughly she was meaning to imply she had given up her hope of harnessing the Langton nature. I was also trying to comprehend that she'd just admitted before Duckett that she'd cared to hear about her husband's condition and, after all the fear and secrecy that Mrs Abbey had worked upon my sympathies, in truth Duckett was entirely indifferent to the lie.

He wasn't really listening anyway. In fact, at present, he was mesmerised by the letter. All of a sudden he wasn't quite so calm after all, because those few paragraphs were making his brows pucker. It was like the time under the hospital arches, only this time his anger at his ignorance was amplified because the letter meant nothing to him when he thought it should.

'May I see?' This was from the policeman.

Surprised, Duckett complied. I noted that he kept the Webley ready just in case the policeman was intending to rush him, but he wasn't. Detective Fleece seemed merely curious. We all watched spellbound as he read the letter through.

Duckett's voice was tight. 'It's nothing to do with me?'

'Nothing,' confirmed the policeman. Then he folded the letter in half and, apparently for the sake of tidiness because the tabletop was so cluttered, slipped it into the pocket of his coat.

I thought Duckett should have demanded it back. Instead he was staring at the policeman, briefly repulsed. I was silent too. I didn't quite dare to mention that Abbey had left the letter for me to find. It seemed impossible that Abbey had foreseen this moment, but every note of caution was remembering the way his wife had spoken about the Langton family and that nothing they had left had been designed to do anyone any good. Now I was noticing the way Abbey's head had turned as Duckett had betrayed his nervousness. And now Duckett seemed to suddenly be focusing on me without anyone needing to steer him into it. He was reaching a hand into a coat pocket to draw out another piece of folded paper. This one was a small square of brown. He handed it to the policeman.

'Read this,' Duckett commanded with the beginnings of a smirk. 'That man has a habit of writing meaningless rubbish about women.'

There was a momentary caution in the detective's movement as he reached out his hand. There was an intensity of curiosity in Mrs Abbey's. I believe she and the detective had both misunderstood. They both thought that Duckett was offering another note by John Langton. There was a glimmer of anticipation in the way the policeman unfolded the paper. Then that brief spark of interest abruptly dimmed once again and instead of pocketing this one too, Detective Fleece surprised me by reaching across the table to me. He told me, 'This one is meant for you, I think.'

I felt the twist in Mrs Abbey's interest; the disappointment as she learned that this note was only written by John Langton's other brother. The feeling in her turned to daring that nearly made her step across the room with a demand to see it too. I don't know what I would have done if she had. As it was, she seemed to change her mind halfway through the act and instead moved past the table into the space of the kitchen counter behind me.

It left me free to meet the detective's hand with leaden

fingers. The paper was the brown wrapping that had contained Richard's sandwiches yesterday. This note was very short and the disappointment for the detective was that it was by Richard's hand and not John's. The joke for Duckett was that this was the second time that Richard had revealed some of his feelings. This note began:

> *Sir. We haven't been formally introduced but I saw your encounter with my friend Miss Sutton just now at the docks. I am, as you may have gathered, a captain in His Majesty's Armed Forces. My home is London and I'm here for a matter of days at the most. It is as long as my commanding officers can spare me from my duties, which are of an independent nature.*

It was, to all intents and purposes, a bland reassertion of his credentials. No threats, no warnings, beyond the statement that he wasn't exactly an untrained weakling. Just a reference to the fact he'd been a witness to Duckett's unpleasantness on the waterside outside his office and perhaps a hint that Richard understood the delusion Duckett was under about my relationship with Abbey. Richard's own cool assertion that he was my friend was his answer to the mistake. The paragraph that came next was the part he must have added as an afterthought at the very end of the discussion we'd shared under the shade of that hospital porch.

> *In fact, given what you and I have just heard, and the hint it bears about Miss Sutton's criminally overlooked capa-*

*bilities, I think I should ask her if she would like to come
along on my next job. The work doesn't prohibit contact
with members of the public and I think she'll enjoy the
challenge of travelling as I do, if she doesn't think it all
too soon. Don't you agree?*

Yours, Captain R Langton.

He meant Greece. He meant his trip to Athens. This was
what had prompted him yesterday to comment on the change
in the way I'd spoken about my former hope of joining my
cousin's next foreign holiday. I'd slipped into setting the plan
firmly in my past; presumably while telling myself very
earnestly that I'd learned in the midst of one of those intrigu-
ingly bewildering debates with Richard that my idea of
searching for liberty abroad was instead drifting vaguely into
the new-found and mildly hesitant thought that freedom
might dwell wherever my life chose to put it.

This principle was a falsehood, of course. I must have
known all the while that the change was really motivated by
the rather less worthy but significantly more emboldening
consideration that if I wanted to see more of Richard, I might
enjoy the chance of it if I stayed in London.

But in writing this note, Richard knew this was different.
This wasn't some dream of mine of little outings to coffee
houses or the pictures and trusting that life might be allowed
to take its course without testing my confidence, for once. He
cannot have expected me to have the chance to read this note,
but still, it was as though it had been penned for me all the
same.

Because if I were to go with him on a job, we would have to be married first. And how long did you have to wait before you could marry these days, thanks to the anxious habits of couples who had met during the war? Barely longer than it took to get the licence.

I was dragged out of the brief forgetfulness of a furtive smile by the chill of being reminded that the man's forbidding, fragile old father was right by my side. The movement of that old, stern hand on the back of my chair was what had roused me, but he wasn't staring at the note in my hand any more, or my face, if he couldn't read Richard's handwriting at that range. If those severe grey eyes had been reading the change in my expression at all, now the Colonel was suddenly reacting to the way that Abbey had stopped hovering in an impotent kind of way by that dresser.

The taller man wasn't particularly threatening me now. He seemed to have developed a maddening compulsion to pick things up and put them down again. Presumably it had been his nervous hands that had moved the Colonel's pots and pans onto the table. Now he was picking up a jug and setting it down again. Then he picked up a plate and then a teacup. I was fascinated for a moment. His fingerprints would be everywhere. Then I turned my head once more to the man leaning hard upon the hand that gripped my chair and I saw the old man's face.

It was as if the Colonel were receiving a physical assault. It was shattering him to perceive this deliberate contamination of the one room in this great sad house that had lately, through the ministrations of his son and perhaps me too, taken on some semblance of being his home. It made me straighten like a bolt in my seat and forget the injunction against action long enough to cry out, 'Stop it. Stop it! Can't you see what you're doing to him?'

'That's enough.'

Duckett's voice came coolly across the room. It was a command for Abbey and he jumped as if he'd been shot. Duckett seemed to have succumbed to the same urge to touch as well because he had taken up both the spare oil lamps from the window ledge near the door, only he was still wearing his gloves.

Duckett was hugging the two lamps to his chest. They were the sort that had bulbous bases to contain the oil and frosted glass globes to spread the light. Briskly he told Abbey, 'I think you've left enough proof that you were here, Paul. Let's get this done.' Abbey turned like a puppet towards the table where I was sitting perched in my chair, only to freeze when Duckett's voice flung itself impatiently across the room to address the woman messing about at the kitchen counter behind me. 'What are you *doing*, Florence?'

Mrs Abbey appeared to have spent the past minutes moving about, quietly opening drawers and cupboards in the space where the oven stood. She made a show of discovering that all the glassware had been moved to the table. She selected one and bore it to the sink to run a tap into it. 'Getting a drink of water.'

She wasn't pouring the water for herself. She stepped around the Colonel and reached to slide the glass across the table at me, on a course that didn't upset the stacks of crockery her husband had set there. She stayed there, leaning across the table, expecting me to take the glass from her. I stayed clasping the seat of my chair with whitening hands and didn't move.

'See?' remarked Duckett tersely. 'She doesn't want it.' Then he straightened briskly with his lamps rattling in his arms. 'Paul? Bring her. And you two gentlemen can walk before me.'

Florence Abbey could presumably make her own choice about where to walk.

Then Duckett hesitated. Rather clumsily, he had worked the pair of lamps into the crook of one elbow and now he was staring at the weapon in his hand, as though it were a faintly unsettling discovery. He asked the policeman in a way that gave a brief kick of hope, 'What did you say about this gun?'

The question came as Abbey twisted across the room and reached past his wife for me. I thought he would stop again; keep himself clear from the line of fire as he had every time before. He didn't. Something had changed. This wasn't controlled. My skin was crawling away. This was because the touch of Abbey's hand through the thin sleeve of my frock felt like he was leaving his prints on me as he had with the plates and the jug. He wasn't remotely acting any more like a man who thought Richard must appear at any moment to save him. This wasn't about making me call Richard. Even his own shout might do that. Or his wife's. She was standing there only a yard or more behind him.

Abbey had allowed himself to be brought here. He'd obeyed Duckett's command to leave a nice array of marks for the fingerprinting dust to find. He was obeying more orders now

486

and it was because clearly for Abbey escape depended solely upon the fact that he'd given Duckett that gun. Only, judging by the way he was beginning to panic, equally clearly Duckett's interest in those lamps represented his failure.

I was still resisting his efforts to prise me from the chair. But his weren't the only hands dragging at me because the old man was huffing and snatching at me too. The Colonel's grip upon my arms was as excruciating as the way Abbey's fists were forcibly working my fingers free from the seat of my chair. Practically standing above me, the Colonel was trying to use his shoulder to barge Abbey aside. Futilely, as it turned out, and it was evident that the Colonel hadn't been remotely worrying about his pots and pans just now; he'd been conscious of their irrelevance when it came to the danger here for me. And that made it awful because this was the protectiveness of an old soldier whose last shreds of dignity belonged to the sense of honour where even old men had to defend women and children.

Before I even knew it, I was stopping fighting and was out of the chair and standing in Abbey's grip and saying on an urgent undertone to no one in particular, 'The warehouse fire.'

And then, while the Colonel was muttering a breathless, 'Eh?' I was turning my head to Duckett and saying incredulously, 'Abbey's terrified of fire. You know what the warehouse smoke did to his lungs and you're torturing him with the threat of more. So he gave you the Webley because it was a stolen gun and he did it because it was the only thing he had left that might save him once you'd caught him, even though

he knew full well he'd already personally left his mark with his own idiotic attack on Richard down by the pump house.'
I had to take a breath. Abbey's grip was hurting and he seemed to be trying to get a hand over my mouth, only it was easy enough to twist away. Then I was flinching away properly within the restraint of his grip because he was abandoning silence for the sake of attempting instead to strike me. This time it wasn't for any calmly conceived strategy. He didn't like the way I was talking about fire. It was hard to fend him off without fighting.

But as I twisted, I saw the flicker that passed across Mrs Abbey's face even if Duckett didn't. She hadn't known before this moment the depth of their failure at the pump house. She could see that I had fixed my nerve upon unseating her husband's plan and I didn't care that it angered him or that she might feel it endangered her. Because I absolutely was not going to wrestle with Abbey to the extent that Duckett would be forced to restore order.

Abbey had lost control now and instead of trying to subdue me, he was roaring at me. He was bellowing, 'I didn't give him the blasted thing. He caught me as I was running home to my wife. He'd been nosing about your cottage. It was the cottage that gave me the idea of bringing Brian here. He might have planned to use my wife's home to prove I was the one who'd been running around burning things. So I distracted him by telling him that I've been staying at the tithe barn since the housekeeper left, because the alternative was Eddington and my children are there—'

488

'Don't mention them.' The caution from his wife was spoken urgently.

'The hayloft in the tithe barn has been your haunt for several weeks?' The policeman's voice masked her plea. His question was given clearly with the practical calm that made it seem as though he were merely continuing his interrupted interview. 'How were you never seen?'

Abbey's wandering gaze, as it snapped over my head, was wild with incomprehension. He too was shaken by how little the detective seemed concerned by Duckett. The detective was studying Abbey gravely, with only a brief allowance of a momentary glance past me to the Colonel. I couldn't read the message in his eyes. It wasn't meant for me. Perhaps he was noticing the way the old man was panting. Then Abbey was drawing the policeman's attention back again because he was muttering, 'There's another door. A hatch where the hay gets brought in. It steps straight out into the lee of the road and the watershed above the church.'

He meant the patch of ground where Mrs Abbey's car had been parked on the day that my cousin had come spinning around the bend on her bicycle.

'Is the hatch into the hayloft locked?'

The policeman's query was loud and it made Abbey's face cloud into deeper puzzlement. He jerkily nodded his agreement. 'The key is on the set left by the housekeeper.' I saw him gulp and then, when the policeman seemed to have satisfied himself with that peculiar run of questions, Abbey gabbled almost plaintively, 'I had to hide there. I hadn't got a choice. Brian's been in a high state of aggression ever since I got out. He acts as though everything might have been fine between us if I had only gone to his office and brazened it out like a man, but it's like the girl says. Brian's been hunting me. He's been turning everything to ashes for weeks, even his mistakes.'

Abbey's head turned to me. Then he added with quiet desperation, 'Except he didn't quite count on meeting you. Brian exposed himself to you.'

The sudden twist in his voice terrified me. It was a sudden return to the attack. Power for him lay in the chance to nudge Duckett into focusing upon me. It made me race to contradict. I snapped, 'Duckett hasn't exposed anything. Don't be absurd. Your wife laid me out as the decoy when she first sent him after me. Everything you both have done has been designed to make another person act out your crimes for you. And now you're trying to make this man here use that gun because you think it'll pass responsibility for everything to him. Only you know full well your hopes of remaining at large are for naught because you've already shot a man with it today and you were seen. By more witnesses than me.'

'Shut up.' A snatched intake of air. A shake of Abbey's grip, which set me against the table and made the crockery clatter. Abbey jerked his head aside to note that Duckett was there and listening intently, then he turned back to me and he suddenly steadied. I could feel every grain of the rim of the table against my thigh as he remarked quite seriously, 'Anyway, don't you think it's a good job that you came to the pump house?'

There was an intensity to that pale gaze. I didn't quite understand his sudden calm. I saw the drift as the policeman considered creeping closer, only to check the movement when Duckett uttered a sharp tsk. The policeman's eyes turned right, found Duckett and received one brief discouraging shake of the head. I understood suddenly why Duckett was allowing us this time to speak. He was fiddling with one of the lamps and in danger of dropping the lot because he had to do it without loosening his hold on the gun.

Abbey's lips were shaking. 'If you hadn't come,' he was saying with a voice that was heavily glossed with a desperately false kind of satisfaction, 'no one would have been shot and I'd have still been following my wife's profoundly convoluted idea of escape. I'd have been left issuing vague threats towards the good name of this old Colonel Langton, but it would never have been enough and, anyway, look at the state of him. This old man couldn't have coped with the strain.'

Abbey barely gave me room to turn my head to the Colonel before he jerked his hands to straighten me again. The act drew an involuntary sound from me that sent a shiver through every muscle and made me press my lips tightly shut because this was why I'd stopped fighting. Abbey wanted me to call out, to struggle, to protest; to do anything that would escalate this debate to the point of requiring Duckett to settle it.

But Duckett wasn't moving; he wasn't intervening nor even paying very much attention while Abbey said on a gratified note, 'Personally, I don't think I need to convince Brian that you are the danger here – he already knows you've seen everything. You've been hounding him for days. I know you have. Because I was upstairs when you disturbed him while he ransacked this house. I'd run to ground there after helping myself to a bottle on the Colonel's spirits trolley. I was frightened and I made some accidental sound, and you saved me by dashing through just at the moment that Brian was starting up the stairs. So I don't have to do anything any more. I don't even have to coerce that man of yours into stepping in because Brian's already proved that you can ruin him.' Abbey stopped with an entirely dismal grin, then squeaked breathlessly, 'I've done nothing except defend myself and Brian's here and exposed and whether he sets that gun down or makes his attempt on a life and escapes, every action is a mistake now; because it'll all be for you.'

For me.

That last wild, optimistic declaration ran on and on in the air around us. It was the confession I'd expected, but still my mind stumbled. It was impossible, but he really seemed to be inciting Duckett to do it.

This was precisely the opposite feeling to the responsibility I'd been feeling for every other life in this room. Abbey meant capitalise on the opportunity he and the others would win while Duckett was distracted by his assault on me. Abbey was pretending that there would only be an 'attempt' on my life, swiftly suppressed. But Richard and I had noted earlier that these people seemed to take advantage of every changing circumstance. Why on earth would a desperate man like Abbey settle for implicating Duckett in a crime that might only cost the man a few years in prison, when there were other charges that would carry a more permanent sentence? Such as hanging for the murder of an innocent young woman, for example.

As it was, I didn't know that it mattered what Abbey thought. I'd seen the expression on Duckett's face as I had stepped down off the stairs into this room. Duckett didn't need to be told what I was to him.

And yet Duckett wasn't acting upon it. He was still midway between the table and the door, cradling his lamps, and he was suddenly laughing in a way that bordered on hysteria. He was saying, 'So, Detective, did you make note of that? I'm the innocent party. He's just broken into this house and performed an act of vandalism on the Colonel's kitchen and now he's admitted that he's trying to drive the girl into the path of violence here.'

The madness of the moment was playing through the grip Abbey's fingers had upon my arms. They were conveying the message that I'd saved him here once already this week. Now he was telling me that I was going to save him again.

For a moment I thought he was mistaken. For a moment, I still had the giddying belief that my wildly flawed attempt to continue the detective's idea of showing Duckett just how much Abbey had made a mess of things had put an end to this after all. I thought Duckett was going to hold out the Webley. I thought Duckett was going to surrender the proof of Abbey's crimes to the policeman and slap him on the back and show him Abbey's wrists for the handcuffs.

Then, as a perfect illustration of why it was imperative that none of us frightened Duckett and why it had been a risk too far to even hint at the prospect that Abbey might be already facing a return to prison, Duckett shuffled the lamps and the gun into one arm. His other hand reached into a pocket for his matches.

He was never going to let us go. Abbey's terror hadn't been imaginary. And Duckett really was here for me. It didn't matter to him now that I was bringing two additional characters into his sights – the policeman and the old soldier. A course of memory followed on a little haunting note; what he'd said about the firemen who had suffocated in the warehouse attics. That no man who had taken human life was ever quite the same again.

He'd lit that fire as well; the one that had claimed the lives of those men. And this was the betrayal he dreaded. This was the reason he had hunted Abbey through all these weeks since Abbey's release from prison and why the man's wife was so appallingly afraid. The betrayal Duckett was fighting to curb was the one where someone found a way to prove who had really destroyed the warehouse under the cover of the air raid.

And now he had decided I was a threat to him for the very flawed reason that I could accuse him of a pathetically small crime that tied him to this area, when he wanted to claim he had never climbed the hill out of Gloucester. So this time the coming blaze wouldn't be a mere sacrifice of walls and timber. The loss of life wouldn't be accidental. And this time it would all be fully attributable to Abbey by the lucky fortune of being able to leave us with the evidence of his stolen gun.

For a moment, just a short moment, I almost pitied Abbey and his wife and the efforts they'd gone to in order to cling to someone else for safety. They'd been trying to escape the desperate wrath of the guilty.

There was a clatter beside me as the Colonel staggered a little into my discarded chair. Even standing there in the fierce lock of Abbey's grip, I turned to him.

It came at the same moment that Duckett decided Detective Fleece was moving to seize that gun.

Chapter 31

I swear it was that way round. I swear the gun levelled a fraction before the fierce determination showed on the detective's face. The next is a crystal clear memory that I wished was a blur. The gun hand lifted, steadied and I shouted a warning, with hands thrusting at the man before me. But I wasn't shouting at the finger drawing white upon the trigger or the sheer fantasy of hope that it would be possible for the detective to close the range in his fearsome dive for that gun hand. But at the Colonel who was on the floor, propped against his kitchen counter, grey, head back and eyes closed, gasping for breath.

The report of the gun firing passed unnoticed. Unnoticed, that is, by all but the policeman, who had the horrific experience of being flung to the tiled floor by the force of a bullet passing through the muscle of his upper arm.

Then Duckett was panicking because the report of the Webley deafened us a second time and it drew a yelp and a flinch from everyone and I honestly didn't believe Duckett had ever considered the possibility that he would actually shoot anyone. He'd meant Abbey to do everything. But suddenly this wasn't a careful incrimination of his enemy but his own crime and the warning had been given twice by his own hand that would bring a small army of policemen running, and a retired old soldier's breath was rasping in his throat and the detective was down with a hand clapped over his left sleeve and blood was staining the tiles beneath him.

'Oh hell, you've still got the gun. I didn't want it to come to this.'

It was the detective, shouting but breathlessly, as well he might, as Duckett abandoned his lamps amongst the clutter on the tabletop, scampered around its perimeter and bent over the Colonel from the other side. The detective's words were an effective warning to the rest of us that Duckett's power hadn't been overcome.

'Oh God, oh God, oh God!' Duckett was saying as he bent. 'Did I shoot him too?'

The policeman was watching him and twisting onto one knee when he looked as though he would have liked to have stayed writhing on the floor for a while yet to give full release to the shock and pain of his injury. Instead he was up and on his feet and staggering a little, with his hand clamped over the wound so that his left arm was held immobile against his side, and from the way his gaze was fixed he too was clearly very much focused upon the state of the Colonel. I was dropping into a crouch beside the old man so quickly that I crashed into the chair I'd recently left and had to pause to set it aside before trying to crouch again.

My hands were mirroring Duckett's as we both reached to

loosen the collar about the Colonel's neck. The old man was alive but gasping, as pale and blotched as ever, and collapsed with his head against the neatly painted panel that boxed in the base of the heavy stone worktop. There was, I saw after the first frantic second, no blood. The second gunshot had missed us all and embedded itself harmlessly in the wall above the sink.

The Colonel's breath was rattling. I whispered frantically to no one in particular, 'It's his heart. We must have finished his heart.'

Duckett had the collar and a twitch of his wrist cautioned me to resist the impulse to compete with him for control of the invalid, so I had the old man's right hand. It was lifeless. Nervous fire ran quivering through every corner of my body when fingers suddenly slid about my waist from behind. After the first frantic second while instinct decided that this was Abbey's attempt to reclaim me, I realised it was Detective Fleece's arm and it was begging me to draw back a little from the Colonel. I didn't want to go, but the policeman was insistent. I went with him, even though every part of me that dwelt in fear was focused on the knowledge that there would be blood on the policeman's hand. My brain clung to the idea that it wasn't the blood that frightened me but the violence it represented.

Unfortunately, because the violence was in the kitchen with us, this didn't remotely help.

Duckett still had the Webley. He was bending close to the Colonel; he was abandoning the throat and reaching for the old man's wrist in a quest to test his pulse. As Duckett moved, the detective's touch suddenly hardened and snatched me back from the careless aim of that weapon. The shock of our movement made Duckett start and crack his head on the overhanging worktop. He leapt back as if we'd attacked him. I thought I knew now why the policeman had dragged me out of the way. That gun was close to going off again. Duckett was barely in control of the way his finger lay upon the trigger. He was too busy screaming out orders to the Colonel. 'Get up. Move! We're going to the car.'

And the Colonel made some sound, a wheezing groan as nothing obeyed the command except one flailing hand and I was lurching instinctively towards him again to try to help him breathe, but Duckett was snarling and the detective's good arm had come about me securely now. He held me. It was probably for the best. I was gibbering and Duckett was trying to marshal us into order and the Colonel's mouth was working for air like a landed goldfish. Richard's father looked finished.

Across the Colonel's floundering form, I found that Duckett was fascinated by me again, staring with more of that blankness that seemed to be a precursor to action and all the while he was still hovering over the Colonel as if to drag the poor old man from the floor. I was snarling at him. And clinging to the detective now as he gripped me, and sobbing all at the same time. I was saying, 'He *can't* move to the car. Look at him. And who's going to carry him? Detective Fleece? Abbey?'

The detective could barely support the weight of his left hand and Abbey was shaking his head. Abbey could have managed me, but the Colonel must have rivalled his weight. I saw Duckett's eye stray to the gun. The finger shifted slightly on the trigger.

'Don't you dare.'

I didn't know I had it in me to growl like that. It made Duckett flinch. In a raw, alien tone, I hissed, 'Don't make this your death. I did this by seeking shelter in his house. If it's his heart, leave him be.'

In my head was the desperate will to drive this point home. That Duckett hadn't killed him. He hadn't killed anyone yet – at least, not willingly, even if we included the poor unfortunate firemen at his warehouse. He could leave the Colonel here, leave him to gasp his last. And I could live with the hope that whatever else happened to the rest of us, there was one small chance that this wasn't as bad as it looked and Richard might arrive in time to save his father.

There was a pause; a momentary consideration. I felt the detective adjust the grip of his arm about me. I was clinging to him fiercely now. The policeman was panting and sweating too, like the Colonel had been. He was feeling the strain of a body put to injury but still trying to function. He and I gripped each other while Duckett made his decision.

'Give her to me. Bring the lamps.' Duckett's voice disturbed the sanctuary of stillness in less time than it took him to move around the fallen man to join us. He was very close. He robbed me of my last chance to see the Colonel. The yard outside the kitchen window was fearsomely bright but empty. If anyone had heard the two gunshots, they weren't near enough to make a difference here.

'Bring the lamps yourself. They're your problem if we're stepping out there.' The detective's voice was loud again. His grip drew me a step away. His arm was strong. The policeman wasn't surrendering me for anything, but not solely for the purpose of protecting me any more. Because the man who held me must believe we'd reached the point where anybody's life might rank now in Duckett's mind as useless as the Colonel's fading gasps, and the policeman was specifically considering the value of his own. It changed everything; the idea that if Detective Fleece allowed Duckett to separate us here, the act itself would almost certainly lead Duckett to think of him as an aggressor once more rather than my support. It was an awful concept to consider how swiftly Duckett might lurch into realising that it would be simplest to leave the policeman behind here to keep company with the Colonel, and in a similar state of health.

Responsibility revived and with it came awful hopelessness that was like an angry sickness. I supposed that ever since I had entered the kitchen I had presumed that the policeman was only waiting. That I could depend on him to know what to do if only the balance of the odds against us were changed, but he was no more in control than I was. I'd been making the same selfish mistake that Mrs Abbey had in thinking that a man with experience would know what to do to make all the difference. But, in truth, training stood for nothing against the insanity of an impulsive decision made by a man who was holding a gun.

So I gripped him like a woman caught in a paralysis of horror and saved him, and in a moment Duckett was distracted by his habit of believing that control might always be restored through fire.

'Florence,' he said and directed Mrs Abbey to collect up the lamps before proffering the matches with shaking fingers.

Mrs Abbey's expression was stony as she reached out a hand. She took the matchbook and led us to the doorway. The Lagonda stood there and it waited patiently while she poured the contents of the first lamp over the back seat. Under Duckett's whispered instructions she lit a match and cast it, spinning, to join the spreading sheen of oil. I startled her when I shook off my supposed stupor and snapped out, 'Release the handbrake at any rate, would you?'

Surprised, she braved the creeping fire enough to reach in and release the handbrake. Now I understood the value of a car whose doors were hinged at the back. It was easy enough for her to step clear as the car began to slide gracefully backwards down the slight slope. It was carrying that fire away from the ancient timbers of the house. It was just in time too, because while the flames had seemed content at first to simply lap away within the patch of oil, now they were investigating the leatherwork and their newfound freedom.

I was bustled across the yard with the detective and Duckett was hiding in the midst of us – in case anyone should be looking, I supposed, since he made sure Abbey was placed in an incriminatingly prominent position. Duckett was shouldering open the door into the tithe barn and then I was stepping of my own volition before him into the blinding dark after all that sunshine. The last thing I saw before Abbey shoved the door shut was his wife's fear-bleached face, flooded in an unguarded moment with hate, which passed over Duckett and moved, slowly but surely, onto me.

I watched, spellbound, as hate merged with a determined kind of triumph. She still believed in her blackmail. She still thought Richard could save us.

Chapter 32

'Tell me about the warehouse, and quietly.'

The detective's whisper was an urgent request in my ear. He must have heard my exclamation in those last few moments before the Colonel's final collapse. Detective Fleece didn't know the details of Abbey's original downfall, of course. He had been brought here by his interest in anything that touched upon John Langton's estate. Now he was frantically trying to understand the history of these people while we hurried along at the head of the group, moving quickly along the row of stables through the harsh shafts of light coming in through the narrow lancet windows. He had a hand on me still, but lightly now, at the midpoint of my back. He wasn't clinging to me any more. This was more the automatic guidance of a person who wanted to chivvy me into a run but didn't quite dare. His touch was nothing like the comfort that Richard would have brought. And there was always the blood.

Today the row of empty stables in this ancient barn looked like prison cells. They had iron bars rising from shoulder height to the low beams that supported the rough-hewn floor of the hayloft overhead.

The detective steered me rapidly along the row. He was instilling a sense of ordered haste into our movements and he was doing this when any sudden move might have made Duckett decide to cut his losses and finish this swiftly. This, at last, must have been a mark of the policeman's training – the training of war, I thought, rather than that of a newly commissioned detective. This was the veteran's ability to break through the incapacitating bonds of fear into constructive action, and the experience to know what happened to people when they dived headlong into doing too much. There was no room for a stand-off here, nor negotiations. Duckett didn't want to be talked down, so it was a very good job that no one had disturbed us in our dash across the yard.

In this claustrophobic space, Duckett was panicking still, but clinging once again to that wish that he might yet get away unseen. He was at the back of our group now; secure enough with the door shut upon the outside world so that no one could approach us unawares. He believed there were no secret witnesses who could place him here. I thought he must have forgotten the gasping Colonel, or else put it out of his mind. And it was a good job he had because I was reasonably certain that our survival beyond these immediate seconds depended on the faith that man still had in his power to use fire to sweep away his crimes.

I could see it in the gloom of this passage. I could see his face, lit by harsh angles of dusty light beyond the grim forms of his other captives, sweating and clutching at that weapon while his hand shook.

'Why *did* I have to burn the car?' Mrs Abbey's voice was a

curious drift on the still air. She was scurrying along behind the policeman after a gap of three or more yards. From her tone, she might have been passing the time of day with an old friend. 'And why, exactly, are we in here when we could have just run?'

The man with the gun was treating her like his friend as well. I imagine he was still attributing her deception as I had; as the frantic deflection of a desperate woman, only he wasn't really bringing himself to question where the desperation lay. Perhaps he'd seen the bruises on her cheek and about her wrist and knew they were by Abbey's hand. He told her, 'If we'd run, someone might have seen us, but thanks to your shrewd idea of letting the car roll, they'll think Paul bungled an attempt to get the girl away in it. They'll be trying to pick up their trail for hours now in the valley and all the lanes and trackways that lead to all the outhouses around here. And that,' he confided, as if this danger needn't quite reach Mrs Abbey, 'gives me just enough time to do what needs to be done.'

And while they discussed the way I might have unwittingly sent help further away, I was telling the policeman as swiftly as I could, in a whisper, the idea I had about the origin of the warehouse fire, and the manslaughter of the firemen, even if Duckett mightn't be fully accountable for their murder.

'You're sure?'

The policeman's serious gaze was a gleam in the last of the light. We were arriving at the foot of the stairs to the hayloft. They were more like a ladder, really. They rose steeply at the end of the row above a void where heavily barred doors had once allowed carriages to slide into the space behind the last of the stables. There was no banister rail, but the left-hand side was made marginally less treacherous by the wooden wall of the goat stable, which rose up to meet the heavy beams that supported the hayloft. The goat was watching us with nervous interest. Above him, the steps veered left at the very last moment into a darkness that smelled thickly of mouldy things. Down here the air was increasingly perfumed with smoke. The sharp tang of poisonous fumes from man-made things such as tyres. The smoke must be sending up a beacon, but I couldn't hear any trace of movement out there.

The policeman was hurrying me up the first of the steps. I was climbing by keeping hard against that stable wall, because every instinct told me not to go. I was leaning very firmly upon the dirty wooden panels and wishing very deeply that I was leaning against Richard and yet also hating myself because it was a piece of the corruption that I despised in Mrs Abbey. It was with the sour taste of need in my mouth that I told the detective, 'You need to look again at the evidence of Abbey's fraud. The police only discovered it after the warehouse was lost in the blaze and the insurance company started getting nervous about the validity of the claim. They said arson. So Duckett put them off by handing in the few surviving records of Abbey's dealings. He told me the company records were usually stored in the warehouse attics. He said that he'd passed on what he had in his office to the police when Abbey didn't die. Abbey was lucky to only be convicted of the fraud. Everyone thought he'd been covering up his tracks with the fire. You need to ask how Duckett knew to remove the papers from the archive in the first place unless he'd discovered the fraud and set a lure to bring Abbey to his death.'

'As simple as that?' The policeman was grim. His eyes were scanning the stairs, up and down behind us, as if there were any other routes. Head turned away towards the darkness ahead, he said, 'Whatever happens up there, don't try to use this to influence Duckett. We've got to either get you out or disarm him. Without that gun he's as harmless as you or I.'

That last part didn't quite ring true, I thought. I couldn't help mimicking him. 'Simple, then.'

His attention abruptly returned to me, utterly serious. 'As you say. So work with me, would you?'

I nodded. I knew why he was cautioning me to keep quiet. I'd just turned myself from the woman who could prove that Duckett had at least visited this place into the woman who had visited the man at his office and could recount every little detail that had slipped out of his mouth. It was hardly proof enough for a conviction, but it was certainly capable of antagonising an already dangerous man.

I thought we'd done it in the next moment. A sharp command from Duckett wrenched us both round at the turn, heart racing and ready to cringe. 'Stop right there.'

The policeman had been on the step just below mine, so he was between me and the rest and he was also the first to look guilty. Duckett didn't see. He hadn't overheard our exchange. He was nervous because we were moving away from him up the last of the steps, while he was trailing behind Mrs Abbey and had barely reached the little kink where the passage turned past the stable that housed the goat.

The last short flight of steps was there above us and then the blackness of the hayloft. I was high enough to make out the apex of the roof hanging upon its great triangular frames many yards overhead and, beyond, about three or four yards away, there was the ghost of the distant end wall. It was rough stone and at its heart was the deeper shade of a recess that was just tall enough that a person could stoop to pass through. It was barred by a wooden door at present. It was the hatch; the means by which the season's fresh hay was gathered in. It was the discreet exit that opened onto the patch of ground between the church and the watershed that Abbey had been using for days, safe from notice from the labourers and Danny returning by night to the machine barn.

My heart began beating strong, steady strokes. I thought that was why the policeman had gone to such lengths to uncover the details of Abbey's route into the hayloft. Detective Fleece had taken care to find another exit that might be forced open and allow us to slip away while Duckett was still climbing the stairs; never mind that it proved that all the time we'd been in the kitchen the policeman must have planning for the likelihood that we must have always ended up in here. And now it was there, tantalisingly close and tempting me.

I jumped when Detective Fleece's hand met my sleeve. I hadn't even realised that I'd been bracing for that final impulsive lunge. He was urging me into caution. All the same, he was backing us, step by step, up the last of the stairs, while contradicting it all by saying unexpectedly clearly, 'We need to get you out of here while there's still time.'

I couldn't quite tell whether it was a command to move or

509

more of a wish. And Duckett was smirking like it was a joke and shouldering his way past Mrs Abbey and her husband and insisting that we waited while he lit the second oil lamp. I dithered, every nerve singing for liberty while the detective gripped my sleeve and Duckett fumbled and dropped a match. The metal base of the lamp was heavy, I think, and it was hard for him to manage that and the glass cone that covered the flame and the Webley, all while trying to strike a match with hasty fingers. He managed it, then sent the match spinning down the stairs to the cobbled passage. It landed near Abbey's feet. It flared for an instant on a scrap of old straw, until it extinguished itself with a sharp plume of smoke. And that was the moment I truly understood the power this man held over his former business partner.

The effect on Abbey was instant. It was as though Duckett had physically assaulted the man. He was suddenly clutching at the wall. He was shuddering from the non-existent flame and suddenly his wife wasn't looking like Duckett's friend. She was snarling out a protest while Abbey's thin and haggard features were being cast into fierce relief by this new lamplight.

I only stared. Various people in my life had quietly wondered if my foibles meant I had been Blitzed. Now I was witness to the appearance of a man who had really experienced the unendurable. Poor Abbey was finally acknowledging the likelihood that he had failed to escape a second time. I understood at last what had driven him to such uncontrollable panic that he had launched unnecessary attacks on innocent passers-by such as Mr Winstone. At this moment, his face was sagging with every memory of gasping breaths and the dying screams of those firemen. And his spirit was collapsing beneath the gaze of the man who had orchestrated it.

Duckett had forgotten him already. He had his lamp lit. It was sending inky lines across his features and upon the wooden panels beside us. He was halfway up the stairs. The policeman had me backing around the bend. The injured man was moving with that deliberation that went with extreme weariness. It wasn't an act. He had a dark stain on the left sleeve of his grey suit jacket – grey in daylight and even greyer in this light. He was using his uninjured arm to act as a barrier between me and Duckett, pushing me back, but discouraging me from moving so quickly that Duckett should decide we were taking flight.

I was moving in short ungainly jerks. My muscles didn't know how to behave. My foot missed the last step onto the hayloft's roughly made floor. I stumbled but caught myself by throwing one hand out against the ancient wooden frame that passed close by my head to the roof and the other onto the detective's shoulder. Blessedly, it was his unharmed shoulder. I felt the sweat through his clothes. Bullet wounds took a harsh toll upon a person.

But Detective Fleece's voice remained clear. He uttered what amounted to a desperate plea to the silent rafters. 'We've got to get her out.' Followed almost in the next instant by a harsh, *'Too late!'*

Duckett was coming. He had discovered the hatch only yards from my side. I saw his beady eyes fix upon it in the ugly yellow lamp light. Everything else swept away into blackness beneath heavy frames that ran in hollow triangles to a distant end. There was nowhere to run. But Duckett pushed me aside anyway. He was up here with us so that I shrank back and collided with the clammy warmth of the policeman when for a brief insane moment I'd thought the detective was bracing to intervene. I believed Detective Fleece had been wildly convinced that help would be on the other side, ready to reach in and snatch us out of range, but no one was there. And anyway, Duckett was in the hayloft with us now. If anyone burst in at this moment, they'd have the terrible experience of finding the man and that Webley between themselves and us.

Instead the only thing that burst in on me was relief when the policeman merely snapped out, 'The hatch is locked. Abbey used the housekeeper's key and then put everything back to how it was when the Colonel came home. So it's still locked.'

Mrs Abbey tried it and it rattled conclusively.

Hay was running along the length of this space like a turbulent sea with a narrow causeway of drowning floorboards at the heart of it. Dried drifts rose to left and right like waves with rotten old partitions acting like breakwaters between one great crest and another. I was waiting for the impact when the tide broke and it came barely three seconds later. The faintest crinkling sound of paper beneath my heel marked the perimeter of the rubbish that had spread from Abbey's lair. It hadn't been spotted in all these weeks by Danny on his daily visit to feed the goat because this deepest end of the loft was where the oldest and most damp hay lay. This dark cave hadn't been cleared out in years. Abbey had added to the rot of time the debris of many lunches and a deep crust of newspaper – because, I supposed, he must have needed something to fill the long hours while he waited for dusk, never mind that sitting with a lighted lamp in this place was tantamount to suicide. Blessedly, he appeared to have been cleaner here and there was no stench of human waste to mask the faint musk of rats.

Duckett puffed along behind us. He wasn't a fool. He had guessed that the policeman had been attempting an escape of some sort. He didn't know how, so he concluded that we had Richard hidden in the haystacks. We hadn't, but Duckett had found a metal bar from somewhere. It looked as if it had been a long handle to a pitchfork at some point in its life. Now he was using it to probe the stacks as he arrived and began scoffing, 'All modern conveniences laid on, I see, Paul. But I'm afraid the stuffing may be coming out of your armchair.'

Abbey had truly made himself very much at home during his weeks here. Unlike the gloomy stables below, this attic was hot and airless because the sun was beating upon the stone tiles overhead. This space also held furniture of a sort because we could perceive by the light of Duckett's oil lamp that Abbey had sculpted himself an armchair and a footstool out of the last haystack behind the final partition.

Abbey was instructed to sit in his chair. He went quietly. He went like a man for whom hope has long since fled. Mrs Abbey was set down upon the footstool. The policeman was directed into the corner, where the triangle of the end wall met the base of one of the vast frames that supported the roof. Detective Fleece sought my permission to leave me before he allowed himself to be bullied onto the floor to nurse his arm in the corner there. It was the furthest point from me and more particularly from Duckett.

Duckett was breathing jerkily and he didn't trust that the policeman wouldn't try for the Webley again. To be honest, though, I didn't know why he was worrying. I had practically been eager to encourage the policeman to take his place on the floor because the detective's skin shone terribly in this light. Detective Fleece looked very much like a moment's pause to collect himself was all that stood between him and collapse.

I was made to stand behind the partition. It was about four feet high and had encountered woodworm.

'You must really love him.' Unexpectedly, Mrs Abbey was speaking to me. 'I saw your face as you read his letter.'

She had already moved from her footstool. She was sorting through the pile of rubbish that her husband had left against the rough stones of the end wall. The heap contained those missing bottles from the Manor's drinks trolley and discarded items of clothing, which must, presumably, have been more relics of John Langton's wardrobe. She was tearing the sleeve off a shirt and passing it to the detective to serve as a pad to press over his wound.

My hands were empty. I hadn't thought before this moment, but I'd still been clutching the note when her husband had dragged me from my chair. It was certainly gone now. I'd probably dropped it when Richard's father had fallen to the floor. It made me think, in a fiercely intense burst of something like revenge, that at least one piece of Duckett's trespass would remain there for Richard to identify, once Duckett's fire had claimed all the rest.

It gave me the resolve to settle my hands quite steadily upon the partition while Duckett dithered beside me. I thought Duckett must act now and swiftly, but he was too busy building imaginary imposters out of the hay. I thought it was with a conscious effort on his part that he curbed the impulse to go on jabbing at the nearest stack and instead set the pitchfork handle down against the end of my partition. He still didn't seem to fully count Mrs Abbey as one of the hostages. It didn't do her much good though.

In the act of placing the lamp upon the post at the end of my partition, he asked her with the hoarse kindliness of excitement, 'Where are the children, Florence?'

I saw her flinch. She was fidgeting about in the heart of the gable end, where timbers that would have amazed my father met in a point at the apex of the roof. Dramatically framed by their harsh lines in the lamplight, she told Duckett quickly, 'With Mrs Winstone. They'd had enough walking by the time we'd left the shop and made it back to the village.'

This wasn't another lie. I thought she must have left them with Mrs Winstone before approaching the Manor kitchen. She would never have dared leave them alone after nearly losing them to Duckett's car the other day and I could guess how strongly she was feeling the luck of the instinct that had made her refrain from bringing them here.

My hands were gripping the coarse rail that topped the partition. Clutching the wood was how I managed to remain still while Duckett passed behind me and my skin crawled.

He was checking the dark void of collapsed hay that ran to the point where the floorboards met the rafters. The space was utterly silent, naturally. No help was conveniently waiting there.

I didn't know what the delay was. I'd understood that escape for Duckett depended on swift action before anyone conducted a thorough search. Perhaps Duckett was simply enjoying himself. Duckett had returned to his position just beyond the post at the end of my partition. The lamp was lighting his job of counting the rounds left in the chamber of his revolver. There were four from a possible six. He reached into a pocket and drew out some spare rounds. Abbey had given him the ammunition too. He really was a fool.

I wondered if Duckett was a fool too. The detective was right; the man's power began and ended with that gun, but its hold on us would be superseded by a greater threat at the moment he tried to light his fire. A bullet might account for one of us, but that fire would claim us all, so we would have to act, and there was every reason to think that all natural sense must unite us to act against him. All the same, though, the thought was hovering unpleasantly at the back of my mind that at the moment we all lunged for Duckett, it was possible that I might find myself having to fight off Abbey. That his terror might lead him to seize the chance to hurt me when anything that befell me in the confusion might easily be attributed to his enemy.

The thought made me notice the pitchfork handle. It was still propped against the post, barely a yard from my right hand, and I wasn't one of three old firemen climbing blind into a trap. My eyes sought the policeman's, but he had his jacket off and was gingerly peering beneath the rag at his wound, testing to see whether it was still bleeding.

It was.

Mrs Abbey's voice cracked through my wince like a whip. I was burning already. It was suffocating up here and my own blood was running in thickened beats. She said, 'I heard at the shop that you've been collecting their groceries. I suppose the Captain's got you cooking their meals?'

I blinked. I believe I'd been waiting all this time for her to begin a coded conversation between two determined women. I'd imagined that she had been preparing me for it when she'd made that comment about my feelings for Richard and his letter. This didn't feel like that sort of speech though. This felt like the beginnings of a fresh allusion to John Langton. It was hard not to automatically perceive it as a threat. Particularly when she added condescendingly, 'Do you think it's attractive to crawl about like a slave for them? Do you honestly think he'll like you for it?'

It was beyond me now to feel compelled to explain that I wasn't weak, or conniving, or whatever else I was judged to be these days. That, at least, was a lesson I had learned and learned well. I might have had to wonder how Mrs Abbey's criticism balanced in the woman's mind with her own dedicated efforts for the sake of her husband in recent weeks. I also had to wonder if she was ever going to be capable of simply telling me plainly what she was really thinking.

Naively, I tried to find the truth by answering her questions. With uneasy honesty, while every other part of my mind watched Duckett as he closed the chamber on his gun, I told her, 'Actually, it was my choice to do the cooking. Richard's father needed feeding and Richard himself was already managing all the old man's letter-writing and telephoning and every other duty imaginable that he's been performing without a murmur ever since his arrival here.'

It clearly wasn't the reply she wanted. Particularly when I conceded rather less generously, 'I suppose, Mrs Abbey, it could be considered rather too typical that the kitchen work should have fallen to the first available woman. And I suppose on that first night I *could* have taken myself home to make my own dinner and left them to sort themselves out between chores while I ate in splendid and dignified isolation. But it wouldn't exactly have been nice, would it?'

I actually made Duckett give a little laugh, which hadn't been my plan at all. He thought I was a lovesick girl advocating servility. But I wasn't speaking for him; I didn't imagine he could understand the difference between exploitation and giving help where it was truly needed. And it had been a foolish thing to say anyway because speaking sympathetically of the Colonel didn't disarm Duckett; it didn't convey friendship to the woman who believed she had been a friend to his son. It all just served to remind me of the man we'd left in the kitchen and the way he had looked that first night after Richard had asked me to cook his dinner. And how Richard had only asked me to stay at all because it had been a way of managing the threat to me without adding to my strain after what had amounted to a very stressful day. At that time we hadn't even known just how dangerous these people were.

Mrs Abbey was drifting away from her place against the end wall behind her husband's shoulders. It brought her a little closer to me. I didn't trust her at all when she said, 'You mention that the Captain's been doing the letter-writing for his father since his return. The Langtons do seem to like their letter-writing, don't they?'

We were there at last. We were back to mentions of John Langton. And I knew now that, for her, his name counted as disguise.

She said, 'That letter of mine you were waving about in the kitchen just now was left to give your soldier a little hint about everything else I have from John. I can tell you what John said about the purchase of my house, and the account he gave of the financial ruin your foolish old Colonel accelerated with his excesses in London. Since you're so friendly with the family now, I suppose you know what the Colonel did, don't you?'

She wasn't, of course, talking about the tireless hours and weeks spent in London hectoring Richard out of his fevered exhaustion and onto his feet. The repulsiveness of her question made me forget Duckett and his lamp long enough to find a retort. 'No,' I said tartly, 'I don't know what the Colonel did. And you don't, either, because despite all your efforts to pry, Matthew Croft won't tell you, will he?'

For some unfathomable reason, I'd made her smile.

She shook her head to ward off my temper. She had her hand out to appease it. I had to wonder if she meant to goad me into creating a scene, as a brutal parody of the trick her husband had lately worked upon my mind.

Duckett was working on my mind too. He had the lamp in his hands again now and was tilting it so that he could examine something that was etched upon the glass shade that spread the light. When my attention strayed, Mrs Abbey told me quite unnecessarily, 'That picture John mentioned in his letter is still in my kitchen, by the way. I never did sell it.'

'I know,' I said, without withdrawing my eyes from Duckett. He was turning the little key that adjusted the wick. 'You need to hang it further away from your smoking stove.'

She didn't hear. 'I told you this morning that I had to find the money to pay for Paul's lawyer. The man was John's contact and John came up with the idea of buying my house to work a little benefit for both our sakes. It didn't matter to him that the estate couldn't really afford the purchase. If the Manor had been solvent, he'd have lost the lot to death duties just as soon as the old man died anyway. But John was set to come into a little windfall of his own that would at last give him a little independence. He was going to buy my house on the proceeds and, when I had the money, I was going to buy the services of this lawyer. I was supposed to return the rest by buying back the house. Only then John died and I had to start all over again in a less convenient way with the meagre substitute Danny Hannis could offer.'

Now I looked at her. I remarked slowly, 'John Langton was hoping to conceal the origins of his sudden wealth by running it back and forth through the sale of that house, and the lawyer was the equivalent of your handling fee. Well, well.' I added dryly, 'At least this plainly criminal undertaking makes more sense than the rumour that this painting of yours was proof he'd left you custodian of his lost hoard of treasure.'

She was suddenly possessed by the sort of stillness that went with the intense realisation that she'd made an error. The lamplight was casting strange shadows across her staring eyes. She thought that I was going add the other rumour – the one where John was paying off his guilt for a lovechild – for the very simple pleasure of doing it with her husband sitting there. As it was, I couldn't help wondering who had the better idea of John's real motives – her for believing he would share his spoils and perhaps even his future life with her, or me for believing the lure had been John's means of ensuring he got his way.

I came very close to saying it. The unpleasantness of the temptation set my jaw. Then it fixed an ache on my soul. It was all a part of this manipulation upon manipulation, where talking about John Langton became, in this instance, a means of confronting me with my feelings for his older brother and I had to stop in case this claimed me before Duckett could even begin to try.

I had to ask her with the sort of incomprehension that runs close to grief, 'Have you no empathy? You're forcing me to fight for Richard's nature when I believe you're really still waiting for him to save you, and it's *inhumane.*'

I saw something peculiar twist in her face. A misunderstanding that blazed like exhilaration. She had her hand out to me again. She agreed with me desperately, 'Yes! Brian is inhumane. I can't escape this without help.'

I thought this was the moment she would explain. I thought she was about to give me a hint of what hope really lay here for her because I thought she certainly still didn't agree with her husband's view. But she didn't say a word. And Duckett was just beside me and so was that pitchfork handle, solid and tempting. Yet all the time it was also whispering warnings because if I were to reach for it, it was inescapable that someone would be hurt.

Or rather, I was afraid that I didn't have the commitment to make sure that the particular man in question would be hurt enough to be stopped.

Then I noticed that Duckett was moving again by the post at the end of the partition. The lamp seemed to be fascinating him. He was turned slightly away from me, strangely vulnerable with the Webley juggling in his hands, and at that moment it struck me, with a sudden bolt of sheer terror, that there was another manipulation being worked upon me here.

He wanted me to reach for that pitchfork handle. Because then he could turn with that gun and finish me and tell himself quite honestly that he had only acted in self-defence.

That was what he'd been waiting for here. This was the cause of the delay. Deceit worked hard and ran headlong into agony because no one here felt they had the power to escalate this to its conclusion without harnessing my help. I really had been right to blame myself for the Colonel's collapse when Duckett had thought to put the old man down in the kitchen. Duckett really didn't like to think of himself as a killer, even though this was the path he was setting himself on. So he'd tried to incite a more desperate impulse in me.

And while fear blazed like fire through every nerve with the force of needles, the policeman caught my eye and seemed to be trying to caution me of another great danger here. Then Mrs Abbey swept in to apply a little more pressure of her own upon my mind.

She abandoned John Langton for something that seemed painfully like the truth.

'I'm not the criminal here, you know,' she told me almost pleadingly. 'I've shown you the scale of the burden I've been living under for years, without even one word of help from anyone. I've described the pressure that stalked me while we were waiting for Paul's trial and we still lived in Gloucester. You can imagine the burns on my husband's shoulder and his lungs and the lucky escape that took the form of his arrest in his hospital bed and carried him straight from there into court, but what good does it do?'

The policeman's reply was so sharp and so unexpected that it made Mrs Abbey jump. 'Don't talk about those days here. And don't move any closer to Miss Sutton.'

I couldn't quite define how the policeman was doing it, but he suddenly seemed taller against his patch of rough stone wall and yet without ever actually moving an inch. He also awoke Duckett to the failure of the pitchfork handle and I watched as the man with the gun took up his heavy bar and set it down against the partition on the other side, well away from me.

Mrs Abbey watched him do it. She was distracted, but determined to speak in a grim little voice made breathless by her nearness to letting Duckett understand that the terrible betrayal he dreaded was already here. She told me, 'There are no words to describe the threat that man held over me in

Gloucester, with his little visits and his little offers of friendship. He was never going to let Paul go. He wouldn't believe—'

'Did you try?' I asked.

'What?'

'Did you even try to explain that your husband wasn't a threat?'

'Of course I did.' She actually looked appalled. 'I've been *trying* to stop this. All along, all I've tried to do is give Brian enough time to leave sufficient traces of himself to give us a chance to satisfy the police that he's been hounding us. That's all I've done. I'm not responsible for any of this. There was nothing I could do to stop him. And Paul was always going to come to me when he got out.'

Confirmation came in the form of an unexpected croak from her husband. He had lifted his head. That was all the energy he had. His hands were slack on his knees. His eyes were hollow. His hoarse voice told the policeman, 'Brian would never have believed me if I'd told him I only wanted to be free. He won't believe I can admit what I did and that I'm sorry for it. I just want to be free to be a father to my children.'

'Don't mention them.' His wife's correction was sharp. Mrs Abbey was barely a yard or more from the partition and her pinched mouth was suddenly hardening to real agitation. Her eyes were for Duckett and the way he was watching her. We could all see the calculations running behind his eyes. I thought she desperately didn't want to experience that moment when his mind strayed from his contemplation of the worth of my life in this play for escape to the usefulness of Abbey's children.

She was almost too late. His eyes followed her as she crept a little closer to me and whispered, 'Brian's been in a high state of panic ever since that lawyer of mine got Paul's sentence reduced to time served. They did it by raising doubt about the severity of the fraud, but Brian thinks my husband got out because he's leading the police into rethinking their conclusions about that fire. Brian was going to come after Paul and get him, and we had nothing to prove Brian's guilt. The only thing we could do to stop him was kill him, and we couldn't do that.'

She might have been confessing that she and her husband had been inhibited by the worry that no one would believe the innocence of their motives. But this wasn't a justification for trying to draw violence from Richard instead. She was trying to explain that my accusations had been wrong, they'd been an invention of my imagination, because she was like me and murder wasn't a solution that belonged to her.

'Miss Sutton!' This was a caution from the policeman. I blinked at him rapidly. I thought for a moment that he had been alarmed by Mrs Abbey's bald reference to that warehouse fire but I couldn't quite see what he was warning me about. Duckett was distracted by a change in the air that had been enough to make the lamp dim and then glow again.

I was waiting for the policeman to explain his alarm but Mrs Abbey's hand was out again. The bruise and her bandage about her wrist were just visible against all the other strange shadows that the lamplight was casting across her skin. I knew then that this was the real lie she'd told. Neither mark had come from the difficulty of reclaiming Mrs Cooke's keys.

She'd been hurt when she'd been forced to surprise a frightened man in his lair for the sake of explaining that I hadn't caught the bus after all.

I thought it was no wonder, in a way, that it had occurred to her to try to control Richard. Because she was a woman who had been failed by every one of the men who had been supposed to be on her side – her husband with his fraud and his insistence on leaning on her for support; Duckett with this hateful pursuit when he ought, simply, to have remembered that he was her friend; and John Langton for dying when she had probably loved him.

Her recent words rang true. There was nothing she could do to stop Duckett. Paul Abbey was always going to come to her when he got out. And I alone had been trusted from the first moments with at least some partial truths because I was a woman, but I hadn't quite shown enough sympathy for her plight to prove myself capable of trying to help.

I couldn't help stammering then, 'I'm so sorry.'

Her reply was to take a last step and claim my hand. Her fingers closed over me as I gripped the wooden partition. I felt her drag my hand free. I let her do it. It was a terrible mistake. It was what she had wanted from me all along.

She drew on my hand to bring me against the partition. Unlike her husband, though, she wasn't visiting violence upon me. She was expressing a more decisive version of what I was feeling – that the only power we had as Duckett's future victims was the power to decide whether or not to do nothing. The proof of how she personally had settled that debate lay in my presence in this hayloft. It lay in this disguise of conversation when I ought to have been noticing how she was acting. There were no lies in what she'd said and yet none of it had actually been the truth. Mrs Abbey had long since abandoned her scheme to make Richard save us here. She didn't need Richard at all because now they had me.

A moment later, Duckett was lurching in. I was already flinching back, but her move hadn't been the cue for Duckett to finish me. He stepped straight past my partition and swung his fist to fling Mrs Abbey hard away from me. He must really have liked her because if he hadn't, I swear instinct would have made him blast away her life with that gun. As it was, he merely sent her back to her husband with such force that she crashed off him and the only thing that saved her from flying onwards to the floor was her husband's wild snatch for her arm. She had a hand up to her face where Duckett must have caught her. There was a trace of blood at the corner of her mouth and yet, in that desolate place beyond Duckett's idea of restraint for the sake of friendship, I thought she must be considering herself very clever.

Because concealed in my hand was a small vegetable knife.

Chapter 34

Mrs Abbey must have decided to select a knife from the kitchen drawers while her husband had been declaring his intention to use me as a sacrificial victim. She'd made a great fuss about pouring a glass of water, but she'd never meant to give me a drink. She'd been working all this time to arm the victim for her defence.

It was a good job too because Duckett was coming back for me.

We'd tipped him out of his stupor. Unnoticed by Duckett, the policeman was suddenly taller against his wall. His warning was a repetition of my name. It was a caution again. A determined negative. But Duckett was coming for me. I had a hand gripping the partition as I turned to meet him. That hard boundary of wood was all that stopped me from stepping backwards into the useless corner, where the hard angle of the roof met the hay.

Duckett rounded the turn. The spread of light from the lamp on its post was casting one half of his body into golden relief. The other was black and only his beady eye shone out from the void. His mouth was slack, like his collar, where the ugly tie had been loosened at his neck.

From her place on the floor Mrs Abbey was bleating out shrilly, 'You asked about John's treasure, Emily? The only treasure I have is with Mrs Winstone.' She had no hope in these men. Her words were for me and desperately well played. 'Not John's pictures or wealth, but mine and truly precious.'

She meant her children, waiting painfully near to hand if Duckett should ever get away from here.

'Miss Sutton, don't!'

The harsh injunction from the policeman's mouth came just at the moment I put out my hand. Detective Fleece had seen Mrs Abbey take up the weapon in the Manor kitchen. All along he'd been trying to convey to me how she meant to use it. Now the blade was lying hard and sharp behind the screen of my hand and I was pointing at Duckett's chest. Heart beating, maddened by my own nerve, I startled a terrified man by waggling my hand to indicate the shadows beyond him.

'Look!' I cried. 'They were hiding there.'

Duckett twisted obediently. Richard wasn't stepping out of the lee of the great frame that supported the roof. This was my own lie. Duckett turned and turned again. Mrs Abbey was screaming. Shouting at me. And Detective Fleece was using the wall as a brace to climb swiftly to his feet. Duckett didn't see. He was frantically glancing back at me for confirmation and crowding me, with the gun held ready, because he would have let loose a shot had Richard been in the darkness beyond the opposite partition as I'd said. Duckett's flank made a perfect unguarded triangle as that arm lifted clear.

All I had to do was use enough force to break the skin. He might not even die. And when I'd struck him there, I would have to slash a second time at his hand as he wrenched instinctively round to face me. I imagined that even if he were gravely hurt, he'd still spasm into bringing that gun to bear. I had to be ready to make him drop it. I could see how. They'd planned for a trained man to do this, but I was here instead. The policeman was injured; no one would blame me, not the coroner, not even me in my nightmares.

Mrs Abbey was screaming again. In the blink of a second she had drawn breath and begun again. I knew why. Duckett was twisting again towards the policeman. He'd seen the policeman move. The detective was lurching forwards and shouting my name with his own instruction because Duckett was still turning towards him and then it might be too late.

I put out my hand again.

Not to strike Duckett. It's terrible to say it, but at the moment of decision, almost the strongest influence against it was the knowledge that Mrs Abbey thought it right that I should. Instead the knife ran from my hand and skittered shining silver through the lamplight across the wooden boards, to be lost in the distant haystack.

The knife did what my shout hadn't. The shock of movement jerked Duckett's instinct into letting off two shots uselessly into the dark. They punched past the haystack to drive two holes through the roof tiles. Sharp needles of daylight fired back. And then I was stepping forwards and laying hold of his gun hand with a commitment I didn't know

I had. This was my plan. Mine, forged when the policeman had made the point that Duckett's only power lay in the bullets of that gun. It had been held waiting until the policeman had been fit to help. It was a small kind of arrogance, I suppose, to wait for this and believe I had found another way, where these people had decided that escape came with savage corruption. But there were only six bullets to account for. Or there had been. Now there were four.

Duckett was writhing. Twisting. One contorting thrust of his free hand across my throat and shoulders nearly forced me away. I was saved, if that was the appropriate term for the experience, by the painful discovery that my ribs were crushed between him and the partition. It stopped me when I might otherwise have fallen.

'Up. Get his hand up.' A scuff of feet and the policeman's hands passed across the post where the lamp had stood to join mine.

His command was a snarl. A strain of effort. It was vital we managed it. It was so we didn't accidentally shoot anyone. I could feel the detective's grim determination as he shifted his weight around the limit of the wooden barrier. It helped me prise myself free of the agonising crush of the partition. I was reasonably sure this wasn't what the policeman had been nudging me towards all this time with his little cautions because I'd surprised him as well as everyone else, but this was our chance. Only Detective Fleece's hands were slipping. His left was almost useless, so then there was only his stronger right while his injured arm thrust limply against Duckett's shoulder. And Duckett was flailing again.

'See to that fire and *get her out!*' The policeman's next desperate bellow deafened me, but this time it wasn't an order for me.

It was a roar that carried the full length of the barn and it was because all my fears about Abbey were proving ground-less. Abbey wasn't seizing his chance to attack me. He wasn't helping us either. He was screaming and hurling himself and his wife back into the corner because that crushing collision with the wooden barrier had knocked the lamp from its post and the oil was burning a slick film across the loose hay.

The fire was smoking where the hay was rotten. It was a poisonous curl of fumes. I remembered this about fire. I'd seen it often enough in the Blitz. The smoke was as dangerous as the flames and all it needed to do to fully mimic the horror of those wartime days was to carry the scent of something terrible cooking in the ashes. This fire was only small – blue-tinged fingers standing up from the mat of oiled hay – and yet the space seemed abruptly brighter. Blinding, really, after the sudden darkness when the lamp had dropped. I remember the faint surprise that such a delicate spread of flames should have made such a difference.

Blood and sweat on the policeman's palm was making his fingers slip on mine and then tighten savagely as he forced his grip to hold. We worked the writhing man's fist up into the space above our heads. Duckett had partly carried it there himself, in that instinctive way people have of reaching upwards in an effort to shake us off. His free hand was clawing at mine. He was marginally taller than I was, or at least longer in the arms. And by virtue of build and gender, considerably stronger. It was against all odds that I managed, teetering and using the policeman's one-armed strength as my anchor, even as Duckett wrenched at my wrist, to curl my fingers over the fingers that gripped that gun.

There was sudden tug. A blast so loud it drew a cry from me and closed my eyes, and a second blow that made me call out again because I had to duck my head low against the shelter of my upraised arm to protect my face as fragments of stone tile and ancient dust came clattering down on us.

It wasn't me who was screaming though. We were terrifying Duckett because he couldn't shake us off. He knew what we were doing. All we had to do was get the bullets from that gun. He wasn't stupid enough to release the trigger this fourth time. He was still screaming. He had his fingers clamped tight and his other fist was brutally enfolding my wrist and I was smaller than him and tiring and I couldn't get him to release his finger from the trigger enough to allow the revolver mechanism to engage the next bullet. I was straining, both for breath and to reach as my hands slid a little. I felt the crush as the policeman's grip over my fingers changed. It crushed me. It tore at my skin. The next grip wasn't his or Duckett's. It was steadier. New hands were joining mine. Familiar and secure. And I didn't know how Richard could do it, but he had eased me aside so that I surrendered the fight to him, gasping, very briefly without even understanding that I'd let him stand before me. It was worse, somehow, because a moment ago I'd been mentally preparing for the instant that my grip failed and Duckett had mastery of my wrist enough to tether me for those last few seconds while he took aim.

Now it was a different expression of sheer terror that gripped me because Richard was here too.

It was in the space between one heartbeat and the next, while my body staggered free to the partition – and hung there to rest a moment in the harsh beam of light cast from the newly opened hatch before gathering itself for the effort of redressing the balance – that Duckett stopped screaming, as though panic ran on a switch. That frightened face shone and hard black eyes settled shockingly upon Richard's face.

'You.'

The rough purpose contained within that single word from Duckett made me realise what I'd done. It took barely a moment for him to speak, but my innocence took an age to die. The change in him came like a footnote to his humiliation outside the hospital.

Suddenly Duckett wasn't fighting to lift that weapon clear. He was allowing Richard's stern grip to draw his hand downwards. Duckett allowed that weapon to slide smoothly into the gap between them. It was almost like a surrender, only there was a snarl in that slanting light. They were face to face. The gun was against Richard's stomach, and against his own too, with Richard's hand folding over the hard black line of the barrel. The policeman was scrabbling uselessly to part them. Now I did scream. A desperate plea to avert the unimaginable.

It was swallowed instantly in the numbing misery of realising the idiocy of my intentions and the sluggishness of my limbs compared to their rapid movement. It was smothered by a last cry from Mrs Abbey as she struggled beneath her husband's panicked urge to shield her from the encroaching fire. She begged him in bewildered desperation, 'Why couldn't she just end this?'

She was right. There had been no moral superiority in my actions. I hadn't chosen a course that preserved all of us, even the criminals, from harm. As I thrust myself uselessly forwards in this airless cavern, panting from a reckless tussle that had absolutely failed, I finally understood. I'd left London because I'd felt a desperate need to find freedom after the stifling life of a war-torn town; and I'd discovered it within a few hours of arriving here through the decisive act of choosing to answer a telephone. But just as the man I'd encountered on the other end had, in fact, been dwelling all that time in the city I'd only recently left, the idea that any decision of mine had any greater influence was fantasy. The world didn't change and I was unshakeably me. The Colonel had described to me once how, in the course of war, you see the opportunity to finish your enemy and then you don't need any other cause at all.

I thought it was a dismal rule for living when this wasn't war but the responsibilities were just the same. There was a choice between acting and passing the burden along the line. She'd armed me when the toll upon my soul for my self-defence would barely have counted. Others had borne the sacrifice long before me. Duckett was staring up at Richard's face like they were lovers. And when those hands moved – his and Richard's on the weapon that pressed between them – I knew at last that nothing I ever did could change the fact that my refusal to play my part in the face of the awful truth made me as culpable here as a murderer.

Chapter 35

There was no sound. Everything in me was blinding antic- ipation, with every nerve straining for confirmation of what I had seen in the final fullness of a gunshot.

Only it never came. After a day when no one had done any of the things they had been accused of and only did something else that was worse, there was a different bang. It was the crash as Richard changed his grip – he wasn't trapped there in a struggle for control over that gun. He was twisting behind its muzzle and keeping close and fixing his other hand over the back of Duckett's neck. Detective Fleece was there too and suddenly a man was on the ground and the light was poor again because of the rush of bodies all pounding into our space between the haystacks.

They jostled me. The fire was our meagre light now. It was low, still behind the partition, but it was feeding and casting a crimson hue upon the stone roof tiles overhead as it crept, finger by finger, towards the stacked hay. It smoked greedily and it smothered the sharp scent of spent ammunition. I was reaching to help Richard. I was reaching for Duckett's outstretched hand – it was being pressed into the floorboards by my feet, but the man's fist was still armed. Duckett had cried out as Richard had put him face down upon the floor. Now he was still. Richard had his knee in Duckett's back. It looked painful because Richard was leaning across him to get that hand with the revolver in it firmly pinioned. I could see that Richard's other hand was hindered by its duty of keeping the man's shoulders down. It was like bending through a racing current when I dropped into a crouch before Richard and placed my own hands to help secure that fist.

Duckett wasn't struggling. He was limp, passive, and then it was my own foot that moved the Webley harmlessly away. Someone, a uniformed policeman with more decision than me, was kicking the Webley fully clear. That gun, that evil thing, finished by skittering, rattling to a stop against the base of the partition that had quietly been my support for what felt like so long.

I was in the way. A crowd wanted my space. Richard's heart was racing, I could tell. He was rapidly surveying the disarmed man's prone form like he always did when he was reassuring himself that the threat was being managed and no new danger had been overlooked. Then I felt the jolt as his gaze lifted to fix on me. We were inches apart. In this dark space his eyes were betraying an intensity of thought that wasn't like his at all. His hard stare had purpose and it belonged to the brutal run of alternatives that had threatened just before. Each one a terror that went beyond danger, beyond anger, and yet, like all the rest, hadn't happened at all.

It was disturbing to see my feelings reflected there. I stood. I stepped sharply back. I'd expected to find I'd been wrong.

For a brief moment in the stillness of helping to restrain Duckett there had been a disorienting sense that it had been my own confused interpretation of everyone's intentions that had made the danger here. I understood nothing and nothing I had dreaded had come to pass.

But that was a lie too. The dark shadow of the Colonel and what those people had each tried to do to me was as certain as the way Duckett was being crushed into the ground by my feet. I was told to move, gruffly, by a policeman who wanted to do his work. I retreated a few steps more because about half a dozen more wanted to crowd in. I had a grip on the wooden post. I put the back of a hand to my forehead to sweep some grime away. It was a gesture made on the edge of distress, or disbelief, or something. I couldn't tell. But I knew the clarity of standing by my post as Richard exchanged rapid words with his neighbours was crueller than the madness of the past minutes because I felt again the stain of fearing the unimaginable ugliness of seeing Richard shot. And from there I unavoidably slid into the real criminal awfulness of acknowledging that I had very nearly been just as afraid that Richard's hand would send a bullet the other way into Duckett.

Then a smaller crowd went past with the Abbeys and I was free at last to turn quite blindly to the corner to retrieve Detective Fleece's discarded coat. Bloody or not, I took the wretched thing and used it to beat out every raw feeling on the growing flames of that neglected fire.

Fighting the fire made the hayloft darker, mainly because I could see very little else but the bright flares of smouldering strands of hay. We were lucky because the spreading blaze had to work its way along each blade of dried grass in turn and the ancient oak floorboards beneath were tougher than they looked. The worst of the job was keeping the disturbed wisps from taking root in one of the stacks. Or drifting down through the boards into the stables below. I didn't dare step past the crowd to go and look because if I'd found everything as it ought to be down there, it would have left me with nothing to do except find the Colonel.

Instead, through the messy smog I created I must still have perceived some of the movement in the crowd around Duckett. I knew Detective Fleece was standing on the far side of the partition, pressing a fresh bundle of cloth to his upper arm. He was a sagging shape in the smutty air. He tried to hand his handcuffs to someone who was passing by – someone in ordinary clothes with lighter hair, who was Danny, perhaps – but they ignored him because they were coming to help me with the fire. Anyway, PC Rathbone was already there and he was the only man on the scene whose face wasn't set into savage lines. This was his first arrest and he was loving it.

And then someone was able to relieve the exhausted detective from the job of standing guard over that gun and he, in his turn, could move to place a hand on Richard's shoulder. I saw Richard turn and look up at the detective. I watched them exchange a few grim words. There was a glance at me. Finally Richard rose to his feet and let the detective take his turn at bending low over the unharmed but frightened man.

Then Richard dusted off his hands and came to me.

I hadn't noticed that the person who had added a more

practical hand to my efforts with the fire had left me alone again. And that the light was almost entirely absent here now because the air was unhealthily thick, the fire was out and the distant hatch in the end wall was open but obscured by busy policemen. Richard was putting out his hand to lightly dissuade mine from beating any longer at the floorboards and saying with a definite roughness in his voice, 'For someone who hates grand gestures, you certainly seem dead set on performing as many as you can of your own for the sake of saving my home and my people, wouldn't you say? Father told me what you did.'

The shock of finally finding time for calmer thought in this dead space of darkness and heat pierced the other shock that was embedded deep into my heart. He had found his father alive. I felt I should be worrying and instead I was asking in a voice so level it sounded wrong, 'What ... what did your father tell you?'

I think Richard must have felt my pulse through my hand; it was the contradiction to my voice. His own voice was so steady now that there was almost a lick of humour in it when he told me, 'Father was very proud of his play-acting while he built up an image of a heart attack in the kitchen. He told me how you ensured he was left behind, as if we hadn't already heard it for ourselves. But he was also, I'm afraid, the reason why we missed every fresh chance to get to you. Until the last one.'

The sudden deepening into apology made me uneasy. My hand stirred restlessly within his. I felt his fingers soothe mine as I asked, 'You were there?'

'Of course.'

That oddly level voice of mine was back again. 'Did Detective Fleece know?'

'I think he hoped.'

After a moment, Richard told me, 'We had a small team in the dining room, but I was outside at first. Beneath the kitchen window with PC Rathbone and a few others. We were there when you came out. Did you notice how Duckett came out in the midst of you as you passed from house to barn? I imagine he thought it was an effective way of preventing anyone from taking a pot shot at him as he came out, which it was.'

It was helping me that he was speaking so unemotionally. We might just as easily been talking about a strategy for catching a bus. It allowed me to pretend that I could speak as plainly as he did. I asked, 'How much did you hear of what was said?'

'Enough. That is, enough that my father's actions were entirely unnecessary. Noble, but unnecessary. We'd certainly heard Detective Fleece's loud instructions to prepare for Duckett's retreat into the barn and if we hadn't, we would have learned where you'd gone pretty swiftly. The alarm was raised by the fellow who'd been called out of the interview to hear the warning that Duckett's car had been found. He saw Abbey's dive into the kitchen when he was coming to relay the news to me at the watershed. They all knew I'd want to get back to the house if Duckett was loose in the vicinity. Unfortunately, my father didn't know any of this and didn't wait long enough for anyone to tell him. He crashed about through the house and finally located me just as we were moving on Detective Fleece's instructions and trying to find a way through that hatch into the hayloft. Meeting my father was why our usefulness was limited to hanging onto the hatch for grim death when Mrs Abbey tried it, I'm sorry to say. Father insisted I had to know what you'd said about the warehouse. I suppose he felt I should know precisely who we were facing. He also had the housekeeper's keys, as if we needed them, because Abbey had lied there too, as it turned out – presumably to reduce Duckett's ideas of escape. The whole contraption was tied up with a piece of string and a stick.'

It had been an act. The Colonel's gasping had been an act, at least in the main. And the policeman must have been aware of it as well to have known to keep me away and to distract Duckett from testing the old man's pulse.

Richard's voice deepened. He added rather less easily, 'By the time Father had finished running about, he really had worked himself to the point of collapse and it took us a while to get to the gist of the message that he felt was so important to convey. He wasn't exactly ... coherent. But he did talk about you.'

Richard was watching my face. He let me understand the seriousness of the Colonel's present condition, and then he added grimly, 'I think ... I think he did it for me. Because he knew that you mattered.'

There was a shuffle beyond the partition as Duckett was hauled to his feet and taken away. I watched him go for a moment and then I said gently, 'I'm sorry, Richard.'

It was hard for him that this costly and unnecessary act was his father's plea for redemption. This had been the desperate self-sacrifice of an old warrior run along far more ancient lines than any recent model of war. The Colonel had been fighting to retrieve some lost honour and leaving behind a frantic wish that the gift would be judged and accepted. It was a relief for me, really, that Richard would never know how his father's plans had failed to communicate themselves to me. Because while Richard was once again being forced to temper his reaction for the sake of shielding the old man's dignity, this time there was also a sense that for both of them this was the moment they laid John's memory to rest.

It was easier then to ask in a stronger voice, 'Where is the Colonel now?'

'In hospital, I should hope. I should say he isn't very well and although it would have been the norm to put the man to bed and call the doctor, since all they do is prescribe aspirin and rest when it's a problem with the heart, we knew he'd never stay put. So Hannis and your cousin took charge of purloining Matthew Croft's car for the trip to Gloucester. They'll get him to the hospital there and I trust them to care for him until I can get down in person later ... Emily?'

Duckett had creaked his way out of the hatch to a waiting car. I risked a glance at Richard's face. And had the disconcerting suspicion that Richard knew full well that I'd been oblivious to the lie. That he was observing the resolve in me as I claimed the right of guarding this secret. The sense of it shook away my stupor and this strange reserve at last. I was free. It was very much time to find some fresher air.

I eased my hand out of his grip. I led the way down the stairs, not out of that low hatch into the space above the church where that police car was bearing Duckett away, but on and down, retracing my steps past the goat stable, which was empty now. Presumably the poor creature had been taken outside by some kind-hearted person who had thought to act in case the whole loft should have gone up with the spilled oil from that lamp.

Then I was taking that first step outside and it came as a shock, somehow, after all that gloom, to remember that the world outside was busy and it must now be no later than mid-afternoon on a glorious summer's day. I'd been meaning, I think, to go into the Manor, but the kitchen was overrun with policemen who were recording every small detail of the scene. The telephone was ringing and answered in the house. So I stalled there on the threshold of the tithe barn, in the brief island of stillness where the sunshine met the weathered stone wall. This was the place where a day or so before my bicycle had rested. I found I was hugging myself, drawing life from the sun and the sudden release of seeing the busy effort of all these people working to restore order.

I said inconsequentially, 'We destroyed your car, I'm sorry.'

'Pretty thoroughly, yes,' Richard agreed. The air out here was scented by the ruins of that proud Lagonda. As I had hoped, it had rolled safely away from the house, but unfortunately it had come to a stop against the machine barn. Unlike our little pool of oil in the hayloft, the fire had fought a longer battle out here. A chain of men were bucketing water over the blackened skeleton of metalwork while the high timbers of the barn doors showed where flames had begun crawling their way upwards to the roof.

Richard's dry humour as he remarked on it made me give my tension a little shake, all of a sudden, until something easier appeared in its place. It came with a little sideways glance that carried some of the warmth of the stones at my back. He was still with me. He was beside me, already propping a shoulder against the stone corner that framed the small tithe barn door. I claimed the support of the wall and leaned back. He was much taller than me when we stood like this. And reassuringly companionable too while a rush of men and a few women scurried past us uphill, muttering about setting a hose to the tanks in the watershed.

Richard tipped his head at the departing backs. 'I feel as though I ought to go and help, but somehow I think it's good for him to be given the chance to wreak his own idea of order at long last upon the Langton estate, with full benefit of law and necessity.'

He was referring to the man who had marched past at the head of the group. This was the man who had been at the scene of Duckett's arrest and had helped me with the fire. And the man who had, now I came to think about it, only really left me when Richard had climbed to his feet.

I caught Richard watching me. I asked him, 'Who is that? I thought it was Danny.'

'Matthew Croft.' A corner of his mouth twitched. His arms were folded too as he leaned against the stonework, but unlike me he was relaxed. The bandage about his hand and wrist was grey now. His suit jacket was dusted and unbuttoned and the recent exertion had darkened his hair just a little. The stone doorway framed him perfectly, dark behind and glorious sunlight on his face. He was the man who had written that easy little note about his trip to Athens.

My eyes took it all in, every vivid little detail of his presence cast in high relief as, oblivious, his gaze ran downhill again and he told me, 'Mr Croft came steaming down here in his car about a minute after the first gunshots. On any normal day the crack of a gun wouldn't have raised so much as a murmur, since we're in the depths of the countryside, but after the chaos he'd already witnessed today he was hardly going to presume it was a gamekeeper bagging pigeons.'

I could see Detective Fleece and he was looking like a man who was about to come and ask us some questions. And at the same time the determined rhythm of the work at the machine barn showed just what fire meant to these people at harvest time.

Richard waited for me to turn my head. Then he shared some of his grimmer thoughts for the first time. 'Do you know,' he remarked slowly, 'I think he actually *meant* to give the thing to me.'

He meant Duckett. He was exposing the memory of those things I wished could be forgotten; the devastating shadow of what Duckett might have done, or Richard might, which my mind still half believed had happened and that my beautiful freedom in this space outside was a dreaming denial of it.

As I shivered, Richard added, 'I think Duckett knew he wasn't going to get away and he was making one last great effort to shake off the evidence against him. I think he must have paid enough attention to the accusations you'd been levelling at Abbey to imagine that I might be relieved to have the chance to hide the thing. He believed I'd conceal it for him for the sake of my father.'

The chill grew worse when Richard's disbelief and his sheer grateful relief for the narrowness of his escape made me recall vividly just how precisely this man knew already what it felt like to be struck by a bullet. It cast a rather different slant on the horror of that brief struggle with the long barrel of the revolver against his stomach. It released a fearsome restless energy in me that became an ache in every limb as I confessed in a lurch, 'I couldn't do it. Mrs Abbey gave me the tools to stop him and I couldn't do it. I could have stopped him. But I didn't. I wasn't fierce enough. I don't think I could quite believe it was necessary. And I suppose it *wasn't* necessary. Because clearly, beneath all the madness and revenge, Duckett never was actually a murderer.'

I checked. The contradiction was like a scar on my memory, because the intent had been there. Beside me, Richard was quick to feel my distress. His voice was suddenly utterly firm. 'Didn't you hear what the detective was saying to you just before he gave us the command to come in?'

I gave a hasty shake of my head.

'Detective Fleece was shouting at you to hold your nerve for a while longer. He just wanted you to give him the time to close the distance between himself and Duckett. It was a matter of yards, at most. He just wanted a few seconds.'

I was biting my lip. And blinking fiercely. This reassurance was the wrong thing for him to say. It was proving that this idea I had that the sunlight was all I needed to be able to shrug off every tension – after all, what had happened to me really? – was a sham. This strange alienation I was feeling was all too real. I couldn't quite get my behaviour right. I was standing against my wall and feeling suddenly the clumsiness of smiling, or not, as was very much the case at this moment, without ever truly knowing if either was the correct expression to be wearing.

Beside me, Richard gave me a moment to absorb his point about the policeman's motivation, which I singularly failed to do, and then he told me very plainly, 'The policeman's just like you and me and every other person who possesses a halfway decent hope of rebuilding some normality after the war. Today, in that kitchen and then the hayloft, he was trying to establish a way of arresting those people for the crimes they'd already committed. He wasn't waiting for them to goad each other into committing something even more depraved. And I can tell you that he was absolutely, uncompromisingly certain that the first real violence wasn't going to be forced out of you. If you'd struck with that knife, they'd have succeeded in making you the only killer in that little piece of hell.'

That final word rang on for a moment, before he added grimly, 'I can hardly even bring myself to contemplate the destruction you'd have wreaked upon your peace of mind if you'd been left facing that. And the same rule applies to the cost of my own actions. So, while I'll admit that you were taking a terrible risk by trying a path of disarmament, and another time you might have been proved devastatingly wrong, you weren't mistaken this time. And you weren't even making that choice alone. Because although you didn't plan for it, I was there.'

There ought to have been peace in those forceful words. But I still couldn't quite break free of those last minutes in that hayloft. And now I abruptly had the discomfort of knowing that although I didn't want it to, my awkwardness was abruptly persisting in ringing on and on upon the principle of Richard's presence in that place too. I had the sudden guilt of knowing that if I didn't get my manner quite right this time and shrug off this growing distress, he might begin to think I was blaming him for intervening, when he knew full well I had resolved to bear no more sacrifices.

Only I wasn't. How could I, when I'd already accepted his father's idea of heroism and every muscle of mine still ached with the memory of grasping Duckett's deep bitter lesson that some things went beyond right and wrong and the simple mechanics of the thing had meant that I'd *let* Richard step between us? And the truth was that after all my deep protestations about the wrongfulness of that kind of burden, I'd been utterly, criminally glad of it because otherwise I wouldn't have stood a chance.

It was at that moment that Detective Fleece sidled a little nearer. My entire mind shied from having to explain all this to him too and while it was doing that, I heard Richard say abruptly and quite carelessly, 'I love you.'

The statement was at complete odds with the bitter thoughts that were racing through my mind. After a day of manipulations and couched demands for things that ought to have been left well alone, it was a contradiction that hurt every nerve. It dragged my head round sharply. I peered at him through a confusion that was a kind of headache and said blankly, 'What?'

He stood there beside me, still propped against the bright stone wall, and told me calmly, 'I love you.' The statement probably shouldn't have needed an explanation, but it did. It came on an almost conciliatory note. 'I'm just cancelling out the venom they've been working on you.'

I was supposed to feel my liberation. I was supposed to smile. I blinked numbly instead. 'Oh.'

It was an idiotically useless thing to say. Suddenly he had eased himself away from the wall. He was stepping round before me. It wasn't for the sake of enfolding me in his arms, though my befuddled heart wished he would. One hand was by his side and the other was perhaps drifting nearer me and he seemed braced, all of a sudden. Businesslike. As though this marked the end of a conference. And the policeman wasn't here for me. He'd merely left the crowd by the smouldering car because he hadn't yet found time to have his wound dressed and he was craving a moment of peace in order to test whether the flow of blood had stopped. It had, but the blood had dried in vivid lines down his wrist.

'*Richard!*' My voice abruptly framed itself on an urgent undertone as I turned my head away from the policeman. I could suddenly feel everything. I thought with a blindingly panicked bolt that Richard was leaving me; going, now when I hadn't yet said anything of any use. I swear it was this sudden wrench and not the unexpected clarity of seeing what Detective Fleece was really doing that made my heart race and made me straighten suddenly and bolt towards Richard.

Naturally, instinct worked quickly in Richard, as always. His arm came around me, gripping me to hold me against him as I gripped him in my turn, and my forehead found safety in his shoulder. I felt his mouth duck towards my ear and heard his murmur. 'Not a real phobia, indeed.'

He was shielding me from the blood. Only I wasn't shivering because of that and I certainly wasn't trying to hide. I had my arms around his neck, hands restlessly moving on again to find his hair and I was drawing back enough to lift my head. I made him stay still to let me study those poorly disguised shadows on his face. The faintest of questions coursed through the warmth of his skin beneath my touch and his doubt unleashed the urgency of feeling that dwelt in me at last and it changed everything. That policeman was irrelevant. Nothing else mattered except this.

I was saying in a pleading rush, 'I'm so sorry. Don't go yet. Please. I'm sorry. This is what reaction does, I suppose. I feel muddled and wretched and I'm sorry, because I feel like I ought to be able to prove I'm fine, but I can't do it. Because I *do* feel altered, Richard. I feel utterly numb. I can't even begin to digest the bitter reality of this experience. But I should have trusted ... I should have understood that you were like me and I wasn't alone in thinking as I did in there. You said something once about the scope of your vocabulary. I think I saw it in action today in the way you engineered that scene of arrest and I should have known precisely who you are.

Instead I'm making you feel like you have to reassure me when ... when the only explanation required here is mine and there are some things I ought to be able to say without needing to feel confident first. It's shameful that it's taken me until now to admit this.'

My voice cracked on the word *shameful* and I gasped and put my face down to his shoulder again. This wasn't a controlled explanation. I never was very good at saying what I felt under pressure and this was frantic because it truly mattered and I was shaking as I clung to him.

In my brief pause to draw breath I felt his other arm slowly lift to close around me. He followed it by saying rather quietly, 'Emily, sweetheart, I'm not leaving you. I've just been trying to give you time to piece together what happened. I wasn't going to make you talk about anything important now. It's enough that I know you're here and with me and I didn't let you down. Is this because I told you that I loved you? Because I'm not demanding anything from you at this moment, I'm really not.'

It was a plea to stop, to let the shock ease first before making any decisions. I knew he could feel the quiver that ran through me as his grip tightened to thoroughly enclose me in comfort. He believed I was warning him to brace himself for a withdrawal, a rejection. Because the strain of being required to remember how to love the man as well as being grateful for his recent protection was too much to bear. But still I was clinging to him. I had my eyes tightly shut and pressed hard into the curve where his shoulder met his neck, while every nerve in my body was deeply conscious of the tightness of his arms. In a variation of Phyllis's concern, he had thought this must be the end of something, but he didn't know what this was.

I made his doubt worse when I dived headlong into speaking about Mrs Abbey. 'She was the real hostage to those men, you know. She really was trapped. I saw her afraid today because her children were nearby and she didn't show it for the sake of any trick. There was no scheme in the fear. She had absolutely no idea whether Duckett would leave her room to take those boys away, or use them to punish Abbey absolutely.'

In quite a different voice, Richard said very carefully by my ear, 'Do you really believe that? Or are you being kind to her?'

'I don't know,' I admitted desperately. 'I know she's very good at working me up into a sense of wretched sympathy for every motive she's had.'

With a shiver that lurched into an absurdly frustrated note, I finally began to confess what was really keeping me trapped in that awful place. 'I feel like each of them was working so hard to steer each other into making their crucial mistakes that they all kept on madly contradicting each other until they agreed on one thing. And that was that they all thought they could control me. None of them knew what they were doing. I don't think any of them ever really acknowledged the scale of what they were working towards. Ever since Duckett stepped into that kitchen today, pretty much all any of them did was lecture me about how it was all someone else's fault that they'd each got themselves fixed upon a certain path. And now Mrs Abbey has almost wholly managed to steer me into believing that, since it was impossible for her to escape either Duckett or her husband's determination to cling to her, I can't blame her for the way she let me work myself in deep enough that I could save her instead. Only I didn't work myself into anything, Richard – she did it. She gave Abbey a reason to think of using me. She made sure Duckett came for me. And I hate that, even after I've seen the truth behind the choices she made, I *still* feel sympathy towards her because I know she was only ever fighting for her children and she really was trapped.'

I stopped. The memory of that letter was there too, the one the policeman had slipped into his pocket. I knew that because of it Detective Fleece was going to encourage me to keep a tight hold of my empathy. He was going to want to use me to ease the pressure on her while he kept her free to reclaim her life as a mother and therefore sensible enough to answer a few critical questions about her relationship with John Langton. My breath checked.

John Langton's part in this was over for Richard and his father, yet that man's memory could never be truly laid to rest. It was a reflection of the true part of the damage these people had done to me by forcing me to accept, even briefly, that their world was the norm. I could escape it, but I wasn't fully free of it. I whispered, 'I suppose it's a good sign that I can still worry about her like this because it means that they can't have changed me very much. But I can't help seeing the pattern of the trap she was working and feeling as if I've discovered that I'm just like them after all.'

'Why?' Richard's voice was suddenly severe. 'Because for a brief moment you were afraid I'd choose to shoot Duckett?' He had noticed my guilt there and his almost angry dismissal of it gave me a jolt. Presumably he hadn't been entirely certain himself.

I turned my head a little against his shoulder to give a faint negative. Knowing he'd already guessed the rest made it hard to say this. It came on a whisper. 'Because I didn't want to be cruel like that former love of yours, and the Abbeys and all the rest, who, in their way, have tried to take whatever they needed from you. I read your note.'

'My *note?*' I suppose as confessions went, it didn't really make much sense. I felt the moment when surprise was briefly followed by relief because he too had heard about the discovery of the letter he'd written to John. He thought I was worrying about this other love. He remarked considerably less seriously, 'The detective told me you'd found my brother's letter when he relieved me of my guard over Duckett. He was warning me that he means to subject it to all possible scrutiny. And I'm sure he will because, whether he means it to or not, I expect this day'll notch a few more marks in the ladder to his next promotion and you can't tell me that a policeman who pursues his investigation in the midst of a scene like this isn't as driven as they come. But Emily, you have to know, I *don't mind.* I said something like this to my father last night and I'll say it again to you now. That letter represents old news.'

It was a kind of joke on that former lover's article. It made me smile a little, but I was already rushing on to say gingerly,

'Not that one. Duckett's. I read what you said about Greece ...'

I learned how Richard felt about that in the way his hand clenched in its grip upon the fabric of my frock.

His reaction drove mine. He made me blunder onwards into admitting the harder things. I added clumsily, 'I thought I was helping you. I thought it was a good thing if I worked to prove that I didn't want to lean on you in the way they do. But when I read your note it was like borrowing a little bit of your confidence. It carried me through and it was wonderful, only they ruined it because I can't tell any more if it's right I should want to go to Athens or if you should even ask me for both our sakes, because if I can't shrug off a scene like today's, I certainly can't cope with a brush with your work. And it's all part of the trap of that old, reluctantly confessed, horror of war. I'm making you believe that I've been led at last into that awful place where some unspeakable cruelty has succeeded in teaching me that I have no choice but to accept the inequality of being me and depend absolutely on the bravery of people like you. But the truth is inescapable and I ought to have told you long before. Because I *do* need you, Richard. I really do.'

Suddenly, this was easier. Any other man would have interrupted this floundering struggle to explain. Only he didn't make a sound. He didn't correct me. All the while he held me with his head down beside mine, submitting to the way my fingers coursed through his hair, leaving me the room in which to speak while I raced on to say it all in one breathless jumble and probably made him believe this really must be rejection after all.

It wasn't rejection. Or, at least, it was, but only of my own habit of denying his right to help me in any way he chose, even while he trusted me with the responsibility of trying to help him. This was real bravery and it was small and personal and made no difference to anyone except the man within my reach. And it began by risking this last little part of me.

I drew a ragged breath and made a final effort to explain. Unexpectedly, my voice was steadier. I said emphatically, 'The truth is, I've always needed you, Richard. I really have. In all sorts of small and harmless ways. Just you. This way I feel now – which is so powerful it feels as if my heart might tear – it's unshakeable and decisive and it's got no parallel except for the way you make me feel when I see that you've been moved again by some little gesture of mine. And it grows from finally having the courage to let you, in your turn, give whatever you want to give, and trusting you for it too.'

Trust. It was a quiet refrain of that old question he'd levelled at me in the car outside the station, when he'd asked if I might not simply trust him. This time my reply staggered him in a very different way.

I felt his hand move in my hair. A brush of his hand across my ear and onto the tangles of my hair, so that it encouraged me to lift my head.

It was hard to do it, but I managed it. My hands drifted from their hold about his neck, to settle more easily upon the lapel of his jacket. I had to work hard to dare to lift my eyes to his face. I found something very serious there.

His hand was still against my hair. I turned my cheek a little into the warmth of his palm and felt a whisper of real comfort. I think I might have discovered grief at that moment. Only I didn't. Not quite. My heart was beating in slow, powerful strokes as I caught the way his breath checked. I felt the tenderness as he brought his mouth down to mine. This was relief after fear. This was an intense fire that gripped us both almost to the point of oblivion and it was part of the exhaustion of terrors of that day.

Then there was the simple normality of being confronted, after all, with what was for me a familiar sense of being wrong and easily contradicted when his head lifted and his hand smoothed my hair again and he confided, 'I really wasn't going to leave you just now when I stepped away from the doorway.'

His touch encouraged me to return to the sanctuary of his shoulder once more. As his arms closed about me, I knew a slow smile was forming on his mouth. I felt it as the merest whisper against my temple. There he added softly, 'I was thinking that if this nastiness had worked itself through all your memories from these few days of knowing me, I should ease at least one of the worries in your mind. I was going to see if you felt like simply starting again, properly, as it ought to have been done in the first place. I was going to put out my hand to you. I meant to introduce myself.'

He did it now. He put up his left hand to cover my right where my fingers were tangling with his collar. His hand was steady over mine. So was his voice by my ear as he said gravely, 'Hello. I'm Richard Langton.'

'Richard?'

'Yes.' His brisk agreement drew a shy smile from me before he added gently, 'I wonder if it might be about time that I provided a meal for you. If, that is, you can bear to wait while we go through the inescapably difficult formalities of getting away from the people here and find a means of travelling down the hill to check on the health of my father. And, of course, hopefully find him well enough to be left for the night. *Would* you like to have dinner?'

There was a distant shout that momentarily dragged both our heads round, but then his gaze returned to me. It was a shock, somehow, to acknowledge the personality burning in those eyes. It felt like a first introduction after all. There was still strain there, in him and in me, but beneath it was an electrifying hint of that energy in him that I thought I was beginning to know so well. It grew stronger when his hand abandoned mine to instead trace an arc across my cheek. It was for the sake of brushing away a speck of debris left there by the burning hay.

I found my true nerve at last. And with it, I managed to lift my chin and say with creditable calmness, 'Given that we can be reasonably confident what our feelings will be once we've had this dinner, do you think by the end of it I might have managed to find a simpler way of telling you that I love you too?'

I was brave enough to silence his reply with a kiss that belonged to my very soul.

Reluctantly, my certainty was followed by the compromise of leaning against his shoulder once more, but this time with my hand gently laid against the line of his jaw and my cheek turned against the warmth of him, so that I too could see what lay beyond us on the busy yard. His arms enfolded me in comfort and assurance. This was because we had both found room, at last, to become conscious of the chaos the car had caused. There had been a crash of damaged timbers down by the machine barn as the farmhands began to make a full survey of the roof in case the flames had got into that dark void. The yell had come from Matthew Croft as he worked with them and it had been designed to politely – but not entirely tranquilly – let Richard know that responsibility was waiting for him there. I hadn't forgotten that for Richard the day's work was not yet over. It probably wasn't for me either. There would be a difficult statement to give.

But for now, at least, Richard's worry about what he would find at the hospital during his visit to his father eased a little with the knowledge I would be there with him. So did the complicated moment of approaching Matthew Croft to see what was needed. The record of old conflicts ran on and on in every shadow and every memory of this place, but the measured greeting he would receive from that man would carry a murmur of Richard's own identity this time and that in itself was a new kind of liberty.

Because this present feeling had nothing to do with other people's grand schemes and lies any more. This was about the small things we each could control in the pattern of our own choices. This was about the little peace we were creating for ourselves.

A Letter from the Author
to the Reader

Thank you for reading *The Antique Dealer's Daughter*. I absolutely loved writing it.

The original idea for this book came from a chance conversation. I'd just finished writing my second novel, *The War Widow*, and my mind was toying with a new idea about the challenge people must have faced after World War Two to establish life on a different footing now that peace had come. I'd read about the lives of the older women who were called up to the war effort to work as Land Girls and WRENs and in the munitions factories and so on, and I'd certainly understood a reasonable amount about the experiences of those younger children who were evacuated. Then I delivered a talk about books and writing to a WI group in Gloucestershire and met a wonderful lady called Vivian. This was the chance conversation that started it all. Only, in truth it wasn't entirely chance because of course I'd chosen to speak at that WI in the first place.

Vivian told me about her own experiences as a teenager in wartime London. She was only in her mid-teens in the early days of the war and she was able to tell me how schooling became a nightmare of disrupted lessons in air raid shelters.

She explained how, like many young people, she left school and took up the counter work that the older women had left behind.

Vivian made me think about how strange it must have been to have had her entire adolescence consumed by conflict. She made me think how hard my heroine, Emily Sutton, might have had to work to adjust to life after the war, and how the reality of the newfound peace might not have quite been how she'd expected it to be. Vivian also, because of the varying aspects of chance and choice involved in meeting her at all, made me think about how Emily's life might have been changed through the single act of answering a ringing telephone.

Chance features a lot in Emily's account of her story, or rather, those choices that other people make, which are out of her control. There's the powerlessness of her adolescence in wartime London, which was filled with the blackout and rules and ration books. There's the pressure she feels now to mould herself to a future she doesn't want within her father's antiques business, and the steadfast way she resists it which ultimately brings her into Richard's life. Finally, there's the burden of being the only person brave enough to step into the squire's deserted house for the sake of answering his telephone. That single decision brings Richard home to confront the unhealed memories of his brother's last criminal acts, only to find himself face to face with fresh danger.

That being said, though, every loss of control is underpinned by Emily's effort to assert her right to make her own choices. It is her choice, after all, to believe Richard is who he says he is when the gossip-mongers get to work. And it is her choice, too, to help him and to learn to let him help her in his turn.

I have loved discovering how Emily will find her own path through life. I know she's determined enough for the task, even if she doesn't fully believe it at first. I'm so glad you've joined her.

Acknowledgements

There are many people who have been wonderfully helpful to me in the course of writing this book. My particular thanks go to Jeremy, my husband, who, as ever, has been an unwavering source of encouragement and support.

Thank you also to my editor Suzanne Clarke for her excellent advice, and to Charlotte Ledger and Eloisa Clegg at HarperImpulse for all their help.

Thank you to Brenda and Robert Brookes for answering my endless questions about Gloucester after the war. Thanks to Judith and Stuart Samuel for all their ideas, and also to Penny Wright for giving me so many location details. Finally, my grateful thanks go to Vivian for sharing her childhood experiences of life in 1940s London.

The appearance of buildings and streets in Gloucester during the post-war period was drawn from the photographic record in 'Gloucester: A Pictorial History' by John Juřica (Phillimore

564

& Co. Ltd, 1994) and *'Gloucester in Old Photographs from the Walwin Collection'* compiled by Jill Voyce (Alan Sutton Publishing, 1989).